The Problem
with Him

An Opposites Attract Novel

Rachel Higginson

The Problem with Him

An Opposites Attract Novel

Rachel Higginson

Other Romances by Rachel Higginson

The Five Stages of Falling in Love

Every Wrong Reason

Bet on Us (Bet on Love Series)

Bet on Me (Bet on Love Series)

The Opposite of You (Opposites Attract Series)

The Difference Between Us (Opposites Attract Series)

Keep up with Rachel on her Newsletter

Connect with Rachel on her Facebook Page

Follow Rachel on Twitter and Instagram

To my Prickle,

The group of women that have picked me for sisterhood.

You inspire me, you challenge me, you encourage me.

I am better because I know you.

Thank you for being #squadgoals and my ride or die

And all the things that make friendship lifelong.

Chapter One

*I*f I were a vegetable, I would be… kohlrabi. Mildly difficult, but not overly so. A little spicy. Versatile. And highly underestimated.

Also, kohlrabi starts with a K. Like my name—Kaya.

Basically, it's my spirit vegetable.

These were the thoughts that occupied my mind at the end of a hectic night of service as I watched the braising parsnips with sniper-like sharpness.

Earlier tonight, I'd already decided that if I were a fish, I'd be a sea urchin.

And if I were a fruit, I'd be a jackfruit.

I was a little concerned that every persona I picked had bumps or spikes of some kind. Obviously, I'd picked the sea urchin for its cool factor. And because it was one of those dishes that people either loved or hated. I was so that kind of person. Uni and I connected on a level even higher than spiritual.

Metaphorically speaking, of course.

Uni was basically the gonads of a sea urchin. That part I couldn't relate to at all.

And I connected to jackfruit because of its versatility. It was also high in fiber. So. There was that.

Shaking my head, I pulled the pan off the flame and decided not to think too hard about my choices. It didn't hurt that most children would be afraid to touch any of the items I picked. And even adults were afraid to eat them. That didn't mean anything. This was a dumb game to pass the time since I'd been shuffled to the sides station tonight, instead of my favorite station—protein.

As the sous chef in one of the hottest kitchens in Durham, North Carolina, working the sides station was a major insult to my talent and I needed something to entertain and distract myself.

None of this mattered.

Except that my parsnips looked fantastic and they were ready to finish. I scooped them out of the boiling water and added them to a bowl, so I could salt them before tossing them with the maple syrup reduction.

My lips pressed into a frown aimed at the parsnips and stayed there while I plated them. Adding chopped candied pecans, I rethought my life choices—at least my food-as-soulmates choices.

If I were a dessert, I'd be… ice cream.

There. Not spiky.

Liar, my inner voice taunted.

Shut up, I spat back. *I love ice cream. Ice cream is my favorite.*

12

Which of course was another lie.

Key lime pie is my favorite. The tarter, the better.

Again, I decided to ignore whatever direct implications that had on my personality and focused on work.

Handing over the parsnips to one of my coworkers, he added a sloppy looking chicken roulade to finish the dish.

If it had been an hour earlier, I probably would have called him on his crap preparation of the protein, but I was too tired at this point. And it was past the hour food bloggers and critics would have a table. Or at least I hoped it was.

My boss leaned in and studied the plate like it held the secret cure for cancer. If only he could read the signs in the parsnips, we could save the world.

I swallowed the urge to clear my throat and get his attention. It wouldn't lead to anything good. I had a sneaking suspicion my true intention was to flash my middle finger at him because of how he glowered at my handiwork. And the extra few seconds he took to wipe the edges of the plate as if I had done a poor job of it myself.

Of course, he didn't notice the roulade. Why would he? That eyesore was prepared, cooked and finished by a good old boy. Someone he could rely on strictly because they sported uni and egos the size of North Carolina.

Tart was an understatement. If I were a key lime pie at this point in the night, those limes would be downright bitter.

Wyatt Shaw placed the plate on a tray and called a waiter forward to take it.

"Charlie forgot to take out the toothpicks," I said in a relaxed tone that could have been mistaken for a suggestion instead of a warning.

Wyatt kept his back to me, his shoulders stiff, his body rigid. He didn't critique me out loud this time, but I felt his disdain as it hung heavily in the air. The waiter shifted the tray toward Wyatt, so he could remove the toothpicks and save the diner from accidentally impaling the roof of their mouth.

Once finished, he jerked his chin down in a subtle cue for the waiter to disappear. The waiter did, scurrying to the dining room with perfect parsnips and mediocre chicken roulade. Wyatt watched him go without bothering to turn around and thank me for noticing what could have been a terrible mistake.

That was okay. There was no need. I was much better at having that conversation in my head anyway.

Crisis averted, asshole. You're welcome.

I was also very good with passive aggressive texts. We were supposed to be a united front in the kitchen, a dysfunctional mom and dad to all our little bastard children. Since Wyatt was the head chef and I was his second in command, I found it easier to communicate all my angry thoughts via SMS.

Not that Wyatt was an amateur. He knew his way around insulting emojis better than anyone I knew.

For instance, much earlier today he'd texted to remind me to be early for deliveries, something the two of us usually handled together. I had texted back that I remembered all on my own. He had hit me back with the surprised cat face.

Butthead.

His texts always riled me up and earlier in the evening I wouldn't have held my tongue. I would have poked the bear out of need to rile him back, forced him to say what he was biting his tongue not to say—which wasn't thank you by the way. But it was so close to quitting time now, I didn't have the energy to fight with Wyatt. He could be disappointed in me all he wanted, I wasn't the one that forgot about the toothpicks.

Plus, my parsnips, just like all my side dishes tonight and every night, were perfect. I'd made over a hundred and fifty of them in the last several hours, and not one complaint had made its way back to the kitchen. At least not about me.

Scowl until your face is full of wrinkles, Wyatt, those parsnips kicked major five-star ass.

Arching my entire body backward, I stretched my arms over my head and released some of the tension curling like a tightened fist in the center of my back. My feet ached. My legs had gone numb an hour ago. There was a migraine crawling up the back of my neck into the base of my skull. And I smelled like duck fat and cilantro. It was time to go home.

I loved my job. I loved it more than anything in this world. Except for maybe Wyatt's job. I felt fairly confident I would love running this kitchen as executive chef. I mean, *really, really* love it. But, there wasn't any difference in the physical part of that job and my current job. Executive chef responsibility wouldn't change how often I had to stand on my feet or how exhausted I would be at the end of the night.

Wyatt currently looked like he'd been mugged at some point tonight, and then dragged through a carwash backwards. Not even his tall chef's hat could hide the unruliness of his dark hair.

Anyway, I loved my job, but I also loved going home at the end of the night. There wasn't anything better than working your absolute hardest for a solid fourteen hours and putting your feet up at the end of the night when you knew you had absolutely nothing left to give.

Which I planned on doing in T-minus forty-one minutes.

As I started to let the blissful daydream of a shower fill up my head, Wyatt's deep voice boomed through the noisy kitchen, snatching my hopes and dreams from the air and shoving them into his filthy pockets. "A friendly reminder that we're deep cleaning tonight, so nobody take off until your station has been checked out."

"Son of a bitch," I growled at the still dirty pan in my hand. Now that Wyatt had said something, I vaguely recalled getting an email about this two weeks ago. But in my current exhausted state, I'd chosen denial and daydreams about a hot shower and a cold bottle of beer the second I got home. Yes, both. Simultaneously. Shower beers were basically what I lived for.

"There go my plans for the night," the sassy blonde to my left, who had also clearly forgotten about our monthly kitchen ritual, mumbled beneath her breath.

I looked at my friend Dillon and quirked an eyebrow. "I'm sure Mr. Random Stranger will be happy to wait for you."

She stuck out her tongue before crouching to wipe the bottom shelf of a stainless-steel counter that was already pristinely clean. "Aren't we judgy tonight, Ky?"

Letting out a frustrated sigh, I leaned on the counter next to where she worked diligently. "I wasn't being judgy. I was… reassuring you that you're worth waiting for."

She blinked up at me. "Bullshit."

I couldn't help but smile. "Fine. I was being judgy. But only because I'm jealous of your steady stream of action." The admission tasted like dirt as I forced myself to speak the truth I preferred to ignore, deny, and convince myself wasn't true.

It was a hard thing to admit you were envious of your friend's sex life. Especially since mine had a neon vacancy sign blinking into the dark night like a dilapidated country motel everyone avoided. Because they were afraid they'd get sliced and diced by the local serial killer.

Not that I was a serial killer. Just a serial relationship ruin-er.

16

Okay, that was a little harsh, seeing as I'd only had one long-term relationship in all of my twenty-seven years. But man did I do all that I could to destroy that one. Straight up annihilated whatever happiness and trust we'd managed to build together.

Afterwards, there had been a series of bad decisions in an effort to forget and move on. Those had also ended terribly. The worst of which I was still forced to work with.

Fast forward to today, when my closest relationship with a man was the maintenance guy at my apartment complex because of how often I needed him to unclog my drain, and it was easy for me to feel like the damage I'd done all those years ago had some lasting effects on my current dating life. Or lack thereof.

Dillon knew me well enough by now to know my apology was sincere. She stood and nudged my elbow with hers. "I'm sure Mr. Random Stranger has a friend if you're for real. No need to be jealy of my social life. You could have one of your very own if you didn't work yourself to the bone every single night."

My heart dropped to my stomach from the weight of disappointment, because that wasn't going to happen. But I didn't want to turn down Dillon yet again. We'd been inseparable since she started working at Lilou with me eight months ago. Our friendship was new, but strong, in the way only those friendships you wait your whole life for are strong. We had obviously been destined to meet since the beginning of time.

I might not have had luck meeting a guy, but I'd been lucky enough to find my friend soulmate and that was good enough for me.

Dillon was a rising star in the kitchen. Her brother, Ezra, was our boss. Like the top boss. He'd put her in his five-star, Michelin award-winning kitchen shortly after she'd graduated culinary school.

17

I'd immediately wanted to hate her. I'd assumed she was everything I loathed in the female world. Ridiculously gorgeous. Unfairly tall. Impossibly skinny. She had family money, family connections, and family that loved her and wanted the best for her.

Undoubtedly, she was everything I wasn't. I had expected her to be spoiled rotten. But more than that, I had wanted her to be dangerously green in the kitchen and completely untalented. I hadn't wanted competition. And I really hadn't wanted a friend. Somehow Dillon turned out to be both, in the very best way.

On the flipside of the coin there was me. I didn't think I was ugly, but most of my days were spent with a bandana over my short-ish curly hair. I wore zero makeup, and always dressed in greasy work pants. I wasn't tall. And therefore wasn't model-thin. I was short and curvy, and a ballbuster thanks to a lifetime of working my ass off to get my foot in the door of one of the toughest, most competitive industries, in one of the best restaurants in the city.

Nobody handed me this job out of charity or familial loyalty. I'd had to fight my way past cocky assholes who thought they were better than me— men that would chew me up and spit me out if I gave them even a millimeter of room—and the constant stereotyping of a tiny, intelligent woman that could cook circles around anyone that wanted to go toe to toe.

So when Dillon walked through the door, practically glowing with nepotism and natural beauty, it was no surprise I despised her immediately. That lasted approximately five minutes.

She'd set her things down next to mine and said, "I think I'm going to puke." When I'd turned to look at her to see if she was being serious or sarcastic, she'd ripped open her chef coat and started fanning her armpits. "Look!" she'd said with bugged out eyes, her gray undershirt drenched with sweat at only ten in the morning. "This job is going to kill me!"

18

"You'll be fine," I had tried to reassure her.

She'd stepped into me and winced. "I'm a total basket case. My one goal today is to not slice my thumbs off." She'd winced again. "I need my thumbs."

I hadn't been able to stop myself from laughing. "Didn't you just graduate from Charlotte? And doesn't your brother own this place? You'll be fine."

"Yeah, I just graduated. And I was perfectly excited about getting a job at Applebee's and then my stupid big brother was all, you can't work there! And I was like, watch me. And then he was like, I own a bunch of restaurants, dummy. And then I was like, I hate you. And then more stuff happened that I can't totally remember and here we are."

It was her armpits that had endeared her to me. She wasn't the plastic Barbie I'd pegged her as. She was sweating, nervous, and real. I had suffered the same way my first day at Lilou.

Okay, to be honest, I had handled myself way better than Dillon, but I never had that choice. I was forced to suck it up and face the kill-or-be-killed environment, especially since I didn't have a boss-brother to run to. Not that Dillon would. She was all about making a name for herself without relying too heavily on Ezra.

Still, I couldn't blame her. Lilou was an intimidating kitchen with competent, experienced chefs. Ezra probably thought he was doing her this big favor and she knew better than anyone that she wasn't ready for a kitchen of this caliber.

Luckily, she had me. I'd shown her the ropes and helped her get settled in. Now she was catching up to the rest of us at lightspeed, a slightly terrifying thing to watch.

She was good at this. Hungry for it. One day she might even be better than me if I didn't continue to bust my ass. That was another quality I loved about her and that helped cement our friendship. She pushed me to be better,

19

to get better, to not ever get comfortable with what I'd already accomplished. And she would never, ever let me settle for mediocrity.

Despite how much Dillon and I loved and supported each other, we couldn't have been more different. Other than our noticeable physical differences, Dillon was the bubbly socialite, and more importantly, a kind, generous human. I preferred to keep to myself and sleep in my bed as opposed to some random stranger's that I'd met at a club two hours earlier.

And I was not kind. I mean, I wasn't necessarily mean. But there was a reason other chefs kept their distance. I could be… prickly. Like a porcupine. Except with my very select few friends.

Fun fact: Do you know what a group of porcupines is called? A prickle. My girls were my prickle. And that was enough for me.

Most of the time.

"No worries," Dillon assured with a casual shrug. "The only man waiting for me tonight is my brother. Molly wanted me to come over to their place after work and hang for a while before they leave on their trip."

For some reason my stress level dropped back to normal. I came off snarky and sarcastic, and obviously I had my own set of issues, but I really was worried about my friend. Dillon was the most trusting human I'd ever met. If I wanted to hook up, I had an entire checklist the other party needed to fill out. Including an appointment at the local clinic to ensure I wasn't going to catch something gross and permanent. I was basically one step away from a full-on background check before second base made it to the table for discussion.

Dillon was the opposite. And that scared me for her and her liberal choices of bed partners.

"I thought they were morning people." The words came out with a clear tone of disgust that she matched with a nose wrinkle and eye roll. When you worked our hours, morning was a curse word you didn't use lightly. But

Molly and Ezra kept normal working hours. Er, Molly did. Ezra basically worked all the time. They went to bed at what some might call a decent time, to ensure they could wake up at the butt crack of dawn and get all those worms the early birds were always talking about.

I preferred tequila worms after midnight myself. But hey, to each their own.

"Usually," Dillon agreed. "But they're taking four weeks off for vacation and they wanted to hang out before they left."

"Four weeks? Holy cow. Where are they going?"

She let out a longing sigh. "Somewhere tropical. And warm. And doused in piña coladas." She paused so we could both take a minute to reflect on how nice it would be to have Ezra's money and Molly's flexibility—she worked for Ezra, managing his PR and marketing. They were one of the most perfect couples I had ever known.

I was friends with Molly and I liked her a lot. I was mostly terrified of Ezra. But that was because he was legitimately terrifying. Together though? They were disgustingly adorable.

"An entire month somewhere tropical? I want to be them when I grow up."

"Right?" Dillon laughed. "Ezra's never taken a vacation before. Can you believe that? Never. Not once! So Molly is making him cram a lifetime of missed opportunities into one big shebang. I'm house sitting for them while they're gone. They're supposed to show me everything I need to know."

An obnoxious pang of helpfulness punched through my gut. "You should go then. I'll cover your station."

Her blue eyes bugged. "You can't do that. It will take you forever to get out of here!"

21

I shrugged, letting her know it didn't matter. "Put in a good word for me with Ezra, yeah? Tell him how amazing I am. And how competent. And that I could totally run this kitchen by myself."

Dillon's gaze slid sideways toward Wyatt. "You totally could."

"Yeah, no kidding." I refused to look at him, knowing it would only make me angry. "Pretty please tell your brother?"

Her smile was bright and grateful. "I will. I promise." She leaned over and kissed my cheek. I'd gotten used to her ways. And I endured the flashy display of affection because it was Dillon and I loved her. Before she all but fled the kitchen, she paused and asked one last time. "You're sure? I mean, super sure this is okay?"

I rolled my eyes. "Yes. Go!"

"You're the best!" she called over her shoulder as she made a beeline for the exit.

"I know!" I hollered at the big metal door that was anything but quiet when she pushed on the handle.

The kitchen was always hot, sweltering. But when Wyatt realized Dillon was in the process of abandoning her post for the night, the temperature dropped at least thirty degrees. A chill crept down my spine as I watched his sharp gaze snap from me to her.

"Where do you think you're going?" he growled as the door closed. He jerked around to face me. "Where is she going?"

Moment of honesty? Sometimes Wyatt scared the living hell out of me. We grew up in this kitchen together. It was the first job either of us had in any kitchen. He beat me by four years, but he was hardly farther along in his career by the time I arrived. We'd both started right out of culinary school. It wasn't fair that he was four years older than me.

We'd been working side by side for five years now and we'd been through a lot together. But that didn't mean we'd bonded over our struggles.

Or that we even knew each other at all. Even as head chef and sous chef our relationship was decidedly strained.

I would love to say that since we'd worked together for so long I knew everything about him. But the truth was, Wyatt had always kept to himself. He'd always been private and mysterious and a bit of an asshole. Sure, before he was my boss, we were friendly-ish. But he was the kind of guy that kept his cards close to his vest. It made sense, because it would suck to be forced to make friends only to end up stabbing that person in the back on his way up the ladder.

And with me, he was totally standoffish to avoid hurting our friendship. Or at least that was what I liked to believe. I was the only one in the kitchen that could compete with him. I was his major competition. That was why he kept his distance, why he always went out of his way to avoid or ignore me. Or bark at me over text.

Competition or no, he had a few things I didn't that catapulted his career ahead of mine. Mostly they appeared in the form of industry connections. And he had no issue cashing in on them.

It had paid off for him. Killian Quinn, the Michelin decorated, James Beard award-winning, and former executive chef of Lilou, had named Wyatt his successor. That pushed Wyatt even farther from my orbit.

Now, he was way, way up there. And I was still on the ground fixing his mistakes and making sure he got all the credit.

The culinary world had been downright apoplectic over Lilou's fate after Killian left. And Wyatt was more than happy to step into shoes that were way too big for him and claim the glory for himself.

Most of the time, I found him irritating. And difficult. And rude. Honestly, I was the same. Especially to him. But when he was like this—a sudden thunderstorm, lashing out, lightning flashing and thunder rolling— even my knees trembled.

23

"She has a thing with Ezra," I answered, purposefully name-dropping our boss. "I told her I'd cover for her."

"You're not responsible for her station," he snarled. "Now it's going to take you twice as long to finish and get out of here. That means I'll have to stay here twice as long to make sure you do a good job. And Benny will have to stay here twice as long waiting on me to make the nightly deposit at the bank. And Endo will have to stay twice as long because he can't do his work until you finish yours. Next time you want to do your friend a favor, why don't you try thinking about the rest of us."

See? Irritating. Difficult. And definitely rude. "Or you could clean her station for me. Then nobody has to stay late. Win-win."

He took a step toward me, and I knew it was a subconscious, slightly murderous response to my taunt. He wanted to strangle me. He wouldn't obviously—at least not with so many witnesses present. But he wanted to. "Excuse me?"

"Before the pay raise, that was your job, Shaw. Or don't you remember?" I refused to call Wyatt chef. It was his rightful title, earned and owned by the position he occupied. But I could not bring myself to say the word. And that pissed him off more than anything else I said or did.

His jaw ticked once, and I savored that visible angry flex that always gave him away. I loved pissing him off. But he also had a ridiculously attractive jawline, and it looked best when he was furious.

Okay, after everything I'd said about him, I knew that sounded crazy. But Wyatt was one of those people that no matter how much you hated him, he was still very attractive.

Sometimes you got to know someone and if they had an awful personality they got uglier the longer you were forced to interact with them. But Wyatt was pretty much the opposite. The more I got to know him, the more I couldn't stand him. And yet, he was so unbelievably attractive that his looks never seemed to diminish.

He was tall, at least six-foot-four, and even though his frame was thin—probably because of the whole height thing, a concept I was totally unfamiliar with—he was tightly muscled. I mean, muscles were everywhere. Long, sharp, cut muscles that wrapped around his body in sinewy bumps and bulges.

His hair was artfully styled in a hipster swoop with the sides recently shaved, and the longer top pushed to one side. His eyes were deep brow, like melted milk chocolate.

And then there were the tattoos. The ones that covered Wyatt from his wrists to biceps and his entire torso, front and back. Images even snaked up his neck in a visible display of eclectic individualism. His entire body was a work of art. One I wanted to paint or photograph. Or trace with my tongue.

He was everything I shouldn't want, like, or notice. Not because of the tattoos. Or even because of the piercings he'd removed once he'd been promoted. He was the kind of guy I should have been able to ignore entirely because of how opposite we were, because of how much we hated each other.

This rivalry had been simmering for years, and if I'd learned anything in that time, it was that he didn't change his opinion. Not ever. Once he decided something, that was it. And he'd decided a long time ago that he didn't like me.

That should have been more than enough for me to keep my distance and my mouth shut.

But Wyatt had the kind of body and personality that demanded attention. And I was as helpless as everyone else. He walked into the kitchen and immediately we all stood up straighter, straightened our coats, focused on our tasks. And when he left, we exhaled gigantic breaths of relief.

25

For as beautiful as he was to look at, the man was a dictator in the kitchen. Rationally, I knew that was his right. This was his domain. He was the captain of this ship. Lilou lived and died by his direction.

There was even a part of me that was jealous of how he commanded so seamlessly. His decisions were calculated and well thought out. He'd stepped into Killian's shoes and not once faltered. Even if he didn't always make what I considered to be the best decisions, he never revealed regret or insecurity. He was almost entirely emotionless.

Except for anger and irritation. Usually directed at me.

Like right now.

"I remember, Kaya." His voice had pitched low, causing goose bumps to scatter over my arms and the back of my neck. "Do you realize that it's no longer my job?"

I swallowed a lump of resentment. He knew I had been gunning for his position. And if I'd had a little more time to prove myself, I could have made a good run for it. But Killian had left so suddenly that I never had a chance to throw my hat in the ring. One night I was dreaming of the day that Lilou would be mine, the day that Ezra Baptiste, the city's foremost restaurateur, finally hired a woman to fill one of his executive chef positions, and the very next night it was gone. I was back at square one, looking at a position that would never open up again. At least not within an acceptable window of time.

Because of this man.

Because of this arrogant, obnoxious chef I was supposed to call boss.

Holding Wyatt's sharp gaze, even though I desperately wanted to look away, I nodded. "It's impossible to forget. You're constantly reminding us."

"Reminding you," he countered. "You're the only one in this kitchen who manages to forget I'm in charge."

The kitchen fell silent as my coworkers turned to watch the drama. They loved when we went after each other. They loved the intrigue and gossip that came with it. Mostly they loved that Wyatt's rage was totally focused on me and not them.

I shrugged, playing the indifferent, blasé part I knew drove him the craziest. Wyatt was all fire and brimstone. He had no patience for apathy. "Guess I'm a slow learner."

His jaw ticked again, and my heart jumped with it. I could pretend I was unaffected all I wanted, but the truth was so opposite. My insides were tingling with adrenaline, my blood rushing through my veins at warp speed.

"Let's hope you're not as slow at cleaning." He turned around, giving me his rigid back and stiff shoulders. "Get to work, Swift."

Unable to stop myself, I threw up an exaggerated salute with my middle finger. "Aye, aye, captain."

Chapter Two

*T*hree hours later, my feet were begging me to take them home, and I was covered in sweat and kitchen grease. I would probably have to burn my clothes. There wasn't any amount of laundry detergent that could cut through the grime that covered me.

I'd shed my coat as soon as we'd closed the kitchen. That wasn't as easily replaced as a pair of black pants. Well, it could have been. But I liked this one. Call me superstitious, but it had weathered a lot of stressful nights with me. It was the old friend I could always count on.

Stripped down to a tight black tank top and my loose black pants, I stumbled my way to Wyatt's office. I'd been as slow as he'd foreseen cleaning the two stations. But I had also been thorough and meticulous. Throughout the late hours, I'd watched him berate my coworkers when their work had gotten sloppy. I'd gone with the do-it-right-the-first-time method, hopefully saving me from a bitch fest.

But knowing Wyatt, he was bound to find something to nag at me about.

I knocked on the heavy door to his office and waited for his invitation to enter. I was the only one left in the kitchen. Benny and Endo were around somewhere. I had a suspicion they were in the dining room sleeping while they waited for me to finish. Unsurprisingly, nobody had offered to help me. Working in a kitchen was like willingly spending your evenings in a shark tank. Without a protective cage to save you from getting bitten.

After waiting for what I considered a lengthy amount of time, I knocked again. Harder this time. Still no answer from the other side.

Since the office was located at the back of the kitchen, I was confident Wyatt hadn't left. I'd watched him walk inside after he'd checked out the expo station and shut the door behind him. Unless I was so focused on my work that I hadn't noticed him tiptoe past me, he was still in there, probably maniacally plotting my demise, or at the very least, world domination.

I pushed open the door and found him sleeping.

The adrenaline came back in full force and I wasn't sure why. This was the most nonthreatening I had ever seen him. Even when he wasn't my boss, he'd always carried around this razor-sharp bite that scared away most people.

The only person I'd ever seen Wyatt behave nicely toward was Vera. But since she didn't work in our kitchen but owned a food truck across the street at the time, she wasn't considered competition. Killian, his idol, had also fallen for Vera and that was all the seal of approval Wyatt had needed. I'd even seen them laugh and joke around together. It was like watching an alien invasion.

30

Wyatt didn't joke around. And he didn't smile. He preferred to snarl, snap, and wear a scowl that was giving him massive forehead wrinkles. Vera was the only person I'd seen him chill out around.

Seeing him asleep at his desk, his head resting on his folded arms, his body totally relaxed and loose, did something to my dislike of this man. My heart, for an insignificant millisecond, turned squishy and soft. How could someone so domineering all the other moments of the day, look so incredibly inviting in this one? How could someone that preferred to growl and bark and never say anything nice become so boyish and gentle-looking?

I was tired. That had to explain my momentary lapse of reason. And maybe, possibly hallucinating. That was why I felt a weird ache bloom inside my chest. That was why I let my gaze linger along the lines of his face, tracing the curve of his jaw and planes of his cheekbones, the fan of his eyelashes against his cheek, the tousled hair that had fallen over his forehead.

There was something about him like this that made me forget what a douche he always was. His eyebrows furrowed, creating little creases over his nose and I had the strongest urge to rub my finger over the spot and whisper something kind to him.

My eyebrows bunched together in utter confusion. I couldn't imagine what that sweet nothing would be. I wasn't exactly the poster-child for soft and feminine.

He awoke with a jerk as if my thought had scared him awake. I jumped in tandem, my heart hammering with the same fear. Thankfully he didn't notice my reaction. He didn't even seem to notice me at first.

Sitting up with a giant inhale, he rubbed his face with both hands. His sleepy eyes slowly moved to me, and I was thankful my hand had been frozen in the shape of a fist against his door. I hoped he thought he caught me in the middle of knocking. And not standing there ogling him like a total creeper.

31

"H-hi," I said shakily and immediately regretted it. I never said hi to him. Never.

His eyebrows drew down even more and his grimace said everything. "Are you finished?" he asked in a sleep-roughened voice.

Afraid of what I would say next, I opted to nod instead. Watching him sleep had done something to my brain. Like made it stupid. Plus, I was tired, I reasoned. Plus, Mercury was in retrograde. Plus, they found zombie-like leeches in a lake somewhere down South. See? I had all kinds of rational reasons why I suddenly felt overly warm and flustered.

Wyatt braced his hands on his cluttered desk, readying to stand. "Are you ready for me to come look at you?" Our gazes crashed together, running into each other with the force of a high-speed car crash. "I mean your station," he clarified, clearing his throat. "Are you ready for me to come check out your station?"

I nodded again. My tongue had apparently lost the ability to form words. I blamed the bleach I'd been up close and personal with for the last few hours.

He continued to stare at me. "What's the matter, Kaya? Cat got your tongue?"

I shrugged, cleared my throat, and faked a yawn. "I'm just tired," I managed to say.

He rubbed his eyes with his fists and I considered getting my head examined. Why was that sexy? It shouldn't be sexy. And yet there was something about a sleepy, disheveled man that made my heart go pitter patter.

But honestly it could have been any man. It could have been Endo. And he was almost fifty, balding and missing at least two teeth.

"Me too." He sighed. "Come on, let's see how you did."

I stepped back against the doorframe, letting him lead the way. I hadn't opened the door all the way to begin with and as he walked by me, his

32

shoulder brushed against mine. Wyatt and I never touched. We kept our distance on purpose.

Probably because when his warm, muscled shoulder touched mine, energy zinged between us. A sharp, hot current of tension. I jolted from the shock of it.

And someone gasped. But it couldn't have been me.

God, I was starved for sex if contact so insignificant produced that much of a reaction from me. But it wasn't only my lonely self-exile from the male population that forced a response from me. It was Wyatt. He seemed made of electricity. Hot and buzzing and intensely magnetic. It was like all that friction between us had been superheated and turned on high.

Wyatt seemed to notice, pausing halfway through the door. His gaze moved toward me slowly, as if he had to mentally brace himself for what he would see.

"I dare you to find something," I blurted, hoping to cover my stupid reaction. My voice held strong despite my quivering courage.

His eyes heated from my challenge, darkening in color and an inexplicable something else. He leaned down so that he could better capture my gaze. "And what do I get if I win?"

The air between us surged with an electrical pulse. My eyebrows raised at the deep rumble in his voice, the way his cheeks warmed in the same way his eyes did. What was this? Some misplaced, late night impulse? Sleepy sexual confusion?

No, those were crazy thoughts. If there was any confusion it was on my part only. Hadn't we already established my absence of recent dates? Hell, my lack of social life period? I was exhausted and burnt out from working my ass off. And fine, maybe I was a little desperate for attention. But that didn't mean I needed to throw myself at Wyatt—the very last person that would ever be interested in me.

"Satisfaction for a job well done?" I suggested, turning my voice as platonically bland as possible.

I expected him to roll his eyes or throw out an insulting barb. Instead, his voice dipped even lower and he murmured, "When it comes to you, Ky, satisfaction seems impossible."

I let out a sharp exhale as he walked away from me toward the two stations I'd cleaned. What was that supposed to mean?

I sucked in my bottom lip and caught my teeth on the small hoop piercing in my lip while I watched him squat down and examine my work. Was that an insult? It felt like an insult.

It also didn't feel like an insult. It felt weird. I felt weird. And like someone had popped a bottle of champagne inside my body.

Wyatt's strong, tattooed hands moved equipment around, checking every nook and cranny. I watched him work, leaning back against a stainless-steel counter and crossing my arms over my chest. Typically, I would have immediately thrown something back at him. But at this point, in the wee hours of the morning, I didn't have it in me. Instead, I stood there like an idiot waiting for him to find something to snipe at me about.

He examined everything with a meticulous eye that I wanted to hate. Or at least resent. But I couldn't. He had to be this thorough, this strict. It didn't make working for him any easier, but at least this part of him I could respect. It killed me that he'd been given his job without so much as a consideration for anyone else in the kitchen. Okay, maybe he wasn't horrible at it. I wouldn't go so far as to say he deserved the job but he worked hard for it.

I could be an honest, rational person and admit that.

He turned around and caught me staring at his back. He didn't flinch or call me on it. Instead, he retaliated with a slow perusal of my body. Starting at my Doc Martens boots and working his way up my body, pausing almost imperceptibly at my boobs that were pushed up in my tank top thanks to my folded arms. I shivered. And didn't call him on it.

Tit for tat. That's how we played.

"Did you wipe down the sous vide?" he asked, all business... all dark, mysterious man.

Shit. I glared at the machine. This was part of Dillon's station and I hadn't realized it until now. Although now that he'd pointed it out, I had to admit it was obvious. I swallowed the bitter taste of pride. "I forgot..."

I expected shouts and curses and frustration. Shockingly, he lifted one shoulder and said, "All right. I'll deal with it."

I belatedly tried to hide my surprise. "It will only take me a minute," I argued. "It's my responsibility."

"No, it's Dillon's responsibility." I opened my mouth instinctively to defend my friend, but he cut me off before I could get any words out. "It's late, Kaya. Don't argue with me. Go home and go to bed."

My spine straightened, and I felt the irrational sting of his dismissal. The normal part of my brain immediately threw up its hands, warning me to back down. He wasn't trying to be mean or pushy. He was doing something nice.

But that was where the emotional, sometimes illogical part of my brain stepped in, full of suspicion and serious crazy. "It's fine. I should have done it before I bothered you. Not a big deal."

He shook his head and I could see frustration spreading through him. "I know it's not a big deal. That's why I'm going to do it."

"What? Are my standards not high enough for you?"

His expression darkened. "Is that what I said? I'm trying to be nice. You have to work tomorrow."

"So do you."

"For the love of— Woman, you've got problems."

A burst of anger exploded inside me, like a firecracker exploding. Not the whole big show, just one singular Black Cat. A crackle of gunpowder and quick rage. "Yeah, no shit. My problem is you." Even though I was furious with him, this was more familiar territory for us. We were back to normal and so, even in my insanity, I breathed easier. And for some reason that made me braver than usual. Stupidly brave and dangerously cocky. I poked him in the shoulder and said, "You're my problem, Wyatt."

It was the second time we'd touched tonight and, like before, that charge of electricity snapped through the air and shocked my exposed skin. I tried to pull away, but he was faster than me, snatching my hand in his bigger, stronger, rougher one.

"I realize that, Kaya. The whole fucking kitchen realizes it." He stepped closer, his hand closing around my wrist and managing to make me feel tiny and delicate and overwhelmed all at once. "So how about when I'm trying to be nice, you let me."

Licking dry lips, I examined the emotion in his intense eyes, wondering if he was sincere or if I was unwittingly walking into some master trap. And while I was contemplating my next move, the demon witch that sometimes possessed my body, and more specifically my mouth, took control and the argument I'd been wanting to have for hours fell out unchecked. "Only if you let me finish the duck tomorrow night. Mine's better and you know it."

His jaw ticked, and I struggled to swallow. He was so close. He'd shed his chef coat like I had, leaving most of his tattooed arms and neck exposed. The thin t-shirt he wore did nothing to contain the body heat radiating off him. And for some reason he smelled good. Too good.

We'd been working for hours, trapped in this sweltering kitchen, surrounded by all kinds of food and spices. He should smell like grease and sweat at the end of a long, hard day. Contrarily, he smelled like fresh herbs, lemon peel, and the faint, woodsy scent of whiskey.

36

I ran my tongue over my bottom lip again, suddenly feeling inexplicably thirsty.

"I need you on sides," he argued.

"I'm better with protein."

Half his mouth kicked up on one side in a taunting smile. "You're leveraging with the favor I'm going to do for you?"

The demon inside me nudged my body forward, brushing it against his. "I'm going to let you clean the sous vide machine and in return I'm going to let you put me on protein, yes. Win-win."

He shook his head back and forth slowly and let go of my wrist. "That's the second time you've said that tonight. I think our definitions of winning are different."

I took three steps back and grabbed the counter with both hands, the sharp under-edge of it cutting into my palms, curbing the instinct to grasp his t-shirt with two fists instead. "Thanks, Wyatt. You're the best."

"I haven't agreed to anything, Kaya!"

Grabbing my chef coat, I headed to the kitchen staff cubbies to retrieve my purse. Before I made my escape from the kitchen, I turned to face him and winked. "I think we both know you did."

I didn't wait around for his response, but I thought about the half smile he was wearing as I hurried across the dark parking lot to my pride and joy. I drove a 1988 Toyota Land Cruiser. She was vintage and sassy and unexpectedly cool. She also wasn't in the best condition. I mean, she was thirty years old. Older than me. But her engine was solid and what she lacked in air conditioning, she cranked out in super lukewarm heat during the cold months.

The night air revived my senses during my quick jaunt to my SUV and gave my brain renewed energy. That was when I realized how ridiculous I had behaved. My body thought Wyatt was flirting with me, but my mind had

37

finally realized that this was Wyatt, and Wyatt didn't flirt with anyone, let alone with little old me—his arch nemesis. Exhaustion and the chemicals from the deep clean had momentarily erased my ability to think clearly.

The fresh air renewed my semblance of sanity. Rational and realistic once again. Wyatt wasn't flirting with me. And he wasn't sexy, even when he was sleeping at his desk. And I didn't enjoy it the few times we'd accidentally touched each other tonight.

Obviously.

That's why I had stopped thinking about him and my skin had stopped buzzing from where I'd felt him.

Or I had done the opposite of those things. Argh!

I dropped my forehead against the faded steering wheel and laughed at myself. This was out of control. What was wrong with me?

I grabbed my phone from the depths of my purse and ignored the billion notifications from a solid day of ignoring it. I hadn't checked it since before I got to Lilou. Now it was pushing two in the morning and I had a lifetime of social media to catch up on. Only it wasn't going to happen tonight. And tomorrow I was due back at work at the same time… Maybe I could finally sit down and re-engage with society this weekend. Or maybe not.

Dillon had texted me hours ago. I had intended to open her message and accept her well-deserved gratitude for cleaning her station. My next planned move was to demand that she find me a date to make us even and to make me sane again. Clearly, I needed to interact with the outside world. My workaholic propensity was driving me insane and if I didn't do something about my libido I was likely to throw myself at the newest dishwasher. The actual machine, not Endo's seventeen-year-old nephew. I was desperate, not a criminal.

But her text totally derailed me, and I forgot about my weird night with Wyatt and my worrisome social calendar altogether.

Dillon: Ezra said his head chef at Sarita quit tonight. YOU SHOULD GO FOR IT!

What? What-what-what?!?

Call me tomorrow, I demanded, knowing she was in bed by now. **I want to know every single thing.**

Sarita was one of the four restaurants Ezra owned. All of them featured premier city dining and reputations of excellence. But recently, Ezra had struggled to find loyal chefs to head them. It wasn't a total anomaly for our industry. Ego went a long way in this business and it was hard to find a chef that could back-up his claim to fame. And on the other side of the coin, Ezra was notoriously hard to work with.

Before Killian left Lilou, Bianca lost her executive chef over creative differences with Ezra. Lilou had always been the shining jewel out of the four restaurants. Even with Wyatt, who had never been EC before, she still managed to maintain her top spot. But now that Sarita was without a chef, Ezra had to be freaking out.

The constant turnover was a testament to how persnickety Ezra could be as a manager. This was not a secret. Even Killian had struggled working for him, and they were best friends.

Ezra was opinionated, stubborn, and emotionally invested in every aspect of his restaurants.

I'd enjoyed watching Wyatt struggle for the past few months. It was fun for me. Not so fun for him. Ezra and Wyatt argued about everything. I'd walked in on them several times having explosive menu disputes.

The same had been true when Killian worked at Lilou too, but the difference was Wyatt managed to be more stubborn. Or maybe Ezra was tired of fighting the same battles. Regardless, Wyatt had actually been winning lately and I had been excited for the small changes he'd managed to make to the archaic menu.

39

But Dillon's text changed everything. Bianca was still without a head chef, leaving Ezra extra vulnerable now that he had to deal with Sarita too. That, in turn, made him prone to make decisions he might not ordinarily make.

I slumped in the driver's seat and clutched my phone with two fists. A mixture of fear, courage, hope, and despair churned inside me. I wanted to believe I was good enough for this, that I could handle a kitchen of my own. This was what I had been working for since before I graduated high school. This was what I wanted more than anything.

Could I run my own kitchen? Could I convince Ezra I could handle it?

The number of women executive chefs compared to men was abysmal. We were highly underrated throughout the entire world. In of the top four restaurants in Durham, did I even stand a chance?

My hands shook as I set my phone down and started my car. They didn't stop shaking the entire way home. Or as I showered and washed my face and climbed into bed. This was it. This was my chance.

Of course, I was going to take it. Of course, I was going to do whatever it took to make that restaurant mine, to prove what a kickass, capable chef I was. Sarita was the perfect restaurant for me. The vibe, the food, the culinary profile? It was everything that I was.

I was made for that restaurant. And there was nothing anybody could do to stop me. I would throw myself into this wholeheartedly, dedicating all my resources and time to get this job. I would do whatever it took to land this once-in-a-lifetime position.

I merely had to stop thinking about Wyatt's stupid half-smile first and the text he sent right before I drifted off to sleep.

Proteins are yours again, Swift. But only if you do them as well as you cleaned your station tonight.

He'd finished the text with a winky face emoji just to be smartass. And I accidentally fell asleep smiling.

Chapter Three

I woke up the next morning later than I'd wanted. It was a little before

eight in the morning when I finally dragged my butt out of bed, but since I

didn't finally nod off until after three, I felt justified sleeping in.

I growled at my clock. Was this really considered sleeping in? Five hours

of sleep was overdoing it? God, I was a masochist. And the crazy thing was

that I knew I was asking for more. If I ever landed an executive chef

position, whether it was Sarita or something completely different, I could

forget about sleeping altogether.

Wyatt, for example, didn't leave until after I did, and he would already be

at Lilou this morning accepting deliveries and taking care of the business side of his job. It wouldn't be like that forever of course. Occasionally, Wyatt and I accepted deliveries for Killian to let him catch up on sleep. But it wasn't like Killian took vacations. Wyatt was the same. He would never be able to entrust Lilou to someone else.

And if I managed to finally secure the job I wanted? I would follow suit.

What had Dillon said about Ezra? This was the first vacation he had ever taken.

This was a special kind of club for people that would rather work than live.

Yes, this was my dream job and I loved it with every ounce of my being, from my very bones to the metaphysical pieces of me that didn't even have a name. This was what I was born to do, this was my gift to the world, what I would give away and give away until there was nothing left of me. But I also hated it sometimes and the payment it required from me.

My soul had been given purpose and my life had been gifted meaning, but the blessing of finding the thing I was meant to do required daily sacrifice. I was convinced I would live my life doing what I loved, but that what I loved would eventually kill me.

It was a morbid way to think about my job, but it was true. And it was true for all of us. Food was art for us. And we poured ourselves into it, into the creation, perfection, reputation, and also the branding and legacy. Working in the culinary field took everything from us and we welcomed it willingly.

Because we loved it. I loved it. I had never loved anything more than this... cooking... creating... working with food. Cooking defined me. It was my sum total. And all I wanted to do was grow. I wanted to get better and better and level up in big ways in my career, but those felt like natural progressions as my love for this thing got deeper, consumed more of me, as we moved together through this little life of mine.

44

I couldn't continue as Wyatt's sous chef forever. Not only because we had the most dysfunctional relationship in the history of culinary arts, but I wanted more than second in command. There was more to me than working for Wyatt. I was as good as him if not better. I needed my own kitchen. I would do anything for it.

On top of that reason, there was this thing inside me that would never be satisfied living in another man's shadow. Maybe especially Wyatt's. Call it pride or drive or a greedy fucking monster, but I could not spend my life working as hard as I did just to hand the credit to someone else.

I wanted the glory. I wanted the fame. I wanted the massive responsibility that could go up in flames in any given second. I wanted it.

And I was going to get it.

Sarita was the perfect dining experience for me. We were made for each other. She was Ezra's most eclectic restaurant, specializing in tapas and craft cocktails. She had flamenco nights, live bands, and a chef's table that featured a fifteen-course meal. Sarita had personality and a gypsy vibe that made my heart ache with solidarity.

I'd grown up in rural North Carolina, a little town called Hamilton. My parents and two younger sisters, Claire and Cameron, still resided there, living the small-town life and surviving on local gossip and small mindedness. I'd fled the town at the first opportunity.

I was the total cliché. The bad girl that never fit in. The rebel without a cause. The goth/hipster/emo chic that struggled to find her place in a society that didn't even acknowledge her.

I was desperate to be anything but the high school cheerleader that married her quarterback boyfriend and never left town. I couldn't stomach the idea of not doing anything with my life. I didn't live expecting to get pregnant, hoping to breed future cheerleaders and quarterbacks, surviving on all the happenings around town— who was sleeping with who, and what little punk was selling drugs, and oh my God, did you know that so-and-so filed for bankruptcy?

I could not do it. I couldn't even pretend to approve of that pathway for anyone else.

My rebellion made me a huge disappointment to my parents, who wanted nothing more than a prom queen daughter and future prom royalty grandchildren.

In protest, I'd spent middle school smoking under the bleachers and high school ditching class and avoiding team sports. And I'd almost made it out unscathed.

It was junior year and I was at my wit's end with my parents and my shining star sisters that were happy to drink the Hamilton Kool-Aid. I met someone who got me in a way that nobody ever had. He listened to me and thought it was cool I liked to read instead of cheer. He liked the boho way I dressed and that I dyed my hair every color of the rainbow. He even liked that I wanted to leave Hamilton, that I saw my life bigger and better, and more purposeful than what that town had to offer. Because he wanted to leave too. Or, at least that's what he'd told me when we talked about the future.

That's how I ended up dating the star quarterback. Nolan and I had been friends since childhood, but in junior high, he'd gone his way and I had gone mine. Until eleventh grade, when Fate had partnered us for pig dissection. What had started as a familiar friendship quickly turned into something so serious I was still recovering from it.

And the worst part? Worse than falling in love with someone who lied to me, led me on, promised to marry me and did all that he could to trap me in that stupid town? I ended up accepting everything I didn't want or like—high school politics with popular best friends and small-town dreams.

46

I was willing to give up everything for him. My parents saw Nolan's power over me and jumped on the opportunity to trap me.

They bribed me with a sweet car to encourage me to go to school consistently. Homework was easy for me, so the good grades followed. They turned a blind eye to the partying because that's what all the kids in town did. My parents carefully encouraged when Nolan started talking about the future and what life could be like for us once we'd graduated. They dropped helpful suggestions about where we could live and how quickly we could marry.

Nolan wasn't the life I wanted, but I was in too deep to remember that. I loved him more than I had ever loved anything. And with our parents' support, I slowly forgot my dream of leaving Hamilton and making something of myself. I forgot about doing bigger and better things than playing house.

He loved me too after all. And he didn't want to leave Hamilton anymore. He liked it there. Plus, if we were going to get married so young, we should stick by our parents' because they could help us if we ever needed it. And what about kids? Didn't I want to raise them in a town I trusted and make sure they had the same idyllic childhood I did?

His argument tasted sweet and safe and it was embarrassing how easily I gave in.

Of course, I would stay. Of course, I would marry him. Of course, my plans could evolve now that I had him.

Everything changed the spring of my senior year. I had signed up for a semester of fluff, so I could skate through to graduation. One of the classes was a cooking class. My teacher, Mrs. Wilton, wasn't the most inspiring mentor ever, but she didn't need to be. All she needed to do was give me sharp knives and the opportunity to find myself in food.

And I did find myself. In the best way.

I ignored all my local college acceptance letters where Nolan had also been accepted and secretly applied to culinary schools. When I get the letter from the culinary arts program at The Art Institute at Raleigh-Durham, I cried tears of real joy for the first time in my life.

Not only was it one of the best programs in North Carolina, it took me far away from Hamilton and the life I'd been willing to settle for.

I kept the news a secret until after graduation, but even when I told Nolan and my family the change of plans, I made it seem like the AI was only a detour from the original plan. Not a total deviation in the trajectory of my future.

At the time, it was what I believed too. I hadn't planned to leave Nolan. I hadn't planned to abandon the plans we made for our future. And yet when it came down to it, I couldn't make myself go through with community college. I couldn't stomach the idea of living there a second longer, even if we were saving up for a place of our own.

Culinary school had been less of a carefully crafted alternative and more of a panicked, wild-eyed desperate last-ditch effort to save my soul. It sounded dramatic now, but that town had crushed my spirit. I couldn't breathe there. I couldn't be me. And I knew that if I stayed, I would never be happy either.

My parents were pissed of course. They couldn't understand what I would do with a culinary degree in Hamilton. To this day, they were still waiting for me to regain my senses and come home. Every time I called them, they tried to lure me in with local drama and reminders that Nolan still hadn't found anyone to settle down with.

I gently reminded them that I had landed my dream job and I was still able to pay rent on time, but I'd call them the following Sunday and we could do the song and dance all over again. We hadn't ended a conversation pleasantly in years.

48

Mostly, it was my mother. She blamed me for ruining her life, for letting go of Nolan, for screwing everything up like I was so prone to do. My dad was disappointed he couldn't see me whenever he wanted, but he didn't try to emotionally blackmail me to move home.

And then there was Nolan.

For as young as we were, our love was real. We stayed together for way longer than we should have. Seven years of my life had been spent holding onto something neither of us was brave enough to let go of. We fought all the time. He kept promising to follow me to Durham. And I kept believing him. It was only a matter of time before we self-destructed.

At first, he would visit me on weekends and we would look for apartments we both liked and Google jobs he would enjoy. As the years piled up, he stopped visiting as much and I stopped expecting anything from him. Eventually all the reasons we should be together stopped making sense. We wanted different things out of life. We'd grown into new people that didn't have anything in common. We said we still loved each other, but if it was love it was selfish and entitled. Neither of us had been willing to compromise. Neither of us had really wanted to change—no matter how many empty promises we made.

Seven years. Seven years with a man that couldn't follow through on anything. From when I was seventeen until I finally let go three years ago at twenty-four, he always had an excuse for why he couldn't transfer schools or quit his job at the high school or move in with me. Seven years of phone calls full of awkward silences and disappointed weekends when he would cancel our plans. Seven years of making the arduous back and forth, trying to make a long-distance relationship work between two people totally unwilling to try.

He even proposed. Right after he'd graduated with his teaching degree and accepted his position at Hamilton High School, he showed up on my

49

doorstep with a black square box and a tiny diamond. "I love you, Kaya." He promised. "I want to do right by you."

My poor, frustrated, neglected heart had soared. We were finally going to have the life we'd been dreaming about for so long. I was finally going to be able to give up Hamilton for good and settle into my Durham life. I was finally going to get to be full-time with the man I loved.

Only his plans had changed. He'd rearranged our future but didn't tell me until after I'd said yes to marrying him. He'd decided he no longer wanted to move to Durham by then. He'd bought a little house on the outskirts of town and loved his new job.

I knew I could never move back. No matter how quaint he promised our life would be. There wasn't anything in that town for me. And yet still, I hadn't been willing to give him up. Stupidly, I thought that if he loved me enough, I could change his mind. Eventually, he would realize I was worth the move.

As our engagement dragged on and on without a wedding date to plan for or any real motivation by either of us to get married, I too-slowly realized we were over. I finally acknowledged we had been over for a very long time.

It killed me. I had poured years into that man. I had truly believed I would spend the rest of my life with him. And I knew he felt the same way about me. Admitting that everything had been for nothing did something irreversible to my heart, added layers of paranoia and skepticism that scarred me. His lack of motivation to be with me felt like rejection in the worst way. Why wasn't I enough for him? Why didn't he want to be with me more than he wanted to be comfortable in that godforsaken town?

By the end of our relationship, I felt brittle, hollowed out, and empty. I knew it wasn't entirely Nolan's fault. I hadn't been willing to change. I hadn't been open to moving. But that didn't stop the insecurity from slipping inside like an evil ninja and setting up residence in my heart. I wasn't the

50

kind of girl men moved for. I wasn't the woman that men wanted to spend their life with. I was safe and comfortable and throw away.

I broke up with him over Christmas when I was home and staying with my parents. It hadn't been messy. He said he'd known it was coming for a while, but he didn't want to be the one to hurt my feelings.

That New Year's Eve, he went to a party with all our old high school friends and hooked up with Delaney Cooper, former head cheerleader and prom queen. I'd found out about it via social media and the walls around my heart had grown barbed wire and electric fence.

Of all people, her? Of all parties, that one?

I had still hoped he'd come after me, move to Durham, prove I was worth the fight. For years after, I clung to the hope that he would wake up from all of the hooking up and dating random girls and realize I was better… what we had was better than the meaningless, shallow life he lived now. But he never did. Or I wasn't worth it after all. Face to face with his true colors, I had to acknowledge that he probably never loved me. He merely loved the idea of me.

He'd broken my heart. And maybe I had broken his. Maybe him. He still texted every once in a while, when he'd been drinking too much and the girl he went home with didn't do enough to help him forget how much he hated his life. But that wasn't my fault.

I'd spent three years having this argument with myself and it always boiled down to that toxic town. He could leave. He had a degree in high school education and experience coaching the football team. Nothing was holding him there. He had family, but it wasn't like he had to move to the moon.

Some nights, I would text him too. When I had been drinking too much. And when guilt and heartache and nostalgia for what we'd had all those years ago threatened to eat me alive. I would reach out to him and ask him to come visit me.

And he would counter that I should come home to him.

There were also the times I went home to visit my parents for holidays or birthdays or whatever…

The problem was that Nolan was as lethal as the town. He would lure me with his all-American smile and quarterback muscles and I would get lost in the bliss of being eighteen and invincible all over again.

The last time we'd hooked up had been eighteen months ago. I'd been in town for my parents thirtieth wedding anniversary and had had too many white wine spritzers at their country club garden party.

My parents had the love story Nolan and I had tried to have. High school sweethearts, married at twenty-one, kids at twenty-four, retirement on the horizon. And despite my hang-ups with them, they truly loved each other.

Calling Nolan that night had felt inevitable. I'd been drunk and lonely and he had been happy to pick me up. That night he'd been as familiar and lackluster as I remembered him to be. I woke up the next morning surrounded by Hamilton High football t-shirts and empty PBR cans and felt sick to my stomach.

No matter how much I'd tried to convince myself differently over the years, Nolan was the same as he'd been when I'd fallen in love with him. That small-town, rudderless life was enough for him. He didn't want anything more than that. By the time I'd put Hamilton in my rearview mirror, I had decided to be happy for him. And why not? He wasn't going to change.

And neither was I. The small town wasn't for me. Not even if it meant the house and the husband and the two-point-five kids. Cooking was worth the sacrifice, worth the loss of everything else. It was worth the chaos and the long hours and the exhaustion. Even the critic reviews and the never-ending, suffocating pressure to get better and do better and become the fucking best.

52

And if I got Sarita… I couldn't even think that far ahead. I had to figure out if there was someone in-house that Ezra would handpick.

My heart dropped to my toes at the very thought of it. Grabbing my phone, I quickly typed out a text to Dillon.

Want to meet for coffee before work?

The text dots started dancing immediately. **I'm headed to Vera and Killian's restaurant. I have to drop something off for E. Want to meet me there?**

My plan was to grill Dillon for every last detail she'd learned from Ezra about Sarita, but Killian and Vera would be even better. **Yes! Going now?**

I'll be there in ten.

See you soon.

I hauled ass to the shower and skipped shaving. I mean, I was wearing pants all day, there was no point. Scrunching my hair with enough product to encourage global warming to keep up the good work, I let my chin-length, bright pink hair air dry while I threw on minimal makeup. I was ready in record time.

There wasn't a whole lot to my uniform other than a clean pair of pants, the right shoes and a tight cami under my chef's coat, which I didn't wear until I got in the kitchen. I grabbed a gray silk duster for the cool morning air and my messenger bag and headed out the door with a banana in my hand. It wasn't necessarily the breakfast of champions, but it would do for today.

I'd grab coffee later. Ugh, the thought of not having a cup before I left nearly killed me. Coffee was essential to life. I wasn't even very smart without it. Without my morning cup, I turned into this un-caffeinated, bumbling idiot that couldn't remember words or social cues or anything beyond zombie-level hunger.

Undoubtedly, this was the perfect time to feel out my dream job with three other stellar chefs who probably didn't even need coffee to have coherent conversations before noon.

I rolled my eyes at myself and hurried down the stairs of my apartment building. The sun was warm as I stepped out to the small parking lot attached to my midtown building. For a single person living in Durham, I made a decent enough living. But I was all middle of the road. Medium salary. Medium part of town. Medium apartment. Yes, I was on the nicer end of the spectrum, but it wasn't enough.

What scared me the most about my ambitions was that I would never have enough, be enough, do enough. That I would always want more.

Those starving pieces buried inside terrified me. Would I ever be totally happy with what I was doing or where I was in life? Would I ever feel joyful contentment? Or even moderately good enough?

There was a certain level of striving that I was okay with. I didn't want to lose my drive or my standards of excellence. Those qualities required fierce tenacity and ferocious hunger. My long-term goals required me to push, to keep rising and become a better chef.

Yes. Those were good traits, but what about the darker side of those same desires—the gaping abyss inside me that wanted to consume everything in my path. Would that desire ever be filled? Satisfied? Exhausted?

I shivered despite the warm day. Did I even want to consider those questions without a cup of coffee first?

I yanked open the rusty door to my Land Cruiser and decided my crazy musings could wait until after caffeine. My foggy brain didn't have the energy for serious self-examination right now.

Thursday morning traffic was as difficult as every other day of the work week. Durham wasn't an overly populated city by any means but driving downtown was always a special experience. Traffic made me rage-y.

By the time I got to Killian and Vera's restaurant, Salt, I had devolved into a furious, cursing caveman. I noticed Dillon's Lexus in the parking lot and breathed a minute sigh of relief. It was comforting to have an ally in life in the nearby vicinity. Knowing I was meeting up with Dillon soothed some of my frazzled edges and whispered rational thought back into my haggard brain.

Although, after wrestling my purse from the passenger's seat and walking the short distance to the main entrance, my traffic frustration and subsequent calm had turned to buzzing nerves and a flurry of internal butterflies.

I didn't know Vera enough to call her a friend, but she had always been nice to me. If we ran into each other in a public space, I wouldn't hesitate to walk over and say hello. Killian, on the other hand, was intimidating as hell. Like some kind of brutal warrior from Greek mythology that was willing to kill you over a stolen wineskin. My courage shriveled to an embarrassing shell of itself.

He was mortal, I reminded myself. Exactly like me. Fine, four years of my life had been spent working for him, listening to him yell at me, perfecting my craft so he wouldn't yell at me, trying to do whatever it took to avoid him yelling at me… But he was as human as me.

I should thank Killian for those difficult years. He'd given me the tools for success that I planned to use to climb my way to the top of this city's culinary upper echelon. He'd helped mold me into a competent, experienced chef. He'd promoted me to one of his coveted sous chef positions and demanded perfection and because of that I was confident I could produce perfection.

Still, I'd lived over four years of my life balancing the growing pains of maturity against trying desperately to not cross his line of fire. I'd seen him at his worst, throwing dishes across the kitchen and snarling at anything that breathed near him. And I'd seen him at his best, earning awards and stars and

55

accolades from the most important organizations and people in our industry. He was hardheaded and cocky, but also fair and talented, and pretty much a genius with food.

He was everything I wanted to be. That said, walking into the restaurant that he'd abandoned Lilou for was like some kind of religious pilgrimage for me. A restaurant like Salt was the big goal, the destination. I was convinced this was what was at the end of the long, arduous journey I was willing to struggle my entire life to reach.

I had no false hopes that I would be able to accomplish what Killian had in the time that he had accomplished it. Killian was kind of a freak when it came to success. I was on the right path and I needed to remember that.

My fingers trailed reverently over the bright blue doors that opened into the main dining room of Salt. They were the only bright spot of color in an otherwise starkly white layout. My breath caught in my throat as I took in the rest of the space.

The restaurant might as well have been glowing with an angelic hue for all the wistful and slightly jealous emotions rushing through me. It was the first time I had been inside, and the first time I realized it was so close to completion.

Vera and Killian had both left amazing jobs—dream jobs—to pursue opening a restaurant together. Killian had abandoned a lot of his claimed awards by leaving Lilou, ones that were specific to Lilou's kitchen. Vera had given up her food truck for this. And they had no guarantee that it would succeed.

I was as impressed with their persistence as I was worried for them. They were both unquestionably good at what they did. But was good enough?

For a lot of great chefs, it wasn't. There had to be more than good food to make an acclaimed restaurant. Where the real awe in my assessment came from was the "it" factor they had nailed with the décor and ambiance.

Between the big wooden rafters and the garage door walls that would open to the outside during the warmer months, I already felt comfortable in this space. I already looked forward to the food. I was already planning girls' nights out here. I couldn't wait to book a reservation and discover the menu.

They'd nailed it. And I tried not to hate them for it.

"Hello?" I called out when I realized I'd been standing frozen on the stone entryway floor for long enough. "Is anyone here?"

Dillon popped her head through the swinging kitchen doors and waved me back. "We're in here."

My eyes dropped to the mug in her hand. "Is that coffee?"

She smiled at me, waving her cup in the air. "It's fresh. Better get back here before Vera drinks it all."

My respect for Vera leveled up knowing she was as much of an addict as I was.

The promise of caffeine took the edge off my nerves and I entered the kitchen totally unprepared for the gleaming glory that awaited me. Lilou's kitchen was spotless. Especially after I spent hours scrubbing it last night. But it was also old enough to have lost some of the shiny sparkle that brand-new kitchens possessed. Like a cartoon with an illustrated glow, every surface, every appliance, every inch seemed to wear a halo.

"Wow," I heard myself say with childlike awe that I couldn't help.

"Welcome," Vera greeted, as pleasant and kind as I'd always known her to be.

I tore my eyes from the expensive machinery to focus on the chef I had come to admire and respect over the last year. "This is crazy."

Her cheeks turned pink. "It *is* crazy."

Her embarrassment only endeared me more. "It's nice though, yeah?"

She laughed self-consciously. "There's more room than the truck. That's nice for sure."

57

I looked around at her massive kitchen space, mentally comparing its size to Lilou's. Salt had it beat by at least five feet on every side. "This kitchen is amazing. I can't wait for you to open."

Vera raised her eyebrows behind a sip of her coffee. "Why? Looking for a job perchance?"

It was my turn to blush. It was a generous offer from her. And unsubstantiated. "I, uh, I-I like Lilou."

"That's a lie." Dillon snorted, sharing a friendly look with Vera. "She hates Lilou."

"I do not!" I defended quickly "I love the restaurant."

"Fine." Dillon sighed. "She hates Wyatt."

Vera laughed again, but it sounded surprised this time. "What? Why?"

Dillon snorted again, hopping backwards to sit on a steel counter. I inwardly cringed at her irreverence but held my tongue. Dillon didn't have the same kind of worshipfulness I had with kitchens. Or with anything really. She was pretty much aloof when it came to social cues and expected behavior. Which were my favorite things about her. Most of the time.

"He's an asshole," I blurted, feeling safer with Vera than I probably should have. They were friends. This would have been a good time to hold my tongue.

Vera laughed again, more subdued this time though. "Every good chef is. It's the only way they can protect their fragile egos."

Dillon canted her head at Vera. "You're not an asshole."

Killian's voice boomed from a doorway that led to a hallway at the back of the kitchen. "You've never cooked with her."

Vera's eyes narrowed at her fiancé. "Poor, abused baby."

He grinned at her and I had a sympathetic pang for Vera. How could she stand him looking at her like that all the time? Killian had to be one of the most beautiful humans on the planet to begin with, but then add in that

58

adoring look in his eyes and the way his whole body seemed to warm and lean toward her? How did she survive it?

I would have died by now. Or gone into permanent shock.

She was for sure a lucky woman. But she also had to be one of the strongest out there. Not because of how beautiful Killian was, but because of how difficult he could be too.

"I am abused," Killian agreed, closing the distance between his bride to be and the doorway in long, stretched strides. "Thank you for noticing."

She rolled her eyes and looked at me as he put his arms around her middle. "See what I mean?"

"Yeah, well, Wyatt is an asshole in a totally different way than"—I waved my hand at them—"whatever you two have going on."

Dillon made a sound in the back of her throat and gave them a disapproving look. "It's like this all the time, Ky. You should be around when my brother and Molly are here too. The four of them in the same room is downright disgusting."

"What do you mean disgusting?" Killian demanded.

I turned my back on all three of them and went hunting for coffee. I found a French press near one of the stovetops with a saucer of creamer next to it. Yes. Please.

While I poured, Dillon exclaimed, "Are you kidding me? Y'all are like a Hallmark Christmas movie, but all the time. I didn't even know it was possible to get sick of love. But I am chronically grossed out these days."

Vera and Killian laughed, too far gone to be bothered by Dillon's comments. "Your brother is way worse than I am," Killian argued. "He's like a smitten puppy."

I turned around just in time to watch Dillon give a pointed look at Killian's arms still firmly encircling Vera. "And you're not?"

59

Killian only grinned at her. "Obviously I am. I'm just way cooler about it than he is." He turned back to me. "Let's get back to the topic. Why is Wyatt an asshole?"

This wasn't something I wanted to talk about with my former boss. And my current boss's friend and mentor. Time to deflect. "You've met him. It's self-explanatory."

Killian's smile died. "Regardless of what Vera has led you to believe, we're not all awful. And I don't think Wyatt is at all. He's hard maybe, precise. He knows what he wants and isn't afraid to go after it. But I don't think that makes him an asshole."

"Maybe," I said noncommittally.

Killian wasn't fooled by my halfhearted answer. "It's probably hard for you since you used to work with him and now have to work for him. It's not that he's an asshole, it's just a difficult adjustment."

"It's not that at all," I admitted when I knew I should keep my mouth shut. "I don't mind perfection. I worked for you and didn't complain."

Killian's eyebrows rose slowly, and I knew I'd said too much.

"Much," I added quickly.

He cracked a small smile. "He's good for Lilou. He's good for you."

The back of my neck prickled, and I took a sip of coffee to hide my urge to rub it. "I don't know about that. Maybe he's good for the restaurant, but we butt heads in the worst way."

Killian's smile stretched. "He doesn't like that you're as good as he is."

The compliment spiraled through me, warming me from head to toe, slightly thawing some permanently frozen place inside my chest. "I don't think either of us like it," I admitted, suppressing the ego swell.

His smile disappeared, and he straightened. It was like he put on a different persona. Gone was the man in love and in his place appeared a wise father figure that was about to offer sage advice. I shifted again. I had never

60

been great with authority. "He needs you, Kaya. He was the best for the job, yeah? I didn't give it to him to spite you. I gave it to him because he deserved it. But that doesn't mean you aren't important. He's kept you as sous, right?"

I shrugged. "Yeah, but he also threatens to take it away from me every single night."

"He won't." Killian's affirmation was confident. "He can't. There's no one else in that kitchen that's ready."

"Hey!" Dillon cried out in protest. Killian gave her a look and she wilted, folding her arms over her chest and sticking out her bottom lip. "Fine, Kaya's amazing, blah, blah, blah."

Killian's gaze moved back to mine. "Support him, Kaya. Support his role completely before you move on."

My eyes narrowed. The boost to my ego from his compliment a few seconds ago was replaced with the sharp, raw feeling of vulnerability. I hated that he saw me so clearly. I hated that he'd managed to motivate me to stay with Wyatt while making me feel valuable as a chef all at once. I didn't want people to see this much of me. I wanted to remain hidden, mysterious. Yeah, fine, I wanted my talent to be known, but I didn't want that to give anyone insight to my insides.

"Why do you think I'll leave Lilou?" I asked him, needing to know how obvious I was.

He shrugged and looked around the kitchen. "Because you're never going to be satisfied with being number two. You don't have it in you to support someone else forever."

"I can't tell if that's an insult or a compliment."

He smiled again, but this time it was at his future wife. "It's admirable." He turned back to me. "But EC is hard as shit. A lot of chefs want to get to the top, but few have it in them."

61

I laughed to make light of his warning, knowing he was right. "I'm okay with hard."

"That's what she said!" Dillon giggled from across the kitchen, her arms raised over her head in victory like she'd won something for being the first person to ever say it.

We all groaned at her terrible joke, but inwardly I was grateful we could move past the life lessons portion of the morning.

"This is why you're still single," Killian teased her in that older brother way.

She stuck her tongue out at him. "Speaking of being single…" She paused dramatically and we all waited to find out where she was headed with this. "What's happening with Sarita? Ezra was on the phone all last night and I fell asleep before he decided anything."

Killian rolled his eyes. "If he was smart, he'd sell the damn thing. He should piece off all of the harem except for Lilou. They're more trouble than they're worth."

The harem was how we lovingly referred to Ezra's group of restaurants, all named after ex-girlfriends.

"He won't do it," Dillon stated simply, but with all the confidence we knew she had the right to have. "He loves them too much."

Killian leaned back against the sink. "Which is ironic considering how much he didn't love the actual women they're named after."

Vera snorted a laugh. "If he names a restaurant after Molly, I'm going to punch him in the throat."

Dillon and Killian quickly promised Vera that would never happen. I wasn't totally convinced, but then again, I didn't know Ezra. I knew about him. And I worked with him enough that I knew what to expect from him in a professional setting. But I didn't know anything about his personal life. Except that he dated high maintenance women with exotic names.

But even that was learned secondhand.

"What will happen to Sarita?" I asked, refocusing the conversation.

"We're going to run it while Ezra is on vacation," Vera answered. "Because we hate ourselves."

Killian explained, "Ezra was going to cancel their big vacation, but Vera felt bad for Molly so here we are, running the most dysfunctional kitchen on the planet."

"That's not true," Dillon argued. "Bianca is the most dysfunctional kitchen on the planet. Sarita will truly be better without Juan Carlo."

I bit my bottom lip to keep from smiling. Juan Carlo was as pretentious as his name suggested. He was a beast to work for and a complete egomaniac. Wyatt was bad, Juan Carlo was impossible. But his food was only mediocre in my opinion and he never changed the menu. Still, somehow, he'd created the illusion of a big name for himself and prior to last night, I never thought Sarita would be available.

"You two are in charge until Ezra gets back? Then what?"

Killian gave me an assessing look that again made me feel too seen, like a kid in trouble with her parents. "Then the search begins."

Looking everywhere but at Killian, I asked, "Do you think he'll hire in house?"

"Hard to say," Killian replied. "It's always hard to say with Ezra."

That response got me nowhere. I downed the rest of my delicious coffee and rinsed the mug out in the sink.

"Just set it there," Vera directed. "I'll get it later."

"Are you sure?"

"It's not a problem," she promised, offering me a smile.

"Thanks. And thanks for the coffee. I needed it today." I caught Dillon's eye and nodded my head toward the exit. "We should get going."

"Oh, yeah." She hopped off the counter and turned to Killian, launching into something about how Sarita opens and delivery information.

Vera moved to my side and started walking, indicating that I should follow her. So, I did. Once we were back in the dining room, she nudged me with her elbow. "Do you want Sarita?"

I swallowed a lump large enough to be my heart. "Wh-what?"

"Don't play humble with me," Vera laughed. "Do you want it?"

Rolling my eyes at her so she knew I didn't appreciate being called out, I admitted, "Obviously, I want Sarita. I'd have to be crazy not to want her."

Her voice dropped, and she whispered, "He's not going to give it to you."

I would have felt devastated if not for the mischievous tone in her voice. "Why not?"

"Because you're a girl."

"I've never taken Ezra to be the sexist type."

She shrugged. "He's not necessarily. It's the industry. It's all men. And Ezra has never had a female executive chef before. He doesn't even know it's possible."

She wasn't telling me anything I didn't know. The first day of culinary school I realized I would have to work twice as hard as the boys in my class that outnumbered me three to one. "Not even Dillon?"

"That's what I mean," Vera said quietly. "He's definitely going to hire Dillon for Bianca. That's already in motion. You're either going to have to beat her or convince him to give two of his restaurants to women."

I hadn't thought of that. The floor seemed to drop out from underneath me. My fragile dream curled up into a ball and rolled out of reach. "Shit."

It wasn't possible. And not because I wasn't good enough. Vera was right. If Ezra planned to give one of his restaurants to Dillon, there was no chance in hell I would get the other one. And I couldn't compete with my best friend over a restaurant because it was the only option.

64

Besides, I wouldn't be a good fit for Bianca. My integrity wouldn't even let me apply for the position. I didn't want to do fussy French food. I wanted spicy tapas and a sexy, smoldering atmosphere. I would suffocate Bianca. Or the other way around.

"Prove him wrong," Vera coaxed. "Prove that Dillon is a fine hire, but that he'd be crazy not to give you Sarita."

I looked at her, feeling helpless and lost. "How do I do that?"

"First, you're going to have to convince Wyatt. And Killian. And me." She winked. "But spoiler alert, I'm already on your side."

"You're not making me feel better," I whispered, my guts exploding with butterflies and bumblebees and razor-sharp wasps.

She smiled at me. "Don't wimp out on me now, Kaya. Continue showing me the strong, independent woman I know you are. The kickass chef that can outcook and outsmart literally any other man. Do your thing, woman, and the rest will follow."

Her words were like a gust of wind on the dwindling fire inside me, reigniting the fight and flames that had gotten me this far. "This means I have to be nice to Wyatt though, doesn't it?"

She laughed. "Sleep with him if you have to."

I nibbled on my lip ring again, hating that I didn't hate that idea as much as I should. Or at all. I made an amused sound to cover my reaction. "Pretty sure that would only make things worse between us."

She winked at me. "Obviously, I'm kidding. But you have to at least try to get on his good side." We reached the door and Dillon burst through the kitchen, quickly catching up with us. Vera slapped me on the shoulder. "Hey, it's worth a shot! Bye, Kaya."

"Bye, Vera…"

That didn't go anything like I thought it would. Hell.

Chapter Four

$\mathcal{D}$illon and I walked into Lilou through the side entrance laughing about having coffee with Killian and Vera at Salt and the possibility of running restaurants in the same city together. It wasn't a conversation I let myself indulge in often, but she wanted to know what Vera had said to me and I couldn't keep a secret from her.

"What are you going to do? How are you going to get him to like you?" she asked.

"Vera said I should sleep with him," I told her, giggling my way through the sentence.

Dillon laughed harder until it completely died on her lips. I looked up to find Wyatt, the very topic of our conversation, looming over us, staring at me. More like glaring at me.

My smile wobbled, but I managed a sarcastic, "Hey, boss."

His eyes narrowed. "Can I see you in my office?"

That was the last place I wanted to go. I had food to prep and a menu to study. And a separate restaurant to takeover. "Uh, sure."

Dillon stepped away from me to head the opposite direction, but not before she whispered, "Now's your chance," which made me cough and laugh at the same time.

Wyatt's head snapped around to see what I was doing. I waved at him and continued to cough and also plot Dillon's murder. That was the worst thought she could have planted in my head before I was forced to be alone with the man.

He held the door open for me and my mind immediately raced to memories of last night and his body touching mine… his late-night text that almost felt flirty. My thoughts sped forward and wondered if sleeping with him was even possible? Not because of the job. My integrity would never stoop to that level. But because… well, hell, because it was kind of impossible to not thinking about sleeping with Wyatt now.

Would he reject me outright? Or was he the kind of guy to never turn down free play? That thought made my nose wrinkle. I could hardly tolerate Wyatt in a professional capacity, but I didn't think he was a douche in his personal life. In fact, the entire time I'd known him, he'd never bragged or even talked about nightly conquests. Around the time I broke up with Nolan, he'd started dating a girl and I thought it had gotten kind of serious, but they had broken up at least a year ago because she hated his hours. Since then if he hooked up with random girls or started dating someone new, he'd never said anything to anyone.

68

Oh, my god, why was I even considering this? It wasn't like I'd let myself move forward in my career that way.

I pressed a hand to my forehead and tried to push the perverted thoughts out of my mind.

"Are you okay?" Wyatt asked from behind me.

Jerking to face him, I tried desperately to school my features into anything but guilty. "Yes. Of course. Why wouldn't I be?"

He watched me compose myself without another comment. I found him particularly unsettling today. He hadn't donned his chef's coat yet and his black t-shirt clung a little too tightly to his biceps and broad chest, tattoos on full display.

His tattoos were familiar to me now, at least the ones I could see, making them even more dangerous for some reason. The single feather that transformed into a bird stretching elegant wings wrapped around his neck. The fork, spoon, and butcher knife laid out on his right forearm like it was set for service. The outline of a pig on his left forearm with the cuts of meat dotted and labeled. There were more, so many more. They made full sleeves over his forearms and biceps, and I could only assume reached across his chest and touched the visible ones around his neck, but I'd never seen the ones beneath his shirt. Only the ones peeking out.

He wore tapered jeans and stylish gray tennis shoes that probably cost more than half my paycheck. His hair wasn't disheveled from work and stress yet, artfully settled in lush waves.

When my eyes dropped to his stubbled jaw and tired eyes, the pang of sympathy for his late night was the wake-up call I needed. I was checking out my boss—the same boss I drove crazy with my presence.

This was Vera's fault.

Sarita danced around my thoughts, taunting me, calling me with her Siren song. I met Wyatt's mysterious gaze and wondered how I could get him on my side. On one hand, I imagined that he was dying to get rid of me. This was his opportunity.

Maybe. If the position at Sarita opened to the public.

On the other hand, did I have a chance in frozen hell that he would admit what a great chef I was? Especially to Ezra?

His eyes darkened as we stood there silently, staring at each other. His jaw ticked, and I realized how foolish this dream was. He was already pissed off and I hadn't even said anything yet.

I cleared my throat and took a step back. We weren't standing particularly close, but suddenly there wasn't enough room in this whole damn kitchen to put between us. "Did you get any sleep last night?" The question came out differently than I meant it to. It sounded like a criticism when I'd meant it as concern. His eyes narrowed, and I knew he felt the accidental judgment.

He rubbed a hand over his face and turned away from me. "Not much." With short, precise movements, he took a seat behind his desk and leaned back in his swivel chair. "That's actually why I brought you in here."

"I get it, Wyatt. You don't have to berate me. I won't cover for Dillon again. I realize now that it screws everything else up."

He rapped his knuckles on the desk and continued to look at anything but me. "I appreciate that, but that's not why I wanted to talk to you."

My shoulders drooped in response to my disappointment. I had been expecting a fight. At the very least, a riled-up argument. But the tired tone of his voice made it clear he wasn't up for sparring. And considering Sarita, I shouldn't have been either.

I wasn't going to sleep with him. Obviously, that was crazy talk. But I could get on his good side. I could get him to warm up to me. I could maybe even convince him that I wasn't always the villain.

70

It wouldn't be easy. And not because of his feelings for me. I would have to be nice, kind... thoughtful. Blech. They were all qualities I wasn't even sure I possessed.

Running a hand through my short hair and pushing it out of my eyes, I decided to make a vision board when I got home. Not that I was confident the universe would simply drop Sarita in my lap if I taped a picture of her to a poster board. The universe didn't work like that. But maybe a physical reminder of my goals would incentivize me to change... work on who I was.

That's when the universe moved. Not when I wished for something, but when I worked as hard as humanly possible to change, to go after the things I wanted, when I didn't give up or quit trying.

I suppressed a grimace. This better be worth it.

"What do you need me for?" I asked in a tone I hoped came off as sweet.

His eyes lifted from the desk and he hit me with that darkened gaze all over again. His jaw ticked once. Twice. My hands balled into nervous fists from some subconscious reaction to him. This wasn't irritation. Wyatt was a complete mystery in every way, but intuition whispered there was something else going on in his complicated mind—some emotion that made a tingle skitter down my spine and my breathing hitch.

Wyatt cleared his throat and subtly shook his head. "Uh, like you said, I'm tired today. And I, uh... this isn't easy for me to ask. And I wouldn't under normal circumstances, but there's a critic from the Daily Durham coming in tonight. I know it's a small paper, but it's my first real write up, so I'd like for everything to operate as perfect as possible."

He paused to take a breath and I decided to put the poor guy out of his misery. "Got it. I'll be on my game tonight. Don't worry about a thing." I took a step back toward the door, ready to escape the awkward tension between us. It was thick and tangling and I wanted to pick a fight with him if only to put us back in neutral territory. But that would be antithetical to my goal. Instead, I reached for the door handle.

"That's great, but not what I meant exactly." His gaze darted to his computer and then his hands, then to the ceiling, and finally back to me. "This isn't easy for me…"

"You already said that," I reminded him in a deceptively gentle voice. Sharp, biting nerves gnawed through me and my guts started churning with the burn of anger. Was he going to fire me? Was this the end of my career altogether? I mean, we fought and bickered, and sometimes I made jokes at his expense, but he couldn't fire me over all that nonsense… could he? I was a good chef, damn it. The best in his kitchen. If he even tried to—

He rubbed a hand over his face again and mumbled, "Right," into his palm. All at once, as if he'd made some kind of internal decision, he dropped his hand and sat up straighter. "I need you to babysit me tonight. Okay?"

The anger dissipated just like that and startled confusion stepped in. "Babysit you?"

"I'm not sleeping well, okay? If I get to bed at a decent time I can manage a few hours off and on which has been enough so far. But I was here so late last night that by the time I got home I couldn't even manage that. I'm worried what that will mean for my performance tonight, and with the review, I'm worried that…" His eyes turned pleading and hopeful. "Can you make sure I don't send anything stupid out? I need you to keep me focused."

"Why me?" The question came out as a whisper.

"Because you'll tell me the truth. You won't bullshit me because you're afraid of me."

"I am afraid of you." Another sentence I hadn't meant to say out loud.

"Yeah, but not in the ways that matter." A ghost of a smile lifted one side of his mouth. "Keep me on my game tonight, Kaya. Don't let me fuck up."

72

I was flabbergasted. And that wasn't a word I used often. Or ever. However, this moment called for it. Flabbergasted. Completely. Totally. Wholeheartedly.

He wanted me to keep an eye on him? He wanted me to micromanage him?

My first thought, and I wasn't proud of this, was why should I? What had he ever done for me that warranted this kindness? But I quickly stomped it down and banished it completely.

I wasn't a horrible person. Sure, maybe I had a "save yourself" mentality most of the time, but it wasn't something I advertised or wanted to be known for. Of course, I would help Wyatt and do whatever it took to keep this kitchen the highest rated in the city.

At least until I ran my very own.

Wyatt's performance reflected on me. And on the giant off chance that I didn't get Sarita, I might want to apply for a job elsewhere. I would need a good track record to get me into a kitchen as good as Lilou.

Besides, this might also come in handy for leverage. I had already decided to get on Wyatt's good side, to do whatever it took to get his recommendation. This was a first step toward that goal.

But again, my mouth detached from my brain and I blurted, "Why aren't you sleeping?"

He rubbed his eyes with balled fists as if the very mention of sleep made him feel tired. "I don't know. I've never been awesome at it. But it's been worse lately."

I wanted to ask if it was because of his executive chef promotion, but I managed to hold my tongue. Sighing deeply, I said, "You can count on me tonight. I'll be the first to tell you when you've screwed up." I smiled, hoping it added levity to the truth in my words.

His mouth moved, forming a small smile, but it didn't reach his eyes. "I knew I could count on you to nag me."

My smile turned fake as his words rubbed at the bad blood between us. "Remember that you asked for it this time."

He leaned forward, resting his elbows on his desk and craning his neck toward me. "Don't let me fire you tonight."

I set my hands on his desk and mimicked his position. "I'd like to see you try."

This time his smile was real. It appeared at the exact moment his gaze dropped to my boobs that were pushed up accidentally for his viewing pleasure. Shit.

His eyes returned to mine a second later and I wondered if he had even meant to look. Maybe it was a guy reflex. Maybe I shouldn't be throwing my boobs in his face to begin with.

Either way, I couldn't help but enjoy the pink tinge to his cheeks and the stalwart way he refocused on my face. "Don't tempt me," he muttered. I had to press my lips together to hide my smile when his eyes widened at his own words.

I stood up, taking the temptation away from him. And then the devil entered my body. My eyelids drooped, and I took a slow, flirty step backwards. "No promises."

Without another glance back, I fled from the office and found sanctuary in the kitchen. My cheeks blazed with embarrassment and incredulity at my behavior. Who was I? And why was I flirting with Wyatt of all people?

Vera was obviously some kind of witch.

Or maybe that's exactly how desperate for human interaction I was.

My fingers itched to text Nolan. But that wasn't human interaction either. That was a bad habit I had already kicked. There was no sense in reopening that gaping wound.

"Hey, what did Wyatt want?" Dillon asked as I buttoned up my chef's jacket next to her prep work.

"Work stuff," I mumbled absently. "Hey, can you set me up?"

She put her knife down and turned slowly to face me. "What?"

Her open assessment of my out of the blue question made my cheeks burn a brighter red. I immediately reached for my apron in my purse and busied myself with tying it around my waist. "I think it would be fun. Do you feel weird about it? Is it weird that I asked? Just ignore me. It's fine. I'll join Tinder or something."

"Oh my God," she laughed. "Don't join Tinder! At least not yet." Her eyes sparkled as she rubbed her hands together. "This is going to be so much fun!"

Oh, no. What had I done. I pointed my finger at her. "No weirdos."

She waggled her eyebrows. "Obviously."

"And nobody in the food industry." I glanced around the kitchen and noticed everyone pretending not to listen to us. Gossips. All of them. Plus, I'd already dipped my toes in these waters and no thank you. After Nolan, I'd made several bad mistakes around this kitchen. It wasn't an experience I wanted to repeat. "I don't want to date another chef."

Rolling her eyes, she went back to chopping. "I'm not a total idiot. Nobody wants to date a chef. We're all egomaniacs that work the absolute worst hours. You have to date from the outside because they don't know any better. You have to trick them."

I blinked at my friend. "Are you serious?"

She lifted her head and seemed to realize she'd said something she hadn't meant to. "I mean, not like really trick them. But you should probably leave all the details about your career and ambition out of the conversation for a while. In my experience, when they find out how much you work and then

75

you tell them you're hoping for a promotion, so you can work more, they tend to run away like frightened kittens."

I felt a pang of sympathy for my friend. She was a catch, damn it. Super smart, super talented and super hot, she was like the holy Trinity of dream girls. She shouldn't have to hide who she was or what she wanted out of life just to get a second date.

Plus, that was the most ridiculous thing I had ever heard. My career and ambition made me who I was. It would be one of the first things I talked about. To know what I wanted in life was to know me. At least in part.

And I knew that to be true for Dillon too. She acted like she didn't care, but she was a shark in the kitchen. She didn't put up with bullshit, she was the fastest learner I had ever met, and I knew she was doing whatever it took to earn one of Ezra's kitchens by rightful skill, and not only because she was his sister.

But this also put her late-night activities into new perspective for me. I had been worried about her approach to dating because I thought she was worth more than random one-night stands. But maybe there was a deeper issue at work. Maybe it was harder for her to find someone than I realized.

Which sucked for me. If gorgeous, perfect Dillon struggled to find someone, I was screwed.

And not in the fun way.

"Are you looking for a date, Kaya? I'll go out with you, chica," Endo called from across the kitchen.

When I turned to look at him, he made kissy noises at me.

I rolled my eyes at him but laughed anyway. "Thank you, Endo. But I'm terrified of Maria, so I'm politely declining."

Endo's twinkling brown eyes turned serious. "As you should be. That woman is *muy loco*. I love her, you know, but she would probably take a baseball bat to your car."

"Have you seen her car?" Dillon asked Endo. "I don't think you'd be able to tell the difference."

I punched her in the shoulder. "We can't all drive a Lexus, richy-rich."

She was unapologetic. "No, I guess we can't."

Wyatt walked in the kitchen and the joking stopped. We stood up straighter, we straightened our chef coats, we stopped throwing barbs. It was a switch that was thrown the second the title of executive chef showed up.

Even if we didn't all respect Wyatt the way we did Killian, the title would forever command our better behavior and obedience. When Wyatt stepped up as executive chef, we swallowed our protests and hurt feelings. We forgot about the times we'd seen Wyatt screw up and the years of growth we'd spent alongside him. He was chef now. And we worked for him and to please him.

He walked to the center of the kitchen and clapped his hands together. We gathered around him, as was our daily routine, and waited for instructions.

Usually I tolerated his pep talks and suffered through his reprimands. He didn't detail everything that was expected of us tonight, but he also took the opportunity to critique our previous night's performance. And Wyatt could come across harshly.

Killian too. But Killian was also such a legend that it somehow made it more tolerable. Wyatt brought out the worst in me—which was probably why we clashed so often. Also, because he was nitpicky and severe. The rational side of my brain argued that he was still making a name for himself and therefore had to be those things. He was still trying to prove himself.

But I rarely listened to the rational part of my brain. Mostly, I told her to shut up so the bitchy side of me could play.

Today was different though. Wyatt stood in the middle of us and I could see how exhausted he was, the toll the job had started to take on him. His eyes were bloodshot and sunken. His face seemed thinner and haunted. His

77

hands had a tremor that I hadn't noticed until after he'd confessed his insomnia and I'd looked closer at him.

My heart lurched in sympathy. I was literally always annoyed with how hard he was trying. I found his efforts to live up to Killian obnoxious and tedious, especially when he blamed mistakes on me. But maybe my criticism of him wasn't fair.

Wyatt was given the chance of a lifetime. He ran one of the best kitchens in the region, an award-winning kitchen that he'd earned by right of being Killian's second in command. Of course, the weight of his burden would be heavy, of course he would struggle to hold it and carry it and live up to it.

I resolved to treat him with more grace in the future. He had a hard job, and someday, hopefully when I stepped into a similar position in my own kitchen, my staff would treat me with grace as well.

Seven hours later during the middle of service, I felt differently.

"What is this?" he demanded in the same tone I imagined the devil used when his evil minions disappointed him. "This is crap, Kaya! You're better than this. Do it again."

"It's fucking perfect, Wyatt. You're wrong."

"It's too dark. It looks burned to hell. I'm not sending it out."

I swallowed thirty synonyms for asshole and decided this was not the fight I wanted to lose my career over. But he was an asshole!

"That's golden brown," I argued, waving my hand at the duck breast I'd pan seared to perfection.

"It's overcooked," he growled. "Our tables deserve better. Do it again."

Cognizant of the entire kitchen watching our exchange, I leaned forward and dropped my voice. "You asked for my help tonight. Remember?"

He dipped his head down, crowding me with the entirety of his body. "That's why I need you to do it again," he snarled. "I would do it myself if I fucking could."

The world disappeared behind a curtain of red and all I saw was this arrogant chef I wanted to kick in the shins. I opened my mouth to scream at him, but he pressed his hand against my lips before I could make a sound. Ignoring the hate lasers I was shooting out of my eyes, he leaned even closer, dropped his voice to a whisper and pleaded, "Please, Kaya."

It was the stupid please that disarmed me. And the matching tremor of his voice and hand. Son of a bitch. I hated this man, I reminded myself. He annoyed the ever-loving hell out of me and treated me like I was less than. The duck was fucking perfect, but he'd said please, so I would reluctantly redo my perfect duck. Goddamn him.

But that didn't mean I wasn't going to fight back. Faster than I could talk myself out of it, I opened my mouth and bit his fingers. He pulled back, shaking them out. Our shocked expressions had to mimic each other.

Oh, my god. I just bit my boss!

I turned around to run away, possibly out of the building altogether, maybe even the city, when his hand at my waist stopped me. His mouth moved next to my ear and I felt his lips brush against the sensitive flesh of my earlobe.

His words were steel, gritty, deadly serious, but I could barely focus on them with the press of his hot hand against my waist and his impossibly soft lips against my ear. "Careful, Ky," he warned in a deep, throaty voice. "I bite back."

He let me go or I escaped, I would never know which of us moved first. But we sprang apart like cymbals after they'd crashed together in a symphony-ending crescendo and staunchly ignored the open-mouth staring of our coworkers. I doubted they'd overheard him whispering in my ear, but they saw it happen.

The next time I brought him the duck breast it was unarguably perfect.

He didn't comment. And I didn't comment. And the duck went out and the diner didn't comment. At least not negatively.

I was determined to totally focus on my job for the rest of the night and completely forget about the weirdly hot moment between us in the middle of the kitchen and the frantic butterflies still swarming around in my stomach.

My resolve lasted for all of twenty minutes when he found a problem with my filet. I decided that I was safe to hate him all over again.

Chapter Five

A week later, an incessant buzzing woke me from the deepest sleep. I groped the other side of my gigantic bed in search of it. The last remnants of my dream flickered in and out of my consciousness. Fingers in my mouth. Biting, but not in a mean way… A hand at my waist… under my shirt… sliding up toward my breasts… then changing direction and heading to an even better place…

The buzzing stopped and started again. I woke up all the way this time realizing the vibration was my cell phone.

Growling at the king-size bed that seemed a little ridiculous for a single girl, I finally cracked open my eyes and found the damn thing buried in my pillows. I'd forgotten to charge it. Crap.

That's what I got for falling asleep reading on my Kindle app. This bed was one of my few big indulgences. I was a wild sleeper and sometimes even this king didn't feel big enough. But I preferred to fall asleep in the very center and unfortunately my charging cord didn't reach this far.

Hopefully whoever had decided to disturb me at the ungodly hour of eight-thirty in the morning didn't need more than eleven percent of my cell battery to convey their message.

"Hello?" I asked, sounding like an eighty-year-old chain smoker.

"Uh, can I speak to Kaya, please?"

The voice sounded vaguely familiar, but since coffee wasn't in play yet my brain wasn't up to the task of figuring out who it belonged to. "This is her."

"Oh my God, Kaya?"

"Uh, yes."

The voice burst into laughter. "I thought you were a man! Did I wake you up?"

I pushed up on my elbow and tried to decode what was happening on the other end of the phone. "Yeah, you did wake me up." I yawned, opening my mouth as widely as humanly possible and asked, "What guy?"

"I'm so sorry, but I seriously thought a man had answered the phone. Like maybe you had an overnight guest and he'd answered your phone."

Not an awesome way to start a Friday morning. "Who is this?"

"Vera."

Vera? Why was Vera calling me? More importantly, why was she waking me up with insults?

I yawned again.

82

"I'm sorry," she said again. "I didn't realize it was so early. Between taking shifts at Sarita and working to open our restaurant, I literally never know what time it is anymore. Unfortunately, I'm awake all the time."

"That sounds rough." I did my best to sound sympathetic, but I didn't know if I pulled it off.

"And you don't sound like a man," she added quickly. "Your morning voice just surprised me."

Clearing my throat, I gave her a break. "No, I get it. I have the worst morning voice." And morning breath come to think of it. I stretched my legs, pointing my toes and working out the kinks in my muscles from last night's late shift.

"I do too," she said quickly. "I blame the kitchen. All those flames and smoked meat. It can't be good for us."

She was right about that. Not that either of us would even entertain the idea of changing careers. "I don't mean to be rude or anything, but why did you call?" As lovely as it was to chat with Vera, a person I barely knew, I really had to pee.

"Oh, right! I was wondering if you would like some lessons."

"Lessons?"

"Like in the kitchen?" she asked, confidently.

Again, she was insulting me. Only it didn't sound like Vera realized it. Was she offering to teach me how to cook? "I don't know what you mean..."

She laughed again, and the sound relaxed some of my bristling back. "Can you tell I'm operating on zero sleep?"

Her question made me think of Wyatt and I got the strangest urge to call him and see how he was doing. Then I remembered how obnoxious he was, and my fingers stopped itching. Almost.

"Here's the deal. Killian and I can't keep up with Sarita and Salt. We're doing what we can now as a favor to Ezra while he's out of town, but I know

83

when he gets back, Killian won't be able to tell him no. In a surprise turn of events, he feels responsible for Sarita's downfall because he left Lilou first, and all the other chefs assume it was because he got tired of working for Ezra. Which is kind of true… but we also had this amazing opportunity and we couldn't say no to our dream anymore. Do you know what I mean? Like we had to go for it or die trying." There was a thoughtful pause and she added, "We still might die for it."

It was silent for long enough that I worried she'd fallen asleep on the other end of the line. "I'm still confused."

"What I'm trying to say," Vera said slower and I could hear the smile in her voice, "is that I can't do Sarita anymore. I need to be done with it as soon as possible. Which means Sarita needs a captain. Which means, I'm willing to coach you right into that head chef position if you want my help."

I sat up fully and picked up my jaw off the bed. "How will you have time to do that?" It was the first question that came to mind and it popped out of my mouth before I could swallow it. I shouldn't have cared about her schedule or whether this one extra thing in her life was going to burn her out. I should have said, yes please, and buried my conscience in a big hole somewhere.

"Well…" There was a tone to her voice that I was starting to recognize as her mischievous side. "You get nights off, right?"

"Two." I admitted quickly. "I mean, I used to get two nights off, but lately Wyatt has needed more help than Killian did."

"We'll get you those two nights back," she said decisively. "I mean, off from Lilou. We'll work together at Sarita. My plan is to have you there enough that eventually you just become the boss, and nobody even realizes we staged a not-so-hostile takeover."

Vera was officially my hero. "That's not a bad plan."

I could hear her smile return to her voice. "I know."

"I'm more likely to only get one night off though."

"We can work with one night," she compromised. "Just make sure Wyatt gives it to you."

"You're kind of an evil genius, Vera."

She laughed. "I know that too." She seemed to think of something at the last minute and her tone changed completely. "Oh, I forgot to ask if that's too much for you. I'd like to work with you as much as possible so that means you probably won't get many nights off. And by that, I mean, you won't get any nights off."

Waving my hand in the air, even though she couldn't see it, I didn't bother to worry about my nights off or sleeping or the non-existent social life I wasn't motivated to fix. I could tend to those things later. After Sarita was mine. "I'm used to working every night. It's not a problem. I can take a day off after I'm the boss." I rolled my eyes at myself because when I was the boss, my work schedule would get even crazier. "Or when I'm dead."

"That's the spirit," she championed. "You're awesome, Kaya. This is going to be fun!"

Fun wasn't the word I would have used for it. But it was an amazing opportunity that I would be a fool to turn down.

"When do we start?" I asked her.

"When's your next night off?"

I squished my eyes shut and tried to remember. "I think it's supposed to be Sunday, but I can't remember if Wyatt asked me to work it or not."

"Make sure you get it off," she ordered. "Tell him you have a family obligation or something. Or that you have to fight a zombie outbreak somewhere. I don't care, just make sure he knows you can't work."

"Got it. Zombie outbreak. I'm sure he'll understand." The truth was, that might be the only reason he'd understand.

"Oh, and Kaya?"

85

"Yes?"

"Let's keep this between us, okay? I'm not totally sure how Ezra would feel if he knew I was interfering this much. I mean, he'll find out eventually, but the Sarita staff is on board with keeping it hush hush for now. As long as you are?"

"No problem," I assured her. "I'm not sure Wyatt would be super pleased to find out I was doing whatever it took to get the hell out of his kitchen."

We laughed together and after confirming our plan and farewells, we hung up. My phone was left with three percent battery and I'd landed the opportunity of a lifetime. That was a pretty amazing start to a Friday.

There was just enough charge left to tap out a quick text to Wyatt that said, **Don't forget I'm on proteins tonight! Also, if there's a zombie outbreak, I expect paid time off.**

He responded immediately. **I don't understand why that would warrant time off? Even zombies need to eat. New menu item, Brains Tartare.**

I rolled my eyes at the phone, because only Wyatt would try to keep his job during the undead uprising. **This is why you'll be the first to go.**

He texted the zombie emoji and wrote, **Then you can finally have my job.**

I sent him the emoji of the thumbs up, when what I really wanted was an emoji of the middle finger.

I scooted to the edge of the bed, plugged my phone in and then hightailed it to the bathroom for the whole getting ready thing I was forced to face every morning.

Truth—I didn't mind waking up. It was when I was forced to move and do obnoxious tasks like take a shower or put on deodorant or wrestle my hair that I could live without.

But I did what I could to maintain my place in civilized society, and by the time I walked out the door with a mug of coffee in my hand, I was only fifteen minutes late and my phone had gotten all the way up to fifty-seven percent. Win-win!

I met Dillon at the side entrance of Lilou and couldn't contain my smile. I wondered if she'd had anything to do with Vera's call this morning, but I was too chicken to ask. If she did, I wanted to give her a giant hug and possibly one of my kidneys should she ever need it. If she hadn't been the one to share my number with her, I didn't want to spill the beans about our secret project. I trusted Dillon completely, but I didn't always trust what she was going to say. I wasn't even sure she always knew what she was going to say before she said it. There were a ton of times I was positive she heard what she said at the exact moment everybody else did.

I loved that about her. And sometimes I was also embarrassed of her. But mostly it was love, love, love between us.

Except when she said things like, "Another day, another opportunity for you to not kill our boss." She yanked the heavy side door open and we sauntered inside.

"Hey, he starts it."

Without missing a beat, she said, "Oh, I'm sure he does. If you'd like to get together at snack time, we can discuss it further over Goldfish and juice boxes before you two are excused for recess."

I gave her a side eye. "Was that a preschool joke?"

"Mmm, more like kindergarten I believe. But seriously, Ky? He starts it? The only thing Wyatt is starting with you is a fire in your pants."

The gum I had been chewing lodged itself in my throat and I promptly began choking on it. Bracing my arms against the wall, I dipped my head and coughed enough times to dislodge the murderous piece of Trident. Then I turned my meanest, I-mean-business glare on my friend. "I'm sorry, what?"

87

She shook her finger at me. "Don't even try to pretend like there isn't something kinky happening between you two."

Kinky? Aw, hell. "That's the most ridiculous thing you've ever said. We hate each other."

She didn't put up with my surly attitude and turned her head enough that I could see her eye roll. "Oh, yeah. You hate each other real hard."

Ignoring the suggestive tone, I decided not to punch my best friend in the bicep and take the high road. "I hate you."

She nudged me with her shoulder. "Only, in reality, that means you love me," she crooned, grinning ear to ear. "See how confusing that is? You say one thing but mean the other. Maybe Wyatt is having trouble deciphering what you mean too."

I slowly exhaled and tried desperately not to laugh at her craziness. It would only encourage her. She didn't need any help from me.

She walked to her station and started prepping her portion of tonight's service. Thankfully, that ended her bothering me about Wyatt.

Argh.

Although now that I was here, I remembered that I needed to find Wyatt and talk to him privately.

I abandoned my prep work and headed out to find him.

"Where are you going?" Dillon called after me.

Without looking back, I said, "Wouldn't you like to know?"

"He's in the cooler," she said in a quieter voice.

"How do you know?"

She nodded at the kitchen clock. "He's doing inventory."

Sure enough, it was the right time and day for him to be counting all the things that needed to be refrigerated and order what we didn't have or more of what required restocking.

I turned away from his office and headed the other direction to the giant walk in cooler. "Better bite him more discreetly this time."

I held up my middle finger and wished a rash to her underboobs. Take that, smart ass.

Wyatt was squatting when I found him, reaching to the very back of a shelf. I shivered, and not because of the cold. The air changed with him so close. It tensed and sparked and amplified every nervous emotion rushing through me.

He turned his head when the doors opened. He nodded to acknowledge my presence and went back to fishing for missed leftovers.

"Hey, Wyatt. Can we talk for a minute?"

He turned around to look directly at me, his eyes dark and ambiguous and unreadable in the poor light of the cooler. "We've needed to talk a lot lately."

His observation made me itchy. I didn't know how to respond to that. Or even how to think about it.

We had needed to talk a lot lately. That was normal between chefs and their sous chefs.

But Wyatt and I weren't normal, and none of our recent talks felt normal either. It was probably best if I fled this restaurant as quickly as possible. Especially because I couldn't even name what was going on between us. Only that it wasn't normal or appropriate or even in the realm of usual for either of us.

"I can come back at a different time…?" I offered timidly.

He stood up slowly, inch by slow inch, until he towered over me. "Now's fine."

Clearing my throat, I had a second of panic that I still sounded like a man. My morning voice had mostly disappeared after two cups of coffee and a Fiber One bar, but now I was too nervous to use it. Not a common trait for me.

Damn Dillon and Vera—getting inside my head. I was perfectly content to hate Wyatt in the normal way before they ever said anything. And now I was second guessing all my loathing for him because of other people's opinions. Dumb. It was dumb. And I wanted us to go back to normal.

That meant ignoring my friends altogether and focusing on our usual relationship status—enemies. Mortal, arch, ride or die enemies.

"What's up?" He crossed his arms and faced me. Suddenly, I felt very nervous.

I bit his finger and now I could never be his mortal enemy again. How stupid was that?

"I wanted to make sure I could have Sunday evening off."

His face scrunched up. "What day is it today?"

"Friday."

"And you want Sunday off?"

I hid my wince at the harsh tone of his voice. "No, I already have it off. I want to make sure I keep it off."

"Hey, if you're not on the schedule, you have nothing to worry about."

"You say that…" I braved his gaze and let him see the nerves I wasn't successful at hiding. "But I haven't had a day off in maybe a month. A little over a month?"

His jaw ticked. "Are you complaining?"

I swallowed. "Not formally."

His head dipped and if he was anyone else, I would have sworn it was to hide a smile. "Okay, so you want Sunday night off. Got it."

"Thanks."

"I mean, it's one of our busiest nights, but if you don't feel obligated to come in, I suppose I can't make you."

The cooler was dark, lit only by a few bulbs not bright enough to reveal if there was a twinkle in his devilish eyes or if I was imagining it. Was he teasing me? Or was he serious?

"I have other plans," I said neutrally. "Or I would be here. You know I would be here."

"Sure. It's fine. You're allowed to do other things besides work."

I shrugged. "We both know that's not true." One of his eyebrows lifted and I could tell he was preparing for a fight. "Not because you're a slave driver. Although you are. It just comes with the territory. This is what we signed up for."

Wyatt ran a hand over his face and nodded. "I guess it is." He turned back to the cooler shelves and started moving things around, organizing them where they should be located on the shelves. It was amazing how quickly things got out of order here. By nature, we were all meticulous and anal with our equipment. But one hectic dinner service shot our best intentions to shit. Someone had clearly forgotten their cooler duties last night.

I hoped it wasn't me.

"Thanks again, Wyatt. I'll be here every other night this weekend." I smiled at the back of his head. "You can count on me."

He looked back at me over his shoulder. "Yeah, thanks for that."

I stood there longer than was socially acceptable, holding his gaze and wondering what the hell to say. He'd never said thank you before. He'd never shown any acknowledgment that he even noticed I was going above and beyond for him.

"You're doing a good job." The words were out of my mouth before I could swallow them. There was just something so vulnerable in the way he was looking at me. And the bags beneath his eyes seemed blacker and bigger than yesterday, and he hadn't yelled at any of us about the cooler. Instead, he

91

was in here organizing it. This wasn't his job. He was the head chef. He wasn't supposed to stoop as low as this.

His eyebrows drew together. "What do you mean?"

"With this." I spread my arms, gesturing to the cooler, the kitchen, this fucking enormous job he had. "With Lilou."

"You don't have to—"

"I'm not," I assured him. "I'm not saying that to make you feel better. You're doing the best you can. And it turns out that the restaurant hasn't burned to the ground yet, and we're still booked solid for the next four months, and you haven't made anyone cry in at least three weeks. Wyatt, you don't suck at this."

Half his mouth lifted in a slow smile, and a rogue butterfly took flight low in my belly. And it must have been on fire, because the quick heat that spread through my body made me lightheaded.

Obviously, that was the butterfly's fault.

"Six months," he murmured in a low rumble.

"Huh?"

"We're booked out for the next six months."

I tried my best to keep my expression neutral, but my traitor eyes bugged, and my eyebrows rose, giving me away. I cleared my throat and desperately grappled for sarcasm. "There. See. I told you so."

The other side of his mouth joined in and he hit me in the chest with a full-fledged smile. What kind of witchcraft was this? Holy hell, Wyatt didn't smile enough. He should definitely smile more. Who knew someone so scary could be so beautiful?

"So you think Killian picked the right guy for the job?"

And there it was—the poison that killed the magic of his mouth. I rolled my eyes, finding it much easier to be annoyed with him again. "Let's not get crazy. Maybe he picked the right guy, but the right person for the job was me." I added a winning smile to soften the blow.

He only laughed, which irritated me even more. "You're so full of yourself, Kaya. I've never met anyone like you before."

I rolled my eyes again and turned to walk out of the cooler. "Yeah, well, you're welcome."

His arm darted out and made a barricade across my middle. His warm skin in the cool air of the refrigerator rocketed through me, kindling the already dangerous fire burning through me. "Is it a date?"

Rotating my head so I could glare at him, I tried to process his question. "Is what a date?"

He didn't look at me though. Even though his arm was wrapped around my waist, he refused to meet my eyes. "Sunday night. Is that why you want the night off?"

My breath caught in my throat and I lost the ability to form words. Why did he want to know? And what was I supposed to say? I couldn't exactly tell him the truth. Vera had asked me to keep our rendezvous on the down low. Beyond that, I didn't want him to know I was moonlighting at Sarita. If missing Sunday night was a big deal, I couldn't imagine telling him I wanted to leave permanently. Especially in his current sleepless state.

But lying wasn't exactly an out either. First, he would eventually figure everything out. Like when I handed in my two weeks' notice and confessed my move across town.

"Not a date," I admitted. "But it's a commitment I can't reschedule."

He looked at me. His head lifted, and he shocked me with his rich, fathomless brown eyes. The intensity swimming in them knocked me back a step. It felt like I'd overdosed on chocolate, my stomach churning from the sugary sweetness that I shouldn't have greedily inhaled.

Ironically, he caught me with the arm that had trapped me. Otherwise, I would've fallen directly on my butt.

He didn't acknowledge my moment of klutziness and I was grateful for his small kindness.

When he was satisfied I wasn't going to topple over again, he dropped his arm and moved out of the way to let me pass. "Okay."

I waited a beat longer, but he turned back to the shelves again. Conversation over. He had work to do and no more time for me.

Okay, fine. I didn't need more time with him. He'd given me his blessing to have Sunday night off. That was the whole reason I'd gone in there to begin with. That was a win.

So why did it feel like I'd somehow lost?

I pushed through the rubber curtains hanging in front of the cooler entrance and rubbed my forearms in an effort to cool down. Or heat up. Or stop the hairs on my arms from standing straight up. Or maybe I was doing all three.

God, Wyatt. What the hell?

The shocking part of the whole exchange was that I had been expecting to hear Wyatt step back from his question. I expected him to assure me my dating life was none of his business. Or that I could date whoever I wanted.

But he hadn't said any of that.

Now I was overanalyzing every single word and looking for hidden meaning, and I hated him even more for making me obsessed with thinking about him.

But at the same time I also hated him less. And that was even more confusing.

I rubbed my temples feeling a headache start to take hold. Sunday night couldn't come fast enough. I needed time away from this kitchen. I needed to clear my head.

94

And my libido.

Chapter Six

*M*y hands trembled as I reached for the door. This was it, the moment of truth. Or at least one of them.

An early one. Probably a baby one.

This was like a prologue to the moment of truth.

But, goddamn, it felt scary as hell.

One of my mentors from school had always said, if you're not scared as shit, it's not hard enough.

This was plenty hard enough.

The door pushed open before I could find the courage to touch it. A guy and a girl walked out carrying empty boxes that needed to be broken down and thrown away. They were both wearing black chef coats with red flowers on the lapel and their hair was hidden behind bandanas, although the girl's springy black curls exploded out the back of hers. They checked me out but didn't stop to chat.

I let out a slow breath and straightened my black chef coat with a flower on the lapel. Mine was a lily though. Not the Spanish rose of Sarita.

Normal people might not notice the difference, but we did.

I slipped inside the kitchen and the exterior door slammed shut behind me. Leaning back against it, I steadied my breathing and took a minute to get my bearings.

Even though I'd worked for Ezra for several years, I'd never seen the inside of the kitchen at Sarita before. I'd eaten here several times and gotten drinks with friends often. But the kitchen had been off limits.

I'd met a few of the chefs at Bianca and Sarita before now, but there was always this unspoken hostility between us. We would never admit it out loud, but we were in fierce competition with each other. We wanted to be the best of the harem. We wanted to be best bitch.

But aside from that, we wanted to be best in the city. And up until recently, when Bianca's leadership failed, we had all been in steady competition for the title.

The constant rivalry made Ezra Baptiste infinitely happy and plenty rich. Because that meant he owned three of the best restaurants in the region. On the other hand, the constant contention made us feral.

Once, when the city had an arugula shortage, Lilou had run out and Killian made me call Bianca to see if they had any extra. The girl on the other end had laughed like a hyena and hung up on me.

There was a rumor floating around that some of the chefs from Sarita had broken into Bianca and stolen all their immersion blenders because they thought Bianca had better ones.

Basically, I was willingly walking into shark-infested waters.

And the Lilou lily was bleeding all over me.

"Hey, you made it!" Vera called across the kitchen that was eerily similar to Lilou's. There was a significant size difference because Lilou was a much bigger restaurant, but the layout was the same. Good.

That made this an easier battle to fight.

Vera felt like safety, so I moved toward her. "Are you kidding? This is amazing." I met her eyes. "You're amazing."

She waved her hand, dismissing the compliment. "I'm doing this for purely selfish reasons." Leaning in, she dropped her voice and whispered, "Get me the hell out of here."

I snorted a laugh. "Is it that bad?"

She looked down at her hands, seeming unsure what to say. Finally, she lifted her head and pierced me with a totally open stare. "It's not mine. That's the issue. It's not mine and I feel it in my bones."

Her words kicked me in the chest and my body started absorbing this moment before my mind could catch up. At the same time, a tingle started in my toes and rose through my body like an electrical current.

This wasn't her kitchen. This kitchen was mine. It belonged to me. Or it would soon.

I smiled at Vera, feeling a change take root in the core of me, a hope and dream that I had never known existed until this moment.

The idea of it had been there for a long time. Even the strong idea of it. But it wasn't until this moment, with the gleaming stainless steel surrounding me and the buzz of voices and chopping and hiss of fry pans and clank of dishes that I fully understood what it meant to wholly, totally, completely want something so badly I would work as hard as it took and for as long as it took until it was mine.

And then I would work harder and longer and tougher and smarter to keep the dream alive.

When I hadn't said anything for long enough that I could tell Vera felt awkward, she clapped her hands together and asked, "Ready to get to work?"

"Hell, yes."

She smiled back. I didn't know if she recognized the hunger I felt for this place or if she didn't know what else to do, but her smile solidified the still shaky parts of me and whispered to be brave.

"Tour first, don't you think?"

I nodded and followed her as she began walking around the kitchen pointing out equipment and people. I continued to nod and smile, desperately but uselessly clinging to names I had no chance of remembering. There were just too many of them and I was still overwhelmed with the unfamiliar electricity rushing through me.

I took deep breaths and settled on figuring out how to get whatever I wanted without having to use names. "Hey, there, champ…" seemed my best option.

She took me back to the office and I blanched at the sight of it. "What happened in here?"

"Right? And Ezra was surprised when he quit. The jackass was a total slob. Killian and I have had a hell of a time getting her right again. This was what the kitchen looked like too."

My hand landed beneath my jaw, supporting my head from falling off my body in shock. "The kitchen looked like this?"

She rolled her eyes. "It was worse if you can believe it. It was amazing this place hadn't burned to the ground from a grease fire yet."

"What about bugs? Mice?"

Her nose wrinkled. "Both. We've had exterminators come out, but we're still working on it."

Bile rose in my throat and real anger settled in my fists. I had worked in plenty of kitchens with bugs and mice problems. I had even worked in one with rats before. It was a difficult problem to solve once they invaded. And if you didn't keep the kitchen in tip-top shape constantly, they invaded quickly.

That was why we were so absolutely anal about deep cleaning at Lilou. And why I would be a total slave driver about it when I ran my own kitchen.

I lowered my voice to a whisper. "How is the staff handling the changes?" It was one thing to deal with the aftermath of a sloppy chef. But if the crew left behind was just as bad, it would be the fight of a lifetime to retrain them.

She glanced over my shoulder quickly before giving me a look. "They're lazy and undisciplined, but not totally worthless. With the right leadership they could turn out to be something special. And I think they want a good leader. They've responded really well to Killian and me and our daily verbal whippings and chores. We have to spell things out for them… but they're at least willing to try."

"Are they talented?"

Making a sound in the back of her throat, she ran her hands through her hair. "Too talented. All they care about is the food. They don't see the point of anything else."

I rolled my eyes and let out a deep sigh. "So not the worst-case scenario."

"I'd rather have chefs I could teach to cook better than filthy ones."

My heart sank. "Would you hire any of them? For Salt?"

Her lips pressed together, and I could immediately see she didn't want to tell me the truth. But she would. And I was grateful for it. I needed the truth. I needed the entire picture. "No. Not one of them." She rolled her neck. "Maybe the dishwasher. He's efficient. Maybe if I couldn't find one I liked better."

A laugh bubbled out of me. "This place is not at all what I imagined."

She smiled. "You thought I was handing over a sexier version of Lilou, didn't you?"

I threw my hands to the side. "Obviously!"

"Oh, young padawan. So much to learn. So much to teach you."

"I only hope it's worth it." I leveled my serious face at her. "Listen, I'm willing to work as hard as I need to. I'm willing to do whatever it takes to get this job and whip this place into shape. But there's still the risk that Sarita won't even go to me. That Ezra won't hire me."

She slapped her hand down on my shoulder. "Sure. That's true. But risk is the best part, right? It keeps us on our toes. Keeps us sharp. If there's no risk, there's no reward."

"Oh my God. You really are Yoda."

She giggled, and using her best Yoda impersonation, she said, "Right, you are. Now, this way come. A shit ton of work we have."

Laughing we finished the tour of the restaurant, taking our time to admire the dining room and how not in shambles it was. Ezra kept front of house spectacular. It would be my job to get the kitchen into fighting shape.

That new hope inside me bloomed with bigger blossoms. I couldn't explain it exactly, but I wasn't afraid of the work. It made me more determined, more desperate to make this place mine. Either way, we were bound together now. I wanted her. And crazily enough, I knew she wanted me too.

Sarita was all sultry reds and cool, hard blacks. While some restaurants with a similar color scheme gave a tawdry vibe or were just plain tacky, she had been designed to radiate passion and wild, uninhibited fun. But it was the passion for food and culture and not sex. Yes, she was a sexy restaurant, but because the ambiance couldn't help but pull that emotion from you.

This was a space you didn't just want to share a meal in, you wanted to stay here to drink, laugh, party, and make lifelong memories.

102

I loved Lilou more than anything, but her insides were stark and cold. The diners came for the food, not to feel comfortable or at home. Sarita's dining room conveyed coming home and kicking off your shoes. Sarita was deep and open. Raw.

I loved her. I wanted her.

We walked back to the kitchen and I couldn't remember being this excited to work. Ever. Not even when cooking was new to me and it was all I wanted to do.

I hadn't known what I was doing back then. My adventure was purely discovery.

Today, I knew what I needed to do. So the adventure was in owning.

Vera stepped up to her spot in the very center of the kitchen. "Have you had a chance to study the menu?"

"Yes," I answered simply, not admitting that studying the menu was the only thing I'd done since her phone call. I'd gone to work. I'd slept what little hours I could. And I'd gone over the menu again and again. I tried to replicate the combinations of ingredients at home to recreate the menu as it was described on the website.

It was hard to cook that blind, especially since menus only told a portion of the story. But I could say I was familiar with the concept of each of the dishes.

"Good," she said simply. "Because tonight, I thought you could wait tables."

All of my soaring aspirations came to a screeching halt inside my chest. "Wait, what?"

Her eyes narrowed. "You've waited tables before, right?"

"Yes." I hated my original response. I amended it. "No." But I felt guilty for not telling the truth, so I added, "I mean, like my first year of culinary school I worked at this little Mexican restaurant, but I wouldn't call that

103

waitressing. There were all of ten tables to take care of and it was almost never busy." Except for every night. I cleared my throat and let her see my desperation, "I can't do it here. Ezra wants his servers to basically have college degrees in hospitality and I don't even know how to—"

"Don't worry about a thing. Currently, Ezra isn't even in the country." She grinned at me. "This will be fun. I brought a white shirt for you. It's in the office. Why don't you change clothes? After, find a guy named Christian out front. He'll walk you through everything you need to know for tonight."

Anger and fear flared to life inside me and I swallowed hateful words that burned my tongue. I'd given up a free Sunday night for this? "I thought you wanted me to work with you, Vera? In the kitchen? Wasn't the plan for you to tutor me and mentor me and get me ready to take over as the amazingly qualified new head chef?"

She smirked. "That's exactly what I'm doing."

"But how is that going to work if I'm not back here with you? Learning the kitchen? Learning how to lead it? Learning all the voodoo that you do so well?" I was not above quoting Salt-N-Pepa to get my way.

Her arms folded over her chest and she squared her shoulders, readying for the argument we were about to have. "I'm sure you studied the menu, but you don't know it. And I'm sure you've eaten here before, but you don't know Sarita's ins and outs, or her deep, dark secrets. I'm sure you can cook the hell out of tapas, but you've never cooked anything off this menu. If you want Sarita, you need to get intimate with her, go down the rabbit hole, find out every single thing there is to know about her. Start with waiting tables and learning about the people that eat here, what walks of life they're from, what they want, what they need from you. Sell the hell out of this menu, be able to recite the dishes from memory, get acquainted with all the dishes. Smell them. Touch them. Taste them. Do whatever the hell possible to become this fucking restaurant. I'm temporary, Kaya. A temporary chef in a kitchen I want nothing to do with. I barely know the menu and I barely care about it enough to make sure it's done right. Don't be me. Don't be temporary. Be the miracle that will save this tragedy of a restaurant. Do everything you need to do tonight to become permanent. Then come back next Sunday and we'll try something else out."

Some of the panic drained from my chest to slosh around in my stomach. I hated the idea of not working back here with Vera. Front of house felt like a missed opportunity. And I couldn't shake the feeling that I needed to hurry up and be amazing. As soon as Ezra got back from his trip, he would start searching to fill this position and if I wasn't game ready by then, I wouldn't get it. "This is some serious Mr. Miyagi shit, Vera."

She smiled again. "You're welcome."

I wrinkled my nose but accepted my fate. I hated to admit that she was right, but she was. I needed to learn this restaurant. I needed to familiarize myself with this restaurant gorilla-style, quickly. I needed to work my ass off and do whatever it took to claim her as mine.

"Goodbye, Kaya," Vera said in a serious tone. "And good luck."

I couldn't help but snicker as I walked back to her office to change into the white shirt she'd brought for me. Vera and I had a similar shape except that she was taller than me. Her shirt fit fine even if it was a little tight over my chest—but I had been fighting the big boobs versus button-up shirts battle my entire life.

Pulling out my compact from my purse, I checked out my appearance. I hadn't wrapped my head in a bandana yet. My bouncy pink curls were on full display. I'd used my amazing, deep rinse conditioner last night, so the pink was fresh and vibrant.

And my curls. They were everywhere. When I first started working in a kitchen full-time, I'd impulsively chopped all my hair off in an effort to survive the heat and chaotic schedule. But recently I'd wanted a different

105

look. The only problem was my hair took forever to grow out. I was currently somewhere between the edgy pixie cut that had been so easy to maintain and a chin-length bob. Unlike when my hair had been short, blue, and styled straight, my natural curls were growing in with a vengeance.

Fishing for bobby pins in the bottom of my purse, I pinned some of the front ones back to give me a softer, 1920s look—something more customer friendly. It was no use terrifying the diners because I looked like I'd just touched a live wire.

Adding colored Chapstick and cute tassel earrings I found at the bottom of my purse, I finally felt presentable. My pants were still kitchen quality and my shoes were still my clunky Doc Martens, but for the most part, I could pass for every day society. At least I hoped so.

Fitting in wasn't something I had ever cared about. Save for my brief hiatus from myself when I dated Nolan, I was way more comfortable in my own skin than trying to squeeze into someone else's. I loved playing with the color of my hair and the shade of my nails and lipstick and eyeshadow— when I wore it. And when I dressed for places that weren't Lilou, I enjoyed taking style risks. I didn't set out to be edgy, I just didn't squeeze into a cookie cutter mold.

My thoughts flickered to Wyatt. There weren't many things I liked about him, but his total self-assuredness was one of my favorites. I had never seen him concerned with what other people thought, save for food critics. I had never seen him try to cover up his extensive tattoos or worry over his clothes. He was perfectly who he wanted to be. And God, I found that ridiculously sexy for some reason. Maybe I liked a few more things about him than I wanted to admit.

On the other hand, there was Nolan. A man so consumed with what the rest of the world thought of him, he'd let them trap him somewhere he hated. My sisters were the same way. Claire had stayed in Hamilton even though she hated it, even though she was dying to leave. My parents had convinced my youngest sister Cameron to go to the local community college to live at home and save money. Cameron was on board, but she had no idea how much she was missing. And she was young enough not to care.

Oh, well. Those were their choices. I couldn't live their lives for them, no matter how much I wanted to help them. All I could do was love my own life. And I did. Even if it was busy. Even if it was hard. Even if sometimes it was lonely. I loved my job and I love who I'd turned out to be and I loved the people I'd surrounded myself with.

I closed my compact and put it away before folding up my chef coat and tucking it into my purse as well. My fingers brushed over the cool stainless-steel counters as I walked wistfully through the kitchen.

Some other day, friend. Someday soon.

Christian found me as soon as I walked through the kitchen doors. "I'm Christian," he blurted excitedly. He was a waif of a kid with ink black hair and a perfectly ironed crisp white shirt. "Vera said she wants me to show you the ropes tonight."

His energy was infectious, and I couldn't help but smile back at him. "She's crazy for making me do this. I cook. I don't know the first thing about waiting tables."

He waved me off. "There's nothing to it." My look must have screamed I didn't believe him because he laughed. "Once you get the hang of it, there's nothing to it."

"How long have you been serving?" He had one of those faces that was deceptively young looking. He could either be thirty or sixteen. I wouldn't have been surprised with either one.

"Long enough to be excited about the prospect of new leadership."

"Was he that bad?"

"Who? Juan Carlo? Or Ezra?"

107

"Juan Carlo. I already know how bad Ezra is." I bit my lip ring and hoped Christian wasn't partial to our boss.

He laughed again. "Oh, right, you're part of the harem."

I rested a hand against my neck, where the stitching of the lily usually was on my lapel. "Lilou."

Cocking his head to the side, his eyes trailed over me, taking my measure. "That seems a little stuffy for you."

It was. "That's why I'd love to move over here."

"You'd be the first to successfully transfer laterally." He rolled his shoulders and sighed, like he was reluctantly giving up information I was dragging out of him. "However, anybody would be better than JC. I didn't mind that he was a diva. Comes with the territory, or so I'm told. But he was completely useless. And God forbid someone lodge a complaint. The man would lose his shit."

I tried to keep my expression neutral, but I wasn't sure I totally succeeded. Under normal circumstances, I would have loved to gossip about any and every chef across the country. It was one of my favorite pastimes. But if I got this job, I didn't want it spread around that I'd had these thoughts about their previous executive chef. Especially if he was a better chef than me.

It was better to play it safe and give the noncommittal answer. Besides, I wanted to be this guy's boss. Meaning, I needed to remain professional and distant. It wasn't the fun answer or the enjoyable one. But it was the necessary one. "He was under a lot of stress."

My reaction must have triggered something for him, because his eyes bugged out and he leaned toward me. "But you must know what that's like, right? I've heard your new head chef is a major douche canoe."

His accusation was accurate, but it also rubbed me wrong. In the worst way. Wyatt was the way he was for a purpose. It was necessary. Unlike

108

Sarita, Wyatt didn't have the luxury of saving a sinking ship. He had to live up to a standard of excellence set by one of the greatest chefs in the current culinary culture. He wasn't walking into a position abandoned by an incompetent diva, he was fighting to prove he belonged in one of the most coveted positions on the east coast. "He's a perfectionist," I explained, ignoring the defensiveness in my tone. "He wants Lilou to be even better than when Killian Quinn was there. It's a hard job."

His expression turned neutral. "I'm sure it is."

Instead of insisting that it was, I let silence fall between us until it got awkward. Wyatt's prowess as a head chef wasn't a hill I wanted to die on, but I also wouldn't let unfair rumors spread through the harem about him. Stories like that spread as quickly as wildfire. If not controlled, every kitchen in Durham and the great state of North Carolina and beyond would hear all kinds of nonsense. I wasn't responsible for Wyatt's reputation, but I did feel enough loyalty to Lilou to protect it.

No, that wasn't entirely true. Whether I wanted to admit all the secret respect I had for him or not, the truth remained. It was okay that he annoyed me and drove me crazy. He was my boss, my problem. And I would defend him and Lilou forever and ever amen so help me God.

"Do you want to give me the general layout of tonight?" I asked after we stood there in constrained quiet for too long. "I'd love to not totally screw this up tonight." I added a smile and that broke through some of the awkwardness.

"You won't," he promised. "I won't leave you totally alone. I don't want to be the dick that abandoned his future boss when she was thrown to the wolves."

My smile turned more genuine. "I appreciate that." Especially since I wouldn't exactly be his boss.

He started walking toward a server station. "Come on, I'll show you how to enter orders in the computer. Then you can help me finish rolling this silverware."

We fell into an easy partnership after that. True to his word, he never left me by myself. Instead of serving on my own, I shadowed him, taking orders when he prompted me to do so and explaining dishes after he'd given me all the details.

Vera was right, I did get to know Sarita this way. By the end of the night, my feet hurt as usual, I'd splashed at least thirty mojitos all over my sleeves and I had developed a full-on hatred for the camouflaged step near the bar, but I knew the dishes. I knew what they looked like. I knew what they smelled like. I knew what a lot of them tasted like thanks to Vera force-feeding me all night. And I knew the vibe of Sarita, her mood, her essence. But mostly, I knew the direction I wanted to take her.

She had great tapas that drew crowds, but all of them could be better. There was a total of three cold dishes for instance. I wanted more. I wanted gazpacho and carpaccio. I wanted a summer flower salad that would blow your mind. And I wanted a chilled watermelon soup with notes of mint and ginger that I dreamed up thanks to one of their most popular mojitos.

As for the hot dishes, several of them were dated. I would easily trade out the classic huevos rancheros for a more modern version with poached eggs and spicy green chili and tomato jam over bite-sized fry bread. And I would toss out the marinated chicken skewers for seared rabbit and a pickled radish chutney.

I had more ideas too. So many ideas. With each new dish I brought from the kitchen, more inspiration would spark, quickly adding to the wildfire blazing through me. The entire night was spent dropping off good dishes and quickly scurrying to a dark corner, so I could furiously take notes on my phone, imagining better dishes, envisioning a better menu and a better restaurant. The best restaurant.

I doubted any of my hurriedly scribbled improvements made much sense now, but that wasn't the point. It was the inspiration that mattered. The deep hunger I had for this place after only being here for one day.

Imagining myself at the helm, I knew I would rip apart the current menu and put my signature on every dish, drink—every inch of this place.

By the time I reached my car sometime after eleven p.m., my cheeks hurt from smiling so much. I shouldn't be this happy. Especially since I hadn't cooked a single thing today. And yet, I couldn't help it. Sarita had so much untapped potential, so much sparkle that had been tarnished by bad leadership and laziness.

I would take this place to the next level. And then I was going to give Lilou and Wyatt a fucking run for their money.

Chapter Seven

"*I* need Sunday off again."

Wyatt's cold, hard stare found mine across the expo station in Lilou's kitchen. We were the first two to arrive at Lilou Wednesday morning and this was the first chance I'd had to chat with him alone.

"Are you on the schedule?"

I braved his glare and shook my head. "No."

"Then why do you keep double checking with me?"

My nerves turned angry at his tone. Like always, this guy had the ability to take me from zero to sixty in approximately three seconds. "Because I'll be the one blamed if you need me and I don't show up."

113

He leaned forward on his hands, bringing us closer together, trying to intimidate me with his size. But I wouldn't be intimidated. I mimicked his pose and leaned toward him. His eyebrows rose at the same time his eyes dropped to my lips, totally throwing me off my game.

Not that I would let him know that.

"Oh, I always need you, Kaya." His head dipped closer. "And I always blame that on you."

My heart jumped in my chest and then took off in a sprint. Something warm and foreign pooled in my belly, some long-forgotten instinct that my brain couldn't name. My vocal chords got on board too, dropping my voice to a softer, sultrier tone. "That seems unfair."

His gaze trailed to my lips again. "It's not my fault. Maybe you shouldn't make me need you so badly."

Butterflies exploded in my stomach, like surprise firecrackers thrown in a poor, unsuspecting mailbox. My body leaned towards him involuntarily, pulled in by the deep tone of his voice and the way his brown eyes had gone dark and hot and so utterly hypnotizing. My body was shaky and overly warm and practically liquid with lust. Good thing my brain still worked. I was able to throw back a sassy, "Maybe you should find someone else to fulfill your needs."

His head dropped again, separating our mouths by only inches. If I wasn't so short, our faces would be smashed against each other right now.

"We've already tried that and it hasn't worked. It's got to be you."

I shook my head, trying to get a grip on reality. Did he mean in the kitchen? Or something else? Something else was crazy right?

This was Wyatt, my biggest problem. And if you asked him, he'd say the same thing about me. Our dislike was obvious by the way his body was leaned all the way over the counter toward me and the way I was pushing up on my tiptoes to get closer to him. It would be clear to anyone that saw us how much we couldn't stand each other.

My body jerked awake with the keen awareness that I was enjoying every second of Wyatt's attention. I pulled back and smoothed out my tank top, trying to find my equilibrium again.

I was reading too much into this. Wyatt meant he needed me here. In the kitchen. Because I was amazing at what I did. And I was his sous chef. Of course, he relied on me.

"You should probably figure that out then, Wyatt. I'm not always going to be around you know."

The heat left his eyes as quickly as it had appeared, and he pulled back into standing, looking more pissed off than ever. "What is that supposed to mean?"

Hot and cold. Fire and ice. Blazing to glacial in seconds. That was Wyatt. He was the same way in the kitchen. He was never calm or even-keeled—his best attributes when he'd been sous chef for Killian. Now he was volatile. Like an active volcano buried under layers and layers of ice.

I'd noticed the change the minute he stepped into his new position. He wasn't the same guy I'd cooked next to for years, the same kid that had a lot of growing up to do before his meteoric rise to fame. He was different. More intense, more focused, more… demanding.

I turned my back on him and started unrolling my knives. Shrugging to diffuse any remaining tension, I said nonchalantly, "It means that I won't always work here as your number two, Wyatt. I want a kitchen of my own. I'm bound to move on eventually." Sooner than that, hopefully. But he didn't need to know all the dirty details. He could find out when I handed over my two weeks' notice with undisguised glee.

"Yeah, eventually. Maybe. Until then... I mean, I thought we talked about this. I need you here, Kaya. You taking a bunch of days off isn't working out for me."

A scoffing laugh dislodged itself from the back of my throat. "Oh, I'm so sorry to inconvenience you, Shaw. I've taken one day off in more than a month, but if you need me to hold your hand that badly, forget I ever said anything. You say the word and I'll be here. Every single night. And hell, why stop there. If you need me to babysit you, I could spoon-feed your meals too. And pick out your clothes every morning. Tuck you into bed at night. Whatever you need, chef. I live to please."

He was behind me in the next second, his hard body pressing against mine, trapping me against the cool stainless-steel counter. I should have been outraged. I was a tiny female and he was a giant man. I should have been intimidated.

I should not have been turned on.

Holy hell. I shivered again, a violent tremble of nerves and lust rolling through my entire body.

His arm slid around my waist, his hand splaying over my hip bone, dipping beneath my chef's coat and tank top. Skin to skin. Flesh to flesh. Wyatt against me. Wyatt versus me in a battle to see who could combust from sexual tension first.

I shivered again.

His mouth dropped to the curve of my neck, his lips brushing against my suddenly sensitive skin. "Say it again," he ordered.

My hands gripped the counter, the edge biting into my tender fingertips as my muddled brain tried to make sense of his request. "Babysit you?" I couldn't say it again without a breathy giggle.

His laugh rumbled through him. I felt it from my neck to my knees. "You know what I want, Ky. You know what I want to hear."

116

Shit.

Shit. Shit. Shit.

I hadn't meant to call him chef. It slipped. It had been my one power play, the one thing I withheld to remind him that I was as good as him. Damn it!

He wasn't supposed to know he had somehow earned my respect in his short time as executive chef. He wasn't supposed to figure out that I admired him and looked up to him and wanted his approval. Those were my secrets. And they were supposed to go with me to the grave.

But with one, ill-timed slip of a title of respect, I'd ruined everything.

"Kaya," he growled against my skin, sinking his teeth into my neck in the sexiest bite of all time. He was getting me back for the one time I'd bitten his finger. Only his was way worse. His was sex and fire and the fucking end of me.

I started to think maybe I'd ruined the power struggle between us in the very best way.

"Chef," I whispered, unable to deny him with his mouth on me.

His entire body stiffened, hardened, springing into action. He spun me around and lifted me to the counter with an impressive display of power. My butt slammed against the surface and my legs instinctively opened for him. He shoved my roll of knives away without acknowledging that they were ridiculously sharp and could slice his fingers open. Or that usually he was meticulous with knives and handling them, taking care of them.

Under normal, sane circumstances, Wyatt would never treat his kitchen with such disrespect.

Not that I was complaining.

Because his disrespect felt too amazing for me to complain about. His touch felt too incredible for me to protest. His body between my legs felt surprisingly right and good and I didn't want him to move away.

For as long as I'd known Wyatt, I'd been physically attracted to him. We'd clashed in the kitchen, two Titans with a hunger for perfection and little room for anyone else to get in our way. But when we weren't cooking, I had always been unable to squash my carnal lust for the man.

I'd been intimate with a couple guys in the kitchen since Nolan, but never Wyatt. And it wasn't just that when he'd been single, I'd been dating Nolan and when I became single, he had Trish. It was more than that.

I had never wanted anything serious from someone in this kitchen. I'd only ever wanted convenient and throwaway. But Wyatt didn't feel throwaway. He felt very permanent. He felt solid and unflinching and like he would sink beneath my skin, wrap around my bones and never let go.

But my biggest problem with him was that I wasn't sure if I would care. The scariest part was wanting him to stay and not knowing if I would be enough for him after all.

His fingers curled under my jaw and he tilted my head, so he could capture my gaze with his. "I like that."

I tilted my chin higher, not letting him have his way. "Is that so, chef?"

"Fuck." The curse ripped from his throat as if he'd lost all control. His forehead landed on mine and I watched in fascination as his eyes fluttered closed and his face scrunched in indecision. "Fucking hell, Kaya. You're going to be the death of me."

I felt possessed, scooting forward so that his waist was cradled more firmly between my legs. It was his turn to shiver and it was the hottest thing I had ever experienced. Instinct told me to back off, that I was playing with irreversible fire. But the demon inside me whispered, "Then I could have your job. Maybe that's my plan."

He pulled back and his eyes popped open, his expression all serious, professional Wyatt. "I fucking believe it."

A slow smile spread my lips into a taunting expression. "Are you afraid?"

118

He moved closer so that our lips were actually touching. I stopped breathing in that second, stopped thinking... stopped being. It was only the two of us here at this moment. No kitchen. No competition. No world beyond us. "I've been afraid of you for as long as I can remember."

And then he kissed me. No more than the slow brush of his lips against mine. It wasn't anything earth shattering. Or it shouldn't have been. It was the briefest taste of his mouth. His tongue was there only enough to remind me that it had the power to undo me. To totally upend me.

To ruin me for all other men.

His hands grasped my waist, forcing me to acknowledge their presence and the intense way I liked them on me. His teeth scraped my bottom lip, pulling a breathy sound from the back of my throat. His scent filled my senses, making me dizzy with the headiness of him.

I stopped caring about our rivalry and our history and the constant competition between us. I stopped worrying about my future and my life goals and just settled in this moment. This was what I wanted. This right here. Him.

Wyatt.

His touch and his taste and the wicked things I knew he would do to me.

It had been too long for me and I was tired of feeling like I'd thrown away my one good chance at a committed relationship when I'd walked away from Nolan. I wanted to feel wanted. I needed to feel needed. I desperately desired to feel desired.

Maybe Wyatt could make me feel all those good things and more.

The problem was I still needed to be able to walk away from him when it was over.

The back doorbell rang, snatching all my hasty, lust-filled choices out of my hands before I'd gotten the chance to make them. Because Wyatt was

119

gone. The loud buzz broke the spell and he'd moved, striding across the kitchen like his feet were on fire.

And I was left to slide off the counter into a puddle of confusion and abandoned desire.

"What the hell was that?"

There was no one there to answer. Wyatt was already outside.

I knew he wouldn't answer anyway. It was his mission in life to torture me. This was another level in our game.

Meaning I shouldn't let him corner me like this again. Now that rational thought had reentered my sex-starved brain, I knew I couldn't let him win. But more importantly, I knew I wouldn't be able to walk away if this happened a second time. At least not with my dignity still intact. I wouldn't be able to push him away. Or deny him what he wanted.

Or convince myself it wasn't what I wanted.

Because it was.

Oh God, I wanted it badly.

Thankfully, I was saved from abandoning all my best laid plans and recklessly throwing myself at him when the rest of our coworkers started trickling into the kitchen. We quickly got to work prepping food for the night after we suffered through our morning meeting and Wyatt's drill sergeant like pep talk. He might as well have looked us all in the eye and said, "Don't fuck up." I knew he thought he was being motivational, but he was only succeeding if he wanted us motivated by fear of him killing us for messing something up.

That was usually the impact he left after his hour-long power trip. But, I had his entire body plastered against mine only a little while ago and was too busy hyper-focusing on getting over that incredible feeling to worry about the consequences of well-done filet mignon. I felt bad for the rest of the crew though.

By the time Dillon and I snagged a break close to opening, I was a sweaty, frustrated, horny mess.

"You seem… out of it today. Are you okay?" she asked as we stepped outside into the cool spring breeze. The trees had just started to bud around the plaza, dotting the industrial brick and stone with brushstrokes of green and white. The sun was warm on my naked arms and my bandana covered head. It calmed some of my frantic nerves and soothed the riotous confusion inside me. I wanted to lay a blanket down and take a nap in the perfection of the day.

Most of all I wanted to forget about the weird energy between Wyatt and me. The barely there kiss. The feel of him.

The way I'd called him chef. Not like he was my boss. The word had spilled out of me as a gift. An offering. Worship.

I turned to Dillon and debated what to tell her. "Vera's letting me cook with her at Sarita Sunday nights. She's… training me to take over."

Dillon's mouth dropped open and I couldn't help but laugh at her shocked expression. "No way!"

I nodded, a gleeful smile taking over my face. "I know! It's crazy. And so kind of her."

"How long has this been going on?"

I shrugged, remembering my inspiring night waiting tables. "I've only done it once so far. I'm going again this week."

Some of our coworkers pushed through the door heading behind the building to smoke. Dillon leaned forward and dropped her voice. "Does Ezra know?"

"No," I confessed. "This is totally Vera's idea. I'm not even sure Killian knows."

Her brows drew together. "He has to know. The whole staff at Sarita knows. I doubt they'd be able to keep that a secret."

121

"I'm not sure what they know. Vera said they're happy to keep our secret because they will do anything to avoid another Juan Carlo scenario. Also, I'm sure they're all terrified of Killian."

Dillon nodded. "As they should be."

"I'm not worried about him finding out though. It's Ezra that I'm hoping to hide this from until I can at least apply for the position with confidence. Vera has promised to whip my tail into shape. Last Sunday, she made me take orders to familiarize myself with the food. She'll probably have me bus tables this week, so I can really get in touch with Sarita's soul."

Dillon laughed at my sarcasm. "No, she didn't."

"She did. I swear it."

"You're like the Karate Kid!"

I snorted. "That's exactly what I said!"

"Still, that's amazing. The job is for sure yours." Her pretty face fell. "And then I'll be stuck here. By myself. Working for the devil. While all my friends run restaurants of their very own."

"Yeah, but not forever," I reminded her. "Plus, there's no guarantee that I'll even get Sarita. Ezra has never hired a female chef before. I'm the first female sous chef in the harem and only by default thanks to seniority."

"Not true," she protested. "You deserved your position. Killian's the one that appointed you in the first place. Not even Wyatt could deny you that accolade." She folded her arms across her chest and hugged her body, staring at her feet. "I don't think Ezra has intentionally only hired men. Unfortunately, I think there are more male candidates to choose from."

That was true. Women were definitely the minority in fine dining kitchens and often left their positions to have families. Kitchen hours were the absolute worst where kids were involved. And because of that, women had to fight harder than anyone to make it in this already cutthroat industry.

"You're probably right," I agreed with her. "But that doesn't make the interview any less daunting." Her lips pressed into a frown. "I don't think your brother is sexist by the way." And I didn't. Maybe naively unaware that his kitchens were dominated by men. But as far as I could tell, Ezra disdained all sexes and people equally. He was an equal opportunity snob.

"Vera!" Dillon blurted, pointing her finger in the air.

I blinked at my friend and her sudden emotional one-eighty. "What?"

"He offered Bianca to Vera!"

This was news to me—I only barely kept my jaw from dropping. "He did what?"

Dillon waved at the general area of where the food truck used to be. "When she had Foodie, and he was dealing with all the drama at Bianca, he offered her the position. But she turned him down because of Killian and Salt."

Hope soared in my chest, creating more hope and new hope and a light at the end of this tunnel. "That's good news."

"Right?"

We were silent for a few seconds before I said in genuine confusion, "I can't believe she turned him down."

Dillon's eyes bugged. "Me either! I guess she only wanted to work with Killian."

Neither of us could grasp a love like that. A love that inspired loyalty and the desire to work together.

I thought about Wyatt. Not that I loved him. Or would ever even like him. But the sexy kiss had put him in my head and it was impossible not to hold him up next to Killian.

Vera loved Killian enough to abandon her food truck and go into business with her boyfriend, now fiancé. I couldn't help but cringe in anxiety for her. That could end so badly.

What if their restaurant ruined their marriage?

Or worse, what if their marriage ruined their restaurant?

Killian had a reputation that could save him. Maybe. But what about Vera? She was risking everything on the miniscule chance that her marriage wouldn't end in divorce and her business partnership wouldn't end in bitter hatred.

It was too much.

Wyatt was one of the best chefs I knew. We didn't even have a friendship to jeopardize, but I still wouldn't risk my future, my business… my reputation on him.

"It's not my restaurant." Vera's words danced through my head and I partly understood her motivation.

Salt was hers. Salt was her home. Killian was worth the risk to have that feeling. And if I had to guess, she felt something similar for Killian.

Maybe I would never know something like that with a man, but I was bound and determined to have that with a kitchen.

"That girl is crazy," I said, referring to Vera. Dillon made a sound that was half laugh, half agreeing. I looked at her out of the corner of my eye and took a steading breath. "Do you think I have a chance with Ezra? Do you think it's possible he'll consider me?"

She dug her toe into the ground and kicked at a chunk of pavement. Burying her chin in her lifted shoulder, she made another noncommittal noise. "I don't know my brother's mind. As close as we are, he can still be a mystery. I think he'll give you a chance though." Her head lifted, and she met my gaze, braving the possibility of disappointing me. "He's fair, Ky. And he wants the absolute best for his restaurants. To like a psychotic degree." The door pushed open behind her and Wyatt stepped outside just as Dillon finished saying, "If you're the best thing for him, then you have absolutely nothing to worry about."

Wyatt's feet came to a screeching halt and his knuckles turned white where he held open the heavy side door of Lilou. Dillon's words landed like landmines around us, falling with the heaviness of a waiting explosion.

God, why couldn't I be a smoker? They congregated at the back of the building, where there was privacy. Where our boss didn't walk into a conversation he had no business hearing.

Instead, I had to hang out here, where the air was clear of lung cancer but strongly lacking in distance to the door. Damn.

To his credit, Wyatt didn't say anything. Instead, he glared at me until my insides started to melt.

"Hey, Wyatt," Dillon said, breaking the awkward tension boiling between us. "What's up?"

He didn't take his eyes off me. "Are you planning on working tonight? Or are you going to hang out here until your shift's over?"

I attempted to swallow, but my throat had dried out to a husk and I couldn't manage it. "Here," I decided. It seemed like a better option than walking back inside. "I'm going to hang out here all night."

His sneer hit me right in the gut, and a deep swell of panic and insecurity washed over me. I wanted to crawl into a hole and hide. I wanted to walk away from this restaurant and never look back. I wanted to… I wanted to feel nothing whenever Wyatt was involved.

That was my biggest issue with him. He made me feel more than any other person on the planet. When he disapproved of something I did, it killed me. When he got irritated with me, it made me want to cry. When he approved of something I did, my spirit soared. When he touched me, I burned. When he kissed me, I exploded.

My emotions were not neutral toward him. I was all over the place. With every other person I could remain nonchalant, totally unaffected no matter their opinion of me. At the very least I could defer to sarcasm without wanting to cry or run away.

Wyatt brought every single feeling out of me. All at once. I didn't want to care about him or what he thought. Yet, here I stood, a buzzing, flailing ball of feeling. If Dillon wasn't here, I probably would have jumped the poor man and picked up right where he'd left off earlier—meaning more kisses. So many more kisses.

I was also contemplating punching him in the kidneys.

It was really anyone's guess what I would do. But the indecision inside me was concerning.

He turned his glare on Dillon. "Can I have a minute with Kaya?"

She crossed her arms and glared back. "That depends. Are you going to be mean?"

His jaw ticked, and I had to fight to swallow again. Only for entirely different reasons. Damn that jaw.

Damn this boy.

"I'm never mean to Kaya."

Dillon rolled her eyes, and the confused, over-emotional crazy person inside me threw her hands in the air and cheered for good friends. "Please."

Wyatt's jaw ticked again. "Go inside, Dillon. I need to have a conversation with my sous chef."

She pointed a finger at him. "Be nice."

His hands dropped to his waist and he glared at the ground until she'd walked past him and disappeared in the building again.

"Am I in trouble?" My voice had more courage than I felt, but I was thankful for the bravado.

His head lifted slowly, his eyes finding mine from behind thick lashes. "You shouldn't let her set you up. I've heard stories about the guys she dates. They're losers."

126

His words made zero sense to me. I blinked at him and tried to put them in the right order. Was he having a stroke? "What?"

"Listen, you're better than that. You deserve more than club rats."

My heart kicked in my chest and I struggled to catch my breath. Was that a compliment? But I didn't know what to say. Or why he was giving me dating advice. I should have said thank you and walked back inside. That's what I should have done. But like all the times before with Wyatt, for whatever stupid reason, I ended up blurting the truth. "I, uh, she's not setting me up with anyone."

His eyes narrowed. "I thought I heard you ask her to."

Belatedly I remembered that I had asked her to hook me up not that long ago. Crap. But had I even been serious? I didn't have the time or energy for blind dates and meaningless hookups. Honestly, a night out with one of Dillon's friends sounded exhausting. Best to move this along. "You must have misheard. Uh, what did you want to talk to me about?"

He remained silent long enough that I wondered if he forgot what he'd wanted to talk to me about. Finally, he said, "There's a chance that Rebecca Jones will stop by tonight."

"Whoa." Rebecca Jones was a food critic in Durham. Lilou had been reviewed by plenty of notable critics while Killian was here and considering the magazines and professionals and acclaimed critics that had reviewed before, Rebecca Jones wasn't that big of a deal. But for Wyatt, she was the most notable critic to dine at Lilou under his new regime.

This was a good sign for him. People wanted to check him out, see if he had the chops it took to handle Lilou.

He shrugged. "It's not for sure. But just in case, I, uh, I need you to be extra on top of things tonight."

Noticing the redness to his eyes and the several days of stubble covering his face, it was easy to see that he still wasn't sleeping. Unable to help

127

myself, I leaned forward and brushed my thumb over his cheekbone. He leaned into my touch, his eyes fluttering closed.

I had the strongest urge to kiss his closed eyelid. My heart squeezed with the need to soothe some of his exhaustion, the burden stress and perfection had dropped on his shoulders. He was too calm like this, too sweet. This wasn't the dictator I'd come to resent in the kitchen, this was a softer, more insecure version of him. A version that made me all squishy inside and prone to make bad decisions.

When I realized what I was doing, I dropped my hand. His eyes opened, and my heart kicked again at how tired he looked. Maybe that was what the kiss was about earlier—sleep deprivation.

"Are you still not sleeping?" I asked gently.

He shook his head. "I think I'm still acclimating."

"You must be doing something right. Rebecca Jones is coming tonight. The city of Durham will soon know you can handle the shit out of this kitchen."

I had been hoping for a smile and I got one. "Yeah, or the opposite."

Rolling my eyes, I moved to walk past him. "Don't worry, I'll babysit you tonight so that doesn't happen."

His arm shot out, wrapping around the front of me. "Thank you," he murmured near my ear.

We heard the smokers returning at the same time. His arm dropped immediately, and I ducked inside before anyone caught us talking innocently and not at all suspiciously outside.

I looked for a surface to bang my forehead against until my rapidly beating heart and rushing blood returned to normal but settled on prep work and hours of chopping instead.

Get your shit together, Kaya. Or you're going to end up as red-eyed and glitchy as Wyatt.

And I did not have time for that right now.

I had an executive chef to babysit and a different restaurant to take over.

It was hard to focus after all that had happened between us today. By the time I got home after a grueling fifteen-hour shift and a successful night of impressing Rebecca Jones—or at least I hoped we had— I wasn't even surprised to find a text message from Wyatt. I might have even been expecting one.

Thanks for taking care of me tonight.

I smiled at the typed words, imagining that they were said with no small amount of reluctance. **Are you embarrassed by how much you need me?** I asked him.

Not even a little bit, he'd typed back immediately. **Pretty sure I've needed you for a long time.**

The demonic seductress inside me couldn't help herself. **You've never said anything before...**

I've never had an opportunity before.

I nibbled on my lip ring and tried to decide if he was still talking about food. **Don't let this go to your head, chef, but I might need you too.**

His reply was simple, to the point, and inexplicably the hottest text I'd ever received. **Good.**

Chapter Eight

"Charlie, do it again."

My coworker cursed under his breath, calling me a dirty name I couldn't make out. I could have guessed though. I figured it landed somewhere in the general vicinity of body parts used to degrade women.

I rolled my eyes. I wasn't going to let him get away with being a crybaby. I'd stupidly made the mistake of sleeping with the idiot a while back. We'd gone out after an epically long shift and gin was involved. One bad decision led to the next... I woke up the next morning with a killer hangover and buyer's remorse. He was a nice enough guy, but so not for me. "Your asparagus is charred to hell and you've murdered that egg."

The poached egg over crispy, lemon asparagus was one of Wyatt's original ideas and it was freaking fantastic. I mean, as hard as it was for me to give Wyatt a compliment, I had to admit it was the best asparagus I had ever tasted.

And Charlie was doing a bang-up job of making sure nobody else shared my opinion.

"Fucking hell, Kaya," he continued to grumble.

"I'm saving your ass," I reminded him. Lifting my gaze off the filet in my pan, I stared him down. "Or did you want to hear it from Wyatt instead?"

Half his mouth twitched into a smile. "You're as bad as he is."

I wrinkled my nose, hating and loving the comparison all at once. "Don't be gross." I threw my elbow toward his grill top. "And fucking pay attention or you're going to burn it again."

"Yeah, yeah," he mumbled but turned back to his food.

On instinct, I glanced back and caught Wyatt staring at us with that signature glare of his. He was either pissed at Charlie for messing up the asparagus for the third time tonight or at me for getting in Charlie's business.

Our gazes clashed together, fire flaming between us. Nope, he was definitely pissed at me. He probably wanted the chance to scream at Charlie and I'd taken it away from him.

Suddenly, the strangest thing happened. A shadow of a smile passed over his lips. He wasn't glaring at me. He was smiling at me!

Nerves bubbled in my stomach at the same time my bones turned to liquid. I quickly turned around and tried to forget that look, that exact expression. I'd seen Wyatt smile before. Once or twice. Maybe. But that wasn't a normal smile. That was sex and sin and very dirty things.

Steak, Kaya. Pay attention to the steak.

It would be a miracle if I didn't ruin this poor filet. And it was wagyu. I'd be damned before I burned wagyu. I needed to focus.

And not worry about Wyatt.

Yeah, right.

I had been telling myself that for two days now. It wasn't working.

My lips still burned where our mouths had touched on Wednesday. I had stopped calling it a kiss sometime yesterday, at like the twenty-four-hour obsession mark. It wasn't a kiss. Kisses were warm and gentle and lovely.

No, Wyatt hadn't kissed me.

He'd branded me.

I knew that to be true, because I could still feel the outline of his lips on mine and the heat of his body pressed into me. The gentle touch of his tongue. The riot of butterflies that migrated through me from head to toe every time I thought about it was unforgettable.

Kisses didn't leave me so disoriented. Kisses were ordinary. Or at best they were nice.

Only nice.

Clearly Wyatt had done something more than kiss me, something wholly irreversible. Now I was stuck with the memory of his touch for the rest of my life.

Bastard.

"Did you read the review?" Charlie asked in a low voice when he plated the now perfect asparagus.

"Which one?" The Daily Durham review had come out last week. They'd raved about Wyatt's successful takeover and seamless transition. Lilou had been hailed as better than ever. They had been especially impressed with Wyatt's new dishes and couldn't wait to see what else was going to come from "Durham's rising star."

133

In a strange turn of events, Wyatt had seemed ignited by the review, instead of pacified by it. He was more desperate than ever to make changes to the menu and improve nightly service. I'd walked in on him yesterday when he'd been on the phone with Ezra, fighting over yet another menu change that Wyatt wanted to make. I could only imagine what another review would do to his already feverish pace.

Rebecca Jones had stopped by a couple of nights ago, but she would visit the restaurant a few more times before she wrote anything up. She never reviewed after her first stop.

"The one on Episessed." Charlie paused to listen to Wyatt's latest callouts. "It came out this morning."

I read Episessed like every other foodie in the region, but I only checked it every so often. They didn't post every day, so I usually caught up on the weekends.

Dread curdled in my stomach. I glanced at Wyatt. His back was to me again, his hands splayed on the counter in front of him. His arms were locked, forcing his shoulders to stiffen, and his head was bowed over order tickets.

God, it was unfair how sexy he was.

That was it. Right there. My hottest fantasy. Not that it was necessarily Wyatt. But a chef that looked like him and commanded a kitchen like he did and stood like that. And also sounded like him. And talked like him. And had an ass like him. Yes, please.

Of course, I was referring to a totally different human. That other person in my fantasy. Not Wyatt. Obviously.

"You should read it," Charlie coaxed.

The dread came spilling back in full force. If it was bad, we were all going to suffer. As we should. They could give Wyatt as many exaggerated honors as they wanted to, but he couldn't run this kitchen by himself. Still...

134

I wasn't sure if he could handle it emotionally if it was negative. He didn't seem to be the most stable person lately.

I tore my eyes from Wyatt and focused on Charlie. "Is it bad?"

He smirked. "You might think so."

Glaring at him, I began plating the slices of wagyu filet over a bed of crispy jicama and sweet potato frites with a side of glazed green beans topped with roasted pistachios.

Wiping the edges of the dish with a towel, I focused more on the plate in front of me than on the annoying cook to my left. "Are you going to tell me what it says?"

"Just read it, Swift."

Holy hell, he was annoying. I couldn't tell if he was taunting me or preparing me. But his suggestion was on my mind as I carried my plate over to Wyatt.

I set it in front of him and ran my lip ring back and forth in my teeth while he inspected my handiwork. "The filet looks okay."

"It's perfect."

"Did you do the green beans?"

"Those are all Benny."

"Hmph."

He started wiping the edge that I'd already cleaned off. It wasn't worth saying anything. This was his way.

Usually I would have retreated to the fire by now, but I had a break in orders and the Episessed review was on my brain. I cocked my hip out to rest against the counter. Wyatt gave me a side glance but remained focused on the dish going out.

"I heard a rumor that Episessed reviewed Lilou today."

He smiled at the filet and my heart kicked with that same obnoxious pitter-patter his smiles always caused. "They did."

135

"The review was a good one?"

He turned his head, that smile still lifting the corners of his too wide mouth. "It was."

Something tugged at my guts, warning me it wasn't all good. Not if Charlie was all but daring me to read it. "Congratulations," I told him, but to be honest, it lacked all the congratulatory feelings.

He didn't say thank you. A normal person would have said thank you. But Wyatt wasn't normal.

Instead, he made a humming noise and then called for a server. The steak went out of the kitchen next to seared rabbit with pancetta and truffle tortellini. My stomach growled at the smell of some of the best food this city had to offer.

"You can take a break," Wyatt murmured in a low rumble of a voice.

I blinked at him again. "What?"

His gaze dropped briefly to my stomach before he turned back to an order of risotto that had been placed in front of him. "If you're hungry. You can take a break."

Was this a trick? "I don't usually get hungry while I'm cooking. I don't know why I am tonight."

He turned to look at me again, hitting me full force with those dark, mysterious brown eyes. "Really? I find that I'm always hungry in this kitchen."

It was a normal sentence. Totally normal. And yet there was a tone to it that made my knees shake and my belly pool with heat.

Was that an innuendo?

No way.

Not in the middle of dinner service...

I found myself staring at him, held prisoner by his hot chocolate gaze and the mystery swimming in the depths there. My mouth was suddenly very dry,

136

and I licked my lips desperately to find relief. His eyes dropped to follow the movement and my breath caught in my chest.

What was wrong with him? This was craziness. He had officially lost his mind.

And the worst part was the confusion. We were in totally uncharted territory and I had no idea how to read him. Was there something going on with him? Between us? Or was I totally reading into stupid little things because I was completely overworked and lonely and secretly, very, very secretly crushing on him?

Leaning closer I caught his scent. He smelled like the kitchen. Fire and herbs and citrus. But there was something beyond the food, something manlier… something so totally consumed with testosterone, my delicate lady parts nearly swooned. "We need to talk."

One of his eyebrows lifted. "Now?"

I shook my head, trying to get my thoughts straight. "No, obviously not now."

He smiled slowly. "Later then."

"Tonight."

His chin bobbed up and down. "Okay, tonight. Come find me."

I turned around and suppressed a scream. There was something about the way he demanded very obvious things that made the hairs on the back of my neck bristle. Obviously, I would find him later and I would talk to him. Those were my ideas. And somehow, he stole the credit because he said them in that authoritative way of his.

Okay, now I was getting irritated with stupid things. Which meant I was nervous. Why was I nervous to talk to my boss? The guy I couldn't stand?

I shouldn't be. This was dumb. I was dumb.

Argh! I blamed all of this on Wyatt. He was the problem. Actually, that was an understatement.

He was the sum total of my problems.

I had work to do, but I couldn't resist the temptation of nabbing my phone out of my apron to quickly pull up the Episessed review. It took the next thirty minutes to read it between dishes, but I managed to get to the end eventually.

I looked over at Charlie. "Son of a bitch."

He cackled. The asshole cackled. "It's a good review for Lilou."

His neutral statement made me want to punch him in the throat. "Yeah, if you're Wyatt Shaw."

He leaned closer, so no one would overhear us. "My favorite part was when they asked him who he could rely on in the kitchen and he said his instincts."

My Santoku knife was sitting where I sliced the filet. I resisted, barely, the urge to grab it and throw it across the kitchen. "He's such a dickhead."

Charlie laughed harder.

"He didn't have to say my name." I tried to sound at least mildly humble. Even if my insides were boiling. "He could have credited all of us. He could have said we didn't flinch with the regime change. We gave him the respect he was due right out of the gate. He could have mentioned us—a general, they're all amazing."

Charlie sobered some, his smile turning confused. "Would you?"

I rolled my eyes. That was a stupid question. "Of course, I would! If I ran a kitchen like this, I wouldn't need to claim all the glory for myself. The food speaks for itself."

He shrugged. "That's the difference between men and women."

It was my turn to be confused. "What does that mean?"

"Men don't like to share. Women lack the bloodthirsty gene."

138

"Not true," I disagreed immediately. "I'm plenty bloodthirsty." My fists clenched thinking about Sarita. I was really fucking bloodthirsty. "But I also know how to appreciate the people that have helped get me to where I'm at."

"So you would thank me in an interview?"

I shook my head. "Not you. You haven't helped me get anywhere. But I would credit Dillon. And… other people." I meant Vera, but I couldn't exactly admit that to Charlie.

"Are the other people women?"

I didn't like his point, but I nodded.

"Okay, so fine, maybe it's a different kind of bloodthirsty," Charlie decided.

I stared at him. "Are you calling me sexist?"

"You said the word."

I snorted. I couldn't tell if he was serious. "Hey, at least I wouldn't credit my instincts."

"That's not sexist," Charlie pointed out. "That's selfishness. They're not the same thing."

"Okay, fine. You have a point." Although it killed me to admit it. "With this one thing. But the kitchen is one of the most sexist industries in the country. You have to admit that."

He shrugged. "Maybe. But also, maybe we're all more like Wyatt than like you. Maybe we're not being sexist. Maybe we're only looking out for ourselves."

"And the catcalls from the line? The crude comments whenever I take off my coat?"

His embarrassed smile added points to my side of the argument. "Again, you're painting those things in a bad light. We're appreciating the opposite sex. We can't help it if you're nice to look at."

I rolled my eyes and turned back to my station. There it was. Point proven.

But maybe he also had a point. I had assumed that the men in this kitchen and in all kitchens didn't take me seriously because I was a woman. But maybe it was less about me. Maybe it wasn't about me at all.

It wasn't that they didn't take me seriously, it was that they were more competitive. In like a savage way. It wasn't only me they wanted to discount, but every single potential threat, men and women alike.

And maybe that was still what Wyatt was doing. Even though he'd made it. He was the alpha. The top dog. He still couldn't let go of his instincts to fight, to keep his job.

Maybe.

Although that was a very generous point of view and I still wanted to punch him.

We were definitely talking later. I had so much to say.

And he had no clue what was coming.

Chapter Nine

I found Wyatt in his office after almost everyone else had cleared the kitchen. I loved working on protein, but my station was a nightmare to clean at the end of the night. And it didn't help that I was a perfectionist.

A polite person would have knocked and waited for an invitation to open the door. Poor Wyatt, because I didn't have any manners left after that Epissessed interview.

He looked up at me from where he leaned over his computer. "Oh, hey."

I slammed the door behind me. Wyatt jerked back, surprised by my outburst.

Waving my phone in the air like a crazy person, I said, "Oh, hey? Oh, *hey?*" He blinked at me in confusion, only fueling my fire. "When you said the Epissessed interview was good, I didn't realize it was because you threw your entire kitchen under the bus! When you said it was good, I didn't realize you meant because it's literally only about you! You selfish, son of a b—"

He cut me off, throwing his body back in his chair and giving the ceiling an exasperated look. "You can't be serious."

"I'm dead serious. They asked you who you can rely on in the kitchen and you said your instincts! Are you for real?"

"I said more than that." He waved a hand at his computer. "They chose to print that. I had no control over what parts of the interview made the final cut."

I rolled my eyes so hard it hurt. "Now it makes sense. You went on and on about how kickass your staff is, and they went with the offhand remark about your instincts. Those dirty rat bastards."

He slid forward in his seat, his posture stiffening. "I did talk about the kitchen, Kaya. I talked a hell of a lot about you. But yeah, I also said my instincts because that's true. My instincts have made this transition seamless. My instincts have known when to push Ezra into new dishes and when to wait for the fight."

"And are your instincts to thank for me saving your ass every night too?"

He stood up and moved around the desk so quickly, I jumped. I wasn't proud of it. But he had the quickness of a jungle cat. And his stupid long legs moved him faster than I could escape. Ugh! More reasons to hate him.

"My instinct kept you sous, did it not?"

"That wasn't instinct, dummy. That was common sense."

His mouth split into a sardonic grin. "I have never met anyone fuller of themselves than you. You're unbelievable."

I folded my arms over my chest and said something I was not proud of. But totally blamed on Wyatt. He turned me into a child. This was all his fault!

"Oh, yeah?" I taunted. "Have you looked in the mirror lately?"

"Good God." He groaned and laughed at the same time. "You're impossible. Is this what you wanted to talk to me about earlier? This? You're pissed because I didn't squeeze your name into a random interview?"

"Yes," I answered quickly. "I mean no. I mean, yes." God, what was the question? I had wanted to talk to him about his weird looks lately, about that kiss that he had not bothered to bring up since it happened. I wanted to figure out what was going on between us to put an end to it.

But now that we were here, I couldn't bring myself to say anything. His actions in the interview had been enough to squash the weird sexual tension I felt earlier today.

"Which is it, Swift? Yes or no? Is there something else you want to talk about?"

He sat down on the edge of his desk, his long legs spreading out to both sides of me. We suddenly felt too close. I wanted to move back, but there was nowhere to go in his tiny office.

I reached for sarcasm, the lifeline to sanity. "I think you being a selfish asshole covers it."

He smiled, and it was so genuine and significant, aimed so wholly at me that it took everything in me not to smile back. I mean, damn, his smile was a weapon.

He hid them so well. Deprived the entire world of that face looking that perfect. But when we were alone? He whipped it out like it was no big deal. Like I wouldn't automatically melt into a pile of goo. Like he couldn't get away with whatever he wanted because all he had to do was smile.

"You drive me crazy, you know that?" he asked, his voice soft, teasing.

143

I held my arms more tightly around my waist. "Good."

His eyes twinkled, catching the affection from the smile. "We're even, see?"

This was a trick. It had to be. Because I should have already stormed out of the office with my middle fingers thrown in the air for good measure. Instead, I found myself leaning against the door, my shoulders relaxing, my scowl fading, my entire body warming to him. "How do you figure?"

"I drive you crazy. You drive me crazy. Win-win."

"I don't think you know what that means." My eye twitched when his smile stretched and I realized I'd walked into a trap. "Yeah, but you should know better. You're the boss."

He leaned forward. "That is the problem, isn't it?"

My righteous anger melted into confusion. "What's the problem?"

"I'm the boss."

"That's been clearly established. Believe me." I stared at him. "Wait, what?"

He stood and towered over me. My heart stopped. He took another step towards me. My heart jumped into a sprint, racing as fast it could go, beating frantically against my poor, fragile breastbone.

"The problem is that I'm the boss." The back of his hand brushed the underside of my jaw. "Otherwise, we could do something about the way we drive each other crazy."

Now I couldn't swallow and my stomach doing somersaults was making me dizzy. I blamed all of this on him. Somehow my voice still came out breathy, forgiving, perplexed. "How could we do that?"

His head dropped so he could whisper in my ear. "Use your imagination." I leaned into him, hating the tickle and savoring the feel of him all at once. He took a step back, depriving me of him too soon. "But I can swear to you,

I'd find a way to work your name in. And I'm fairly confident you'd remember to use mine."

Was he serious? Sex? He was talking about sex?

What the ever-loving what?

He sat back down on the edge of his desk, his arms folded over his chest again, smug and arrogant and so fucking full of himself.

Nope. This could not stand.

He could not do an interview like that, work me into a frenzy like this, smile at me, and then do whatever the hell he just did and get away with it.

I decided I needed to teach him a lesson. And put my libido out of its misery.

Stepping into the space between his legs, I gripped his coat collar with two hands and leaned forward until my mouth was an inch above his. "Don't be so sure of yourself." The wickedness in my plan pulled a smirk from me and I savored the way his breath hitched, and his body went rigid. He had expected me to walk away.

Or run away.

See? He'd underestimated me again.

I let my mouth brush over his. "It's not a given that'd I'd remember your name, chef. You might turn out to be totally forgettable."

"Not a fucking chance." His voice was low, hoarse.

I wasn't sure who moved first. Whether it was him or me or both of us crashing together all at once in a tangle of lips and tongue and teeth. His hands were on my waist, pulling me closer, holding my body against his, searing me with the same heat that had branded my lips.

He tasted like coconut, and his lips were surprisingly cool to the touch like he'd just finished taking a drink of something cold. For as rock hard as the rest of his body was, his lips were the opposite. Lush and pillowy and too addicting.

145

Our kiss was frantic, unfamiliar and wild. I couldn't get enough of him. The more I kissed him, the more I wanted. The more I needed.

And the more we practiced, the better we got too. I learned the contours of his mouth, the tilt of his head, the sound he made in the back of his throat when I sunk my teeth into his full bottom lip. God, this man.

His mouth moved from mine to trail kisses along the curve of my jaw, the length of my neck, the spot just behind my ear. And down so he could nip at my collarbone and do wicked things with his tongue to the hollow of my throat.

I shivered, a full body tremble that he caught with his arms wrapped around my waist. He laid his head on my breasts, holding me to him in an embrace that felt part genuine and part fear. I looked down at the top of his head and couldn't help but whisper, "What are we doing?"

He pulled back and grinned at me. "I think it's pretty obvious." He pressed a lingering kiss to the underside of my jaw. "But I can show you again if you're still confused."

I set my hands on his shoulders, holding him at a distance. "Wyatt, this is crazy."

His smile was less sure this time, but just as powerful. Maybe because it was nervous… insecure… maybe because it wobbled and sort of fell and hit me right in the chest. I wanted to bring it back in full. I wanted to wrap my arms around him and hold him to me, making sure he never looked uncertain again.

That wasn't who he was. He was confident to a fault. Cocky and fearless; completely sure of himself.

So, this vulnerable version needed to go away before it completely slayed me.

"Maybe," he admitted. "But maybe not so crazy either."

I braved those brown eyes, dark with the secrets of what we just did. "What do you mean?"

His arms tightened around my waist. "I mean… it feels inevitable. I know things are complicated since I'm your boss, but it had to happen eventually, right?"

Maybe sleep deprivation had broken his brain. None of his words were making any sense. "Why eventually?"

He glanced at the ceiling, already getting frustrated with me. I nearly smiled at how quickly the bliss of kissing wore off. We would be back to bickering in no time.

"I don't understand why you keep saying that. What had to happen eventually?"

His sigh was frustrated and annoyed. I tried to suppress a victorious smile. "This goddamn tension between us, Kaya. It's been building and building and building. Eventually it was going to come to a head."

I glared at him, irrationally angry that he was downplaying what happened here. I knew it made no sense. I was the one trying to convince him that nothing significant had transpired between us. But I was a female and therefore allowed to be fickle at least once a day. "That's what you think this was? Sexual tension coming to a head?"

His rumbly chuckle chased another shiver down my spine. "No, this was more like a compression leak." His hands moved down my hips, to the backs of my thighs where he gripped me beneath my ass. He tugged me toward him and I had to grasp his shoulders for balance. "We haven't even begun to release the real pressure."

I laughed, even though inwardly I was freaking out. "Wyatt, we're not doing this again." A slow smile spread across his mouth. I pushed at his shoulders, but even I had to admit I barely put any effort into the protest.

147

"Wyatt, I'm serious," I insisted. "This was a mistake. We're smart enough to know not to repeat our mistakes."

"You kissed me," he said, totally catching me off guard.

"What?"

"Tonight. Right now." His eyebrows jumped, insisting that he was telling the truth. "I wasn't going to kiss you, but you practically threw yourself at me."

"You're blaming this on me?" I was too shocked to be pissed. Although I knew that would come later. Right after the shame and embarrassment.

Or maybe before.

It was hard to tell at this point. There were too many emotions clamoring for first place.

His head cocked back and his hold on my waist went slack. "I wasn't blaming you," he said. "I was... crediting you." His eyes flashed with something that looked too much like hope and I wanted to take back my words and swallow them just to erase that look on his face.

But I couldn't. I was too worked up, too out of my depth. As much as I liked to pretend I loved spontaneity, what I really loved was predictability and obviousness. I hated change. And I hated not knowing what happened next.

That was one of the reasons I loved cooking so much. I knew what would happen. I had the variables calculated and my processes in place. If I cooked a specific size protein for a certain number of minutes, it would turn out exactly how I wanted it to. If I used x amount of spice with x amount of other spice, I would get a very consistent flavor profile.

Sure, there was some change and I couldn't predict the future no matter how hard I tried. But for the most part, I could get pretty damn close.

And that was important to me.

148

I'd run from a past that had been way too predictable, but I hadn't left that girl behind completely. She still lurked inside me, a shadow of a past I desperately wanted to forget. But I couldn't. And I couldn't completely forget the girl I used to be either.

"I don't want the credit," I told Wyatt. My eyelids slammed shut, hiding the shame for my cruel words. I took a step back and Wyatt let me go.

He was going to be pissed. The man did not handle rejection well. I knew this from working with him. This would wound his pride, chip away at his testosterone. He'd hate me forever now.

So, I drove the nail into the coffin and let go of this delicious, wonderful, totally unexpected moment of insanity. It was better this way. "I don't want you."

Only his smile turned genuine again. His eyes twinkled and darkened, beckoning all at once. His hands rested on his desk, his fingers curling around the edges. He stretched his body back all cocky arrogance and self-satisfied man. "Liar," he taunted.

"Excuse me?"

"You're a dirty liar, Swift. You fucking want me."

Red. I went red. From head to toe, including my vision. "I don't want you." I stepped forward and pointed a finger directly in his face. "I seriously don't want you."

He sucked in his bottom lip and let his silence speak for him.

"You're out of your damn mind."

He remained silent.

"I honestly can't believe you. Or how you could even come to that crazy conclusion! What have I ever done to give you any indication that I want you? I was being polite, asshole. Nice. I didn't want to wound your poor, fragile ego." I yanked open the door, but before I walked through it I had to turn around and say, "Tomorrow morning you're going to feel embarrassed

149

about all of this. And I'm not going to feel bad for you, Shaw. This is what you get."

I turned my back on him and that's when he decided to speak. His voice still low, he asked, "And what if I want more of it, Kaya? Then what?"

I looked back at him over my shoulder. "Then find somebody else."

He shook his head and mouthed one word. "No."

My body finally reacted the way it should have a half hour ago and I ran from the building like the hounds of hell were chasing me.

If I thought his barely there kiss a few days ago was bad, that was nothing compared to the torment a full on make out session put me through. I tossed and turned for hours, replaying every second of the night.

I couldn't help but wonder what I'd done to lead Wyatt on. And then every single interaction between us seemed obvious and fraught with sexual tension. Hadn't I bitten his finger? How else was he supposed to interpret my actions?

And, God, was he that far off?

Alone, in my room, with nobody to face and no one else to answer to, I had to be honest with myself. Of course, I wanted Wyatt and I had imagined us together. I had noticed his body, his mouth, the way he would casually touch me every once in a while. I had played around with the idea of how good we would be and how he would totally rock my world in every sense of the phrase. But that was a natural reaction to what he looked like. That wasn't my fault! He was objectively attractive.

I was reacting to him as any woman in my position would react to him.

When I rolled out of bed in the morning, he'd sent me an email. There was no subject or personal message other than a link that led to another interview.

The interview had gone live last week on a more popular website than Epissessed called Cocktails and Carnivores. It was a national site and didn't

150

have the promise of local gossip, so I didn't check it often. I read through it three times before I believed the words on the page.

"How has the transition gone?" they'd asked him.

His reply? "Unbelievably smooth. Honestly, I expected a fight. Killian was made in that kitchen and I feel totally unqualified to fill his absence."

"You must be doing something right," they'd said.

"It's the staff mostly," he'd answered. "Especially my sous chef. Kaya Swift. She's stayed strong through the entire overhaul, giving the kitchen confidence to do what it does best—cook good food. I'd be completely lost without her."

I swallowed my tongue. Or nearly did. That should have been enough. That would have been enough to shut me up about the Epissessed interview. But they'd gone on.

"She sounds special," the interviewer had commented.

And in print, in type, right there in front of me, from a reputable website that claimed Wyatt had verbalized these exact words, said, "She is."

So that was basically the sound of my entire world collapsing. Or exploding. Or altering entirely.

Wyatt was full of surprises lately.

It was probably time I decided if I liked those surprises or if I wanted him to get the hell out of my kitchen.

Chapter Ten

"You look like hell."

My lip curled at Dillon as I slid across from her in the vinyl-cracked booth. "Good morning to you too."

"I mean, clearly something's up," she went on. Not the least bit apologetic. "Are you feeling all right? Do you have the flu?"

"No flu."

"It's cancer then." She leaned forward, sliding her hands toward me over the Formica tabletop. "Oh my God. You have cancer. Don't' worry, friend, you also have me. We're going to fight this, K. Fight it with all we got."

I threw my hands in the air before she could touch me. "Has anyone ever told you how obnoxious you are?"

She grinned at me. "Nope."

"You're obnoxious."

Her expression didn't falter. "Yeah, but that doesn't count because you love me."

"I'm reconsidering actually."

She stuck out her tongue and handed me a menu at the same time. Saturday mornings we always grabbed brunch at the Blue Pelican. It was this hole in the wall dive that served the best corned beef hash on the planet.

"This is how I know I'm right," she murmured. "You're so grumpy today."

I raised an eyebrow. "I thought you knew you were right by how I looked?"

She waved a hand at me. "I was giving you a hard time. I mean… your eyes are a little bloodshot today, but the eyeliner helps. It looks good on you. You never wear it."

Staring hard at the menu in front of me, I didn't comment. I didn't usually wear makeup to work, especially not eyeliner. I was more of a waterproof mascara and hydrating primer kind of girl. But Dillon was right about my eyes. And the bags underneath them. Also, how my hair had decided to misbehave and get all wild on me—even with half of it knotted on the top of my head. I was a mess today.

"It's okay," I relented. "I didn't sleep at all last night. I'm exhausted."

"You need a night off."

I smirked at her. "That isn't going to happen."

"You're all…" She made hand gestures that put her at a cross between a zombie version of Frankenstein and a chipmunk having a seizure. "Tightly wound."

She had no idea.

The waiter stopped to take our order. Dillon got the roasted tomato and poblano egg white mini quiches and I got a cup of coffee.

"Are you sure you don't want something to eat?" our regular server, Dan, asked.

"Um, maybe the oatmeal? With the berries and brown sugar."

Dan's eyebrows raised, but he didn't comment. Dillon wasn't as kind.

"Oh my God. It is cancer."

"Shut it."

"Oatmeal, Ky? Oatmeal? How bad is it? Stage four? Stage five? Oh my God. Is it stage ten?"

Staring at my gorgeous, talented, super ditzy friend, I wondered whether to bring up Wyatt now or tackle her severely irrational fear of cancer. "I think cancer only has four stages. I think stage ten is dead."

She pounded a dainty fist on the table. "That's not the point!"

I needed to put her out of her misery. That was the kind thing to do. But I couldn't seem to get the words to leave my mouth. They sat on my tongue, making it numb and immovable.

Rip the Band-Aid, Kaya. Tear that motherfucker right off. "Wyatt and I made out last night."

She slumped back against the booth and blinked at me. She didn't even have to say a word. I felt her judgment fill the small restaurant like helium in a balloon

"Obviously making out with Wyatt was a mistake," I told her. "Obviously it won't happen again."

She still didn't say anything, and I decided I should have let her believe it was stage ten cancer.

"I stopped by his office to talk to him about… I can't even remember what now. But we were alone, and one thing led to another…" Although I

155

was still fuzzy on all the details. One minute we were standing there and the next I was trying to climb him like a spider monkey. "And suddenly we were making out."

She finally spoke, her eyes as wide as I had ever seen them. "In his office?"

I pressed my lips together and nodded.

"Holy shit, Kaya!"

Covering my face with my hands I moaned. "I'm a terrible person."

"You're my hero!"

I peeked through my fingers and saw glee on my friend's face. Her reaction couldn't be right. "Huh?"

"You made out with Wyatt fucking Shaw." She laughed. "That's legendary status."

"Shh!" I demanded, leaning closer. Saturday morning brought out our industry en masse. Either they were gossiping or working while gossiping. And the last thing I wanted was for this piece of information to get around town. "Please. Nobody can know."

She looked truly affronted. "Why not? Don't you think every female in this city has been trying to get in that boy's pants for years? He's basically a locked box. I've played around with the theory that he's secretly wearing a chastity belt. He's never looked twice at me." She didn't say it in an arrogant way, but I couldn't help but smile. She of all people wouldn't understand Wyatt's lack of attention, not when she got plenty of second glances and third glances and fourth glances everywhere she went. "But suddenly, our dear Kaya has the keys."

Her grin made my cheeks blush tomato red. "That's wrong. All of those things you're saying are wrong."

156

She laughed at my flustered denial. "Kaya, he's into you! Like so into you. I see it now. How could I have been so blind all this time? The man has it bad for you!"

"You're out of your mind," I insisted. "It was a fluke. A mistake. He hasn't been sleeping. And I haven't been… sleeping with other people. And it was like the wrong time and the wrong place and we both got caught up in the… the… the whatever it was. It was a one-time thing that can never happen again."

She didn't hear a freaking word I said. "This explains why he's always glaring at you and yelling at you and making you do everything over. He doesn't hate you at all! He's got the hots for you!"

My blush turned from embarrassment to irritation. "First of all, no. Just no. No to all of that. Second, I'm pretty confident—because I have dated guys before, just not recently—that when guys like you they don't spend their time glaring at you and yelling at you, living to piss you off. They do different things. Like ask you on dates. And do kind gestures and buy you things. And smile at you." Although he did smile at me, didn't he? Yeah, okay, maybe not very often, but more often then he smiled at other people.

Shit.

Stop it.

He didn't like me.

"He has kindergarten syndrome," Dillon decided. "He's treating you how a little boy on the playground treats his crush."

"That is the dumbest thing I've ever heard. Wyatt hates me. He's threatened by me. Maybe he tolerates my presence in his sacred kitchen because I'm good at what I do, but if he ever has a chance to replace me, he'll take it."

At that moment a text flashed across my phone from Wyatt. **Stopping for coffee. Want one?**

157

I quickly clicked my screen to black so Dillon didn't see it.

She crossed her arms over her chest and jutted out her chin. "Okay, let's go with your theory then. He hates you. That explains why he's always staring at you when you're not looking and why he makes you work every single night and why he wants you to stay late with him. That's definitely the reason he made out with you last night in his office. Be real, Kaya, there's been weird, kinky tension between you two for weeks. Maybe even months."

My eyes narrowed. "Don't act like I'm the crazy one! Up until approximately three minutes ago you thought he hated me too. One tiny piece of new information doesn't change years of hard evidence." Of course there were other pieces of evidence I was choosing to omit from the conversation, but she didn't need to know that.

Shaking her head at me, she continued laying out her case. "Up until three minutes ago, I agree that I didn't understand his behavior and that he'd definitely singled you out. It was easy to assume he hated you because Wyatt's an asshole and it's hard to read him. But, lucky you, it turns out he doesn't hate you at all."

She had a point, but I couldn't give in. The change was too sudden for me to wrap my head around. There had to be another explanation to his attraction one-eighty. "He's working all the time. He doesn't have time to meet anyone right now. And he's been acting weird ever since he got the executive chef position because he's not sleeping well. What happened is, he got desperate. I am also," I cringed admitting the truth of it, "a little desperate, and when the two of us were alone together something… snapped."

"He's not sleeping well?"

"No."

"How do you know that?"

Another text from him lit up my phone. **I'm getting you one. If you don't want it, I'll drink it.** The text box ended, but I knew there was more I just couldn't see it. My fingers itched to check it.

I hesitated answering Dillon's question because I didn't want to admit the truth. But after a few beats of trying to ignore my phone, I finally fessed up. "He told me. He wanted me to… to help make sure he was getting everything right."

"Hmm."

"Don't hmm me." I pointed a finger at her that let her know I meant business. "I'm his sous chef. Obviously, he would count on me for something as important as that."

"That's another thing." Dan showed up with our food, interrupting our conversation while he set it in front of us and made sure we had everything we needed. I took the opportunity to sneak a look at Wyatt's message.

I'm guessing you're an iced coffee kind of girl. Cream? Sugar?

When I hadn't answered, he'd come back with, **I'm getting you cream and sugar.**

He was right. How did he know that? I mean, there were other options I liked. But during warm months, iced coffees were my jam. And always with cream and sugar. Always.

When Dan walked away again, Dillon leaned forward and dropped her voice again. "He asked you to stay as his sous chef right away. On day one. He didn't even have to think about it. It was like the second he got promoted, he knew exactly who he wanted by his side."

I rolled my eyes. That was the least interesting clue out of the bunch. "That doesn't mean anything. Who else would he ask?"

"Benny."

"Benny's not far off from sous. He's like an honorary. They're BFFs."

"Doesn't that make it strange that he asked you and not Benny?"

159

"I'm a better chef than Benny. And I was a sous for Killian," She gave me a look. "Besides, Wyatt's not the kind of guy to pick his friends over more qualified competition. They might be close, but Wyatt cares about the kitchen more than friendship."

She tilted her head thoughtfully. "Okay, you have me there."

"I have you everywhere," I insisted, except in my recent text messages. "Stop trying to make this more than it is. Whatever happened last night was the product of too much hatred, too little sleep, and a weird moment of insanity. It's not going to happen again. Ever."

Dillon's mischievous smile filled my stomach with nerves. "Don't be crazy. This is Wyatt Shaw we're talking about. Have you seen the man? God, he's so sexy. That body. All those tattoos. His hair! His hair is obnoxiously amazing. Kaya, if you get a chance to do that again, do it. Do it for me. Do it for the women of Durham. Ney, do it for the women of the world. Be our tribute."

I found myself laughing before I could discourage her craziness. "You're ridiculous."

"Was it good?"

Rolling my eyes, I suddenly found my oatmeal to be very interesting.

"Kaya!" she hollered at me.

"God, what? Don't yell at me!"

She was still grinning like a fool. "Was. It. Good?"

I held her eyes, my expression turning serious and furious all at once. "It was fucking amazing."

She threw her head back and cackled at the ceiling. "Ha-ha! I knew it. I knew he would be good!"

"Okay, seriously, do you have a thing for him? Because you've never said anything, and I didn't mean to step on your toes and—"

160

Her laughter died, and she wrinkled her nose at me. "Don't be crazy. I have no thing for Mr. Mysterious and Broody, okay? I like my men open, honest, and much less... yell-y."

He was very yell-y.

"But," she went on. "I've always felt like there was more to him than what he lets the world see. I mean, Ezra and Killian think the world of him. And they are the two opinions I trust most in the world. Clearly, he's not all mean, scary boss. It's nice to see that there's a soul to him. That's all."

He definitely had a soul. There had been times when we were sous chefs side by side that I'd even thought we were friends, maybe even good friends. Yeah, we always found something to clash over, but he had layers. He was so much more than the version I faced off with in the kitchen every night. Not that I would admit that to Dillon. "Being a good kisser does not automatically make someone a nice or decent person. Do you remember when he threw your trout in the trashcan? The whole entire plate and everything? He is the definition of mean, scary boss."

She shrugged. "I'd killed that trout. And I'd managed to drop half the roe on the ground and tried to get away with it. He called me on my bullshit." She buried her face in her hands for a moment and groaned. "I was so green. I'd been working there for all of two weeks or something and seriously contemplated quitting. Yeah, fine, he's terrifying. But he's also right most of the time."

"What about when he's wrong?"

She held my gaze, leaning forward so I could see the honesty in her expression. "Then we know you have our backs. And he knows it too. That's why you're sous and Benny's not. He respects you, Kaya. Give him a break."

I took a bite of my now cold oats. "Fine, he respects me. He knows I'm not going to take his shit. That's as far as it goes with us. The rest was ... sleep deprivation."

161

"Yeah, yeah, keep telling yourself that."

"I will. Thank you."

She laughed, but finally dug into her cold breakfast too.

"Don't tell Ezra," I whispered, nervous that mentioning her brother's name would put the idea in her head.

"What?"

I lifted my eyes and met hers, more afraid of this request than of accidentally making out with Wyatt again. "You can't tell Ezra that I made out with his executive chef. First, it's complicated because Wyatt is my boss. I don't know the exact protocol for intra-kitchen relationships, but I'm positive they're frowned upon. And second, when I apply for Sarita for real, I don't want Ezra to think Wyatt's good opinion of me is skewed. If he even has a good opinion of me. I... I would like to get Wyatt's recommendation without it feeling like a sexual favor."

"Wyatt would never—"

"Yeah, maybe Wyatt wouldn't. But I don't want the perception to be there. I don't want Ezra to think that..."

"Ezra wouldn't," she promised. "I know my brother and I know how much he respects Wyatt. He would never assume that about either of you." I opened my mouth to argue, but she held up her finger and added, "Besides, other people's opinions matter very little to Ezra. He'll only hire a person one hundred percent qualified for that job. He would never take someone else's word for it."

"I don't know if that makes me more nervous or less so."

She laughed at me again. "Seriously? Chill, Kaya. You're so worked up about a few kisses with one of the hottest men on the planet. You said it yourself, it's not going to happen again. Relax and take what happened as the compliment it is. Wyatt Shaw thinks you're a sexy beast. Own it, friend. And stop worrying about all the rest."

162

I sucked in a steadying breath and let the truth in her words ground me. She was right. I didn't know what Wyatt was thinking, but I knew myself. I was strong-willed. Independent. Tougher than fucking nails. I had self-control for days and days.

Even though Wyatt and I had made out once, that didn't mean it was going to happen again. I had that power. I would just avoid him altogether and try not to find myself alone with him ever again. And also, maybe I wouldn't look at him for a while either, because Dillon was so right about him being one of the sexiest men on the planet. I had acknowledged that long ago.

The point was, I wasn't going to accidentally fall into his arms again and let my mouth land on his. Consequently, there was absolutely nothing to worry about.

Besides, kissing him had been a fluke.

A weird, crazy, unbearably hot... fluke.

Tonight, we would be able to work together without any of the tension that had plagued us recently and we'd get back to our normally scheduled hate-fest. I would spend tomorrow night working with Vera at Sarita and I would be one step closer to the dream.

My dream. The one that took me away from Lilou and into my very own, five-star kitchen.

No man was worth losing sight of that dream.

Not even Wyatt fucking Shaw.

Another text blinked across the screen of my phone. **Get here already, woman. I want to see you.**

The butterfly riot that marched across my belly was enough to call me a liar, but I mentally held my ground. *Goals, Kaya. Dreams. A lifelong legacy that did not include my boss.* I just needed to focus and stop daydreaming about that kiss and those deep brown eyes and all those secret smiles that I was too quickly growing addicted to.

Chapter Eleven

*F*our hours later, I had to chant the promises to make my dreams come true like an incantation. I thought if I believed in them strongly enough, they would come to fruition. That was difficult when a certain someone apparently had other ideas in his big, stupid head.

The trouble had started when Dillon and I walked in the door to Lilou, ready to start prep for tonight's service. Wyatt had caught sight of us almost instantaneously. He'd popped out of his office and held up his hand in the smallest of waves. His other hand had offered a creamy iced coffee that I hadn't been able to turn down. Despite Dillon's raised eyebrows and giddy smile.

I'd tried to remain neutral and returned a simple thank you. That was when he pulled out the big guns. His eyelids had lowered to that dreamy, bedroom look that gave me goose bumps all over my body and his lips had curled into a soft smile when he mouthed, "Hey."

A mouthed hey shouldn't have sent me into a tailspin of frantic emotions and even more panicked thoughts, but it had. Why? Because this was Wyatt and up until yesterday, he preferred growling and snarling over actual words!

Things had only gotten worse from there. He'd stopped by an hour ago to help me mince onions and chop herbs. And then ten minutes ago, he'd brought me a cold bottle of water and set it down next to me without saying a word or asking if I even wanted the damn thing. Apparently, he was very concerned with my hydration.

I did want the water. I was always hot in the kitchen and subsequently always thirsty. Maybe I was thirstier than usual today. Fine. I could admit that. Anyone would be thirsty with Wyatt walking around, being nice, not yelling…

Also, the kitchen was very hot today. Did I already say that? The point was, he should have at least asked if I wanted water.

I let out a slow breath and decided banging my head against the wall wasn't going to solve any of my problems.

"There you are." Wyatt rounded the corner, another one of those secret smiles appearing as soon as our eyes met. "Can I go over a few things with you about tonight?"

My breath caught in my throat, but I wrestled it into a shaky exhale. "About the kitchen?"

One half of his mouth kicked up in a smirk. "Yes. About the kitchen." He tilted his head toward his office. "Come on."

"In there? Are you sure?" I spoke softly as to not alert the few people in the kitchen.

But he'd already walked ahead of me and didn't hear my pathetic reservations.

"Strong, independent woman," I whispered to myself. "Tough as nails. Remember that."

I reluctantly followed Wyatt into the office and immediately felt an embarrassing blush creep up my neck and tiptoe across my cheeks. The corner of his desk was a particular place I needed to ignore if I wanted to avoid spontaneously combusting in a ball of nerves.

Taking a seat in the chair across from his desk that was squished between a bookshelf neatly organized with trophies, awards, notebooks, business manuals, and a filing cabinet, I intentionally left the door wide open. Hopefully Wyatt would take that as a sign I had moved on. And also, that I didn't trust him.

Even though I hadn't moved on and I did trust him.

He read the truth all over my face as he sat down in his chair, his smirk becoming more and more wicked with every passing second. "You look a little tired today, Kaya. Did you sleep okay last night?"

"I didn't if you must know," I told him in clipped tones. "I barely slept at all."

He leaned forward, resting his forearms on his desk. "I'm sorry to hear that."

There was something hidden in his voice, some kind of clue that he wanted me to catch and I was curious enough to take the bait. His body seemed relaxed, and I couldn't help but notice that the black bags beneath his eyes were slightly less pronounced. The redness to his pupils had all but disappeared. "You look better rested though."

His grin came out in full force, stopping my heart and tap dancing all over my fresh resolutions to stay away from him. "I slept better than I have in months last night. Like a baby. I woke up this morning and I have to tell you, I felt great."

My lip curled over my teeth for a nanosecond before I was able to smooth out my reaction. "How nice for you."

He made a sound in the back of his throat that sounded like a laugh. Only I knew it couldn't be a laugh because Wyatt didn't laugh. "I think I have you to thank for it."

Nope.

Nope.

Nope.

We weren't doing this. Not now. Not here. Not ever.

The thing was, I was great at denial. The best if truth be known. But if he opened the conversation I thought he was leading to, especially right before dinner service, I was going to melt into a humiliated pile of goo. As a result, dinner service was going to be a disaster and then Ezra was going to fly home from vacation to fire me. I was never going to get Sarita and I'd have to move back home with my parents. And, oh my god, I'd have to marry Nolan.

Hell, no.

Instead of letting Wyatt watch me freak out, I swallowed my laundry list of fears, neutralized my expression and asked, "Did you say you wanted to go over tonight's service?"

"There are important reservations tonight that I wanted to make you aware of."

I pulled a notebook from my apron and got ready to take notes. We were back in familiar territory and it felt good. All I needed now was for him to yell at me later tonight and reduce me to near tears—we would be one hundred percent back to normal.

Wyatt rattled off the VIPs coming in tonight—mostly people with money or local politicians or both. There were also people that were vaguely friends with Ezra and he had promised them a tour. Unfortunately, we would have to dance around that during service and whichever careless waiter was put in charge of the behind the scenes look. Never a super enjoyable experience because it was obnoxious to have people in your kitchen that had little regard for health and safety, and food inspectors, but it was something we accepted. We went over a few more notes about staff and topics he wanted to talk about in our meeting. We wrapped it up with a brief discussion of a new dish he wanted to introduce on the summer menu.

"Fish and chips is hardly groundbreaking," I told him, frowning over his latest nouvelle idea.

"Yeah, but we would put our spin on it. Make it amazing."

"I don't see how battered fish fits Lilou's menu. Ezra likes things old school. Besides, it's not exactly up to par with the other protein dishes we offer."

"That's the point. Lilou isn't accessible. It's outdated and stuffy. I want to make the menu more inclusive, add a few more classic options that feel brand new."

"Isn't that what Vera and Killian are doing with Salt?"

He snapped his fingers excitedly. "Yes! But also no. Vera and Killian are extending her philosophy from Foodie. They're doing all new Americana with a twist. They're taking already trendy food and putting their spin on it. I don't want to do exactly what they're doing. However, from when Vera had her food truck parked across the street, I know there is an outcry in this city, particularly this area, for that kind of familiar food. People want to eat here, but they also want to have a handle on what they're eating. Everybody is a food critic these days. Everybody thinks they're a foodie. Thanks to Netflix and Top Chef, our customers come into this restaurant with an expectation

169

that they can pick apart our dishes with earned expertise. And then they have our food, don't understand what the fuck they're eating and rip us apart afterward."

"You mean in Yelp reviews?"

He leaned forward, his eyebrows drawing together. "Yeah, in Yelp reviews, on Google and Instagram accounts that somehow have garnered thousands of followers. Our social media presence is tanking."

"I thought you said our waitlist was six months long?"

"For now," he growled. "But it's not a sustainable expectation if we keep churning out the same old shit day after day." He slid forward in his chair, growing animated with his argument. "Vera and Killian are going to blow up as soon as Salt opens. That's a given. Those two are powerhouses on their own, imagine them together." He had a point. "If Lilou wants a chance in hell at surviving that kind of competition, we're going to have to mix things up. We're going to have to take risks and try new things. We're going to have to up our game."

"What did you have in mind?"

"A deconstructed hamburger, for instance. It will still have the Lilou flare. Wagyu of course, with heirloom tomatoes and artisanal gruyere cheese. I'm thinking a champagne glaze and maybe some kind of caviar garnish. Expensive, interesting, but comforting."

I leaned toward him, eating up every word, totally enraptured by his vision. It was genius and ballsy and impossible all at once. "What else do you want to add?"

He smiled and pulled out a notebook from the side drawer of his desk. "A modernized Croque Monsieur, with an American twist. It would convey easy, nostalgic, but also elegant and sophisticated; a fancy grilled cheese and tomato soup option. I'd use pork belly instead of the traditional ham; finishing it with whipped brie. We could call La Parisienne to find out what loaves they have available for our kitchen, maybe something with olives and rosemary—the entire city knows their baker is extreme. I've been playing around with these tomato soup bites. Warm soup injected into a hollowed out cold cherry tomato. I want it to be this surprise bite of comfort food that just bursts to life in your mouth. I haven't worked out all the details yet, but I think I'm headed in the right direction."

I stared at him. Who was this man? I had expected a Killian clone. Not a man willing to go head to head with Killian to hold his place at the top of this city's fine dining experience. At the very least, I expected a man that towed Ezra's line because he was more afraid of losing Lilou than his identity. "Have you talked to Ezra about this?"

He nodded. "A bit. He hasn't, uh, exactly approved my direction. But I think he's open to change. I think losing Killian has been an eye-opening experience for him. And it would kill him to lose to Killian at anything, but especially in this."

"The reservation list is still months out though. Ezra doesn't have a whole lot of incentive for change."

He shrugged, hiding his notebook away again. A pang of something bloomed across my chest. His notebook was like his diary, the place where all his most secret and intimate thoughts flowed. It was instinct to hide it away, to protect it. Not only would it expose his still formulating ideas if someone found it, but it would also give them away.

It was like the holy grail. In his hands, his potential for success was unlimited. But if it fell into the wrong hands, his work would be for nothing. They would take his thoughts, his ideas, his innovative risks, and make them their own, claiming their origins.

There probably wasn't anybody in this kitchen with the balls to do that, but this was a cutthroat industry where creativity was questioned every day. It was unfairly easy to accidentally mimic someone's brilliant dish or abuse

171

inspiration based on someone else's hard work. Integrity was preached, but rarely practiced. We were all paranoid at best, raving conspiracy theorists in our worst moments of insecurity.

"I'm not worried about months down the road," Wyatt admitted. "We have this brilliant, complicated menu that makes no sense to seventy-five percent of our patrons. I'm not saying I want Lilou to be known as the best snobby burger joint in the country, or that I want any old Joe to wander in off the streets to order something to go. But I do want to meld together old world culinary with new world innovation. I want to update our painfully outdated menu and give our diners something they recognize, but also something that will change their entire definition of what good food is and how it can change their life. I want to welcome Killian and Vera to the neighborhood and then fucking annihilate them on every level." He grinned, showing his teeth and sending sizzling heat spiraling through me.

My chest squeezed again and this time I recognized the feeling as jealousy. This was brilliant. Incredible. Fucking genius. If he got his way, he was going to be the guy responsible for evolving Lilou into her best version yet. It wasn't a totally original idea, but it was in this caliber of fine dining.

And he was right about Salt. It would kill us the second it opened unless we did something innovative, something that could truly compete with it.

Most chefs, for that matter, aspired to mimic Lilou's style, not skydive off the precipice to become more relatable to the common man. Wyatt not only saw the need to up our game before Salt became real competition, but he also recognized the necessity of keeping our social media game on point. I was blown away by his foresight and insight into the industry. He saw years down the road and knew what he had to do today to keep us at the top.

"I'm impressed, chef. This is a good idea."

His eyes sparked with the compliment, but his words surprised me. "You shouldn't say that."

172

That look was back, the one that had gotten me into so much trouble last night. One part confident, sexy man, two parts vulnerable and open.

"Say what?" I whispered.

"Chef."

"But you are a chef."

His jaw ticked. Anger, I thought immediately. But it wasn't. It was something else. And now it had me questioning every single time I'd seen it before. "And I like it far too much when you remind me."

I laughed a breathy, girly sound. I couldn't help it. Now he was flirting with me? Opening up to me? Sharing his plans for the future with me?

"Wyatt, what are you doing?"

His Adam's apple bobbed up and down as he struggled to swallow. My eyes tracked every second of it.

"I'm trying not to kiss you, Kaya. I thought that was obvious."

Now it was my turn to nearly choke on my tongue. "You're ridiculous."

"You're beautiful."

I stood up so quickly, I probably would have tipped my chair over had there been room. "Are you drunk?"

He shook his head. "Did you hate it last night?"

No. Yes. No. I crossed my arms, hugging my body against the wave of embarrassment that washed over me. "It was a mistake," I told my shoes.

I didn't have to see his face to know that he was smirking. "Hmm, you liked it then."

My head popped back up. "It doesn't matter what I like, Wyatt. You're my boss! We work together. This is insane. And also, there are other reasons." I couldn't remember them off the top of my head, but I was certain they existed. Especially not with him looking at me the way he was, his eyes practically liquid chocolate as they sparkled and darkened, brightening all at once.

173

"We should try it again though."

"Is that a suggestion?"

"A counterargument." He stood up and leaned over, his hands planted on his desk—the desk that remained between us.

"It's crazy. That's what it is." Crazy because I was thinking about it, because that wicked expression on his face had me considering it, had me thinking that maybe we should try it again.

"It's not that crazy, considering."

I raised one eyebrow at him, calling out his sweet-talking tactics. "Considering what?"

"Considering you're the most beautiful, fiery, fierce woman I have ever met. Considering I've wanted to kiss you since the day I met you. Considering the things I want to do to you have only gotten decidedly more depraved over the years."

This was the part where I flailed around for a few seconds trying to catch my breath after I mis-swallowed, the spit dangerously going down the wrong tube. Obviously, I was a sex goddess and why wouldn't he want to do all manner of wicked things to me? I bent over at the waist and desperately tried to wheeze in enough air to prevent myself from dying on the spot.

"Have some of my water." Wyatt tried to pass me his glass, but I waved him off.

I didn't need saving. I needed for him to stop ripping the rug out from underneath me with crazy talk.

"You're telling me you've liked me since the day we met?" My voice was hoarse, still shaky from the ominous threat of more coughing.

He shrugged nonchalantly. "I don't think like is the right word to use. You can be difficult. And a little self-righteous. And from day one you've made it clear that we are in some kind of competition with each other and you're willing to spill blood to win. But…"

My nervous energy flatlined. And so did my patience. "You don't like me, but you want to have sex with me?"

"Geez, no!" He ran a hand over his jaw and wrapped it around his neck, hiding his tattoos from me. His lips twitched, and I knew he wanted to smile. "God, Kaya, it's not like that at all. You can be those things. But you can also be unreasonably kind and patient. You're competitive with me, but your challenge has made me a better chef. I don't know what I would have done without you during this transition, during the kitchen takeover. You've done all that I've asked of you and more. And I've demanded an insane amount from you. I like you a lot. As a person, as a friend, as a chef. But there are times I also want to strangle you. And if I had to guess, I think you feel the same way about me."

He hit the nail on the head. I did like him sometimes. And I respected him as a human and a chef, although I wouldn't go so far as to call him a friend. But I also wanted to strangle him a lot.

Like more than was probably healthy.

"You like me and also hate me, and now you want to make out with me?" Was it possible to get this conversation with subtitles? I felt like I was completely missing something.

His smile was shy, self-deprecating, and irresistible all at once. I wanted to strangle him right now. Because how was it fair that he could look like that and make me feel like this by smiling?

"What I'm trying to tell you is that yes, we disagree, and sometimes yes, you're downright scary, but I have always had a crush on you, Swift. From day one. But you had a boyfriend and then I had a girlfriend. Our timing has always been off. We're finally both single. And now we've broken the seal. We kissed. It happened. And it was fucking amazing." He dipped his head and looked at me from beneath lush lashes. My uterus jumped up and down

175

in my body like it was trapped in a CrossFit session against its will. "Let's do it again."

I sucked my lip ring between my teeth and demanded my feet stay put. I wouldn't run away from this. I couldn't let him see me panic. He had all these inflated ideas of me, that were, fine, kind to my ego, but maybe not entirely true.

Like the scary part. I wasn't scary. I was sometimes tenacious because I got tired of being walked on by bullish men. But that didn't turn me into a villain.

It just made me… assertive.

Except at this moment, I was anything but. I wasn't assertive. I wasn't tenacious. I wanted to put my hands over my radish-red cheeks and flee from the building.

Flee from Wyatt.

I didn't trust myself around him. I was already too enamored with him from kissing him. What happened if we kissed more? Or tried out other fun activities that didn't include clothing?

I would become a full-on fan-club stalker and he'd have to get a restraining order taken out against me to get through dinner service.

Okay, maybe it wouldn't be that bad. But Wyatt Shaw was trouble. Until now he'd been this alluring mystery, a perplexing enigma that piqued my interest and tempted me in the worst way. But now I knew him and what he wanted, and I knew I wouldn't be able to stop this snowballing attraction we had for each other if I gave it even an inch of room. There would be no walking back from this, from him. There would be no coming out the other side unscathed.

If he continued to look at me like this and smile at me like this I was going to spontaneously combust. Or worse, let him get away with his flirting.

And when Ezra found out—and he would find out—without a doubt, Wyatt would keep his job, but my fate was questionable. It's possible I would keep my job. Or get fired. Or get moved to another restaurant in the harem. I sure as hell would never get the head chef position at Sarita.

I did what any sane, rational thinking person would do. Even if I didn't feel sane or rational. I doused the flames between us with ice cold water. "You're sweet, Wyatt... but..."

He looked down at his hands and grumbled. "Fuck."

"I don't think this is a good idea. You're my boss. Also, I fight with you more than I've ever fought with anybody in my life. We're explosive together. Maybe that's fun sometimes, but most of the time we just blow shit up. On a regular basis, we'd be a disaster of epic proportions." I exhaled a shaky breath and jumped off the cliff of finality. "And I'm not willing to give up my career for a fun fling that will eventually end in a flaming ball of fire."

I took a step toward the door, but he stopped me with a sound in the back of his throat. It was both angry and desperate at once. The employee inside me picked up on his disappointed fury and instantly cringed, awaiting his wrath.

"You're looking around then?"

Another question that left me spinning. "What?"

"I've had the feeling you're exploring other options since I took over. I'm not stupid. I know you think executive should have gone to you. I know it's hard for you to work with me."

There were so many things wrong with what he'd said. But there was also a lot right with it. I didn't even know how to begin to tell him the truth. I could barely admit to Vera and Dillon what I was trying to do. There was no way I could share it with Wyatt.

Besides, I got the feeling that the last thing he wanted was for me to leave Lilou. How many times had he already said that he couldn't run the kitchen

177

without me? Maybe it wasn't in that one online review, but it was everywhere else. The way he talked to me here. How he relied on me, leaned on me, shared with me. Despite our weird and warring feelings for each other, we had somehow developed the dependent, symbiotic relationship every great chef had with his sous.

A thought occurred to me. It was absolutely batshit, but so was Wyatt wanting to make out with me. I narrowed my eyes at him as the suspicion started to take root and turn into an idea, and just like that, it grew roots and branches and leaves and became a verbal, anger-driven accusation. "Are you trying to seduce me to stay at Lilou?"

His head snapped back, and his eyebrows drew down immediately. "What? No."

"Tell the truth, Wyatt. I will not be toyed with in your pursuit of greatness."

"That is the most absurd thing I've ever heard. You know me better than that. I wouldn't treat anybody like that, least of all you."

"Good," I said quickly. "Because it wouldn't work. I'm a much stronger woman than that."

Half his smile returned, softer than before, but no less dangerous. "Kaya, if all it took to get you to change your mind was dry humping in the cooler, we wouldn't be having this conversation right now because I wouldn't be interested."

My heart kicked with embarrassment. "You wouldn't like me if I wanted to make out with you?"

"I wouldn't like you if your mind changed that quickly and purposelessly because you were into me. I like you because of your strong opinions. I like you because you're feisty and sharp and unwilling to change for anyone. Not even me and I'm your boss."

His words hit me in the chest like a shove or a slap across the face. I stood there, totally and completely upended, trying to absorb them, understand them. He was the first person that had ever complimented my stubborn will and opinionated personality. The very first.

My friends felt that way. I knew they did. And I felt the same way about them. But most everyone else shied away from people with strong opinions and relentless drive. We were intimidating or weird. Or maybe our ambitions made us too self-centered to relate to. We were always so focused on our career and the path to get us where we wanted to go that we hardly ever picked our heads up and looked around at the needs of the rest of the world. I wasn't proud of that, and I made a concerted effort with my friends, but there had been plenty of people that hated me because they felt trampled beneath my hunger to reach my goals.

My parents were forever annoyed by my sense of self, my need to make my place in the world. They wanted a sweet, docile daughter that was willing to live close to them for the joy of a quiet, uninterrupted life.

Nolan had only pretended to support my ideas and big plans, my drive and overwhelming need to do something with my life. Once I'd left Hamilton and it became clear that he wouldn't join me, we'd had countless arguments. His abandoned promise was one of the reasons I knew I'd done the right thing when I broke up with him. He wanted a compliant wife, a woman to dutifully stand by his side and shut up until asked to speak. He wanted someone content with mediocrity.

Nolan had never been cruel or unkind about what he expected from me, but the belief system was as ingrained in him as it was that entire town. It was a small town that expected small things from its inhabitants. And while that was fine for other people, I could not get on board. Bending to that will wasn't me.

179

I would never be content with small. Hell, I was desperate to get away from medium. I was a go big or go home girl all the way.

"You mean that?" I asked him, my voice barely above a whisper.

He held my gaze, his brown eyes darkening. "Yes. Nice bores me. I like you scary."

We both laughed, his dry sense of humor felt out of place considering the heart palpitations in my chest. But it worked. He lightened the mood and I was finally able to suck in a deep breath.

"That said"—his expression grew serious again—"I can't let you leave. I need you too much. Whatever they're offering you, I'll pay you more. I'll double it if I have to."

My heart quit palpitating. Only because it stopped beating altogether. "You'll double my salary?"

He nodded. "If I have to."

"Now you do."

A deep chuckle tumbled out of him, zinging straight to my core and curling around my heart, coaxing it to beat again. "Who are they? I need to know who's poaching my kitchen."

"Nobody," I assured him, anxious to keep him off the trail of Sarita. "I've been looking, but nobody has offered me anything. It's wishful thinking at this point."

He stared at me for a long minute, taking in my answer, weighing its truth, searching for the secrets I kept hidden away. Finally satisfied, he grunted a gruff, "Good."

My stomach twisted with nerves and I felt inexplicably guilty. I couldn't shake the feeling that I should have told him what I'd been up to and hoped for. At the very least he deserved honesty. But Sarita seemed impossible at this point. Ezra was still on vacation. I'd had one lesson with Vera and I hadn't even worked in the kitchen. There were too many unknowns still.

Better to keep it quiet until I knew if I could even apply for the position.

Wyatt shuffled to the door and grabbed the handle. "If you're not going to make out with me, you should probably get back to it then."

I turned toward him and couldn't resist that wicked half smile of his and the words he'd said to me, the affirmations, the sweet confessions. Did Wyatt really like me? Not just as a sometimes friend or loyal employee, but like girlfriend potential?

It didn't seem possible.

After all the grief we'd given each other through the years, he felt more apt to hate me than want to start a relationship with me. Except if I were honest with myself, fighting with him had never felt like fighting.

Our arguments had always shown how we challenged each other. It was like we were playing tag. Or chess in our more sophisticated moments. There had always been a heart-pounding competition to it.

That would have been enough for me. I enjoyed our headbutting bouts. I had fun with them. Fun with... him. Even if it felt like World War Three between us sometimes. But now he'd gone and said everything else. He'd admitted to liking me for me. Now I couldn't unhear his life-giving affirmations no matter how badly I wanted to.

I paused by the door, knowing this would only complicate things between us even more. But my body was moving on instinct and my fingers were already pressed against his crisp black chef coat.

His body stilled beneath my touch. Enjoying his reaction more than I should have, I stepped forward and pressed my body against his. The kick of his heart beneath my palm was the final incentive I needed.

My left hand slid behind his neck, putting pressure on the warm column, bringing his face closer to mine. "Thank you for saying what you did, chef." His eyes lit with anticipation. "They make me hate you a little bit less."

I pressed my lips to his in a sweet, lingering kiss that only held the promise of something more. He wanted more, but I wanted to give him something more meaningful.

And so, we kissed in that slow, tantalizing way that made my toes curl from the frustration layered between the sweet tease of it. I nibbled his lower lip and ran my tongue across it, promising wickedness I wasn't sure I could deliver. He made a sound in the back of his throat, half groan, half satisfied moan and I wanted to strip us both down and see exactly how far he was willing to take this.

But I didn't.

I pulled back, taking a step away from him to catch my breath. Then I fled from his office and into the safety of the kitchen. I knew my cheeks were blazing red and I was visibly out of breath, but I needed the kitchen, the buzz of it. I needed the clanging of pots and the bustle of my coworkers. I wanted the sweet smells and the sizzle of the grill. I needed my equilibrium to return and for steadiness to settle in my soul.

Because Wyatt had taken them from me. He'd flipped me upside down and turned me inside out and then left me to piece myself back together.

I didn't get giddy about men. I certainly wasn't infatuated with them.

Not even when they said the sweetest things and turned out to be so much more than I ever gave them credit for. Not even when they looked like a demigod and tasted like sin.

Not even when they were Wyatt fucking Shaw.

From this moment on, I would get over him and this new and sudden attraction between us. I knew I kept saying that, but this time I was for real.

Wyatt was becoming a problem I couldn't afford to ignore. A problem that felt too big and too complicated to solve. A problem that also felt like a solution. I shook my head and decided I needed to stop trying to figure it out, figure him out. Mostly, I needed to stop kissing him.

And I would. I would stop all this nonsense and put my career back on the pedestal where it belonged and forget about my crazy, stupid, hot boss.

Starting… now.

Chapter Twelve

"Son of a bitch!" I shouted at the full glass of Diet Coke that slipped

from my hands and crashed to the ground. Miraculously, the glass didn't

break thanks to the rubber mats beneath my feet, but I did end up with sticky

soda all over my shoes.

My shoes would never be the same. Damn it.

"How's it going over there?" Vera called across the kitchen.

I bit my tongue to keep from telling her exactly how it was going.

Because that explanation would have involved more expletives. An excessive

number of expletives.

"Have you ever bussed tables before?" I called back, already knowing the answer. At least I thought I knew the answer.

"I ran a food truck, sweetheart," she sassed back. "I worked the whole damn operation by myself."

I rubbed the sole of my shoe on my pant leg, hoping to wipe off the remaining liquid, then I set my foot down and realized that my pants as well as my shoes were wet now. So there was that. "Yeah, yeah, you're superwoman. But have you ever bussed tables at a real restaurant before?"

The entire kitchen burst to life with "oohs" and "burns" and someone even snuck an "oh, snap" in there. I blushed but held my ground.

Vera's head tipped back, and she laughed at my dig. "Can't say that I have."

Our eyes met across the busy kitchen. "We're not paying our bussers enough money. They deserve a pay raise."

She rolled her eyes at me while the two bussers on shift cheered loudly.

"You're a bad influence," Vera scolded. "You're going to start a riot in my kitchen."

I looked around at the staff unable to suppress a smile. They had warmed up to me a little. Not a ton. I mean, they weren't ready to throw down arms for me like Vera suggested, but they didn't totally hate me now. I was making progress.

I needed more time though. Ezra was coming back soon. I had hoped to inspire fierce loyalty to the point where maybe they would strike if I didn't get the job. At this point they only barely tolerated me. Steps in the right direction, but not good enough.

And Vera hadn't even moved me to the kitchen yet.

I wiped my forehead with the back of my hand and reached for the dish caddy again. "I better head back out there. Stay calm, everyone! We'll save the uprising for next week."

186

Vera threw her fist in the air and laughed. "Keep up the good work, grasshopper."

In the dining room, I waved at Christian and got back to work clearing off tables and wiping them down, so they were ready for the next group of people.

I knew from last week that Sunday was one of the busiest days thanks to the all-day happy hour policy at Sarita. It was a genius business plan and something Lilou didn't offer.

Although to be fair, Lilou didn't need added incentives for diners. The drinks at Lilou were good, but people came to have their minds blown by the cuisine.

Sarita had a more laid-back menu and the atmosphere was vivacious, primed for drinking and having a good time. Plus, the cocktails were the best in the city—that's how she was able to survive so long with her former chef.

Tonight seemed even crazier than last week though. The constant stream of people through the front door hadn't let up in the several hours I'd been here. My feet were already sore, and I smelled like salsa gone bad. The spilled drink coating my legs and shoes didn't help.

I don't remember ever working this hard. Okay, that wasn't entirely true. There were nights in the kitchen that totally and completely kicked my ass. But usually I could end the night at only completely exhausted, instead of the way I was going to end it tonight—*utterly* exhausted.

Another table paid their bill and I patiently waited for them to gather themselves and leave. I took the opportunity to glance at my phone. My focus narrowed on the only notifications I cared about. Three missed texts from Wyatt.

You're not here again. And it's the worst. Benny bumped into Gail and made her drop three plates. I'm never going to get this risotto out of my shoes. I blame you.

187

Seriously, where are you? Are you bored? You should bring me dinner. Something greasy and terrible for me.

I grinned at my phone and wondered when I'd become so totally infatuated with this man. He was too bold and too pushy and too totally ridiculous. And yet my head felt dizzy and the invasive butterflies were back, swooping and twirling and reminding me that his adorable texts were stronger than my will to stay away from him.

Ten minutes ago, he'd texted to say, **Fine, I'll let you bring me tacos. Hector's please.** I realized that I might have done just that had I not been preoccupied. Especially since he'd picked the best taco truck in all the land. There was a serious problem if I was willing to drop everything to take Wyatt supper on my night off.

Sorry, chef. I'm unavailable for tacos tonight. Maybe I'll let you buy them for me some other time though. If you're good.

His response was much faster than I expected. **Too busy for tacos? It must be serious.**

He was fishing. My smile stretched until my cheeks hurt. God, this man. **I'm in the middle of dishes**, I confessed. **Obviously, it's very serious.**

Liar.

Never.

He sent back the halo emoji to which I countered with the kissy face one. I pretended that small interaction didn't make my entire night.

Tucking my phone back into my apron, I hurried over to the now abandoned two-top and started stacking messy plates and ice-filled cocktail glasses into my tub, so I could wipe down the table and set it for the next couple.

I did appreciate how small the tables were here. At first, I had expected them to be an annoyance to diners because there was barely enough room for the towers of tapas and multitude of drinks. But after a couple of nights observing the dining room, I'd changed my mind. The intimate atmosphere pushed couples together. And for bigger parties, the servers simply combined tables.

Unlike Lilou, where everything felt staged and carefully planned, Sarita had a warm, inviting atmosphere that drew people together. Lilou was a dining experience. Sarita was a relationship experience. And it helped that the dishes were shared family style. Customers ordered a number of small plates, so everyone could try a little of everything.

The more I worked at Sarita, the more I loved her. The more I wanted her.

I had come to believe Vera was a genius for giving me this view of the restaurant. On the off chance that I had been hired based on my skill level alone, I wouldn't have seen this side of the business, I wouldn't have had the privilege of knowing her this intimately.

This was a gift. And I planned to use it to my full advantage.

"Kaya?"

Shit.

I took it back. All of it. This wasn't a gift, this was exposure I wasn't ready to face yet. And mildly embarrassing since I was sous chef at one of the best restaurants in the city and I was currently bussing tables pro bono at a competing restaurant.

"What are you doing?" Killian's voice was obviously confused.

I tucked a strand of my curly short hair behind my ear and turned around to face him. "Oh, h-hey, chef."

Our smiles wobbled, mine because I was humiliated and his because he had no idea what to make of the tub of dishes in my hand and the dishrag hanging out of my apron pocket.

"Since when do you work here?" he pressed, his eyebrows furrowing into a concerned expression.

"I, uh, don't."

His eyes dropped to the bucket of dirty dishes in my hand. "That's not what it looks like."

Clearing my throat, I decided honesty was probably the best policy here. Okay, real talk, I couldn't think of a lie fast enough, so honesty spilled out in an open confession. "I want Sarita," I confessed, hating the words once they were in the air between us. They left me too exposed, too vulnerable. I wanted to go hide in the kitchen and not come out until Ezra gave me the job. "I mean, I want the executive chef position. Vera has been, er, coaching me to get it."

"Vera?" he asked, sounding more befuddled than ever. "My Vera?"

"Yeah. She's the only Vera I know."

He gave me a sardonic look. "She hasn't said anything about it."

Oh, shit. I knew she wanted to keep it a secret, but it wasn't like I could get out of it now. Or even make something up that was kind of believable— trust me, I was trying.

There was no way to explain what I was doing here on my one night off, posing as a busser. that could possibly make sense. Except the truth. The truth of it made perfect sense. At least to me.

Although, I could have gotten away with some weird dirty dish fetish. Killian might have believed that. Or at least not asked very many questions about it.

Oh, hey, Killian. I have a depraved obsession with dirty dishes. There's just something about greasy plates… I'm working on it, but I'm, uh, weak.

Then I would have had the super fun experience of watching him run from the restaurant to never speak to me again. Or look me in the eyes.

Yeah, the truth was better.

"Oh, I asked her not to say anything to anyone." Pretty much the truth.

His gaze dropped to the dishes again. "I can see why."

Setting the tub on the table, I took a step closer to him and glanced around at the dining room. Suddenly, I felt overwhelming panic. If Killian had already found me, it was only a matter of time before our little community knew what I was up to.

Maybe that was giving myself too much credit and people weren't as obsessed with me as I feared them to be. But, they were all a bunch of gossips. Every last one of them. That meant none of them could be trusted.

Not even my former boss.

"She has you bussing?"

I gave him a half smile. "Last week she made me wait tables."

An affectionate smile stretched across his face. "She's evil."

"An evil genius maybe. I think her plan is working."

"Yeah? You feel ready to take on Sarita now?"

I didn't like his tone. It suggested that I was nowhere near being ready. Struggling not to glare at him, I confessed more of the truth—truth he didn't necessarily deserve, but apparently, I sucked at lying. "No, not yet. But she wanted me to appreciate the restaurant as a whole, experience it from outside the kitchen. I've seen what's working and what could be improved. I've gotten to know the staff and the layout of the restaurant. If I want a chance in hell of getting this job, the more I know about it, the better off I'll be."

His smile became genuine again. "Knowledge is power."

"Yes! It is. I want to know more about this place than Ezra."

He folded his arms over his chest. "I don't know if that's possible. Ezra is a control freak times one billion. But, you might end up impressing him and that doesn't happen very often."

I chewed on my lip ring, debating over my next question until it kind of flew out of my mouth without my permission. "Do you think I have a chance at it? Be honest with me."

191

His body flexed and twitched as he took a minute to seriously consider my question. I had been expecting an immediate answer and his hesitation made me wish I'd never opened my stupid mouth. I wanted to snatch the words from the air and swallow them.

Finally, he leaned forward and said, "You're a hell of a chef, Kaya. That's indisputable. You're hotheaded though and Ezra is going to do whatever he can to avoid hiring another angry egomaniac. This job is going to piss you off. A lot. You need to know how to handle it without causing a scene and without drawing Ezra's attention."

His words hit like a punch in the gut. I would have snarled something bitchy at him if it wouldn't have proved his point.

The thing was, all chefs were arrogant and hot tempered. At least, most of us. Hell, he was the king of cocky and angry.

"Also," he continued, making me cringe in anticipation for what he was about to say. "You have a tendency to overcook your fish."

I covered my face with my hands to hide my groan. "I shouldn't have asked you."

He knocked me on the bicep with his fist. "Hey, don't feel bad. Fix those two things and Ezra would be stupid not to hire you. I'd be happy to tell him that too."

His comment gave me the courage to drop my hands and brave him again. "You would?"

He smiled. "You're good, Kaya. In this place, you could be fucking great. But you've got to get your temper under control." He pointed a finger at me. "And your fish."

After what he said about me in Sarita, his criticism was easier to swallow. "I can handle those things."

"Hell yes, you can."

"Thanks, chef."

"No prob—" He cut himself off, realizing something. "Does Wyatt know?"

He already knew the answer. "Please don't tell him."

"Kaya…"

"Please, Killian. I want to tell him myself. And so far, I'm only playing at this job. Ezra isn't even back yet. I have no idea if he'll hire me or if he wants to open it up or recruit someone or what. I'll break it to Wyatt… slowly… I need more time."

He frowned, and it made my stomach flutter, remembering what he was like as my boss. "If he asks…"

"Specifically," I quickly cut in. "If he asks you specifically about me and Sarita, I know you can't lie to him. I'm only asking that you don't bring it up?"

His head bobbed back and forth. "All right, yeah. I won't bring it up."

"To Ezra either." His eyes narrowed and I added a fast, "Please?"

His sigh was long suffering and pained. "Fine. Yeah, okay, I can respect that. I will have words with my bride to be, however. She should have said something."

"She was doing me a favor," I insisted.

He made a sound in the back of his throat and I thought for a moment he was going to argue with me, but a man stepped up beside him and clapped him on the shoulder. "Hey, man. Sorry, I was waiting out front for you."

My gaze turned to the new guy and I had to put a hand on my chin to keep my jaw from dragging the ground. Holy hotness, he was gorgeous. All tan skin and wavy auburn hair, rich and full and the kind of red that made you wish you were a ginger too. He had tattoos, but only on his forearms, not like Wyatt's that reached all the way to his ears.

To be honest, now that I'd brought up the comparison, I preferred Wyatt. I liked the full body of artwork on Wyatt. I liked that his tattoos covered almost every inch of him. And this guy had a boyish face complete with dimples full of mischief and a tousled-just-out-of-bed look.

Wyatt's appearance was less mischievous and more straight sin. His face wasn't cute or boyish or adorable. Wyatt looked pissed all the time, his smiles were rare and made themselves present only after a hard fight. This guy was attractive. Wyatt was sexy as hell.

My inner comparison finished, I now wanted to slap my hand over my eyes because I couldn't seem to stop comparing everything to Wyatt. *Get a grip, Kaya.*

"Oh, no worries," Killian assured, turning his body so the two of them could shake hands. "I was catching up with an old friend." He took a step back to include me in the conversation. "Will, this is Kaya Swift. She's Wyatt's sous chef at Lilou." Will glanced down at the dishes still in my hand and the white dress shirt I wore instead of my chef coat. Before he could comment, Killian continued, "Kaya this is Will English. He's the owner of Craft."

I'd never heard of Craft before. That meant it was either new or on the verge of bankruptcy. It was good business to know what else was in Durham. And until this moment, I had not heard one person, blog, or critic reference Craft. I didn't say any of that though. I reached out to shake his hand and said, "Nice to meet you."

He smiled, his dimples striking in full force. If I was a lesser woman I would have swooned. Good lord, he was pretty. "Nice to meet you too." He continued to shake my hand until it got slightly awkward. His eyebrows drew down in confusion and finally he spit out the question I could see tumbling through his head. "Is this like a side job? Or...?"

"Yep." I cleared my throat and avoided Killian's hard glare. "For now. I, uh, like it here."

That was better than claiming a weird dirty dish fetish.

194

"Cool," Will said.

"Is Craft new? What kind of cuisine do you serve?"

His deep, raspy laugh filled the air around us. He laughed often. He had to. He was good at it. Again, I thought of Wyatt and how serious he was all the time.

Except with me.

More smiles.

More laughs.

More… more of him.

I blinked Will back into focus as he answered, "No cuisine. We're a bar. Craft cocktails and craft beer."

That explained why I had never heard of them before. My social life had died months ago. "That's cool," I told him genuinely.

"You should come check us out," he added, finally releasing his grip on me.

I ignored the way Killian frowned at our hands. "Us?"

"I own it with my brother and sister," he explained.

"Ah."

He smiled again.

Flirting. He was flirting with me! My short hair was frizzy as crap thanks to sweating my ass off tonight and I was covered in soda. Either this guy had a thing for girls that looked like they'd been dumpster diving all night or… or… I didn't have an alternative for him. He was clearly a weirdo.

I shook off the insecurity and decided I was prettier than I gave myself credit for. Besides, it wasn't low self-esteem that had tripped me up. It was Wyatt. I felt surprisingly uncomfortable under another man's attention, like I was betraying Wyatt.

Not that we'd made anything official. Still… At any other time in my life, I would have been happy to have Will's attention. I would have flirted back.

Now? Now I was shrinking back and avoiding eye contact so he didn't think I was interested in him.

I blamed Wyatt.

Killian clapped his hands together, pulling our attention back to him. "We're here to poach Ezra's bartender." He winked conspiratorially. "We'll let you get back to it."

My mouth unhinged. "Are you serious?"

Smirking now, he said, "Try to keep that between us, will you? You know, unless he asks you specifically about it."

Was that a threat? I shook my head at him and laughed. Maybe it was insurance. I won't tell if you won't tell kind of thing. "Got it, chef."

"Keep at it, Kaya. You got a chance. Don't fuck it up."

I waved him off. "Yeah, yeah." I turned back to Will. "Nice to meet you. Good luck with the bartender."

He grinned at me and even on that handsome face it felt lackluster. I could tell Will gave his smiles away freely, generously. I had developed a taste for the reluctant kind. "Yeah, thanks. Maybe I'll see you at Craft?"

And those dimples again. They would have once inspired a fluttery response and a soft smile from me. Today I was happy to give him a noncommittal shrug. "Maybe."

They walked off toward the bar and I got back to work, keeping my head down the rest of the night. I didn't want anyone else to recognize me, but I was also serious about doing a good job tonight.

I was desperate to get back to the kitchen with Vera. That meant I needed to kill my job performance in the front of house. I needed to bus the shit out of these tables.

And that's what I did. By the time I put the last few dishes in the industrial dishwasher sometime near two in the morning, I was practically sleeping on my feet. Tomorrow was going to be hell. But today was so worth it.

I was even in a good enough mood to text Wyatt when I got home. **Today was a good day. Thanks for letting me have it off.**

His reply came two minutes later. **It would have been better had you brought me tacos.**

Better for me or for you? I asked, curling up under my heavy blankets as a shiver spiraled through my sleepy body.

For both of us. When we're together it's always better for both of us.

There's always tomorrow, I told him.

Good. I missed you today, Kaya.

My response was quick and familiar. **Good.**

I found the heart flutter and soft smile that had been missing with Will English. They had been waiting for Wyatt.

Chapter Thirteen

*M*y phone buzzed in my pocket, a reminder that I still had it. I was in the middle of Monday afternoon prep, and already hot and irritated.

Hot in the literal sense of the word.

Not hot and bothered because of the way Wyatt kept staring at me across the kitchen. That was more irritating than sexy.

Okay, lie. It was sexy. Super sexy. And only vaguely irritating.

But he was acting like we weren't surrounded by my coworkers and his staff and that he could do whatever he wanted without repercussion.

I supposed that was how he did everything. That was how I'd always known him. But now that all that bad boy rebellion was directed at me, I didn't know what to do with it.

The paranoid part of me wondered if he knew about Sarita and this was his way of sabotaging me. I wouldn't put it past him.

The smitten girl inside me couldn't get enough of him and the way his eyes darkened every time he looked my way.

The buzzing stopped, but started again almost immediately. I pulled my phone from my pocket, worrying that maybe it was something important.

The phone call was my parents.

I was on the fence if the reason they were trying to reach me was important or not. We hadn't spoken in a week. The last time I'd answered, my mom had tried to convince me to take the freshly opened cook position at their local diner. She'd tried to sell me on it by dangling how close I'd be to home, how nice the hours were because even though I'd have to start work at five in the morning, I could be off by one. But the kicker was that Nolan stopped by there every morning for his cup of coffee on his way to work. She'd been unfairly disappointed when I turned her down on the grounds that I was a night owl.

"You could change who you are for an opportunity like this," she'd snapped. "Something like this doesn't come around too often, Kaya Camille. You need to get your priorities in order."

I'd chosen not to remind her that positions like that didn't come around often because there was only one diner cook position in all of Hamilton and the last guy had worked the shift until he'd died of a heart attack two weeks ago. I also carefully danced around the priorities comment.

I had mine in order. And mine didn't include Hamilton or giving up on my executive chef dream. It most certainly didn't include moving home to marry the high school football coach and have all his babies in an attempt to keep the town's population from dipping.

I wanted babies, don't get me wrong. I also wanted a career that set my soul on fire and a husband that made my toes curl. I dreamed of a legacy. A balance of both work and family that screamed into this great big world that Kaya Swift had tried her absolute hardest to make the very best of her one, little life.

I wanted the entire package. And maybe that wasn't possible. But moving back to Hamilton was about ten thousand steps in the wrong direction. More importantly, it wasn't going to happen. I wished my parents would figure that out, so we could stop fighting over it.

Given how things ended last week though, I decided I better take the call. I answered and shouted a quick, "Hold on!" into the speaker before slipping outdoors. The days were getting hotter and hotter as summer approached. I squinted into the blinding light, enjoying the way the sun immediately began to bake my exposed arms and face. The fragrant breeze chased the sensation, washing over me with the scent of flowering trees.

It wasn't exactly quiet outside. The bustle of downtown Durham buzzed and zoomed and occasionally honked. Traffic and pedestrians and the busy life of businesses booming in the plaza sang all around me. But the space was larger, more stretched out unlike the deafening cacophony of inside the kitchen.

Not that I minded the sound. It was like the soundtrack to my life. The clanging of metal together as pots and pans were moved around. The thwacking of knives chopping, julienning, mincing. Water boiling. Sauces simmering. Music playing somewhere. Voices shouting and laughing, ordering things to be moved or stirred. It was our own brand of symphony. This was the warm up, the sound of a hundred instruments preparing for the performance.

"Mom?" I asked the quiet on the other end of the phone. "Sorry, I'm at work."

"Kaya," she sighed. "You're at work already? Don't you have to work late?"

"Yes," I replied patiently. "These are my hours."

She sighed again. "That job is going to turn your hair gray."

I tugged on a faded pink curl. My hair might already be gray. It was impossible to tell after years of dying it whatever fun color of the rainbow I was in the mood for. And my hairstylist was a genius, a true color artist. Unless I specifically asked for gray, she'd never let my hair be anything but the color we decided on.

"I've got a girl, Mom." I dodged her. "She won't let that happen."

She mumbled something that sounded like, "Thank God." I smiled at my shoes. My mom was meticulous about her looks and public persona. Growing up, she'd always say to my sisters and me, "Girls, there are only three women in the world you should trust enough not to let you down. Your mama, your stylist, and your manicurist."

Her advice had stuck. I might dye my hair the craziest shades I could think of, but my hairstylist, Veronica, was a super star.

And don't even get me started on Tina, my nail tech. She could work legit miracles on the fingernails I destroyed on a nightly basis.

My mama, however, was a different story.

"What's up?" I asked when she'd been quiet for what I felt was long enough.

"How are you?"

I licked dry lips and talked myself into relaxing. It was kind of her to ask, but the truth was harrowing. I was exhausted to my bones. My feet hurt. My back hurt. I wanted a four-hour nap. But I wanted Sarita more. As a

202

consequence, this was my life for the foreseeable future and I was okay with that. "I'm good," I lied. "Work is busy."

"You're always busy." This was always her complaint. "Work is always like that for you."

"It is," I answered. "How are you? How's Daddy?"

"Oh, you know us," she tittered. "We can't complain."

"Did you plant your garden?"

"I haven't yet. Your daddy is going to get me what I need this weekend. Although, you know I'm not any good at it. I'd love it if you came home and did it for me. We're going to start it on Friday."

I dropped my head back and blinked up at the bright sky. She knew I couldn't get away this weekend—exactly why she'd asked. She wanted me to feel guilty.

"Work is tough right now, Mom. I can't get away anytime soon."

She made a sound in the back of her throat. "Do you think it would be possible for you to take a break from it for at least a few days?"

My body immediately bristled, readying for a fight. I was afraid to ask her why. With my luck, she'd probably arranged my wedding to Nolan and was giving me a courtesy call to inform me of where to show up and what to do.

Keeping my tone neutral, I asked, "Why? What's going on?"

"Nothing life changing," she said quickly, helping me relax a teeny bit. "Your dad and I want to come visit you. It's been too long since we've spent time together. And since we can't get you to visit us for some silly reason, we thought we'd come to you."

"Oh."

"But we don't want to get out there only for you to ignore us and work the whole time. Do you have vacation days or something? Can we get time with our eldest daughter before we die? Or should we say goodbye now? I can leave funeral instructions with the preacher if you'd rather. You won't

203

have to be bothered with the details. I know how much you hate to be inconvenienced."

I couldn't help but laugh at my mom's sharp tongue. I'd stopped wondering where I got my short-temper a long time ago. But with her it was impossible to tell if she was joking or not. Her voice never sounded sarcastic or teasing. And her expression never ever gave anything away. But surely that was a joke, right?

She couldn't be serious about wanting to spend time with me before she died… right? Or quite possibly this was a new low. Even for her. She was probably trying to lure me back home with death threats.

It was kind of working. I didn't want my parents to feel like I didn't love them or want to spend time with them. I did. Of course I did.

But I also had a demanding job. And there was always that off chance of the zombie apocalypse starting while I was visiting them at home…making it impossible to leave…so I'd be stuck fighting zombies for the rest of my life in the same town I swore I would never live in again. Legit reasons for never going back there.

"Mom, I'd love it if you and Dad came to visit me." I was also kind of dreading it. But this was always how it was with my parents. There was always equal shares of love and trepidation. "When are you thinking?"

"Next weekend," she said quickly, the tone of her voice changing just slightly. She sounded happier… softer. "Is that enough time for you to get one or two days off?"

"I already have Sunday off," I assured her, even though I wanted to kick myself for offering her one of Sarita's days. I knew Vera would understand, but I didn't know if I would. I wanted to work at Sarita again, couldn't wait for it. No matter what job Vera had waiting for me, and let's get real, it could get worse before it ever got better. She could make me fill in the exterminator position, for example, to catch cockroaches by hand. She could

204

send me rat hunting and tell me not to bother coming back until I'd skewered them all.

Just kidding, from what I understood the rodent and bug problem was mostly under control by now. Thank God. Still, there were plenty of jobs that I dreaded.

And for some reason, I trusted Vera to know that whatever she had waiting for me was part of this growing and maturing business. In the long run, it would benefit me. And hopefully, Sarita. That was all I needed.

Bring on the proverbial cockroaches.

Kind of.

If I absolutely had no other choice and my future depended on it.

"Your dad has a doctor's appointment on Monday afternoon, so we'll leave that morning. We'd like to see you while we're there."

"Mom, I told you I have Sunday off." She didn't say anything, but I could feel her judgment through the phone. "And I'll see what I can do about Saturday."

"That's all we ask, darlin'."

I glanced at the door and knew Wyatt would have something to say about it. He struggled to give me Sundays off on a regular basis and that was my actual day off.

"When can I expect you?"

"We'll come up Friday night and entertain ourselves. That way we have all day Saturday together."

It wouldn't be the worst thing to entertain my parents for the weekend, right? I did love them. And I enjoyed spending time with them when they weren't harping on me to move back home.

Even if I wasn't their favorite, they were as devoted as possible to me. My family had always been close, maybe too close. We were always in each other's business. Always overstepping boundaries and butting in when we shouldn't. That was why they could never let me go completely. They were used to being in the middle of my life. They were used to knowing and caring about every single little thing that went on with me. And they wanted to keep it that way.

It was sweet. But also suffocating. And the reason I'd fled Hamilton to begin with. At least one of the reasons.

Mom and I said goodbye and I clicked off my phone. Stepping back into the building, I braced myself against the humid air that enveloped me immediately. It was a different kind of stifling. It somehow wrapped around my body, clenched my lungs with two fists, pulled sweat from my pores and infused every inch of me with its heaviness. And still, it felt like freedom.

This was the familiar feel of the kitchen.

This was the siren call that would not let me go.

My parents' brand of smothering was not like this at all. Their hold on me was like a wet pillow over my face sometimes. Cooking was the opposite—it gave me breath.

My parents were codependent. Lilou and I were happily independent side by side.

I tucked my phone away in my purse and prepared myself for dinner service.

"Hey, are you going to work or stand outside all afternoon?"

I whirled around to find Wyatt standing behind me, hands planted on his hips, growly expression on his stupidly handsome face. I thought back to Will and had to smile. He was cute, but he wasn't my type. If I had a type, one that I was willing to seek out and try to date, it was Wyatt. From edgy haircut to tattoos running the length of his body to his scuffed black motorcycle boots, he was the man I would design for myself.

"Stalk much?" I asked him, raising an eyebrow so he knew I wasn't impressed with his bullish behavior. "I swear every time I step outside you get in my business."

He swayed into me, his hand landing on the wall beside my head. "You were in the middle of prep," he reminded me. "It's my job to make sure we're service ready."

I desperately tried to suppress a smile. "You don't have to worry about a thing, chef. I'm definitely service ready."

His eyes flared with heat and his expression softened. Even still he leaned closer. "Seriously, everything okay?"

I should have pushed him away. He was crowding me, covering my body with his heat and scent, forcing a frustrating desire to touch him. But I didn't. I was used to fire. I worked with it. I used it to create, to cook, to show off my skills. I knew how to handle it.

Instead of backing away from him, I let my finger run down his sternum, enjoying the way his Adam's apple bobbed up and down. "It was my mom. My parents are coming to visit next weekend." Lifting my gaze, I met his and pretended to have more courage than I felt. "I need next Saturday off."

Half his mouth kicked into a smile. "Is that why you're playing nice? You want something from me?"

"Need something," I whispered. "I need it from you."

He didn't say anything for a few moments. His eyes searched mine, looking for something I didn't know how to give him. Or hide from him. He struggled to swallow again, and my breathing picked up in response.

Who was playing with who now?

"Saturday's a big night. I don't think I can spare you."

"My parents don't visit that often," I returned, settling my hand against his breastbone so I could feel the hammering of his heart. I was mesmerized by the whole thing. My eyes were glued to my hand as it rested against his black t-shirt.

It looked tiny against his broad chest—delicate, dainty. He wasn't a bulky man, but his entire body seemed corded with long, slender muscles. He was a force of nature. A priceless marble statue. And yet the racing of his heart told me that he was also, somehow, breakable.

"Please," I whispered, hoping that was all he was waiting on.

"Have coffee with me."

I tore my eyes from his body and glued them to his face. "What?" In my head the word was a screech, a surprised yelp. But in reality, it left my mouth on a whisper.

"Have coffee with me," he repeated. "And you can have Saturday off."

"Are you blackmailing me to go on a date with you?"

"Who said anything about a date? It's coffee."

"I haven't gone on a d—" I cleared my throat and started that sentence over. "I haven't gone out for coffee in a long time."

The other half of his mouth joined the first in an amused smile. "Does that make it a policy for you now? You're anti-coffee?"

"I'm not anti-coffee. I'm definitely pro-coffee. I just usually drink it alone."

"That's cool," he laughed. "I usually drink it alone too."

I blinked at him.

He shuffled back a few steps to put some distance between us. "One time we can do it together. It's not a big deal."

My eyebrows scrunched together of their own volition. "It's kind of a big deal."

He shook his head. "How about tomorrow?"

"You're asking for payment way in advance."

He shrugged. "I'm making sure you don't have any opportunity to renege on your part of the deal."

I rubbed my temples with my forefingers. "Tomorrow's Tuesday."

"And?" His smile was still in place. He knew exactly what day it was.

"Don't you go to the Morning Market on Tuesday?"

"Oh, right," he said. "We can meet there. The coffee's good."

"You've lost your damn mind."

His smile brightened. "Maybe." Then he turned around and called over his shoulder, "Now get back to work before I fire you."

Even after all that flirty banter... even after a scheduled date... I still believed he would fire me.

That made me the dumbest person in the world for being secretly excited about having coffee with him at the farmer's market tomorrow morning.

Chapter Fourteen

*H*e'd texted last night and told me to meet him at seven this morning. My eyes were barely open this early. The sun was barely awake. It felt like neither of us wanted to be here, yet… here we were. Doing our part to give Wyatt what he wanted.

Although I supposed most of the people on this side of the world wanted the sun to rise. It wasn't only Wyatt.

I yawned as I stumbled my way from the gravel parking lot to where he stood next to a coffee stand. I knew this market well. I had shopped it often, but it looked different this morning. Maybe it was the softer, earlier light than I was used to. Or maybe it was the start of the new season as we rolled closer to summer.

Mostly, I thought it was Wyatt. I had never been here with a man before, let alone a man like Wyatt. Dillon and I often came here Wednesday mornings. And there were a few times during Killian's reign at Lilou when he'd sent me in his place if Wyatt hadn't been able to go for him for whatever reason.

I'd brought Molly here twice when she'd wanted to surprise Ezra by cooking for him. Both times had ended in disaster. She'd made me promise to never bring her again, no matter how ambitious Pinterest made her.

Wyatt held out a to-go cup of coffee with that aggravating half smile lifting one side of his mouth and the sun rising behind him. A shiver trickled down my spine and I decided it was worth getting up early this morning to see this—Wyatt like this, gentle, kind... sweet.

I took the coffee from him, our fingers brushing in the exchange, and wondered if I even needed the caffeine anymore. He had managed to completely wake me up by looking irresistible.

We hated each other, I reminded my heart.

No you don't, my heart whispered back.

I don't think we ever did, my brain agreed.

"Good morning." He stepped closer to me and I inhaled the fresh, clean scent of him. His hair had been recently trimmed, the sides freshly shaved.

"You got a haircut," I pointed out, ignoring the tender way he'd greeted me. Not on purpose. It was like my entire body was rioting with a thousand different emotions and I didn't know how to process any of them. Instead, I chose to ignore them. It was a totally mature response and I should probably receive some kind of award for how good at adulthood I was.

He ran a hand over the side of his head a little self-consciously. "Oh yeah."

212

"When?"

"Huh?"

"When did you have time between last night and this morning?" What I wanted to ask was what barber kept those crazy hours?

It was hard enough finding time to do routine maintenance on my body with the kind of hours I kept. Things like doctors and dentist appointments got pushed off all the time. Especially because I rarely prioritized them over hair and nails. Maybe my mom should have included a good gynecologist in her girl squad lectures.

"Oh, I did it," he confessed, chuckling self-deprecatingly.

"Are you serious?"

I had the pleasure of seeing his cheeks heat with embarrassment. "Yeah. Why? Does it look bad?"

Leaning around him so I could take in all sides, I shook my head, amazed at this surprising skill. "No, it looks amazing. You did a good job."

He laughed again. "Uh, thanks."

"How long have you done it yourself?"

"Since I was a kid," he answered. "The way I grew up, I didn't always know if I'd be able to get it cut by someone else. It was easier to do it myself."

"You grew up with Killian didn't you?"

He nodded. "Kind of. In the same circles. Foster care. Eventually I was deemed a troubled enough youth to get sent to Jo's with Killian and Ezra."

I lifted my eyebrows and drank in all this surprising information. "Jo? As in *the* Jo? Farm Jo?"

The smile that twisted his lips made my heart leap into a sprint. It was so affectionate, so absolutely adoring. I immediately wanted him to look at me like that. I was jealous for this expression that I had never seen before. Desperate for it.

213

"Yeah, she took us all in. Tamed us. Taught us to be civil."

His answer did something to my insides, turned them squishy and soft. "I would have liked to see that."

"What?"

"You," I answered, my voice just above a whisper. "Before you were civil."

His grin curled through me, making my toes flex and belly quiver. He leaned closer, dropping his voice while a wicked sparkle danced in his eyes. "I can demonstrate if you'd like."

I licked lips that were suddenly dry, but I didn't know how to reply. "Yes, please," seemed a little too eager. But "No, thank you," wasn't right either.

Changing the subject was my safest bet. "You were wild then?"

"Savage." He ran a hand through his hair again, but this time it wasn't a nervous gesture, it was confident and casual, and totally Wyatt. "My mom tried. For a long time. She was an addict though. Meth or some shit. Anyway, I didn't end up in the system until I was fourteen. I was lucky enough to eventually get to Jo. There were some rough years prior. I was back and forth between group homes and my mom for a long time." He started walking through the vendors, quietly sharing his history with me while we passed peppers in every color and big bouquets of lettuce. The air smelled fresh and herby. I followed alongside him, drinking in every single word with a hunger for him I didn't know was possible. "When I was sixteen, I got a new caseworker and she permanently removed me from my mom's home, if you can call it that. Donna took one look at me and sent me to Jo. By that time, she knew my kind. And she knew exactly who could kick my ass into shape."

"Jo?" I laughed. I knew Jo. Or I'd experienced Jo. It didn't surprise me at all that she'd been the one able to handle Ezra, Killian, and Wyatt. Even as teenage hellions. She was the scariest woman I'd ever met, and I was

214

convinced her produce was as good as it was because she threatened it into obedience. If I were her produce, I would listen too.

He grunted an agreeable sound. "But it worked. She worked." He let out a slow breath and launched into an explanation. "My mom didn't do anything as far as parenting. I basically raised myself. She would have food in the house sometimes, but for the most part I learned how to do what needed to be done on my own. That meant haircuts or showers, homework or sickness. Whatever. By the time I got to Jo, I was wild. I'd never had discipline or an authority figure that I respected. School was something I tolerated because I knew if I didn't go, they would take me away from my mom. But I was a terrible student. And I was bad. That's how CPS found me. The principal kept calling my mom and eventually she answered... high. They knew something was up immediately."

"Oh my God, Wyatt."

His chin jutted out. "It's okay. It led me to Jo. And Killian and Ezra. And it gave me this." He spread his hands wide, gesturing to the nearest produce stand with his coffee cup. "Food."

His smile had turned gently affectionate again and I realized I had never experienced the two of them together before. I'd seen how she spoiled Killian and treated him like he was God's gift to the planet. And I'd seen her butt heads with Ezra and put him in his place. I'd also seen her baby the grown man like he was a wounded toddler. But I'd yet to see her around Wyatt. I couldn't imagine that he would tolerate either parenting style. He didn't want to be adored. And he definitely didn't want to be coddled.

A nervous wisp wiggled through my belly, but I didn't take the time to examine it.

"Do you still see your mom?" I asked him.

He shook his head. "Nah, she passed my senior year of high school." He kept his head dipped, staring at the ground. "Overdose."

215

"Wyatt."

He shrugged, but his shoulders remained stiff and rigid. "Yeah, it sucks. She always had demons, you know? She could never shake them. Never found a reason to."

My breath was trapped in my lungs, unable to escape. I stopped walking and grabbed his coffee-free hand, turning him to face me. "You were the reason," I whispered, my eyes watering with unshed tears. "You were the reason to stop."

He stared at me, saying nothing for a long time. His eyes flicked back and forth between mine, searching and analyzing, deciding if I was telling the truth. Of course, I was. And he needed to know it. I poured all of myself into that look, into the truth of what I told him.

Yes, he was the reason. He was the only reason she needed.

Finally, he looked away and I gasped for breath, but I didn't let go of his arm.

"Like I said, I had Jo. And Ezra and Killian helped. Killian has a similar story. It's nice to know that... you're not alone. I mean, I don't have any biological siblings, but I have lots of foster brothers. Not only Killian and Ezra. There were a lot of kids on that farm. We've all stayed close over the years." He smiled again. "You know, surviving Jo bonds you. It might as well be blood we share."

I smiled with him, finding myself jealous again, but for entirely different reasons this time. I had an idyllic childhood compared to Wyatt. My parents loved each other. They'd never done a drug in their life. I had biological sisters who I adored. But there was something about the way Wyatt talked about his foster brothers that made me envious.

Or maybe it was more like regret. Guilt? His fierce loyalty was so evident. He would do anything for his brothers. For Jo. And I knew Killian and Ezra were the same way.

I didn't have those same feelings for my parents. I lovingly tolerated them. Their pleas and petitions for me to move home were getting old. And my sisters and I were as quick to fight with each other as we were to stand up for one another.

"Have I freaked you out?"

I turned my head, so he could see the sincerity in my expression. "No, not at all." My small smile wobbled. "I was feeling guilty for how much I take my own family for granted."

He winked at me. "I have some of that too."

A single butterfly flapped dragon-length wings through the pit of my stomach and a shiver rolled down my back. God, if I wasn't careful, I was going to develop feelings for this man. The real kind. The never-ending kind. "I have two sisters," I confessed. "Claire is only ten months younger than me. But Cameron is six years younger. She's the baby."

"Your parents needed a break after... Claire?"

"Yeah, the whole Irish twin thing wasn't fun for my mom. It was me though. I know this will be hard to believe, but I was a difficult child." I was still a difficult child. He nudged me with his elbow and we both laughed.

We aimlessly wove our way around vendors, inhaling the fresh market scent and enjoying the cool breeze dancing over our skin. It was a perfect morning. And it took a lot for me to say that.

"Are you and her close?" he asked.

I shrugged. "Mostly, yeah."

He laughed. "Mostly? What does that mean?"

I glared at the sky for a second, hating myself for admitting this to someone. Especially Wyatt. "She's the perfect one, you know? The straight A student, the prom queen, the perfect angel. And I'm... not those things."

"You're the evil twin?"

The mischievous tone to his voice softened the truth. "Yes, exactly."

217

"What does your sister do?"

"She's a teacher," I sighed. "A kindergarten teacher."

He laughed again. "Gross."

I shot him an appreciative smile. "Thank you!" Wyatt put his hand on the small of my back to lead me around a corner and kept it there. The warmth of his hand sunk into my skin and spread through my body, wrapping around my bones, infusing my blood, sinking into deep, secret metaphysical places of me.

God, I was in trouble with this man. Clearing my throat, I added more to my case against Claire. "But it gets worse. She also lives five minutes away from my parents. She stayed home while I fled to the big, bad city. Something my parents have never forgiven me for."

"What?!" he exclaimed, his voice sliding over the word until it reached a high pitch.

I smiled. "It's their life goal to get me to move back home. And until I do, Claire will remain the golden child."

"Where's home?"

"Hamilton. It's about two hours west. Past Greensboro."

"Small town?" he asked, clearly having never heard of it before.

"Very," I confirmed. "About a thousand people. My parents were born, raised, and plan to die there. They'd like Claire, Cameron and I to do the same. But that town is toxic. I... I can't do it." I fixed my attention on my shoes, but the ground blurred in front of me, obscured by my watery vision. "Plus," I added brightly. "They have like one greasy diner and a Pizza Hut— not a lot of career opportunities for a classically trained chef."

"You wouldn't leave Durham, would you?"

"Oh, no. Never. I was kidding."

A thoughtful silence stretched between us, but it didn't bother me. It wasn't awkward. It was weirdly comfortable.

218

Finally, Wyatt said, "Your parents give you a hard time about that?"

"Every single day. All they want is for me to move home, marry my high school sweetheart, and give them thirteen grandchildren. No big deal."

His laugh was a low rumble. "No big deal. Is that what Claire's doing?"

Shaking my head, I felt a twinge of pity for my sister and her tragic dating life. She had the absolute worst taste in men. "No, she's still single. But for some reason my parents are less worried about her. Maybe because she's a whole ten months younger than me. Or maybe because the dating pool in Hamilton is shallow? I have no idea. But for some reason they're convinced I'm going to turn into an old maid and die alone." I laughed, but it lacked the humor I'd hoped to use to soften the truth. "Although, going by current standards, they might be right about that. They know I keep insane hours. And that I haven't been on a serious date in like two years." I paused, giving them the benefit of the doubt and letting my affection for them override my sarcasm. "I think they're just worried about how hard I work."

"They don't get it then," Wyatt said softly... thoughtfully. "How important this is for us."

I inhaled a deep, even breath, appreciating his support in a way I didn't realize I needed until he'd given it to me. "I didn't even notice at first, you know? I just wanted it so bad... wanted to make it, wanted to make a name for myself, wanted to move forward in my career. It's like, I'm waking up to how completely enslaved I am to this thing."

"It feels good though, doesn't it?"

A smile stretched across my face. "Yes. In the best way."

He grinned back. "We're an industry of masochists."

We stopped under the shade behind a stand, the cool air pulling goose bumps from my arms. Or maybe it was the hot look in Wyatt's dark eyes. It was hard to say. "Sadistic, right?"

Leaning forward, he tried to tuck a wayward strand of hair behind my ear. It didn't stay. It was still too short. "At least we have each other."

"At least," I whispered.

Our bodies moved together at the same time, our mouths crashing together in a gasp of breath and touch of lips and taste of tongue. He didn't waste time pushing me gently back against the stand wall, his hands holding on to my waist, tugging our bodies together in a collision of heat and need.

His mouth moved over mine, hungry and inviting, encouraging me to move back, taste back... seduce back. I tilted my head, so he could delve his tongue deeper into my mouth, pulling a sound from the back of my throat that was almost guttural.

God, how could he taste so good? Like mouthwash and a hint of coffee. And Wyatt—a taste I was getting too quickly addicted to.

His fingers moved over my bare skin thanks to my crop top shirt, but he wanted more than the slim strip of skin I offered freely. He wanted everything. And as his hands slid upwards, over my ribs, against the edge of my bra, I made another one of those sounds, inviting him to explore and discover and keep doing what he was doing.

He trailed kisses over my jawline, nibbling on my earlobe, driving me absolutely wild with searing anticipation.

"Wyatt," I gasped as he kissed down my throat, spending significant time along my collarbone and the place just below my ear.

"Kaya," he rumbled, teasing me.

The tiniest slice of sanity returned. "What are we doing?"

He lifted his head, his eyes pitch-black with lust, a smile playing on his full lips. "I'm worried that it's not obvious to you..."

I couldn't help but laugh. "I mean with..." I wiggled a finger back and forth, "us."

The look in his eyes faded, turning careful and guarded. "Is there an us?"

Slapping his shoulder, I let him know that I was frustrated with him. "Wyatt, you tell me!"

He pulled me against him again and I had to work to swallow. His body was so hard, so completely unyielding. Every single part of him. He was temptation and sanctuary all at once. He was irresistible and addicting and looking at me like I was the same thing for him.

"Kaya, I like you," he said in a voice that was as rich and decadent as chocolate ganache, just like his eyes. "And I think you like me."

"Irrelevant," I growled. "That doesn't explain what we're doing. Secretly making out? Wandering around markets baring our souls to each other? What is happening between us?"

His smile returned, and it was enough to send my heart into overdrive. "I'd hardly call having a normal conversation baring our souls. And, I'm happy to make out with you in public places if you're tired of the secrecy." I opened my mouth to call him an idiot, but he cut me off. "My point is that I think we both like each other and that maybe we should see where this goes. Maybe there's enough between us that we should explore it." His fingertips glided over my ribcage, finding their way to my back where he splayed his huge hand over my spine. "Explore each other."

Sex, my brain told me immediately. He wanted sex.

And okay, fine. Maybe I did too.

"This is a bad idea," I whispered, too far gone with desire to put any real conviction behind the truth.

He shrugged. "I like bad ideas."

Holding his gaze, I said, "We have that in common."

His head dipped, readying to kiss me again when a voice called out from several feet away. "Wyatt Shaw, what are you doing to that poor girl this early in the morning?"

221

Instead of his lips, his forehead dropped to mine and his eyes slammed shut. I watched with no small amount of fascination as his entire face turned red.

"Hey, Jo," he called back.

Aw crap.

Finally, he pulled away, exposing me to the most terrifying woman in all of creation. "Kaya, is that you?"

"H-hi," I croaked. "Hi, Jo."

She shook her head, apparently disappointed in both of us. I felt thirteen again, when I'd been caught making out with Danny Brayburn in the fellowship hall of our church by Mrs. Minch, the seventy-year-old organ player.

Jo snorted. "Did you only come out here to make a spectacle of yourselves? Or are you going to buy some produce?"

"That one," Wyatt said, clearing his throat and fidgeting. "The, uh, second one. I'd planned on saving the spectacle for after."

It was my turn to turn the color of a ripe strawberry. Jo let out a shocked cackle. "Then let's get this over with so you can get back to it."

Jo turned and marched off to her stand while I tried to catch the shriveling pieces of my dignity. Wyatt turned back and grinned at me. "You heard her, let's get this over with so we can get back to it."

He grabbed my hand and pulled me after him. "Not happening," I hissed at his back. "That was the last time."

"You keep saying that," he said without looking at me. "You're like the boy who cried wolf. I don't believe you anymore."

We came to a stop in front of some of the lushest produce I'd ever seen. Shiny, oddly shaped heirloom tomatoes and long, bumpy cucumbers. Perfectly round radishes. Juicy strawberries. Jars of orange marmalade and raspberry preserves. We were standing in front of a carefully guarded gold mine. My spirits instantly lifted.

"You're going to be disappointed then," I told Wyatt as my fingers itched to grab for the beauties laid out in front of me.

He leaned in, his breath a whispery tickle over the shell of my ear. "Your denial is cute. But we both know you've got it bad for me, Swift. So, so bad."

Chapter Fifteen

I had a flat of produce that I had no idea what I was going to do with or when I was going to use it, seeing as I worked every single night. But I couldn't help myself. Jo had the best of the best. Her stand was a chef's dream.

And fortunately for us, she worked with Ezra's restaurants almost exclusively. Wyatt had wandered off to check something out for Jo in her truck. Apparently, he was a bit of a mechanic too. That shouldn't have been another turn on, but damn it, picturing him all greasy and shirtless and under a car was pretty much the hottest thing I'd ever imagined.

Everything Wyatt did was suddenly hot. I mean everything. He could have flossed his teeth and I would have worried about my panties melting off my body. It was obnoxious.

Jo eyed me across a pile of figs. "I haven't seen Wyatt with a girl in a long time. Not since the last one that hated food. Could have told you she wasn't going to work out. Personal trainer my ass. She wouldn't eat his food. That was a big enough sign that astronauts could see it from space." She pursed her lips and added, "Not that I don't think there have been other girls. He doesn't bring them around me anymore. He doesn't like my opinions."

I didn't know if that was an insult or a commentary on factual history. Steeling my nerves, I told my courage to cowboy up. I was tougher than Jo wanted to believe I was.

"We're not really here together," I told her evenly. "You caught us at a weird time."

She raised an eyebrow. "You're in the habit of kissing boys you're not with?"

Well, shit. I searched for my usually sharp temper, but I couldn't seem to find it today. Instead, something else came out of my mouth. Something stupid and kind of pathetic. "How many girls do you think there are?"

Her lips twitched like she wanted to smile, but she held it back, reminding me so much of Wyatt in that moment that my chest pinched. "I thought you said you're not with him. What does it matter to you?"

I glanced at the sky, hoping help would fall from it. "Because I'm really not in the habit of kissing boys I'm not with," I confessed. "And…"

"And it's Wyatt," she finished for me, sounding as confused and unsure as I did. "I'll tell you this much, Wyatt has never brought a girl to this stand. Not even one he casually works with. So, you two could have stepped up here as businesslike as you please and I would have known something was up immediately. But you didn't step up here. I think you circled the damn

226

place fifteen times before I caught you smooching. So, all that to say, there aren't other girls, honey. There's you."

My heart kicked in my chest, harder and faster than a freaking kangaroo on the offensive. "I thought he hated me."

"I've known Wyatt a long time. I can honestly say I've never known him to hate anyone."

She didn't know us before the constant making out… "Any words of advice?"

She smiled this time and the expression softened her face, making her look years younger and possibly approachable. "Don't hurt him."

I took it back. She wasn't approachable. She was a grinning viper. Her mouth stretched wide, readying her for her attack. Yikes!

Licking dry lips, I tried to form the right response. "I'm not planning to," came out instead.

"Don't worry about planning," she snapped back. "Don't do it. That boy doesn't trust people. And I mean, not at all. His mama was about as awful as they come, and she messed him up real good. Don't be another woman that disappoints him. Don't give him another reason to stay alone."

Shit. And holy shit. What was I even supposed to say to that? I couldn't promise her those things! I didn't know what was going to happen with Wyatt and me, but happily ever after was a ridiculous stretch of the imagination. More than likely I would disappoint him. Probably even today. Hell, I felt like I had already disappointed him as his employee about one hundred times in the last six months. Don't give him another reason to stay alone? I was like the definition of why men should stay alone. Run. Hide your men. The she-wolf is on the prowl!

Good grief, Jo had messed with my head in about the most severe way possible. And now she was looking at me, waiting for a response. All I wanted to do was throw my hands in the air and run away screaming.

"We're just…" Friends? No, that wasn't the right word.

Enemies? Wrong too. Especially now.

Competition? That felt more like reality, but how could I explain that to Jo in a way that would make the kissing make sense?

"We're uh…" I tried again.

"Yeah, yeah," she waved me off. "I know what you're doing. And I also know that two of his brothers have recently settled down and it's started a fire in that boy that he didn't know needed to be kindled. Now he's out looking for that girl, the one that's going to save him from himself." Her eyes narrowed, becoming shrewder, less trusting—if that was even possible. "My guess is he thinks that girl is you, Miss Swift. I'm asking that if you're not also looking for someone serious, that you let him down before he's too invested, to give him a chance to recover."

I pressed a fist to my stomach and leaned forward, desperate to catch my breath. "Damn, you've put a lot of pressure on me."

She cackled again, sounding more and more like an evil witch from a Disney cartoon movie. "It's only fair to warn you, I love that boy like my own. I want to see him happy." She leaned forward on her hands, bringing her head closer to mine. "But mostly, I don't want to see him hurt. I think we have that in common."

She was right. I didn't want to hurt him. No matter what my feelings were for him. And to be honest, I was still trying to sort through them and give them names. They ping-ponged back and forth frantically between my head and my chest, never landing long enough for me to pin one down.

My head argued that we had a cruel and competitive past together and that absolutely nothing could come out of an attempted relationship between us except more cruelty and a hell of a lot more competition.

But my heart spoke in a language that didn't involve words. It beat with the hope of something my brain couldn't yet describe. And it raced with

228

anticipation for more of the kissing. More touching. More talking. More smiling. More everything.

They didn't agree, my head and my heart. And the feeling of my body being in such staunch disagreement made my stomach flip in protest.

Damn, Kaya, get it under control.

"You're right," I told Jo. "I care enough about him to not want to see him hurt. I'll be careful with him."

She lifted a hand, pointing a stern finger at me. "I didn't say anything about being careful. My Wyatt wouldn't know the first thing about being careful. I'm asking you not to screw this up. He's trying, girl. He's brought you to this place that is sacred for him, for all his brothers. He's trusted you in ways I don't believe he's trusted anyone since his mama died. Don't be careful with him. Just don't fuck this up."

"Yes, ma'am." My response was immediate and triggered by the sharp tone of her voice. My eyes bugged at her curse word, surprised to hear it come from someone who looked, even if she didn't act, like a grandmother.

Her mouth broke into a satisfied smile. "That's what I like to hear."

"Jo, I can't find anything wrong with that truck other than it's a hundred years old," Wyatt exclaimed as he rounded the corner, wiping his hands on his pants. "You're going to have to take it to the mechanic if it keeps acting up on you."

"Oh," Jo answered. "I'll figure it out."

She turned around to reach for a crate of fingerling potatoes in every shape and color and I had just enough time to glare at her back. Evil woman. There wasn't anything wrong with her truck. She wanted to get rid of Wyatt for a few minutes, so she could lecture me!

Her lecture wasn't going to work. Wyatt could take care of himself. He didn't need scary mama Jo fighting his battles for him.

"Hey," he said to me, standing close, popping my personal bubble with his height and body heat and irresistibility. "Sorry about that."

My Wyatt, she'd called him. Only he wasn't. He wasn't hers.

I struggled to swallow and slow the rapid beating of my heart. But was he mine? "Hey."

"I'm going to grab a few things from Jo and then I'll be ready to go."

Picking up my cardboard flat of odds and ends, I distanced myself from him. "Go for it," I said quickly. "I should be going anyway. I need to drop all this off at home and change before work."

His bright expression dimmed. "Are you sure? I'll only be a second."

"It's fine. You're fine." I cleared my throat to get my mouth to stop saying dumb things. "I just don't want to be late. My boss can be a real pain in the ass."

His mouth kicked up in a half smile. "Yeah? Maybe I should say something to him."

"Make sure he knows you mean business." The fluttery, nervous beast inside me relaxed at our easy banter. This was more comfortable territory. This was familiar ground.

Jo had messed with my head with all her talk about fragile, committed, and damaged Wyatt. I needed to disentangle myself from her delusion and remember that I knew Wyatt, and we were only having fun. Or something like that.

It was impossible to date around with our hours. And the pressure and stress of our job kept us isolated, clinging to things we knew and didn't have to try very hard for. That's what I was to Wyatt. And that's what he was to me. End of story.

He walked me to the dirt path that wound between vendors out to the parking lot. "Hey, I know your parents are coming this weekend. You should bring them by the restaurant."

230

I smiled. As if. There were a lot of perks to working at Lilou. Not only prestige and industry-wide respect, but excellent food and access to one of the best kitchens in the region. However, just because I worked there didn't mean I got to drop in whenever I wanted. In fact, employees were only allowed to make reservations once a year. The waitlist was so demanding, Ezra didn't want his employees taking up tables. And when we were able to get our names down, we had to wait in line like everybody else.

"Are you going to set up a table in the alley? Feed us *Lady and the Tramp* style? Because my parents might enjoy it, but hello, awkward party of one." I pointed to myself, shuddering at the image of my parents making out with a plate of spaghetti between them.

Gross. And no thank you.

He laughed at my joke, his eyes lighter and happier than I had ever seen them before. But again, this perspective of him was skewed. I was used to him yelling at me all the time, hating me. Our new… friendship? Or whatever you wanted to call it was seriously messing with my head. And my sex drive.

"Have they ever been?"

It took me longer than it should have to catch up in the conversation. I was lost in that look in his eyes, the one that made them so decadently brown, like rare, smooth whiskey. "To Lilou? No, they haven't. Their style is more, um, how do I put this gently… Cracker Barrel."

His smile stretched and warmed all at once. "I'll get you a table then. For Saturday night? You can show them what you do. Impress them."

"Are you serious?"

"Yeah. I bet they'd love to see where you work. And even though you won't be cooking, they'll get the idea."

"Wyatt, I don't know what to say. That's unbelievably nice of you."

He leaned forward, his grin turning wicked. "I'm trying to unseat your sister. No offense to her, but I can't have anyone thinking someone else is better than one of my chefs."

It was my turn to laugh, the sound bubbling out of me from the bottom of my toes, all the way through my chest, filling my lungs and giving me a fizzy feeling low in my belly. "I appreciate that."

"You're welcome."

"Okay. Bye, Wyatt."

"Bye, Kaya."

I carried my produce back to my Land Cruiser and loaded the flat into the back seat. The doors screamed in protest as I opened and shut them, first for the veggies, and then for me. I ducked behind my steering wheel, feeling like the entire market was staring at me.

They weren't. Nobody cared that my beautiful, vintage beater was noisy as hell. They went on with their business none the wiser that I'd shut myself in my car as quickly as possible, so no one would witness my freak out.

God, why did Wyatt have to be so... likeable. I'd gotten used to hating him. It was easier that way.

My chest ached, and I was positive I was having a heart attack. I rubbed at the pain with the heel of my hand and tried to sort through the riot of emotions trying to trample my insides.

The car started to get hot. The sun was warm today and without the windows down, I had started to bake. Sweat prickled on my forehead, but I still didn't touch the manual window crank.

Instead, I glared at my phone spilling out of my purse on the passenger's seat. I needed therapy. Or aversion therapy at the very least.

Carefully picking up my phone, I swiped my thumb over the screen until it recognized my face and opened past the lock screen. I pressed the Facebook icon and clicked on my search bar. Nolan and I weren't friends anymore. Not in real life or on social media accounts. But his name was the first thing to appear in my search history. Pathetic. I was one hundred percent confident in how pathetic I was.

But I couldn't help it. My social life had been reduced to coffee dates with one of my two friends and working fourteen-hour days.

He was back home dating all the girls in Hamilton. All the girls older than eighteen and younger than sixty-six. He drew the line when they were eligible for social security.

Scrolling through Nolan's newsfeed, I cringed at exciting pictures of him hiking, out drinking with our old circle of friends and selfies the girls he dated tagged him in. He was having the time of his life coaching and living up his youth.

I was working myself to the bone for a dream job I had to convince myself I still wanted.

Lifting my eyes, I stared at myself in the rearview mirror and forced my fragile self-esteem to call bullshit. This wasn't a joke. And I wasn't doing this to prove a point.

I wanted this—Sarita, food, all of it—for me. I wanted it because I didn't know how to not want it. I wanted it so bad I could feel it in my bones, to the depths of my soul. This career was me. Sarita or no, I wasn't going to give up on it and call it quits because my ex-boyfriend looked like he had a better night life than me.

You would think that little pep talk would make Wyatt more appealing. What if we were only having fun? I deserved a little fun, didn't I? I deserved Facebook worthy photos and a few wild stories to share with the gossipy bitches back home.

Shaking those stupid thoughts out of my head, I started my car and pulled out on Franklin Street. I wouldn't do that to Wyatt. I wouldn't use him to make myself feel better.

Besides, there was more to Wyatt than I wanted to admit to myself. I wasn't sure I could handle something casual with him. I got the distinct impression it would be like playing with fire. I would be smart for a short while, but inevitably get burned. No matter how familiar I was with the flame, he was hotter, more unpredictable, and dangerous in ways I didn't even know existed.

No, it was easier to protect my heart from another bad boy with different aspirations. A relationship with that type of guy never ended well for me. And even though I was the one that stayed true to myself, I was the one that kept getting hurt.

At home, I planned to have another cup of coffee and relax for a few minutes before it was time to head in to work. My fake excuse about being late to work was unsubstantiated. I had at least a whole hour and a half to kill. I'd gotten my purchases put away when Dillon texted to ask if I wanted to meet Vera and her at a nearby plant nursery. I texted back that I would love to and would meet them in twenty minutes.

See? I had a social life. Sometimes I worked. But sometimes I went shopping for house plants. Take that, Nolan. You big, dumb idiot.

I changed my high-waisted cotton skirt and chambray cropped tank top for a pair of wide-leg black linen pants and a yellow cami with wide-straps that had a little ruffle along the seam. In another hour I would throw my chef coat over it and be work appropriate, but for now I would fit in with the real world.

Grabbing my crossbody purse, I glanced around my sparse but trendy apartment and noted places that could use a little green. There were a lot of spaces.

I had been wanting to get plants for a while. It was either a house full of plants or a puppy. But I worked too much to take care of something that needed to be fed and walked and required human interaction every day. And I hated cats.

Also, I hated fish tanks. I'd had one break in my bedroom when I was thirteen. I'd thrown a baseball at Claire and she ducked instead of catching it. The ball crashed into the tank and water dumped everywhere. Water and those tiny rocks and itty, bitty, shattered pieces of glass. I had sworn that day I would never own another fish and face a potential twenty five gallon catastrophe ever again.

Plants. I could handle plants.

Maybe I'd even make an herb garden behind my kitchen sink where the natural light could reach it.

Liking the idea more and more, I headed out the door to meet my friends. Er, my friend and the drill sergeant I knew.

The nursery felt like a breath of fresh air when I stepped into the cool building. Deep greens and light greens and every color of flower stretched in all directions, carefully designed to draw the eye and jumpstart the gardener in each of us.

It worked on me. This was like some kind of textile therapy. And after my morning, I drank in every second of the calming atmosphere and aromatic air.

"Kaya!" Dillon called from where she stood by a pallet of succulents.

Ooh. Yes, please. I grabbed a basket near the door and headed toward them. "Hey." I smiled brightly, feeling more like myself than I had five minutes ago.

Vera and Dillon smiled back. "Hey."

"You look cute." Vera grinned. "It's nice to see you not covered in Coke from head to toe."

235

I laughed. "Yeah, it's amazing how comfortable I am in a kitchen, but ask me to carry dirty dishes around for a few hours and I lose all sense of balance and coordination."

"I can't wait to see how you do with reservations."

"No," I groaned. "You're not putting me on the phones, are you?"

She waggled her eyebrows and held her thumb and pinky up to her face, mimicking my future. "Hi, this is Kaya at Sarita, how can I service you this evening?"

"Oh my God," Dillon laughed. "You sound like a phone sex operator." She looked at me. "Please don't ask strangers how you can service them!"

"That could be an interesting career change. My mom would love that." Smacking my hand to my forehead, I made an angry sound in the back of my throat. "I forgot, I can't come in this Sunday. My parents are coming to town and I promised to spend time with them."

Vera pouted. "That's no fun. I'll have to find someone else to torture this week."

Dillon gave her a look. "You look so nice from the outside. Nobody would ever know you're psychotic if you didn't go around announcing it."

Vera flexed her tiny bicep. "Wait till I have a staff of my own." She added some succulent arrangements to her massive cart. "By the way, we're going to start hiring next week if either of you ladies are interested. I can't promise a sane working environment, but we're going to have fun!"

Dillon leaned on me, both of our shoulders deflating. Because… that sounded amazing. I had loved working for Killian. Even if he had been a dictator ninety-nine percent of the time. And even though I didn't think Vera would be any different to work for, I liked her a lot.

"I wish," Dillon grumbled before I could give my answer. "But I'm fairly confident if I quit Lilou to work at Killian's restaurant, Ezra would cut me out of the will and mail me to Siberia."

236

"He wouldn't do either of those things," Vera assured her. "At least he wouldn't mail you to Siberia." She paused and added, "The cost of postage would likely stop him. He's a real cheapskate about those things."

"He would. He'd take it out of my inheritance," Dillon assured her. "And he would never forgive me, which would be worse."

"Ah, sibling love," I groaned. "It's adorable." Both Vera and Dillon had brothers they loved. Which made me want a brother. Clearly, I'd been give the short straw with two sisters. We didn't love each other in that hero-worship kind of way. We loved each other out of obligation, but we didn't like each other much at all.

"What about you, Kaya? Care to apprentice full-time?"

I bobbled my head back and forth. "Maybe? I want to see how Sarita goes first and I don't feel like I should abandon Ezra before I try that. Besides, Wyatt would kill me if I left him right now."

Dillon and Vera shared a look before Dillon asked, "So you guys are official?"

"Official?" My heart jumped to my throat and I started coughing dramatically in an attempt to dislodge it. "God, no. I meant... I meant in the kitchen. If I left him alone at Lilou, he would murder me. And then bring my corpse back to life and make me his sous-chef zombie slave."

Vera snickered. "Sounds kinky."

My face was now the same color as the nearby mini rose trees. "Dillon, I can't trust you with anything!"

She held her hands up. "What? That was juicy! I can't be expected to keep information like that a secret forever."

"It's been one week." I turned to Vera. "How long have you known?"

She pressed her lips together to hide a smile. "Oh, not long. Maybe like a week?"

I glared at the greenhouse-style ceiling and decided these two chatty Cathy's could remain my friends. For now. Until someone better came along. And by better, I meant anyone with the ability to keep a secret.

"You didn't tell Killian, did you?"

Vera's expression turned guilty. "It's just that he's been worried about Wyatt lately. He's been stressed out because of the promotion. We want to see him happy." She cleared her throat. "Also, Killian was pissed I didn't let him in on training you. I needed something juicy to even things out! And you guys as a couple is about as entertaining as it gets."

I rolled my eyes. "Don't get any ideas. There's nothing juicy happening between Wyatt and me." Except for when we made out this morning. In public. In front of his foster mom.

"Why not?" Vera asked, her eyes darkening with worry. "You're so good for each other."

The comfort and freshness of the nursery faded with the intrusion of cold, hard reality. "Not in the long-term sense of the word." At Vera's completely fallen face, I quickly added. "We're having fun. It's nothing serious. It won't ever be something serious."

"Oh, sure." Vera turned back to add more succulent arrangements to her cart. "Yeah, I only meant we want to see him less stressed out. Jo said he was better this morning when she saw you two."

I blinked at Vera. "How has word spread this quickly?"

She gave me a side glance. "We're all on Wyatt watch. We want to see him settled into Lilou and in life. It's nothing against you, Kaya."

"Oh, I'm sure it's not."

Dillon nudged me with her elbow. "Meeting Jo though… That's kind of a big deal?"

My shoulders lifted in a casual shrug out of instinct. "I already know Jo. And this morning wasn't like that. It wasn't like… an official meet the parents moment or anything. It was—"

"She said she caught you kissing!" Vera practically shouted.

Desperately trying to keep my voice softer than shrill, I said, "Oh my God."

"And Wyatt confirmed," Vera confessed, nervous for the first time ever. "They both had unrelated questions, but the conversation naturally kind of… veered to you."

I tried not to fidget as the burning in my cheeks reached an all new level of volcanic hot. "Is this why we're here? You want to interrogate me about Wyatt?"

"We're here to pick out low maintenance centerpieces for Vera's tables," Dillon said nonchalantly, like they hadn't lured me into their trap to confirm all the scandalous details of my not-so-private morning. "Aren't they pretty?"

"Yes," I mumbled, picking up one for myself. There were three different varieties in a kind of rock garden settled into a stone pot. Very pretty. It would look super cute on my island, next to my giant wood cutting board.

"He's a great guy," Vera said gently. "Maybe you should give him a chance."

"It's bad timing," I confessed. "With my attempt at Sarita. And being his sous chef. And, both of our insane, chaotic lives. It's not meant to be."

The eternal optimist, Dillon's eyes lit with hope and she started to say, "Maybe—"

"Look at those mossy things," I said, cutting her off. "I'm going to check those out."

They let me have my space and graciously didn't bring up the subject of Wyatt again all morning. I left with another backseat filled with purchases and a rapidly beating heart.

I could handle ninety-hour weeks like a pro. I worked in one of the most stressful, sweatiest kitchens out there, my boss was a total tyrant and I had to consistently produce perfection to keep my position. Those things didn't bother me. I didn't get anxiety. I was a badass chef and comfortable in my role in the kitchen.

But a harmless conversation about Wyatt? Entirely based on facts? Too much for me. My palms were sweaty, and my stomach had decided to grow an ulcer. I would have called in sick tonight if I would have thought I'd still have a job in the morning.

What was it about Wyatt that turned me into a complete mess? I was so much better when he was yelling at me than dealing with the sweeter, softer, surprise version of him I didn't even know existed until recently.

Steeling my nerves, I said goodbye to my friends with promises to see Dillon very soon and Vera as soon as my parents headed back to Hamilton. Then I went to work. Because that was what I did. No matter what happened with Wyatt or my personal life, work was my center, my cure. I would throw myself into it tonight and forget everything else. And at the end of the night, I'd slip out before Wyatt could get me alone and trick me into more of his delicious kisses.

Or maybe I'd stick around for them. As long as he swore on his kitchen knives that he wouldn't tell anyone this time.

Chapter Sixteen

*H*oly shit! I caught sight of my reflection in the small mirror above the
hand-washing sink and held back a laugh.

My short hair shot out from behind my damp bandana every which way,
frizzy loose curls, frizzier and curlier now that I'd been working almost
fifteen hours. My mascara had smudged beneath my lower lashes and my
cheeks were rosy from running around like a chicken with its head cut off for
the last several hours.

I undid the top three buttons of my jacket, hoping to cool down a little.
The kitchen was extra hot tonight. And we were extra busy.

There were rumors that Lilou, and by default Wyatt, was up for another James Beard award. There was talk that Ezra had entered the two of them into several categories, like he always did in October. The results would be announced soon, like they always were in May, which meant judging was well underway.

Of course, there was no way to know if that rumor was true or what awards we had to strive our best to receive because Ezra wasn't here to ask. Besides, he wouldn't tell us anyway. We had gone through this every year while Killian was in charge. I thought Ezra would give us a couple years to calibrate to new leadership, but apparently, he didn't want to waste time making Wyatt a chef to contend with.

I had expected the rumors to wind Wyatt up, make kitchen life intolerable. Instead, he was in rare form. Completely unaffected by the pressure and operating as efficiently and effectively as possible. At a speed that I quite frankly didn't even know existed.

There was something oddly more relaxed about him, but at the same time his perfectionism had reached a whole new level of demand. I'd gotten through tonight with only one redo, but I'd been stressed out the whole evening making sure every single element of my dishes were without reproach.

I should hate him all over again for what he'd put me through tonight. But these were the aspects about his personality I respected. These were the things I appreciated about him. I had only known head chefs to be totally, intolerably obsessive about their kitchens.

From cleanliness, to the quality of ingredients they cooked with, to the level of finesse at which their dishes left the kitchen, most chefs at this level were control freaks times one thousand. And I gave every single one of them grace.

Their name was on the line. Their reputation at risk. They weren't selling food to hungry diners, they were creating an evening that was memorialized by smells and touch and taste. They were developing moments of excellence that would follow these people to the end of their lives. They were facilitating experiences that would change and mark people.

Think back to your favorite meal. It wasn't only the food. The memory encapuslated the people you were with, the ambiance, the aesthetic of the food, the drinks you ordered, the smile on your server's face, the temperature of the restaurant, the smell, the lighting… every single aspect played a part in creating the most perfect dining experience of your life.

And while the back of house might not have a say in décor and dimness, we controlled the main event of the evening. Wyatt, like Killian before him, wanted every single customer to leave tonight declaring that they had eaten the best meal of their entire lives—the meal every other piece of food would be compared to for all of eternity.

I could get on board with that.

One day, I would run my own kitchen and the same would be true about me. My staff would mumble, "That persnickety bitch," under their breath and I would smile and pat them on the head, because a meticulous shrew was exactly what I would have to be.

Dillon sidled up to me, wrapping her arm around my waist in a quick side hug. She'd already stripped off her chef's coat and we'd only been closed for five minutes.

"Hey, I'm taking off," she said, clearly rushed to get out the door.

"Already?"

"Molly and Ezra asked me to pick them up from the airport," she explained.

I glanced at a nearby clock. It was just after eleven. My heart sank for two reasons. One, that Ezra was back. And two, that Dillon was abandoning me to close without her.

Still, I was a good friend, so I asked, "Do you need me to shut down your station?"

She grinned at me, backing up toward the side entrance. "Wyatt already volunteered you. I think his exact words were, 'Kaya will do it for you. She loves to clean up your shit.'"

My eyes bugged. "That asshole."

Winking at me, she put her hand on the door.

"Can't they get an Uber?" I called after her, but she was already racing to her car.

"They're engaged!" she shouted over her shoulder. "He asked her while they were on the beach!"

My shoulders deflated as the heavy steel door slammed shut. Okay, so that was a no?

Smiling at how loyal my friend was to her family, I turned around and got back to work. If I wanted any shot at six hours of sleep tonight, I needed to get my ass in gear. My parents were coming tomorrow night and I could not, in any way, be running on fumes while they were here. It would get my big mouth into more trouble and I seriously didn't want to fight with them their entire stay.

"Swift," Wyatt called from across the kitchen. "You good with sauté?" He was referring to Dillon's station where she sautéed veggies and made the sauces for dinner service.

"It's my favorite," I told him. It was my least favorite. And Dillon had been especially messy tonight. Probably because of the extra layer of mayhem and her excitement over her brother's engagement. But dang, no wonder she was in a hurry to get out of here.

244

I would be too if my station looked like she left hers.

Wyatt made a noise that from across the kitchen almost sounded like a laugh. It couldn't have been though, because Wyatt didn't laugh in his kitchen.

Benny shot me a funny look, roughly rubbing his closely shaved head. "Was that a joke, Kaya?"

"Shut it," I growled at him.

He grinned at me. Benny was a gigantic man that seemed too large for a kitchen setting. And even though his fingers were as big as sausages, he did amazing things with meat. As the butcher, he carved the proteins and made them look fabulous. Besides me, he was Wyatt's most trusted chef on staff.

"I wasn't prepared for you to be funny. You should warn me next time."

"I've always been funny," I shot back. "You just haven't had a sense of humor until tonight."

"I don't think it's me that needed to find their sense of humor." His gaze darted back to Wyatt and I fought the urge to slap my palm over my eyes and curse.

"Maybe he's finally settling into the role." I shrugged, pretending it was no big deal.

"Maybe," Benny agreed.

We separated, getting back to our work. He finished way before me and disappeared to find Wyatt.

I was left alone in the now empty kitchen space since I had double the workload. Benny and Endo had offered to help me finish, but I'd declined their help. It was late enough. They didn't need to stick around for me. We all wanted to get to bed.

Benny and Wyatt had left twenty minutes ago to drop the nightly deposit off at the bank. I'd watched them walk out the door and breathed a sigh of relief when they'd gone.

245

It wasn't that they were bothering me, it was that I loved being alone in this place.

As sous chef, I had the rare privilege of closing by myself. I had my own set of keys—I could open by myself too. Wyatt and Ezra had entrusted me with a lot when Killian had left, and I was only now feeling gratitude to them.

Dropping my cleaning towel on the counter behind me, I turned around and admired the gleaming kitchen I busted my ass in day and night.

I had been so angry at Wyatt for waltzing into the head chef position unchallenged, so frustrated that the job had been handed to him on a silver platter, that I hadn't considered how hard he'd worked for it before Killian had left.

This had been Wyatt's job during Killian's regime. He'd been second in command. He'd worked these insane hours. He'd never gotten days or nights or holidays off. He'd been here from open till close every single day. There were days he worked harder and longer and more ferociously than Killian did.

I knew, because that was what I was doing now.

And on top of that, he'd had a relationship with Killian, a friendship that existed long before Lilou and James Beard Awards.

The executive chef job at Lilou was never mine. It was never mine to claim or fight for or want.

In the still quiet of the kitchen at the end of a long, hard day, I could finally admit that to myself. I could finally rest in the truth that this job was, is, and will always be Wyatt's.

And that was okay. Because there were other kitchens out there for me. I would take every second of experience and training I could get from this place. I would take the long hours and turn them into an indomitable work ethic. I would take the grueling demands and insane expectations and turn

246

them into my version of perfection. I would take my difficult coworkers, my impossible boss, and the demanding, never-satisfied customers and create my own style of leadership. And I would take my success here, my steady climb up the hierarchy, my stellar reputation, and turn it into more success, more of a meteoric rise, more of an industry-wide reputation that came with accolades and household name recognition.

My rise wouldn't happen overnight or even in the next several years, but I was in it for the long game. This was a marathon not a sprint, and I planned to finish this race as strong and solid as I started.

My fingers wrapped around the edge of the counter, the steel edge biting into my tender palms, but I couldn't help but smile. There was something different about tonight, about being alone in such a renowned kitchen. I could feel success skittering up my spine. I could taste victory dancing on my tongue. I could practically see the future and it included everything I'd hoped for… my very own dreams coming true.

I didn't know if that was Sarita or not. Ezra's arrival back in Durham meant shit just got real. No more practicing. No more pretending. I would have to face him and his judgment. Was I up to that challenge? I might have only gotten practice at Sarita doing front of house tasks, but I had a career in the kitchen gleaned from my efforts at Lilou. I knew how to run a kitchen. But would I be enough for Sarita?

Catching movement out of the corner of my eye, I swallowed a scream and swiveled to face the intruder. My hands patted the counter blindly, searching for a knife or sauté pan or something I could use to defend myself.

"It's me," Wyatt soothed, his voice a calming rumble.

"God, you scared me," I accused him. My heartbeat slowly began to calm down and my breathing returned to normal. "I thought you went home for the night."

"I forgot something," he said.

I ignored the thoughtful way he was looking at me, the way his eyes had darkened and heated, laser focusing on me.

How long had he been standing there? I'd only noticed him a few seconds ago, but he looked so… fixated.

My body knew the answer, but my brain forced my mouth to ask the question anyway. "What did you forget?"

He crossed the kitchen in six long strides, reaching me on the seventh. One hand slid around my waist, bringing my body flush with his. The other glided over my jawline, tipping my head back so he could steal a kiss from my mouth.

His mouth was so hungry, so completely desperate for mine that I couldn't do anything else but submit. I was helpless against his tsunami of desire. He swept me off my feet and into the devastation that was Wyatt wanting something.

And that something was me.

I kissed him back—that was the only logical response, the only reaction my body was capable of making.

It was this man. No matter how much I talked myself out of a physical reaction with him, I had to admit to myself that I wanted him. And who wouldn't?

Yes, he was inhumanly gorgeous to look at. And his tattoos perfectly tempting. But it was more than that.

It was the way he looked at me across our busy kitchen, the way his eyes burned hotter than the flames we cooked with. It was his tragic story he shared with me on Tuesday morning and the way he pulled on my heartstrings because of the little boy he was, the same little boy I sometimes still saw in him.

He'd snared me with his rare smiles and even rarer laughter and the way he commanded the kitchen so fiercely. He'd captured me with the flawless way he cooked and his relentless expectations of perfection. It was the way he respected and trusted me and didn't think he could handle this kitchen without me. It was this thing that had been simmering between us for years and years. This thing that I was only willing now to admit existed. This thing that was threatening to consume me entirely, drown me in the sheer force of it.

I wrapped my arms around his neck and held on as the storm between us grew more electric. Our mouths fought, and our tongues warred. We were comfortable with this now, we knew each other's curves and angles. He preferred having my top lip and I wanted to nibble his bottom. We'd developed this greedy synchronicity between us, our constant push and pull, bringing the desire between us to a boil.

His mouth moved to pay attention to my jawline, my ear, my neck. His hand reached up and flicked open the remaining buttons of my coat that were still clasped. I started to shake off the coat and he helped by tearing it from my arms.

He'd lost his hours ago and stood pressed against me in only a thin t-shirt and pants. But they were too much. I couldn't stand anything separating us. Now that I'd given into this, I wanted him stripped bare. I wanted all of him.

Every part of him.

My fingers gripped the edges of his shirt and tugged. "Are we alone?" I asked as I tasted his earlobe for the first time. God, he was decadent, rich, like the best meal I'd ever had. I wanted more. And more. And more.

"Totally," he confirmed. "The doors are locked."

Together we ripped his shirt over his head and tossed it somewhere… else. He crashed against me, his skin unbelievably hot. He pressed his chest to mine and a breathy moan escaped the back of my throat.

"This is crazy," I murmured, trailing kisses along his hairline as he dipped his head to kiss the tops of my breasts.

249

As if the taste wasn't enough, he cupped my breast with his large hand and squeeze, his thumb brushing over my nipple, teasing, tantalizing, tearing down whatever remained of the walls I'd built to keep him out.

He pulled his head back, so he could meet my eyes. His were so dark, so perfectly deep and warm. "Not crazy," he said firmly. "It's a long time coming."

I smiled because what else was I supposed to do? I wanted to ask him only a hundred questions to get to the bottom of that infuriating and cryptic response, but I couldn't seem to form the words.

He stepped closer to me, letting me feel his body against the most intimate part of mine. I hadn't thought we could get closer.

I was wrong.

His thumb brushed over my nipple again. "Tell me if you want me to stop," he ordered. "And I will."

"Don't stop," I begged, sounding more desperate than I had intended to. "Please, don't stop."

Half his mouth lifted in that smile I was officially addicted to. "Tell me if you want me to. At any time. Tell me, okay?"

I nodded.

"When's the last time you were tested?"

His question shook me awake from the lustful coma I'd slipped into. Tested. Tested for what? Oh, god, that.

"The last time I was with someone," I told him honestly. "It's been a really long time." A really, really long time.

His question effectively doused cold water on my hormones and I was able to cock an eyebrow, demanding an answer to the same question from him. "You?"

"Same," he answered on a mumble. His hands grabbed the back of my thighs and hitched them around his waist. I let out a yelp and clutched his shoulders as he settled me on the counter. "I'm clean."

"Me too," I whispered as his body moved into my core, making my eyelids flutter closed.

His hand wrapped around the back of my neck and then his fingertips dipped into my hair, pulling my head back to look at him. "I've wanted this for a long time, Kaya. A very long time. But if you need me to stop. If you're not ready... tell me. I can wait."

There was this defiant witch inside of me that had to know more. I wanted this too. And maybe, if I was honest with myself, I could admit that I'd wanted it for way longer. But I couldn't let him get away with... getting his way. I was too used to fighting him to give him what he wanted without at least a small argument. "But how long will you wait?"

He didn't seem amused by my question. He leaned forward, forcing me to tip back on my elbows. His chest brushed mine. His tattoos winked at me, inviting me to touch them, taste them... suck on them until I'd left my mark. "A lot longer than you'll make me."

My mouth dropped open. "What does that mean?"

He grinned. No half smile or wicked smirk. This was a full on, blinding, both-sides-of-his mouth smile. "It means, we can play this game till the end of time and two things will remain true. One, you want me. You've wanted me for a long time. You want this to happen. And I'm very willing to oblige you. And two? I want you. I've wanted you for a very long time. I've wanted you for so long, you're the only thing I can remember wanting. I want you and I'm willing to wait as long as it takes to have you. You get me? We can do this cat and mouse thing for however long you need to do it, but I know both of us are ready to play a different kind of game."

His head dropped so he could kiss and suck his way over my collarbone. I closed my eyes and tried to catch the spinning thoughts in my head, to make sense of them.

"Kaya," Wyatt taunted, his voice low and growly. "Yes or no?"

"Yes," I whispered without thinking. No more fighting. He was right. We both wanted this.

We both couldn't stand not having it for another second.

His mouth found mine again, followed by a desperate collision of our bodies, both of us needing to taste each other more than we needed air. He wasn't gentle this time and I wasn't either.

We consumed each other, grabbing, clawing, demanding more and more and more. He tore my tank off, exposing me in a way I hadn't been for so long. I had a second's hesitation, of fear and insecurity, while he pulled back to stare at my nearly naked torso.

"Goddamn," he whispered reverently, erasing whatever self-esteem issue I was wrestling with. "I knew they would be beautiful, but fuck, Kaya. They're magnificent."

I let out a giddy laugh at his assessment of my breasts. "You're ridiculous."

His mouth descended on my left nipple as if he couldn't stand waiting for another second. "You're delicious," he countered, his tongue flicking over the right spot.

He pulled my bra cup down, so he could taste my bare flesh. We moaned together. My fingers fumbled to unclasp the damn thing as quickly as possible. As soon as it went slack in his hands, he tore the thing from my body, covering my breasts with his gigantic hands almost immediately.

I looked down at his tan skin against the milky white of mine, tattoos snaking over his hands, wrapping around his fingers and I nearly orgasmed on the spot. Wyatt's body was a work of art. From the gauges in his ears to the colored ink covering all his exposed skin, he wore his self-expression as skin, daring anyone that could see him to know him.

But did anybody know him?

Jo thought he was fragile. Dillon and Vera thought he was invincible. Killian treated him like a little brother.

All of these titles and perceptions were wrong. All of them.

He wasn't fragile; he was stupidly arrogant, open, and ready to face whatever this world threw at him.

He wasn't invincible. He was vulnerable when the moment called for it. Gentle when I needed him to be. Willing to admit his mistakes and ask for help.

And he wasn't little anywhere. Or in anything. He was imposing and dominating and… overwhelming.

They didn't know him. I wasn't even sure I knew him.

Not completely anyway. And even though the ghosts of my past whispered that now was the time to run, before I got too invested, before he saw too much of me, I couldn't.

Not now. Maybe not ever.

Wyatt had sunk beneath my skin and made a bed in the secret places of me that I'd desperately tried to hide from him. He hadn't been willing to wait or sit back. He hadn't even asked for permission. He'd… taken. And now I was afraid he'd never give back.

While he paid my breasts special attention, I became greedy to explore him. I reached for his belt, bringing his pelvis to my core again. He pressed against me and for a moment my attention was derailed. My eyelids slammed shut at his sharp intake of air.

"Fuck," he murmured.

"More," I gasped at the same time.

My fingers fumbled, desperate to unbuckle his belt, to get rid of these pants that were so irritatingly in the way.

I felt him smile against my skin. "Hey, hey," he murmured, his lips hot and soft against my skin. "Let's go a little slower, yeah? I've been waiting long enough, I think I deserve to enjoy this."

Enjoy this?

Enjoy me?

Oh God.

Still, I couldn't help myself. There had always been a push and pull between us, a constant tug of war that neither of us could let go of. "You deserve to enjoy this? That seems a little entitled."

He pushed my body back on the counter, pressing down fully on top of me, pressing our most intimate parts closer together. His fingers entwined with mine, spreading my arms wide so I felt completely exposed to him.

"I've earned it, chef." His head dipped so he could nip at the curve of my jaw. "I want you slow, Kaya. I want to savor this. Make it last as long as possible. Make you last as long as possible. And I'm going to savor every single second."

Before I could argue, he started trailing kisses down my throat, over my breasts, down my bare stomach until my pants barred him from going further.

He raised his torso enough to flick open the button fly of my linen pants. His fingers hooked inside the waistband of my panties and with one firm tug, he removed both items of clothing.

My legs kicked out at his surprise attack, but he caught my ankles before I flailed too wildly. With complete confidence—the same way he did everything—he rested my feet on the cool counter, my knees bent, my sex exposed to him in a way that made my breath hitch with nerves.

254

I self-consciously covered my breasts with my arms, desperate for some modicum of control. Very suddenly I felt upended, turned inside out. Wyatt had managed to take the lead somehow and I was left struggling to catch my breath trailing after his reckless need.

My heart hammered against my breastbone and my skin prickled with both anticipation and anxieties. I should be thinking about what would happen after tonight, about how we would ever come back from this moment, how we could ever work together again… or look at each other again… or—

His mouth touched the most intimate part of me and my train of thought fizzled beneath a blazing sizzle of desire. He kissed me there like he kissed my mouth, like he couldn't get enough of the feel of me, the taste of me.

He used his tongue, his teeth, and his fingers the way I had watched him cook for all these years, with absolute certainty and graceful deftness. My back arched off the cold counter as my hands searched for something to grasp onto.

The sensation was too much—too sharp, too real, too… intense. "Wyatt," I panted, not knowing if I wanted him to stop or keep going. "Oh God, Wyatt."

He lifted his head to meet my eyes. His were dark pools of desire. His finger slid into me, sending me closer to oblivion. "Don't fight me on this, Kaya," he demanded. Another finger joined the first. "Not on this." His mouth closed around me once more, sending me over the edge into an abyss of light and tensed muscles and the most delicious feeling of my life.

My body contracted around him, trapping his hand within me as my thighs squeezed his head unwilling to let him go until I absolutely had to.

He lifted his gaze to meet mine, his expression was lazy satisfaction that nearly sent me over the edge once again. Slowly, reluctantly, he slid his fingers out of me and I shivered, still so sensitive.

255

I stared up at him, expecting him to move on to the next course. I waited for him to undo his belt or rip his pants off superman style or something. But instead, he leaned over me, his hands resting on either side of my head. He made a contented sound in the back of his throat and belatedly I realized that was all he planned to do tonight.

Huh?

Didn't he want to…?

Taking things into my own hands, I locked my legs around his waist and invited him forward. My cheeks were already flushed. Otherwise, they would have blushed tomato red at the demand I forced out. "We can't be finished yet. We're just getting started."

Half his mouth lifted in that crooked grin I was starting to love. "I don't have a condom," he explained.

I propped myself up on my elbows and looked at him incredulously. "What? Did you check your wallet?"

He dropped his head, laughing at my question. When he looked at me again, it was from underneath his lashes. His eyes still hadn't lost their electricity or their need. A tremor rocked through me again. I could feel him still, his hard length pressed against me, begging for attention, demanding we finish what we started.

"Yeah, you know I've never really carried those around with me. I figure if I want something that bad, I can wait until we've made it back to my place." The planes of his cheeks turned a pale pink. "And I can honestly say until tonight, I have always been fine with waiting."

"Now what are we going to do?" I growled. Clearly this was his fault. And fine, I'd already had a lovely orgasm, but I wanted another one, damn it!

He dropped his head, kissing the hollow of my throat, using his tongue and teeth and seductive witchcraft. "We're going to go out on a date."

That sobered my sex-drunk brain. "What?"

Lifting his head again, he smiled and said, "A date, Kaya. You are familiar with the activity?" And because he was Wyatt, he said, "It's that thing you do when two people really like each other. The guy picks the girl up. You go to a mutually enjoyable public place. There are beverages involved. Sometimes food. Sometimes dancing. Am I ringing any bells?"

I rolled my eyes. "That's cute, smartass. But we can't do that."

"We can't do what?"

"Go on a date."

"Why not?"

Letting out a frustrated sigh, I sat up fully, forcing him to step back. I needed clothes on if he was going to challenge me. "Because you're my boss. And we work together." Seeing the stern set of his jaw, I knew I hadn't picked an argument that bothered him yet. "Also, I'm your sous chef. You can take the night off. Or I can take the night off. But we cannot take the night off together. Who would run the kitchen?"

The bottom half of his jaw slid back and forth as I finally hit a note that rung problematic. "Huh…"

Finishing clasping my bra, I hid my victorious smile behind my chef coat as I slid it on. "It doesn't work, Wyatt."

"Lunch."

I blinked up at him. "What?"

"We already knew this relationship would be unconventional… our dates are going to have to be too."

Wait, did he say… relationship?

"You're not serious."

He blinked at me. "About what?"

Son of a bitch. Where the hell were my panties?

"Don't you think we're going a little fast? I mean, yesterday we hated each other and—"

257

"I've never hated you."

"And we're going in separate directions and we work all the time. A relationship seems extreme in light of everything."

He studied me for a few long moments, seeming to take my measure, deciding something about me that felt like it needed my permission. "What direction are you going in, Kaya, that's different than mine?"

Oh, no. Abort! Abort! This wasn't a conversation Wyatt and I could have in the middle of the night after he'd feasted on my body. I needed cold space before I admitted my plans to him. I needed distance and a clear head and for my body not to feel like it had just been worshiped.

Panties?! Hello, panties??? Where for art thou, panties?

Seeing my obvious distress, he reached down and handed me a bundle of pants and underwear and one of my discarded shoes. I slid off the counter and started yanking everything on.

"It's late," I observed in an even voice. Braving his gaze when all I wanted to do was slink away into the dead of night and never resurface again, I said, "Can we talk about this tomorrow?"

"Tomorrow?"

I stretched up on my tiptoes and kissed the feather tattoo on his neck. "When I get in tomorrow morning? We can figure out the details." Panic had started welling up inside me like an overboiling pot. I needed space to figure out what happened. I needed air to catch my breath.

I needed… sleep.

"Details?" He kept repeating my words as if they didn't make sense to him. "Is this the kind of relationship that has details?"

My eyes squinted shut and I turned away from him, so he couldn't see my regretful expression. I was afraid he would misread it. Or maybe I was misreading it.

What did I regret? What we did?

No… not really. Not yet.

Pulling away from him and treating him like this?

Maybe.

"There are logistics, Wyatt. We can't… we can't… We work together. This could get messy."

If I let it go on. If I didn't figure out how to stop it.

His fingers reached out and gently wrapped around mine. He barely applied any pressure, but he didn't need to. The feel of him was enough to pull me back into the sanctuary of his body.

His other hand wrapped around my waist and he dropped his face to the curve of my neck, my back pressed to his chest. I flinched when he spoke, his voice barely above a whisper. "Okay, Swift. Go home. I'll clean up here."

He wasn't fragile, I reminded myself. Jo was wrong about him.

I knew him.

He was the strongest person I knew.

"Thanks, Wyatt," I told him, my voice shaking with emotion, fear, and regret.

"See you tomorrow?"

I nodded, unable to say the words. I was the fragile one. It was me that was breakable.

He let me go. I fled the building, too much of a chicken to look back at him.

How had something that amazing caused me to run away again? I had never experienced anything like that before. Nolan didn't even have the ability to make a woman feel like that. I was positive ninety-nine percent of the male population couldn't make a girl feel that way.

So why was I still running?

Why was I still trying to avoid this thing that could be so good?

The question plagued me all the way home. It continued to haunt me all the way through my hot shower, stripping the joy of my shower beer and the satisfied feeling of having kicked major culinary ass today. It stayed with me as I climbed into bed, tossing and turning with no chance of falling asleep. And the doubt sat on my left shoulder the next morning, whispering lies and insecurities and all those things I'd thought I'd left behind in Hamilton all those years ago as I tapped out a cowardly text to Wyatt an hour before I was supposed to be at work.

I feel like crap. I think I'm getting the flu. Sorry, I won't make it in today.

He'd sent back a thumb's up emoji, making me feel even more like crap.

See you Monday sat on my phone for the remainder of the day, but I never found the courage to send it. It was official, the same reasons that had sent me running from Hamilton, had now possessed my feet again.

Wyatt isn't Nolan, I told myself.

He's still trouble, my brittle heart whispered back.

He's still going to hurt you, my brain agreed. *You won't be enough for him either.*

I was too tired to argue with my head or my heart. Besides, I didn't know what the point was. They were both right.

Chapter Seventeen

"*K*ay-bug," my dad exclaimed as he pulled me into a hug. "I'm so glad
you were able to get tonight off." My dad, Eric Swift, was the soon to be
retired CEO of Haymill Chicken. He was ridiculously smart, ambitious, and
ruthless at work. At home, he let my mom run the show and enjoyed being
shuffled back and forth wherever she told him to go.

My mom, Dana, our household CEO, spent her days as a part-time
recruiter for the local business bureau. She liked her job because it was
flexible and a gateway to all the town drama she could stomach.

"I wanted to spend time with you guys," I told him. "I never get to see
you."

"That's because you're trying to work yourself to death," he grumbled, reluctantly handing me off to my mother.

"Hi, Mama." I smiled at her.

She took my face in her hands and kissed my forehead. "More beautiful than ever."

Her words soothed an open wound in my chest and I relaxed a little, truly happy to see them. She pulled me into a firm hug, further calming the gaping chasm that had bothered me all day.

"Let me take your things," I offered, leading them deeper into my apartment. My parents had always been good-looking people and old age had done nothing to change that. Sure, they were softer now than in their youth. Their attractive faces still got wrinkles, no matter how many skincare products my mother forced on them. And they weren't toned-and-svelte-could-pass-as-fitness-model-body-doubles anymore. But their beauty had evolved into a dignified kind of handsomeness. They were like a living, breathing ad for AARP. So perfectly small-town America, you wanted to crown them both and slap a "Mr. and Mrs. Successful American Citizen" on them.

I was the opposite—wild. With pink hair to their perfectly cropped, perfectly muted gray. I was lip rings and cartilage piercings to my Mother's habitual pearls. I was boho hipster to their upper middle-class cardigan sets. It was hard to believe I was their offspring. But not so hard to believe why I'd eventually fled Hamilton like my tail was on fire. They had Claire and Cameron to show off at home. They didn't need the black sheep tainting their golf outings and church potlucks.

Setting their small suitcases down in the second bedroom I had spent the morning cleaning and organizing, I was surprised to see my parents had followed me into the room.

Dad checked his TAG Heuer watch. "We don't have much time, do we? We got here later than I had hoped. Cameron's car broke down outside of town—I had to help her before we could take off."

Concern for my baby sister flickered to life. We were six years apart, so we'd never been super close, but I had always felt protective of her. "Oh no. Is Cam okay?"

Mom scoffed. "Don't be dramatic, Eric. She ran out of gas."

He folded his arms over his chest and huffed. "She still needed my help."

"I swear that child would forget her hair if it weren't attached to her body."

I smiled because it was true. "Glad it was only a minor mishap."

Mom turned to me, assessing my yoga pants and white tank top. "What time do we need to leave? How long will it take you to get ready?"

"Ready for what?"

She mimicked my exact expression. There weren't many times where outsiders would say I looked like my mother, but this was one of those moments where I knew we were spitting images of each other. Nobody was better at looking completely dumbfounded than the two of us—usually because of other people's idiocy. "For supper."

I looked down at my clothes, realizing they wouldn't pass my mother's standards for leaving the house. "Oh, did you want to go out?"

Dad laughed as though I'd made a joke. "Did we want to go out," he stated, not as a question. "You're always so funny."

I gave my mother a helpless look. "What am I missing?"

"The reservation." She pulled her phone from her pocket and shook it in front of me like that would jog my memory. "They called earlier today," she explained. "They wanted to confirm a table for three at seven?"

"They?" I asked, suspicion leaking through me, like my heart was a faulty balloon.

"The restaurant," my mother said slowly. I was currently the complete idiot receiving her befuddled glare.

"What restaurant?" I snapped, full-blown panic taking control of my tongue.

"The one you work at, bug," my dad explained in that patient tone I remembered him always having. He was never rushed, never sharp, never frazzled—emotions left for my mother and me. "The one that's so hard to walk right in." He smirked. "Believe me, we've tried. It was thoughtful of you to book us a table. And how fun that we get to eat there with you. You'll know what to order." He smiled at my mom. "And what to avoid."

This whole damn debacle waiting to happen, that's what I wanted to avoid.

I glanced at the ceiling and grappled for my patience. Clearly, this was Wyatt's doing. Right? I mean, this was his idea to begin with. And I'd called in sick... He thought he could force me to face him? While simultaneously doing the sweetest thing for my parents? He'd underestimated my expert ability to run and hide.

Except that this was Lilou... and truly a fantastic opportunity for them. Not only would they finally have that meal of a lifetime I'd been dangling in front of their faces since I started working there, but they'd also finally understand why I loved my job so completely.

But what was Wyatt after? What would he say in front of my parents? Nothing. He wouldn't bring up last night. That would be insane. He wasn't a totally evil person. Dear God, at least I hoped he wasn't. I frowned at the bedpost, because after a quick thought, I wouldn't put it past him.

Shaking my head, I tried to talk myself off the ledge. He wouldn't bother us. Not tonight. I didn't take Wyatt for the kind of guy that wanted to meet any parents. Besides, the kitchen would keep him super busy while we ate. I already knew Lilou was completely booked tonight.

And that begged an interesting question: how had Wyatt squeezed a table for three into the already crowded reservation list?

Refocusing on my parents, I realized Wyatt had already won. I wasn't going to take this opportunity away from them. They'd wanted to eat at Lilou for a long time—ever since I started working there. I had even tried to put their name on this list once or twice, but that never worked out. Either they couldn't make it to town when there was an opening or there hadn't been an open spot when they'd been in town.

"We'll finally know what the big deal is." My mom smiled, her words sounded sugary despite the backhanded compliment.

"You're going to love it," I told her through gritted teeth. "The food will change your life." I leaned over to read my dad's wristwatch. "Did you say seven? We should leave in about forty-five minutes then."

My mom glanced over me again, her eyebrows furrowing over her straight nose. "Does that give you enough time to get ready?"

Weirdly enough, I felt more at home than I had in a long time. My mother's passive aggressive barbs pertaining to my appearance so familiar to me, I felt nostalgic for my childhood. Tucking a pink curl behind my ear, I said, "I'm quick."

She wrinkled her nose at the reminder of my hair choices but moved out of the way so I could hurry to my room.

As soon as the door shut behind me, I started stripping, yanking off the comfy clothes I'd worn all day while I'd cleaned my entire apartment. Throwing myself in the shower with a toothbrush in my hand, I got to work arming myself for Lilou.

It wasn't a random dinner and extended weekend with my parents. It wasn't just eating a meal at one of the most prestigious restaurants in the city. It wasn't one of our usual visits either; I'd settle myself in, excited to eat takeout pizza while I was forced to listen to gossip from back home until my parents passed out from too much wine.

My curiosity was sparked by Wyatt making the next move in our long game. He'd laid down another challenge and I had to do something that would match him. He thought he could outmaneuver me? Also, it was concerning how he got my mother's cell phone number—I would ask him about that later.

But this was so much more than supper and showing off my place of employment to my parents. This was about putting Wyatt in his place, reminding him who he was messing with. I didn't play to tie. I played to win. And Wyatt was going to realize just how much I savored victory.

Thirty-five minutes later, I emerged from my bedroom with springy pink curls pinned artfully to my head and a little black dress that clung to my curves and showed off my ample chest in a tasteful way—since he seemed so obsessed with it.

My heels were sky high and reserved for revenge. Honestly, they were reserved for nights I knew I wouldn't do much standing. I finished my look for the evening with vibrant lipstick the same shade as my hair, and smoky eyes that felt way over the top compared to my usual waterproof mascara and colored Chapstick.

I nibbled my lip ring as I led my parents downstairs to their Range Rover. Compared to my mother's demure silk blouse and high-waisted black trousers, I could have been mistaken for a hired escort, but my confidence refused to dampen.

I looked pretty tonight. Maybe even hot.

If Wyatt wanted to play with fire, I hoped he was prepared to get burned.

It was only a fifteen-minute drive to Lilou, even with the Friday night traffic. We pulled into the parking lot before I'd fully mentally prepared.

Thankfully, my parents paused for a few minutes inside the Rover to take in the outside of Lilou. She was spectacular beneath the dark night sky, all white brick and twining ivy. The landscape lights highlighted the best parts of her, warming the building in their soft glow. She was surrounded by iron and towering red brick on every side, making her standout as a beacon of culture and class.

My mom turned around in her seat and smiled at me. She genuinely meant it when she said, "It's charming, Kaya."

Smiling with pride, I said, "One of the prettiest in the city, I think."

This plaza was one of three main thoroughfares for nightlife, but in my opinion the best of the three. Lilou was obviously the crowning jewel of the square, but we also had two of the best nightclubs in town—Greenlight and Verve. There was Vera's brother's bike shop, Cycle Life. Plus a few designer boutiques that brought in a lot of business.

Yes, our plaza was the best, but we were better when Vera's old food truck had taken up residence in the middle. Foodie had offered a low key, urban vibe that was missing in her absence. And it had been super nice to grab a late-night meal after work. Especially now that I was second in command and left work so late. There was nowhere good open at that hour except Taco Bell, and a girl could only take so much fast food, even if it was tacos.

This was why Dillon and I were such breakfast connoisseurs. We were constantly surrounded by five-star food, but rarely had access to it or the stomach to eat it after we'd been cooking every night.

My parents got out of the car and I followed them. I probably should have led the way, but I rarely used the front door at Lilou and I couldn't help but savor the opportunity.

Unlike the kitchen door that dumped you into stainless steel and abrasive busyness, the front French doors had a kind of magic that was rare and

267

precious. Small square panes of mottled glass outlined in black paint were like the amuse-bouche, teasing and endearing all at once.

Once inside, you were immediately transported to a different world where waiters silently bustled back and forth in all black, contrasting vividly with the stark white linens and the softer white interior brick. Accents of green wrapped around the windows and dotted the tables in the small centerpieces. The lighting was rich and warm, continuing to appeal to the diner's softer sense.

The hostess greeted us from behind a large podium she could barely see over. "Hey, Kaya." She smiled.

"Hey, Erin." She was a nice college-aged girl, studying to be a sports broadcaster. I only barely knew her, but she was a hard worker and didn't start drama—hard to come by in the restaurant industry. I stepped up to her stand and wrapped my fingers around the edge of it. I dropped my voice some so my parents couldn't hear me ask, "Someone called my mom to confirm reservations earlier?"

She scanned her reservations list. "What name would it be under?"

"Swift, I think? Or Dana."

"Oh, here you are. Yep, it looks like Chef Shaw added you at the last minute." She met my gaze. "Lucky. I've been trying to get my parents a res here for months."

I smiled at her, but it wobbled. "This is the first time they've been in and I've been working here for years. Keep trying. You'll get a reservation eventually."

Like when you sleep with Wyatt. Or almost sleep with him—he's super accommodating after some third base action.

She sighed, and I could already tell this was only a temporary gig for her. She wasn't going to wait around years to squeeze in a reservation. We'd be lucky if she lasted the summer. "How many are in your party? All the reservation says is give you the best table. But I don't know how many to set it for."

If she didn't know the particulars of our reservation then who had confirmed it earlier with my mom? Wyatt? Leaning forward, I scanned her paper from an upside-down angle, which meant I couldn't read it at all. "It says that?"

She turned the list around for me and sure enough, in Wyatt's slender, scratchy handwriting, it said, "Swift— best table."

My stomach did a teeny somersault. I read it three more times to be sure I wasn't somehow hallucinating, or my mind wasn't playing tricks on me, forcing me to see what I wanted to see.

Wait. Did I want to see that?

I closed my eyes and I was back on the cold steel counter in the kitchen, Wyatt's head between my legs, my sense of reality and common sense exploding into a million particles of light and fire.

God, what the hell, Wyatt? What were you doing to me?

"I can seat you when you're ready," Erin said softly, her eyes narrowed with concern.

Shifting my shoulders, I forced my brain to focus and stepped toward her. My parents followed as we made our way past blissed-out diners on the verge of food comas. I soaked in every second of this rare vantage point.

I didn't hear from customers or reviewers or critics. As the mere sous chef, my name wasn't attached to anything in the restaurant. Blogs didn't rave about my talents with protein or sauce expertise. Yelp reviews didn't recommend this restaurant because of what I could do with risotto or the genius way I served Brussel sprouts. All the accolades went to Wyatt. And Killian before him.

Still, I knew the plates on these tables were a team effort. And not thanks to me. There was an entire staff hanging out back of house, working, sweating, slaving away to create the most perfect dining experience possible.

These separate elements came together to create a full menu that was nothing short of a work of art. Each recipe was carefully crafted and endlessly finessed. And everything was a living, breathing organism that was constantly changed and tweaked and studied to make sure it was always the best version of itself. That the diners were always getting our most perfect end-result.

Those rabbit legs? They had to be braised for two hours prior to service to make the meat fall-off-the-bone tender and then pan-seared in duck fat at exactly four hundred degrees to lock in the juices. They had to be flipped exactly halfway through the sear to ensure a nice crispy texture on the entire outside.

That filet could only be flipped once, right near the end to make sure the grill marks were uniform on both sides. Flipping it too early would overcook it. Flipping it too late wouldn't give both sides a chance to finish. And I made sure all my beef rested before I ever plated it.

We had only recently decided to add soft-boiled quail eggs to the asparagus. And the microgreens to add a fresh, springy taste to a tried and true favorite. Wyatt had perfected those two elements when he took over for Killian. The additions had blown the previous dish out of the water. The yolky eggs added richness to something familiar, and the microgreens added brightness and a burst of flavor to a dish that had been done and redone for years. The asparagus felt completely new now and so much better than before. Our diners flipped out over it.

Erin led us to a table in the center of the dining room, with a perfect view of the kitchen and the rest of the restaurant. It was the best table and I wondered how many other reservations she had to fight off to save it for us.

She handed out our menus and assured us that Kim would be over shortly to take our orders.

My dad leaned across the table and mouthed, "Wow!" It was all I needed to relax in my seat and finally let go of my fear. I didn't even know what I was afraid of. Only that I was afraid. Wyatt and I had once been friends. And we'd once been enemies. I didn't know what we were now.

Us.

Our.

We.

Him and I.

Together.

These words bounced around in my head, waiting for a solid definition. My brain wanted to give them boundaries and boxes and take away the fluttering in my chest that felt like so much more than a crush, lust, or anything I was ready for.

Our waitress, Kim, appeared. She was one of the pillars of Lilou. She'd worked here as long as any of us and could handle whatever the restaurant threw at her. She smiled at me, and I introduced her to my parents before ordering drinks for the table.

Darius, the bartender, and I were good enough friends that I knew his specialties and the favorites that Ezra had made him remove recently to fit in with the prohibition-era trend sweeping the country. Ezra wanted a list filled with new takes on gin fizzes and Old Fashioneds, Moscow Mules and French 75s. Darius was working on infusing jalapeno into tequila. He'd dip the glass in a cinnamon-cayenne-salt blend to make a spicy, sweet, delicious paloma that would blow minds and start beverage revolutions.

I ordered one for my dad, and a lemon, rhubarb gin thing for my mom.

271

For myself? Dirty martini. Also gin—preferably Irish Gunpowder if he had it. Extra dirty. Extra blue cheese stuffed green olives—like the good Lord intended.

What can I say? I liked a cold beer as much as the next girl, but in heels like these? I needed a drink James Bond would be proud of.

As soon as the drinks were dropped off at the table, I ordered appetizers from memory. I wanted my parents to get the most well-rounded experience possible. I also wanted them to have the meal of their life. I wanted them to see what I did and be impressed by it.

Knowing their taste, I ordered the smoked trout toast with avocado cream, the asparagus I'd just finished mentally raving about and the hand-rolled pistachio and saffron crème gnocchi.

I felt like standing up and mic dropping, but we hadn't even gotten to second plates yet. I decided to hold back until they asked me to roll them out of the restaurant.

Kim smiled at the order and disappeared to put it into the computer.

"That's so much food," my mom complained. "Was that all just appetizers?"

"You don't have to eat everything," I assured her. "I want you to try as much as possible. It will be worth it, I promise." I shrugged, feeling like I needed to add, "Besides, it's my treat."

My dad's brow furrowed immediately. "Oh, we can't let you pay for—"

I waved him off. "It's not a big deal. I want you to have the full Lilou experience."

My mom's shrewd eyes scanned over the menu again. "Maybe we can split something for the big meal."

"Mom," I groaned. "Please accept that I'm a big deal here. I'm not living paycheck to paycheck anymore."

My parents stared at me, trying to pull hard facts from my ambiguous statement. Dad's curiosity won out. "You're really top of the food chain here?"

I smiled. I was. It wasn't first place, but it was a damn good place to start. "I am. The one and only sous chef. I'm second in command in the kitchen."

"Is it stressful, honey?"

They already knew my title and position, but until this moment, I didn't think they understood exactly what that meant. It was a word without a definition until they'd seen it in a real-life setting. And they knew that I worked a lot and they probably could have assumed that my job was stressful. But I had never verbally admitted that part to them. I wanted them to get the message of how much I loved this career, this position. If you'd have asked them before tonight what my life was like? They would have come back with some version of rainbows and butterflies.

"So stressful," I agreed. "But worth it. This is what I love. And I'm lucky I get to do it in one of the best kitchens on the planet. I don't take that for granted." Or I wouldn't any longer. Starting now.

Thinking back to my ungrateful attitude over the past ten months, I wanted to hide my face in shame. I had taken my success for granted. I'd disregarded Wyatt's trust in me and let my entitled attitude nearly ruin one of the best experiences in my life.

Dad looked at my mom. "We asked her to leave this for the diner."

My mom sniffed the air, untouched by guilt or remorse. "I want her close to home. I'm not trying to take her dreams away from her."

But that was exactly what she was asking me to give up. My dreams. My aspirations. My future. "There's nothing for me in Hamilton, Mom. I belong here."

Kim approached with two waiters from the kitchen carrying our appetizers, forcing us to drop the conversation until the first plates were set

273

before us. My dad's eyes widened in awe at the intricacy of each dish while my mom glared at each component as if it were personally responsible for keeping me away from her.

I started plating for them, letting the argument hang in the air for a few minutes. My parents were cultured, but they weren't foodies. Besides, this food was fussy and took some explanation for even well-versed fanatics.

"Is this what you make?" my dad asked after he'd devoured his trout toast.

"Um, sometimes. It depends on the night and who else is working. I'm mainly responsible for proteins, by choice. But I'm the one that suggested pistachio for the gnocchi."

"How'd you come up with that?" my dad asked, scraping his fork against the plate for any straggling crumbs.

I shrugged. "I don't know. It's one of those things. I knew it would fit with the flavor profile and I felt the dish was missing an important crunch component."

"It is impressive," my mom conceded.

Kim came back to check on us and I put in the rest of our order. Our crispy pork belly served over creamy polenta with glazed carrots for my mom. The steak and frites for my dad—Kobe filet served with hand cut duck fat fries and charred broccoli. And I ordered the sweet pea tortellini for me. The tortellini was my favorite dish on the whole menu and one Wyatt made himself. I quickly added the swordfish curry—at least Wyatt's take on curry—over lentils and root vegetables to share.

"Kaya, that's too much," my mom chastised for the second time after Kim had walked way again.

I smiled patiently at her. "You don't have to eat it all. But I promise you'll thank me later."

Her eyes dropped to my midsection. "I thought maybe you'd given up yoga, but now I understand."

Used to her passive aggressive cruelty, I changed the subject without acknowledging her dig. "How's Claire? Is she excited for summer?"

My mom's entire face lit up at the mention of my younger sister. "She loves her class this year, but she's looking forward to the break. She works so hard, you know? Those kids give her a run for her money."

I restrained an eyeroll. My poor sister that had to work normal hours every week and got summers and major holidays off. Not to mention all those paid teacher work days.

Guilt immediately kicked me low in the gut. That wasn't fair to teachers. I knew they worked hard—harder than most. And my sister loved her students, pouring every bit of herself into their little lives.

But the scales were skewed at my house. Claire was revered for how hard she worked, while I was pitied because I had no social life. Maybe it was that Claire had achieved better life balance and I was jealous of her summer breaks. I mean who wouldn't be? Or maybe it was my parents' refusal to pay attention to what I did while Claire was worshiped, but either way, I knew my resentment for Claire was unhealthy. Borderline insane. Claire was wonderful. And we genuinely got along. I had a frustrating amount of misplaced resentment for my parents.

"She's planning to visit you for a few weeks," my dad added.

"Huh?"

"Claire," he said slower. "She misses you. She told us she's going to spend a few weeks with you this summer."

"She hasn't said anything to me," I told them.

They shrugged. They didn't care what I thought. If Claire wanted to spend time with me she would. I didn't get a say.

"Our air conditioner needed new filters last week," my mom said, changing the subject in a weird direction.

I didn't know what to say to that or why she was telling me about her air conditioner, so I nodded and mumbled, "Oh yeah?"

"I had to run into town to buy them. Your father wrote down what I needed, but you know what his handwriting is like. I got to the store and couldn't for the life of me figure out what he'd asked for. I got him to send me a picture of it though." She lifted her eyes to the ceiling, demonstrating her exasperation. "Although I still couldn't find what he needed."

At her pause, I tried to sound sympathetic. "That must have been frustrating for you, Mom."

She looked at me and reached out to squeeze my hand as if my sympathy meant the world to her. I nibbled on my lip ring to hide my smile. I pictured her harping on my dad all week about his negligence while he ignored her to watch golf.

"It was," she said. "Thank you for acknowledging my feelings, Kaya."

I smiled at her again.

"Anyway, while I was wandering around the hardware store, you'll never guess who I ran into."

Oh, man, I had a guess and I wanted to keep it to myself but—

She lifted her hands in excitement and exclaimed, "Nolan! Can you believe it, Kaya? He was right there. Right when I needed him the most."

Swallowing back the sarcastic way I wanted to ask her why air conditioning filters were the things she needed most in the world, I said, "It's not that hard to believe. I mean, he does live a block away from the hardware store."

My mother's smile pinched. "He was so kind," she added. "He found me exactly what I was looking for."

"Oh, thank God. I was so worried about the air conditioner."

276

"Kaya…" my dad warned.

My mom ignored me, her tone turning smug with juicy news. "He asked about you, Kaya Camille."

It was my turn to glare at the overhead lighting. "Of course, he did. I'm the only thing you two have in common. He was grasping for straws trying to make conversation with you."

"That's what I said," my dad grunted. He took an angry sip of his cocktail and I appreciated him more than I ever had in my life.

He had only barely tolerated Nolan. My mother on the other hand… was his biggest fan. President of the Nolan Carstark fan club. She'd probably make t-shirts if Dad let her.

Mom leaned forward, her eyes alight with the information bomb she was about to drop. "He wants to know when you're coming back to town. He said he misses you."

I held my mother's sharp gaze, resisting the eye roll I desperately wanted to unleash because I needed her to take me seriously. "Mom, I know two things about Nolan. And this might be disappointing, but I feel like you need to hear them anyway. One, he doesn't miss me. Maybe in the generic sense of the word because we share a collection of good, youthful memories together. But he doesn't miss me. Not really. And I know this because the only time I ever hear from Nolan is after he's three sheets to the wind and had meaningless sex with a random female whose name he can't remember. That's when he tells me he wishes I would move home and marry him. When he needs a name to remember to assuage his guilt."

"He's said he wants to marry you? He's said those words exactly?" My mother's selective hearing was astounding. Like, legitimately something medical science should study.

"Two." I held up correlating fingers, choosing not to respond to her temporary psychosis. "Even if I did leave my job here, pack up my life and

277

move back to Hamilton, he would only break my heart again. He's the same kid I graduated with nine years ago. He wants nothing to do with commitment or a wife that has opinions or a mind of her own. And he'd just drag out our engagement for another hundred years because, no matter what he's led you to believe, he isn't ready to settle down."

Her eyes narrowed, her mouth flatlining. "He said he misses you, Kaya, that means something."

I shook my head. "He doesn't. He misses a girlfriend that loved him. He misses not feeling guilty every time he gets laid. He misses having someone there to tell him he's amazing and help him match his ties to his shirts. He doesn't miss me." I let out a slow breath and tried my best to shield my fragile heart from the next truth she needed to hear. "He's a narcissist, Mom. He loves himself. He doesn't love me. He's never loved me."

My dad's hand clamped down on my knee under the table and squeezed supportively. "He doesn't deserve you," he rumbled sternly.

Mom huffed and tossed her napkin on the table. "You haven't even given him a chance, Kaya. You left him remember? You left town and never looked back. The rest of us were left to pick up the pieces. That boy was going to marry you and you just… abandoned him. And for what? For this life you claim to love so much? You work a million hours a week. You don't have a social life or a dating life, or hell, any kind of life. You have no prospects. You're stuck on this never-ending hamster wheel where you cook all day. This can't be all you want out of life." She never raised her voice. Her sense of decorum was too strong to cause a scene, but she didn't need to. Her words were arrows, aimed directly at my self-esteem and shaky confidence. One eyebrow rose, and I instinctively shriveled back, knowing she was dealing the final blow. "I raised you better than to settle for this."

The air behind me turned to static, electrified and sharp. I felt the change all over my bare skin. All the little hairs on my body stood to attention, the

278

back of my neck prickling with warning. The sensation was so strong I hardly noticed my mother's sneer at all. Although I couldn't ignore it completely. I mean, it was there. All over her face.

"Hey there, chef," Wyatt's deep voice greeted from behind me.

My body had been keenly aware he was there for a solid twenty seconds now, but the intense warmth in his voice made me jump. I couldn't move right away, paralyzed by the intimate way he said "chef" and the five alarm warning bells clanging through my head. The signal was to run, but I didn't know if it was to run from Wyatt or to him.

"I hope you're enjoying the meal," he said, addressing my parents now.

The nervous feeling zinged through me evolving from hot tension to cold fear. How much had Wyatt heard? Had he caught my mom's tirade? Had he heard about Nolan not wanting to be with me? Oh my God, right now would be such a good time for a cataclysmic earthquake. Or super volcano? Surely there was a hidden super volcano buried directly beneath me.

I swiveled in my seat to stare up at him. He had been waiting for me. His smoldering gaze met mine immediately, the corners of his mouth turning up in that wicked, mischievous way of his. "You didn't have to come all the way out here," I told him.

"I wanted to meet the parents," he said evenly, destroying all of my assumptions about him. Or maybe not all of them, since he had been the one to set up the reservation in the first place, but there was an extra layer to his words that made my heart karate kick my breastbone. "I've heard so much about them after all."

Not wanting to draw this out for longer than I needed to, I jumped to my feet, only tottering a second or two as I adjusted to the height of my stilettos. "I'm going to make you pay for this," I whispered to Wyatt as I settled my hand on his shoulder to catch my balance.

His head dipped so he could whisper, "Promises, promises," against the shell of my ear.

Hiding my shiver, I faced my parents again and waved a hand in Wyatt's direction. "Mom, Dad, this is Wyatt Shaw, executive chef of Lilou." Seeing my mom's still pinched expression, I added, "And my boss," hoping to soften the snarling bitch that had taken possession of her body.

My dad rose immediately to shake his hand. "Pleasure to meet you, chef. Eric Swift."

Wyatt offered a firm handshake I knew my dad would respect and said, "Same to you, sir. Your daughter is a real asset to my staff. I'm afraid I'd be lost without her."

"That's true," I quipped. "He needs me."

His hand settled on my lower back, adding pressure to my already tingling spine. "I do." My breath caught in my throat at the seductive tone to his voice, but he quickly added. "She's the best sous chef in the city. I'm lucky to call her mine."

God, was it me or was Wyatt full of innuendos tonight? Probably just me. Right? One mind-blowing sexual encounter did not a relationship make.

"You're who we have to thank for working our daughter to the bone?" my mom asked, not even pretending to be impressed with Wyatt.

"Yes," I said quickly, trying to diffuse the insult with sarcasm. "Please blame him. He never listens to me when I lodge complaints."

He smiled down at me, taking the bait, but there was something in his eyes that let me know he was only being kind for my sake. There was a gentleness there, meant for me. A sweet question of, "Are you okay?" with a vindictive shark swimming in the background. Wyatt didn't take shit unless it was from Killian or Ezra. He wasn't about to let Dana Swift bust his balls. Even if she was my mom.

"Wyatt, this is my mom, Dana."

280

Wyatt took her hand, but quickly released it, reaching for mine instead. As if we stood like this often. With his hand still on the small of my back, splayed familiarly… possessively and his other hand holding my fingers loosely in his, my body tucked into his like we were a couple. Or two people with zero physical boundaries—the latter probably more accurate.

"Hi, Dana," Wyatt greeted brightly.

She tried to smile, but none of us believed her. "Everything has been delicious so far."

Wyatt looked at me, our eyes connecting in another one of his encouraging glances. You can do this, he seemed to say. You're strong enough for this. And because he believed it, I believed it too. The gaping wound my mom had opened with talk about Nolan and marriage and my priorities began to close, my body ached less, my heart hurt less.

"Thank you," he told her patiently. "You won't eat a better meal in the city."

My mom blinked at him, but his confidence held strong. I also knew he believed what he said. It wasn't bravado for the sake of standing up for me. Lilou was the best. It was worth sacrificing for.

"We see that," my dad said tersely, saving the conversation.

I turned to Wyatt, putting my hand on his chest, realizing too late how comfortable we looked touching each other. His arm that was already resting on my back, slid around and tugged me toward him, settling me against his body and holding me there. I focused on his face, stopping myself from glancing around in a panic. It wasn't only my parents that I was worried about watching us now. His entire staff could see our public display of affection.

There would be no way to stifle the gossip. This was exactly what I didn't want to happen.

And yet… I didn't hate it either. Yes, thinking about my career and the implications this would have on my application for Sarita, I wanted to shrink into a tiny version of myself and race out of here like a cartoon Jerry trying to escape Tom's sinister plans. But, the girl inside of me—the one that controlled my emotions and soul and my broken heart—rested in this touch, this closeness, the way he held me so firmly but so delicately. My heart grew three sizes in his arms, allowing my body to feel comforted and healed and held all at once.

"You should probably get back to the kitchen," I told him, even though all I wanted to do was throw my body around his like a boa constrictor and never let go. "I'm not in there to save your ass tonight."

He smiled down at me, his mouth a sanctuary of affection and his eyes a temple of desire. His expression was nothing short of adoring. God, how had I caught this man's attention?

And how was he still here after everything I put him through? How had he not run away screaming by now? How did he ignore every single word out of my mouth and only pay attention to the signs I was too chicken to say out loud?

"Don't remind me," he groaned. Tipping forward on his toes, he pressed a sweet, slow kiss to my forehead.

I was momentarily blinded by the riot of butterflies inside me. They started low in my belly, but quickly spread to every extremity, making it impossible to think straight or form words or do anything but melt into a sticky, gooey pile of adoration.

Wyatt stepped back and addressed my parents. "Your food should be out in a minute. It was nice to meet, y'all. I'm sure we'll see each other soon." To me, he said, "I'll text you later, yeah?" He started to pull away but didn't. He quickly leaned in and caught my ear with his lips. "By the way, I'm thinking about making this your new dress code. Goddamn, woman, you

282

know how to bring me to my knees." And then he was gone. Back to his lair, while I was left to convince my body it still had bones to hold me up with.

How did he do that? How did he make me feel so completely hot and melty and... soft? I wasn't soft. I was hard, edgy... biting. I was a venomous snake. I was a snarling Pitbull. A barbwire version of what I used to be before unrequited love and devastating heartache had made me completely pull into myself.

Bracing myself for my parent's questions, I collapsed on my chair and turned to face them. They were as flabbergasted as I was. All they could do was blink at me.

Thankfully, our food came out, saving us from trying to speak in full sentences until we'd collected our scattered wits.

Kim went over each dish, reminding us what was in front of us. She took another drink order—I asked Darius to surprise us.

I wasn't entirely sure that alcohol was going to improve the evening, but I was willing to give it a shot. Besides... I still had two days left with my mother. Probably best to soak everything in booze—especially my sharp tongue.

"Wyatt seems nice," my dad said evenly as he cut up his steak.

"Are you dating him?" my mother demanded, her tone shrill and slicing. "Is this what your hang up with work is?"

I took a bite of my handmade tortellini, closing my eyes against the fresh taste of blanched sweet peas and wholesomeness of pasta from scratch. The sauce was perfect tonight, hot and creamy and just a little tart thanks to the sharpness of the aged parmesan. God, I could eat a gallon of this. Carbs and my ass be damned.

"The thing with Wyatt is..." Not real. Too real. So very real. "Early," I cleared my throat. "My hang up with work is that I love it. I love it more than

283

I've loved anything in my life." I pointed my fork at her when she started to protest. "Including Nolan."

"Maybe you should back off for tonight, Dana," my dad tried.

But my mom was a dog with a bone. "You can't hide in a kitchen your whole life, Kaya. Eventually you're going to have to come out. And when you do you're going to find that you're all alone and life has," she made a vanishing gesture with her hands, "passed you by. No man is going to want a shriveled-up spinster, even if she can cook him a good meal."

I slid to the edge of my chair. "Life is not passing me by, Mother," I snapped. "I'm living life. I'm living it to the fullest. I have an amazing job. A job other chefs would literally kill for." I glanced at my dad. "Not literally. But do you know how many other chefs want my job? How many are dying for the day I leave? A ton. So many. And I love my friends. And I love my apartment in the city. And I love my life. I love it. And I have a man. A good man. A smart, creative, super talented man. A man that I love—" the words caught me off guard, sticking in my throat and burning my tongue. I hadn't meant to say that. I hadn't even meant to think it. "To work with," I finished. Calmer, slower, with more intention, I repeated. "A man I love to work with. A man that makes me a better chef. And a better person." I relaxed in my chair, realizing that all these things were true. I not only felt them, I meant them. I didn't have to convince anyone else. I could… rest in their truth. I held my mother's angry gaze, praying she would see the sincerity in mine. "Nolan was never that man for me, Mama. We were kids. And he… he's never grown up. He's still the same kid, still playing the same games, still using the same tricks. But I'm not the same. I have grown up. And my taste has grown up. My qualifications. My preferences. I'm sorry that you think Nolan is this great love of my life, but he's not. And I'm also sorry that you think I need a husband to make my life worth living. Because I don't. I'm

284

happy. Really, truly happy. And I would love it if you would be happy for me."

Both of my parents stared at me, hardly believing the words that had come out of my mouth. For so long I'd been the silent victim to her constant nagging. I'd taken her anger, believing I deserved it, deserved their anger.

I'd felt guilty for running away. I'd felt guilty for leaving Nolan, for leaving Hamilton, for leaving everything behind. And they were so content with their life, so utterly happy with the smallness of it. I couldn't live that way. That life wasn't for me. Those people weren't for me. Nolan wasn't for me.

It had taken almost ten years and an unlikely arrogant chef to help me see it, but I finally felt released from the chains of my childhood.

My mother twisted the napkin in her lap and stared at her untouched pork belly. "Well." She sniffed.

Surprising everyone, my father barked a low, "Enough, Dana. Eat the damn good food and give her a break for once."

I had to shove some tortellini in my mouth to hide my smile. My dad never stood up to my mom. Like ever.

But then again, neither did I.

It might have been my imagination, but our dinner tasted even better after that. The conversation fell to safe topics like my sisters and how good everything was and the genius that was Darius the master barman.

My dad and I even laughed over the different names of dishes as I explained the rest of the menu and how frilly everything sounded. My mom never quite got over her ruffled feathers, but that was okay. I was willing to risk hers if it meant mine could be left alone.

By the time we got home, I was exhausted. All of us were ready for bed. I said goodnight to my parents and headed to my room.

Mindlessly working through my nightly routine, I saved plugging my phone in for last. I knew I'd have a text waiting for me. I had several— precisely what I expected after Wyatt's full on possessively affectionate act tonight.

There were several waiting for me from Dillon and Benny, even Endo had texted a WTF?!?! But it was Wyatt's and only Wyatt's that I was interested in opening. There were four of them, sent throughout the night.

Keep thinking about you and that dress, Kaya. Damn.

Five minutes later he added, **But it's not better than you stripped naked for me. Need to see that again real soon.**

An hour later he sent, **Hope I didn't piss your parents off too badly. To be fair, I was on my best behavior. At least considering the circumstances. Don't remember being that irritated in a long time.**

And then twenty minutes ago. **PS, who the fuck is Nolan?**

I typed back, **He's nobody**. For the first time in too many years, I meant it.

Chapter Eighteen

A week later, I was back at Sarita and felt more at home than ever. Not just in this restaurant, but in my own skin.

After my parents left Monday morning, I'd grabbed some breakfast tacos, headed over to Lilou and enjoyed some one on one time with Wyatt. We'd spread out in his office and laughed over the total headcase that was my mother.

I thought he was going to be as exhausted with her as I always was, but he had been surprisingly endeared. He claimed that he loved to see how much she cared about me, even if it drove me crazy. And knowing his story with his mom, I relaxed. My mom made me see red most days, but Wyatt was right, she loved me more than anything.

He'd asked about Nolan and I had reluctantly shared—not because I was afraid of what he would think or of reopening my old wounds, but because Nolan finally felt like my past. I finally felt like I could let him go and move on. It wasn't even hard for me to admit that Wyatt had played a major role in my new-found freedom. He had helped me see that I was worthy again, that I was desirable. He'd helped me shed the prison of not feeling wanted, not feeling good enough.

And yes, Wyatt's affection and desire helped speed the healing process along. But it was more than that too. It was his respect for me, his utter belief in me. It was the way he lifted me up and chased after me.

I'd let one bad relationship define me for too long. Wyatt had opened my eyes to a whole new way of thinking. Nolan's rejection didn't get to have a hold on me anymore. I truly was the strong, independent, capable woman I had claimed to be for so long. And I might forget that sometimes in the future, but I would make sure Wyatt always reminded me. Or Dillon. Or I would tape sticky notes all over my house that screamed the truth at me. Never again would I let someone else decide my self-worth.

Our conversation had ended with secret kisses and wandering hands. We'd locked ourselves in his office until our coworkers started to show up and we were forced to act professionally again.

We'd been playing the same game all week. And I thought we'd been doing a pretty good job of being discreet until yesterday when Dillon had caught me walking out of Wyatt's office with my chef coat undone and my lacey bra beneath totally disheveled. She'd been texting me nonstop today. I'd been faithfully ignoring her glee.

Vera spun a plate in front of her and nonchalantly mentioned, "Ezra's going to stop by tonight."

I focused on plating scallions atop bite-sized circles of bacon-wrapped scallops. Albeit reluctantly.

This was a dish I would change in a heartbeat. No more bacon wrapping anything. If we were going to add bacon to a plate, it was going to be the feature, damn it. Not the saving grace to an otherwise bland, boring and outdated yawn-fest of a dish. And we wouldn't cut corners by gift wrapping mediocre seafood with overpowering salt parties.

No, the right bacon could stand on its own. And the right scallops should stand on their own. I would take this dish and make it into two. Scallops diced over toasted lavash, with sharp asiago cream sauce sprinkled on top, and a mint, cucumber drizzle finish.

For the bacon dish? A thickly cut piece to feel like steak, crispy on the outside, perfectly done on the inside, served with a tomatillo and jicama chutney and a microgreen salad on top.

The thoughts spiraled through me, anchoring my feet to the ground when all my body wanted to do was float away.

I could do this. I could impress Ezra.

Maybe.

Hopefully.

Okay, at the very least I could manage to get through casually meeting him tonight without un-impressing him. That was my goal—don't un-impress him.

I cleared my throat, hiding the wobble waiting in the wings. "Oh yeah? When do you think that will be?"

She lifted one shoulder in a helpless shrug. "I have no idea. Who knows why or when the man does the things that he does."

I had been in the kitchen all night, working alongside Vera and getting a feel for the Sarita kitchen. Service was so different here. I hadn't expected to feel quite so out of my depth.

Most of the reservations at Lilou were for two-tops, seating two people, and the occasional four-top. Because the reservation list was so many months out, most people only risked including one other person—usually a person they were legally bound to by marriage. Or on a date seriously trying to impress the other party. But at Sarita everything was a massive party. And I didn't mean the vibe of this place. Every table had four plus diners. And they ordered copious amounts of dishes thanks to the way they were served stacked on top of each other.

In Lilou's kitchen, our normal table needed two plates finished at the same time. Here we were talking an average of six to eight plates ready all at once. And twice tonight, we'd had three orders of fifteen plus plates.

I had stopped thinking terrible thoughts about Juan Carlo three hours ago. I'd decided that he was a saint to put up with this for as long as he did. I also understood why this kitchen was messier than I was used to. At the speed people moved around this kitchen, it was no wonder it had been total chaos. These people didn't just cook, they flew.

Vera paused over the dish she was finishing in tandem with mine and smiled at me. "Don't be nervous," she encouraged. "You're fabulous."

I was sweaty. And maybe smelly. Like, I said, tonight had been a doozy. But to Vera, I said, "Thanks. And thanks for doing this with me. Even if I don't get the job, this has been a great experience."

Her smile widened with genuine kindness. "First of all, if you don't get this job, Ezra is bananas. Because you're amazing. And second, there are plenty of other positions around the city that you would be great for. This isn't your only shot." She leaned in. "For instance, I know of a great little up and coming restaurant that could use good staff."

I laughed. "Is it that new place called Pepper?"

She frowned immediately. "Don't joke. That's literally my biggest fear. Killian wants to name the baby Pepper. He's all, get it? And I'm like, OMG, stop."

"The baby?"

Her eyes widened until they were the size of the moon. "Oh my God. I didn't mean to say that!" Her head whipped right and left checking out who had overheard. Satisfied that her words had been lost in the clatter of dinner service, she leaned in and begged, "Please don't say anything to anyone, Kaya! We're keeping it a secret for a while longer. We haven't even told our families and they will be pissed if they're the last ones to find out."

"I'm so happy for you," I told her, my smile so big it hurt my cheeks. "I won't say anything. But I am so, so happy for you!"

Her cheeks turned pink, but the panicked look on her face softened. "Thank you. It's super early. I mean, I haven't even been to the doctor yet. I've only peed on a stick. And puked my guts out for the last two weeks. All signs point to baby." She smiled down at her nonexistent tummy. "But I'll feel better after my first checkup."

"Gah!" I squealed again. "This is so exciting!"

She laughed. "And also, maybe the worst timing ever with Salt opening in two months and the wedding coming up. But at least I won't be showing too badly for our wedding. I would die if I had to take my dress back. It's too pretty to part with."

My shoulders sagged, and an ache spread over my chest. "Listen to you, Vera. Has your life ever been this perfect? You literally have everything going for you right now."

She shook her head. "I don't know about that."

I held up a hand and ticked off reasons why she was my superhero. "You're engaged to one of the hottest chefs in the country. And he's good-looking." I winked at her to be cute. "You're also having his baby. And

291

getting married. Oh, and you're opening your dream restaurant. I mean, seriously, you are the definition of happily ever after."

"Hey, happily ever after is a lot of work." She frowned again. "It's also been covered in puke lately."

I laughed with her, but I couldn't help but feel jealous. And something worse. Something like despair. Standing next to Vera, I felt wholly unqualified to work in this kitchen or in this industry or even as a basic human. She was a true superstar. She had this amazing fiancé and an incredible business that was bound to take off with the two of them involved.

And she was going to have Killian Quinn's child. I mean, could you imagine the palate on that baby? It was bound to come out of the womb wielding a sauté pan.

She nudged me with her shoulder as she finished the final touches to the plate in front of me and handed it off to the server. "Seriously, Kaya, you're sweet, but there is nothing to be jealous of. You'll get your version of happily ever after too. It won't look exactly like mine, but it shouldn't. You deserve your special thing and for it to be tailored to you." She smiled gently. "And you'll find it too. Whoever it's with... whichever restaurant you work in... whatever you end up doing... it will work out. It's probably going to be completely different than anything you thought you were going to do or be or marry. Life has a way of taking all of our expectations, flipping them on their heads, and then laughing at us while we flounder around in search of which piece goes where."

"That's..." I cleared my throat, searching for something polite to say. I didn't find anything. "Interesting."

Her head tipped back, and she laughed harder. "That was supposed to encourage you."

"Oh, it did," I deadpanned. "I can't wait for my life to be so totally different than what I actually wanted. That sounds awesome."

She grinned again and accepted new plates getting ready to leave the kitchen. "I didn't want to marry a chef," she confessed. "I was in a terrible relationship during school and after. He was a chef. And he abused me."

I sucked in an audible breath. How did I respond to that? How was a person supposed to react? What was the social code? Who the hell cares about the social code?

"Oh my God, Vera." I swallowed down the quick rage against any monster that would put his hands on a girl, but especially Vera—who was kind, and so generous, and one of the most kickass chefs I'd ever met.

She waved a hand in the air, swatting away the past. "It's over now." Her gaze grew distant and her shoulders jerked with a shiver. "Thank God, it's over." She faced me again, clear-eyed and somber. "What I'm trying to say is this. After Derrek, I was convinced I would never be able to cook in a commercial kitchen ever again. I never ever thought I'd date again, but if I did, I knew it wouldn't be a chef. Never, ever again."

"Derrek is a chef?" I asked quietly, unable to quell my curiosity.

She lifted one shoulder and rubbed her chin on it. "Derrek Hanover."

Holy shit! He was a decently big deal in North Carolina. He didn't have the national acclaim that Killian did. I'd never been impressed enough to find out more than he owned a mildly popular, newly opened restaurant.

"Vera, I'm so sorry," I told her.

"He was the worst," Vera whispered. "After we, er I, ended things, I gave up on my dream of working in a restaurant completely. But then I opened Foodie, my consolation prize, and I met Killian. Now here we are, opening a restaurant together. And I never thought…" She paused, looking down at the counter and hiding the emotion in her eyes from me. "I never had a clue a relationship could be this good. Or that a man could be this amazing. Or that it was possible to have all the things that I wanted so badly, but for them to look so different. I would never relive those years of abuse or giving up on

293

my dreams. But they led me here, to this place, and it's so beautiful and so fulfilling that I don't know that I'd totally give them up either."

Now my eyes were watery with unshed tears. "You have a powerful story, friend."

She only shrugged. "It didn't feel powerful while I was going through it."

I put my hand on her shoulder and squeezed. "You're amazing, Vera. You're the strongest woman I've ever met."

She laughed and held up her scrawny bicep. "I mean, check out these guns, right?"

I laughed with her. "That is not at all what I meant, and you know it!"

She pulled up the next plate and smiled at me. "I know. But I didn't share that for you to think I'm amazing. I'm the idiot that got involved with the psycho to begin with. I'm only trying to say that no matter where you're at right now, you have the potential and the grit to do what you want to do, Kaya. It's up to you. Whatever it is you want, you have to go hard after it and trust in the journey."

Her words hit a chord inside of me, plucking the taut string with deft fingers and sending the reverberation of sound echoing through my body. She was right. I just needed to trust in the journey.

Weirdly, I wasn't even thinking about Sarita in that moment. I was thinking about Wyatt. And the fear and panic that had crippled progress with him.

"You got out," I told Vera, deciding she needed to hear truth too. "That doesn't make you an idiot. That makes you amazing."

She rolled her eyes. "You have no idea how long it took me though. And I—"

"Stop." It was an order and a plea. "Vera, seriously, stop. Stop downplaying what you did. You got out. You're a hero because you got out."

294

"Thank you," she whispered sincerely. "I need to remember that. Sometimes I feel amazing, like he can't touch me ever again. And sometimes I feel like a weak, spineless girl that let herself be abused. But I'm neither. I'm somewhere in the middle. I'm healing. I might always be healing. You're right though. And Killian reminds me all the time. He's the villain, but I'm not the victim. I'm the hero."

Smiling at her, I blinked away tears and focused on the plates again. "I love being right."

We were laughing again when the kitchen door whooshed open in a dramatic, slow motion sequence. The dramatic, slow motion sequence might have been in my head.

Regardless, Ezra entered this sacred space and nearly all motion ground to a halt for a solid five seconds before jump-starting again with new vigor. The boss was here and everybody in the kitchen felt the pressure. It wouldn't have surprised me if the diners suddenly started eating with more gusto and better manners too.

I swallowed down the gurgling nerves that wouldn't settle no matter how many rational whispers of affirmation I told myself.

This isn't the interview. If this doesn't work out, there will be other opportunities.

Ezra's not as scary as you think he is. Molly likes him, and Molly is a totally rational, normal, chicken just like you! If she can handle him, you can handle him.

He surveyed his kitchen as I imagined a general inspected his troops before battle. His shrewd eyes bounced from one person to the next, to the equipment and the food leaving the kitchen. He saw everything at once and had already passed his judgment. For better or worse, we were what he had to work with. It was impossible to tell if that pleased him or infuriated him.

A few staff members waved or said hello, but he merely nodded in return. For a man recently engaged, he wasn't exactly the shade of matrimonial bliss.

"Hey, Ezra," Vera greeted sweetly as she passed another stack of tapas to a waiting server. "Long time no see." Her gaze swiveled back to mine and she explained, "Killian and I met them for a celebratory lunch today."

He rubbed his red eyes. "We drank too much."

Vera smiled. "You drank too much. I had to work."

He blinked at her. "Yeah, I thought Killian was going to be here."

"Killian is working at our restaurant." She paused, and I thought she might have been waiting for that to register with him, but he didn't comment. "Anyway," she went on, "I'm doing you this huge favor tonight so Kaya can work alongside me."

Ezra's attention moved to me as if noticing me in Sarita's kitchen for the first time. "You don't belong here."

It wasn't a harsh statement, more like a neutral observation. He wasn't accusing me of anything, only sliding the missing puzzle piece into place.

I didn't know what to say though. Apparently, he was drunk or maybe just tipsy or on the other side of either heading toward hungover. However, all of those scenarios were less than ideal because he seemed cranky.

Pitching myself to the regular version of Ezra, who was terse, demanding, and obstinate in general, was hard enough. But having to convince him I was right for this restaurant was an entirely different beast of impossible.

Straightening my spine and steeling my courage, I lifted my chin and said, "I beg to differ."

"What does that mean?" Ezra asked through a yawn while he rubbed his eyes again.

"I think I could belong here," I ventured, swallowing the wobble in my voice. "If you let me try. I think I could be your executive."

296

He focused on me fully while Vera moved down the stainless-steel island to give us space. "You want to be Sarita's chef?" He rested his body weight on his hands. "Kaya, you want to leave Lilou for Sarita?"

Isn't that what you did? was on the tip of my tongue, but I decided making jokes at the expense of his dating life probably wasn't the best way to land my dream job.

"Yes," I told him, feeling the truth of that one simple word down to the bottom of my soul. "I want her, Ezra. I think I was made for her."

His eyes narrowed thoughtfully. "Will that put Wyatt out?"

I shrugged, knowing I should be more professional, but now that the truth of what I wanted was out there, I couldn't play coy. "He has other options. This is a once in a lifetime chance for me. I want to at least try."

"I have several people interested in the job. You're going to have to apply like everybody else."

"That's okay," I told him honestly. "I'd love the chance to show you that I'm the best."

He smiled at my sassy reply.

I held my game face in place even though the words were more bravado than anything else. My knees were currently trembling, and my nauseous scale was tipping towards violent. "I also have good references." I inclined my head toward Vera.

He made a sound in the back of his throat. "References that are highly motivated to get out of doing the job themselves."

Vera's hands slammed playfully on the stainless steel. "Because we have our own damn kitchen to run."

He smiled at me, ignoring Vera. "I see my ploy to hire them back isn't working out like I'd planned."

"Ezra!" Vera gasped.

I laughed because I could only hope that was a joke. If it was true, I was in trouble. There was no way I could compete against Killian. Not because he was such a superior chef. I mean, there were plenty of those out there. But because Killian owned the real estate on all of Ezra's kindness. I supposed Molly got a portion too.

Ezra wrapped his knuckles on the counter. "Okay, Kaya. One shot. Make me a meal that will change my life. I want three courses and a dessert in the style of Sarita. So at least ten plates, but I'll accept up to sixteen. The best you've got. I'll also need a resume, references, and a letter of recommendation from Killian and Wyatt. I know you've been Wyatt's sous chef for less than a year, but that should have been enough time for him to know your style and if you'll fit in over here."

I'd pulled out my phone to quickly take notes on everything he said. "When?" I asked, feeling breathless and weightless and scared shitless.

His head bobbled back and forth as he decided. "You can have one week. Next Monday, Sarita is closed over lunch. Is that enough time?"

"Yes." *No.* "I can't wait." *Oh my God!* "This will be so much fun." *I'm going to die.*

His smile was knowing, making it—and him—evil as he turned and walked away.

He knew Monday wasn't enough time to put together the ten to sixteen course meal that would change his life and make him hire me at Sarita. It was nowhere near enough time, but that was probably his design. I couldn't help but think back to my conversation with Dillon, praying and hoping she was right, that he wasn't sexist, that he wanted to hire Vera.

Because if Vera had a shot, then so did I.

Hopefully.

Maybe.

We'd soon find out.

I turned to Vera and gave her a shaky smile.

"Oh, my god!" she squealed before I could talk. "That was amazing!"

"I think I'm going to puke."

She put her hands on my shoulders and shook my body roughly, apparently not caring about my puke warning. "You're going to rock the shit out of this interview!"

"I think I should sit down."

"Do you know how he, like, never does that? Like ever? I've never seen him take an interview like that. Never. I mean, last I knew, he was planning on hiring headhunters to look for the replacement. I know there are people interested in the job, but he's very particular this time around."

"Are you trying to make me feel better?" I shook my head rapidly. "You're not making me feel better."

Her smile stretched. "You've got so much work to do."

"I feel like you're enjoying this."

She laughed, the sadistic little nymph. "So much. This is so entertaining to me."

"I hate you."

She laughed harder, but it quickly died. "What about Wyatt? Have you told him you were trying for this job? Do you think he'll write you a letter of recommendation? Or sabotage you to get you to stay?"

Covering my face with my hands, I groaned. "Oh my God. Wyatt. He doesn't know anything. He's going to freak out."

Her lips pressed together in a frown. "What do you think he's going to say?"

I thought about how sweet he'd been lately. How kind. I thought about his dinner reservation for my parents. I thought about the way he'd been relentlessly pursuing me. His smiles. His kisses. His mouth on me in my most intimate of places.

And then I thought about how much he relied on me. Needed me in the kitchen. Begged for me not to leave him…

My answer was obvious. "I have absolutely no clue."

Chapter Nineteen

Can we talk outside of Lilou?

It had been a simple enough text on my part. Straightforward. To the point. Without innuendo.

As in a date? Had been his stellar reply. **Breakfast tomorrow? Benny said he'd cover deliveries.**

He already had substitutes in place?

When I hesitated to reply, he sent another one. **Come on, Swift. Play hooky with me… Promise we'll have fun.**

I had tried not to smile as I paced my apartment Sunday night and contemplated how to answer him. God, I was smitten with Wyatt.

Completely head over heels. Maybe it had always been simmering underneath the surface. The way he would tease me. The way I would challenge him. How I always felt his eyes on me. How I always knew where he was. But, God, I was so stubborn. So obnoxiously pigheaded. I don't think I would have done anything with my crush had Wyatt not kicked down my walls of resistance for me.

And it was embarrassing to think about it now, how messed up one relationship had made me. It was so long ago and yet I was still carrying around the fear that I wouldn't be good enough. That there was something in me that would inevitably push Wyatt away.

Ridiculous, right?

The fear was still there though. Still burbling inside me like an accidental nuclear waste spill. I wanted to get rid of it so badly. I wanted to cleanse my body of the toxins. But even if I did the hard work and cleaned it up, there would always be trace particles lingering in the air, hiding in buried places within me, leaking forever into my confidence and self-esteem.

I was tired of the way my personality split in two, this frustrating dichotomy always at war within me. I could protect my heart and be open to new relationships. I could also hide and shrink away, terrified of change. I could be kind and considerate and also guarded and careful. I could snarl, act a raging bitch, but still remain loyal to my friends and generous whenever I wanted to be.

Maybe it wasn't only me. Maybe all humans had these battling personality traits. Endless characteristics that didn't always match up, but always made sense in light of who we were.

We were complicated and intricate, made up of a billion different experiences that have shaped and molded us to who we are. For better or worse.

That was how I felt now. Both better and worse. Both completely confident in my skills in the kitchen and terrified that I wouldn't be enough for Ezra, or that his taste would be outside the realm I could cook in.

I one hundred percent loved my parents. I was grateful for all that they had done for me and the way they tried to support me and loved me, even though I wasn't living the life they wanted me to be living. I was also totally frustrated with them and felt as though I'd earned some distance. Mostly from my mom.

And more importantly, I was falling for Wyatt. Hard and fast and irrevocably. And here I was, still trying to protect my stupid heart, still trying to quickly build defenses from the rubble inside me that could save me from the inevitable heartbreak.

I didn't want to find out I wasn't good enough for Wyatt.

I didn't want for things to fall apart if I left Lilou because we wouldn't see each other all the time and there wasn't enough substance there to keep us together.

I didn't want Wyatt to give up on us because I wasn't worth pursuing.

I'd already had that relationship. And it had killed me. Damaged me. Left me as this skeptical, paranoid person that couldn't even try at relationships anymore. I couldn't go through that again.

But a date couldn't hurt, right?

My heart thumped twice. Yes. Do it.

My brain gave a weak, common sense protest, but my fingers were already typing. **How early do I have to get up?**

I swear I could feel his smile all the way through the phone. **Eight-thirty. It's worth it. I know the best little place.**

Not even his early choice for breakfast could turn me off to the idea. Still I couldn't help but give him a hard time. It was too ingrained in me. Besides, I knew he liked it. **Okay, fine. I'll meet you there. Where is it?**

Been waiting to do this for a long time, Kaya. I'm glad you said yes.

My heart had exploded with butterflies. I'd collapsed on my couch in a fit of old-fashioned heart palpitations.

But now as I pulled up to the address he gave me, I was second guessing my choice. This wasn't a restaurant, but a house. Possibly the scene of a murder. Or my future murder. Not that the house was scary. It was the opposite.

The perfect square of a ranch had a detached garage, the door opened to show off a big, black muscle car with the hood popped open and tools laid neatly in rows on one of those manly workbench things. He drove an Acura to work and I didn't know anything about it other than it was fast. This one seemed to be along the same vein.

The Acura was parked in the second bay. Leading me to believe that this was not only Wyatt's house, but he had a thing for fast cars.

I tried to pass a snotty little judgment on him, as was my way. But I couldn't come up with anything. It wasn't stupid that Wyatt liked fast cars. It somehow fit perfectly in line with his personality. It wasn't such a surprise to find that out as it was an obvious addition to all of the facts and truths I already knew about him.

Filing it away, I tried to talk myself out of imagining him driving the sleek muscle car with the white racing stripe down the center. But it was too late. I'd already imagined him. And I already found it unbearably sexy.

There was that.

The house itself was completely isolated and perched on a bluff. Tall, towering trees surrounded the property and left little grass to be found. Instead, pine needles lay in a blanket of brown, only interrupted by the occasional bush or shrub.

A cozy wraparound porch made the walk up to the front door especially inviting. I could tell immediately that Wyatt took pride in his home. The

304

walkway and porch were both swept of the relentless pine needles. The shutters looked nice framing the large windows. And there was even a porch swing hanging from the ceiling.

Either he was going to murder me all the way out here or charm the pants right off me.

The navy-blue door was opened, but I still knocked as I stepped inside his domain. I paused in the doorway, inhaling the scent of him in his house, and checking out the spacious layout.

There wasn't an abundance of decorations or anything hanging on the walls, but his furniture was rich, chocolate leather and he'd filled in all the right spaces so it didn't look as though there was anything missing.

His lamps, coffee table, and dining room setup were all a mixture of modern and mountain. It shouldn't have gone together, but because it was Wyatt, it did. His aesthetic wasn't accidental. This was his taste. This was him laid out before me in such a way that I felt like I was turning the pages to his autobiography.

He poked his head out of a room I could see was the kitchen, a smile already on his face. "Hey."

I suppressed a smile and shook my head at him. "I hope you got reservations. This place looks packed."

His smile stretched. "Don't worry, I know the owner," he assured me. He disappeared again, and I took that as my cue to join him.

Toeing off my shoes, I dropped my purse by the front door and closed it behind me. I walked around the corner and joined Wyatt in his real-life kitchen.

It wasn't terribly different from Lilou. His appliances were all stainless steel and nearly as big as what we kept at the restaurant. His gas stovetop was gigantic and the copper hood over the top was one of the few bright spots of color in the whole space. But somehow it worked.

305

Again, there was that strange mix of modern and mountain, but everything that was modern was state of the art, and everything that was mountain cabin felt cozy and warm.

"You know you should warn a girl before you invite her over to your super secluded cabin," I said as I sidled up across the island from him while he chopped green onions and cooked bacon. "So, she doesn't assume you're luring her to the middle of nowhere because you're secretly a serial killer."

He looked up at me and winked. "I didn't want you to have the opportunity to decline."

My gaze strayed to his tattoos, the bird on his neck, delicate and dainty compared to the hard, masculine design of him. I swallowed so loudly I was positive he could hear me.

"That's exactly what a serial killer would say."

He laughed and shook his head. "This once, try not to think the absolute worst of me."

I stuck out my lower lip and explained, "But I've been doing it for so long. It's like an irreversible habit now."

His smile warmed. "I have faith you can manage. We're way past fighting now, Swift. We've finally gotten to the good stuff."

My eyebrow raised without my permission and my mouth blurted the dumbest question. "The good stuff?"

He set his knife down and leaned into me. "This, Kaya. You and me. What's happening between us. This is the good stuff."

I struggled to swallow again. How could he be this sweet? And this hot? And this totally, one hundred percent amazing person. Even though I would deny all of this if asked in public.

He waggled his finger back and forth between us. "You don't realize it yet. But I'm telling you, woman, this is where it's at."

"I believe you," I said quickly. "I do know this is good." And I did. It didn't only feel good in the carnal, greedy sense of the word. Although there was that. There was my lust and desire for him to touch and kiss me again, and do wicked, depraved things to my body again. And there was the infatuated good too. The kind that made all of my thoughts revolve around him, and my fingers itch to check my phone constantly to see if he texted, and my heartbeat speed up whenever he was around.

But then there was the deeper level of good. The wholeness of this, the healing in him. There was a lightness to this attraction that I'd never experienced before. My feelings for Wyatt didn't feel heavy or weighted with impossible expectations. They were honest and genuine, fun and flirty, real and exciting. But most of all they weren't holding me back. They weren't... holding me under them.

His grin stretched across his face and my lungs forgot how to do their job. My heart also decided to throw its hands in the air and quit. I mean, honestly, how was I supposed to function when he looked like that? It wasn't fair. And probably the reason he was so much further along in his career than me.

For real, if I could smile like that I would probably have my own Food Network show by now.

"Yeah?" he asked me. The insecurity in his voice was like two defibrillation paddles to my chest. All at once everything inside me kicked into high gear via his electric current.

"Yes, Wyatt. You're the good stuff."

"Mmm," he hummed. "I like to hear that."

Rolling my eyes in a last-ditch effort to hold onto my heart, I changed the subject. "Okay, since you didn't bring me out here to kill me, what can I help with?"

He focused on cracking eggs into a mixing bowl. "Uh-uh. I'm cooking for you this morning, Ky. Sit down. Relax. But don't try to lift a finger."

Hiding my smile, I took a seat at one of the square-style wooden stools tucked into his island. "Gosh, you're so bossy."

He looked up at me from beneath thick lashes, his eyes turning stormy and electric. "Only because you like it that way."

I sucked in my lip ring and let him see what I thought. My gaze heated, my cheeks flushed, my entire body screamed yes please! I took a breath and asked, "What's on the menu, chef?"

Using his knife as a second hand, he picked up the green onions and bacon and tossed them into whisked eggs and then added sautéed spinach, mushrooms and peppers. "Quiche."

His answer surprised me for some reason. It was so… simple. "How French of you."

He added handfuls of cheese and milk to his mixture and laughed. "Shocking, I know." Pulling out a pie crust that I had a feeling he hand rolled himself, he added. "It's worth it. I promise."

I couldn't help but ask, "Do you make quiche often?"

He shrugged. "I don't make an entire one for myself, if that's what you're asking. But if the opportunity arises, I like to. It's one of the first things I ever learned to make well. One of those dishes that kickstarted the whole love of cooking for me. You know, beyond my obnoxious need to keep up with Killian and Ezra."

"My kickstart dish was a good roulade." I confessed. "We learned how to make them in high school Home Ec and mine was exceptional. Ever since then, I always feel like a superstar when I pull off a good one."

"That's exactly it." Adding more cheese to the top for good measure, he slid his secret signature dish into the oven and set the timer. "I'm not going to lie, I've been playing around with the idea of bringing one into the Lilou menu."

"What's stopping you?"

308

He splayed his hands across the island and leaned toward me, giving me his full, heart-stopping focus. "Because I know it would be totally gratuitous. It wouldn't add anything to that menu other than I would have added something personally nostalgic there."

"Isn't that your right?" I asked him, leaning closer to meet him halfway. "If you've earned executive, haven't you also earned the right to put your adorably nostalgic dishes on there too?"

Some of the light dimmed from his eyes. "That's the thing about the executive chef, it's all an illusion. You assume there will be all this freedom and control. But the truth is, you're a slave to the restaurant and what the restaurant wants. It's an almost impossible question to answer by the way, because the restaurant is fickle and picky. There's an owner to answer to and the limitations of your staff. Not far behind are the thousand opinionated diners and reviewers and critics." He dropped his head, hiding his expression from me. "It's going to suck out my soul before I ever figure out how to please the greedy bitch."

A sharp pain cut across my chest and it had nothing to do with me or my ambitions. I ached for Wyatt, for the struggle to make his place in this industry. For the pressure he felt and the constant fear of disappointment he had hanging over his head. "Is that why you took out your piercings?"

He nodded, still looking at the counter. "Yeah. I'm trying to be, uh, more professional. Besides, it was time. I'm thirty-one now. I should probably take life seriously. Not just this damn job."

I smiled at his levity. "I liked them."

His head lifted slowly, his eyes sparking with challenge. "And now you find me hideous?"

Laughing because I couldn't help it, I shook my head slowly. "Completely. I can barely look at you."

"Liar."

My breath caught in my throat, trapped there by the butterflies swarming through my body like it was migration season. The look on his face was so adoring, so completely enraptured. He stared at me like I had always yearned for, like I was his sun and moon and morning star. God, it did things to my insides. It turned my hard edges soft and squishy. It melted my frozen heart and razed my impenetrable walls.

"Prove it," I dared him.

He stalked his way around the island, his strides long and sure. I swiveled in my chair to keep him in my line of sight. Nerves fluttered inside me, dancing like windchimes in the breeze. God, this man. He did something to me. Without consciously deciding to, he made my nerve endings buzz and my blood rush through my veins.

My entire body came to attention under his dominating gaze. Like a sunflower reaching its face for the light, I stretched and preened and leaned toward him whenever he was around. I used to assume that was because he was my boss, and before that, my superior. I wanted to impress him. I wanted him to notice me. Now I realized it was more than that. Since I'd met Wyatt, he'd pulled me toward him. I had always reached for him. I had always wanted him. And now, I was finally going to get him.

"Challenge accepted, Swift." His arms caged around me. His words were a rumble in his chest, a sweet temptation and wicked threat.

His mouth descended on mine like a gasp of breath. We connected in an open-mouthed kiss, our tongues tangling as our hands grappled to get to each other.

My legs opened in an invitation, one that he gladly stepped into. His hands landed on my cheeks, while mine curled into his t-shirt, tugging him closer.

I loved the taste of him, and the way he kissed around my lip ring and then scraped it with his teeth just when I'd forgotten about it. I loved that his tongue dominated mine, leading the kiss in every way. I loved that his hands held me in a way that made me feel cherished and adored, but his mouth was anything but soft. Greedy, hungry, all-consuming, he kissed with fire and passion—the same way he cooked.

Our mouths separated so we could explore the rest of each other's skin. He kissed my jawline and toward my ear. I nibbled his earlobe between my teeth and pressed a kiss to his temple. My hand slid beneath his shirt and when I touched his bare skin, he shivered.

"Fuck, Kaya," he mumbled in my ear. "It's been too long since I've touched you."

I laughed against his skin, loving the feel of his stubbled jaw against my lips. "Not that long."

"Any amount of time is too long with you," he countered, always arguing, always needing to be right. And I loved that about him because I was the same way.

He kissed up the column of my throat, forcing my head back. His teeth grazed against the underside of my jaw. I gasped when his hand palmed my breast, his thumb brushing over my nipple, making it peak, bringing it to life like every other part of my body.

"I want you all the time," he murmured. "I can't stop thinking about you. I can't stop wanting you." His head lifted so he could meet my gaze and drown me in desire and feeling and him. "You're my weakness. I see you across the kitchen and I crumble. I lose my train of thought and I forget what I'm in the middle of doing. I see you and there is only you. You're going to get me fired."

My lips lifted in a love-drunken smile. "Then I could have your job."

He stole the desire straight from my lips by kissing me to oblivion. His fingers tugged at the thin straps of my flowy, floral maxi dress. "Why am I not surprised this is your play?" He laughed against my skin, his scruff tickling my throat. "But the joke's on you. If you would have dangled sex in front of me months ago, I would have gladly handed it over to you."

I pulled my arms free from my dress and it slinked to my waist. He didn't bother to wait for me to acclimate, his hands moved to the back of my strapless bra and deftly flicked it open. I tugged at his shirt, not wanting to be the only one topless.

"Now who's the liar?" I asked, totally breathless.

Forcing my eyes to stay open, I took in the sight of him and all his glorious tattoos in the natural sunlight from his big kitchen windows. God, he was breathtaking.

I traced my fingers over the very realistic eye drawn over his right pec, a single tear welling up in the corner of it. On the other side, an anatomical heart had been reimagined with fissures snaking out in every direction. It looked so real, except it was shattering, breaking apart into little, destroyed pieces of itself. The words forgive, focus, and fear made a triangle beneath his ribs. And all of it was connected by intricate designs and meaningful swirls.

My fingers traced over the word triangle curiously. "What does this mean?"

"My mom," he rasped, his eyes intently watching my fingers move over him. "It's a reminder to forgive the people that have hurt me, focus on the things I want most and rise above the fear."

I made a sound in the back of my throat, feeling oddly convicted by the words he chose to live by. I could learn a thing or two from them.

"And the bird?" I asked, trailing my fingers to his neck.

"More of my mom. It's like a memorial to her."

My throat dried out until it was sandpaper and gravel. "You were close to her?"

312

He jerked his chin once and it seemed like the one simple movement took everything out of him. "She had her demons, but she loved me. She wanted to take care of me, she just… couldn't."

Tears wet my eyes. I laid my hand over the broken heart on his chest, knowing without a shadow of a doubt that it symbolized the real one hidden beneath skin, muscle, and bone. My voice was a strained whisper, grating against the rocks in my mouth. "I'm so sorry, Wyatt." The words were so inadequate, so completely wrong. I was sorry, yes. But I was more than that too. I was devastated and grief-filled and angry on his behalf. I wanted to take him back in time and shake his mom until she got it together, until she saw how fucking precious her son was and how desperately he needed her to take care of him.

"I'm okay," he told me. And I believed him. "It was a long time ago. But I… I don't think I'll ever stop missing her." He blinked against glassy eyes. He pointed to the toque next, the giant chef's hat tattooed on his side. "I got this the week Killian left Lilou. It was my promotion present to myself."

And just like that we'd moved on so effortlessly. His eyes cleared, and his voice steadied. He'd slid back into his comfortable skin. His hands caressed up my sides and settled on my back, bringing us closer together.

"That doesn't surprise me." I leaned to the side, to get a good look at it. "I'm surprised there isn't an 'I Hate Kaya' tattoo somewhere on you." I checked around the other half of him. "Or something like 'Sous Chef Must Die'…anywhere?"

He shrugged, nipping at my collarbone with his teeth. "Again, I feel as though you're missing how much I rely on you. How I've always relied on you." His head lifted, and our gazes slammed into each other in a head-on collision that would shut down an interstate for hours from the force of the impact. "How much I've always liked you."

My belly flipped. "Lies," I accused.

Shaking his head slowly, he pressed a sweet kiss to my lips. "Day one, Kaya. You walked into the kitchen—all cotton candy blue hair and sharp teeth—and I lost my fucking head. I had never seen someone so cutthroat and sexy all at once. I burned everything I touched that night because I couldn't concentrate on anything but you."

I remembered that night. I had been a ball of nerves, ready to puke at any second, but my own screwups had been ignored because Wyatt's mistakes were way worse. Killian had chewed his ass all night.

"You've never said anything until now." My words were a whisper of disbelief. I thought about all the times I'd been mean to him, snapped at him, challenged him unreasonably. God, I'd been a vindictive bitch all these years.

I thought about our texting through the years. And our recent make outs. I thought about the way I let him win sometimes. How I'd practically killed myself working so he could transition to EC easier.

Okay, maybe I hadn't been horrible the whole time.

"You had a boyfriend," he reminded me. "Or I had a girlfriend. Or God, you were sleeping with fucking Charlie." His face wrinkled with disgust. "The timing has always been off for us."

It still was. He didn't want to admit it but working together and sleeping together was a bad idea. And then there was Sarita… This was what I would call a pickle.

And he was right. For all these years, we had missed each other. Now, at least we were both single. And what we had was too good to let go. I needed to explore it. Explore him.

"The timing isn't exactly awesome now…"

His biceps flexed around me and his jaw ticked in that way I liked so much. "You think I'm going to let working together stop this?" He shook his head, determined. "Kaya, finally." His breath snuck out of him in this

314

relaxed, delicious way that forced my body to react. I felt him in my bones, down to my toes and the places beyond my physical body. He was settling into something permanent with me and I was helpless to stop him. "Fucking finally." He grabbed the sides of my head and tilted it back, forcing me to meet his intense, consuming gaze. "This is real, yeah? This is fucking deep. And if you're in, then let's fight for this. Work, our friends, your parents, whatever is out there that wants to get in our way is just noise. We decide what we do, what we want. We decide how hard we want to work for this and when we want to walk away."

After all these years, I had to admit that I wanted this as badly as he did. Maybe I'd wanted it as long as he had too.

"Do you think you will?" I cleared my throat, old fears and insecurities resurfacing. "I mean, walk away?"

His smile reappeared, lifting the corners of his mouth slowly, in that way I loved so much. "Kaya, I've been trying to walk into this relationship for five years. The plan is to figure out how to get you to stay forever."

"Forever?" The word rushed out of me in a whoosh of disbelief.

The look on his face devastated me, tore apart my heart and stomped on my soul and then somehow pieced it all back together again. His brown eyes twinkled, and his smile brightened and everything about him radiated permanency and hope.

"You're such a chicken," he taunted. "I've known you for all these years and I can't believe I'm only just now realizing that you're one huge chicken."

I sat up, pushing my body into his, closing what little space remained between us. "I am not," I argued, lit up by his challenge. "I just think you're moving too fast."

"Yeah, of course you do. Because you're chicken."

315

Grabbing his nipple, I twisted quickly, causing him to jump back and fend me off. "Now you're violent! I'm rethinking this entire relationship."

I ignored the way my heart kicked at the word relationship and my stomach flipped with fear. I couldn't let him be right about me. I couldn't run from this good, beautiful, honest thing between us because I'd been hurt in my past.

"Now who's chicken?" I taunted, reaching for his other nipple. He laughed at my efforts. "I'm in it, Shaw. You want long term. You got it. I can out-relationship you any day of the week."

He shook his head at the tug-of-war that never ended between us. "Good." He held out his hand and I took it, thinking he was going to be sweet and gentle. But then he grabbed my wrist, playfully yanked me out of my seat and tossed me over his shoulder.

I screamed in surprise. "Put me down!"

"I intend to," he promised darkly.

"Where are we going?" I demanded as he ran through his house bouncing me on his shoulder the entire way. The top of my dress was hanging down but did little to cover my breasts. I grabbed the back of his jeans and pressed my upper body to him, holding on for dear life.

We burst through a door and from my upside-down position, I realized it was his bedroom. Hunter green shades hung over a giant picture window that looked out past a deck to a glorious view of the bluffs. His furniture was all rich browns and soft tans, mingling together to make a masculine but tasteful space.

He tossed me on his bed and I witnessed his huge, sleigh bed first hand. King size. Could he be more perfect?

He hovered over me. "You're in this, Kaya? No prisoners?"

I smiled up at him. Wondering if he treasured my smiles as much as I cherished his. "No prisoners, Wyatt. You and me. For better or worse or whatever. It's you and me."

And there it was. His smile to end all smiles before it. He leaned over me and I scooted back. He followed quickly, our bodies parallel but not yet touching.

"I've been waiting so long to hear you say that."

"I've been wanting to say it." And I realized I had.

"I've been waiting for this too." His eyes darkened.

"For what?"

"To have you, Kaya. To have all of you."

Chapter Twenty

His hands moved up my thighs, dragging over my legs. His thumbs brushed over my sex and I shivered in anticipation for what was to come.

"Finally," I rasped.

His eyes flashed with lightning. "You've wanted me too?"

I nodded while my belly pooled with heat. There was something so indescribably sexy about Wyatt hovering over me. His skin was so perfectly decorated in colored ink, his cut biceps on full display as he supported his weight.

Everything about him interested me. He was breathtaking and overwhelming and mine.

My body jerked at the word in my head. Mine. He was mine. And I was his. Even before we stripped naked and learned every inch of each other's bodies, he had already emotionally committed to me. There was no denying the taut cord of connection between us.

And I knew I had already committed to him too. Even if we weren't about to have sex right now, I had rammed head first into the chemistry that had been simmering between us for years. And now I could give myself over to Wyatt in the best way possible.

"I've been waiting longer," he assured me, finding something to argue about even in this.

I smiled at him. "I know."

His laugh was a rush of surprised breath. He arched one of his strong eyebrows. "You're letting me win?"

Trailing my fingers over his chest, running them up his neck and hooking them behind his head, I savored the spikey shaved part of his head. "Only because I want something more than winning right now."

"Say it then."

"You, Wyatt," I whispered, bowing my back to draw his eyes to my breasts. "I want you."

His heated glance at my chest was carnal and greedy. Our mouths met together in the space between us, hungry and desperate and adoring all at once. We didn't draw anything out though. We knew what we wanted and there was no stopping us this time.

His hand slid down my waist, over the top of my thighs to palm me. He applied the most delicious pressure until I was gasping against his mouth and trying to wiggle out of my stupidly voluminous dress.

He laughed at my efforts, hooking his thumbs into the sides and divesting me of the obnoxious thing. My underwear went with them because... that was how he did things. Finally, I was laid bare before him, completely stripped of my clothes and my doubts and the defenses I'd carried around for way too long.

His gaze moved over me slowly, drinking in every inch of my body. I wanted to cover myself. I wanted to turn off the daylight that poured through his too-big window. I wanted to start over in three months after I'd made that Pure Barre class a priority.

I knew he was attracted to me. I knew he wanted sex. But this was too much. God, what had I been thinking.

Staring up at the ceiling to spare myself embarrassment, I cursed my insecurities. Why did being a girl have to be so hard? Why was I so confident in the kitchen and fragile everywhere else in life?

At least all my grooming was up to date. That would have made enjoying this intimacy we were sharing an utter catastrophe. I preferred to be practically hairless, except for my arms, from the neck down. I knew all the important places were in tip-top shape. But I was also firmly in the "curvy" category when it came to body shape. Fear whispered that my thighs would be too bumpy, and my stomach wouldn't turn him on either. I was terrified gravity had somehow ruined my boobs—apparently one of his favorite places on my body when supported with the right push-up equipment. And what about my armpits? I had always been particularly self-conscious about my armpits…

"How are you more beautiful than I imagined?" Wyatt demanded. "Fucking gorgeous," he murmured. He splayed his hands over my thighs and spread them apart, causing a fierce blush to rush to my cheeks. But I couldn't help but search out his gaze. I had to know how serious he was.

"You've imagined this?" I tried to tease him, but the intensity waiting for me set my entire body on fire with need.

"Kaya, yes. More times than is probably normal. It's been a real problem for me. I can't even cook in the same room as you most of the time because

321

all I can do is picture you naked… under me… exactly like this." His lips twitched in an embarrassed smile. "But I don't think this is going to cure me. You'll be the end of me, woman."

I shook my head. "No. I refuse to be the end." Feeling my insecurities drain and disappear, I leaned forward with renewed confidence and the lovely feeling of being wanted by someone who truly knew me. Someone who cared deeply about me. "I want to be the beginning."

He nodded rapidly and then kissed me senseless. His hand disappeared between my legs again, only this time there was nothing to impede his progress.

One of his fingers dipped inside me, sending a shockwave of blissful sensation zinging through me. I clutched his shoulders, loving how strong and hard and immovable his fingers and hands were. They grounded me as a second finger joined the first, filling me, stretching me.

"Wyatt," I panted.

He smiled against my mouth but kept kissing me. His fingers moved in and out, teasing, seducing, drawing me closer and closer to the edge of my sanity. When I couldn't keep up with his incessant kisses, he moved to my jaw and the column of my throat. He paid special attention to the hollow of my throat, tasting, sucking, driving me mad with all the different places he was touching me.

Shifting to his side, his free hand wrapped around my waist and tilted my hips. His fingers reached deeper, finding new places to bring to life. His mouth closed around my nipple at the same time his thumb found my most sensitive place. My back lifted off the bed in a jolt of intense pleasure.

He continued to thrust his fingers inside me until I could do nothing else but chase the fireworks his magic fingers promised to ignite soon. He continued to lick and suck at my breasts, moving from one to the next. He pressed my thighs farther apart and did something wicked with his thumb again.

Light exploded behind my closed eyelids, my body coiled and tight while sparks ignited through every single one of my muscles, stretching to my fingers and toes and the back of my neck.

The rush of my orgasm continued to pulse through me when he didn't remove his hand. His fingers moved slower, more deliberately, not allowing me to let go of the feeling completely.

When I was finally able to open my eyes, I found him hovering over me. He was a fallen angel like this, something more than human… more than mortal. Dark and so intense and strained with need.

"That was the most beautiful thing I have ever fucking seen," he rasped, his voice completely raw.

I blinked at him, feeling the exact same way about him. Lifting my head so I could kiss him. "I need you, chef. Now."

He had to exert some effort to reach his nightstand where a condom was tucked into the drawer. That was the amazing thing about king beds. There was so much room. But I had to laugh at how he was forced to scramble over me, not missing the opportunity to smack his ass when he took too long.

By the time he'd stripped off his pants and settled over me again, I was breathless and tingling with anticipation.

"You're my biggest weakness, Kaya" he whispered as he lined up his hot, hard, perfect body intimately against mine. My thighs cradled his waist and I felt him everywhere. Over me and against me, and in one, slow, mind-blowing thrust, inside me. "And my greatest ally." He peppered kisses along my jaw and collarbone, slowly sliding in and out of my body as I struggled to comprehend what he was saying and the English language in general. "You're my biggest challenge, my biggest problem. But mostly, you're my salvation. From the kitchen. And from myself." He paused over me and cradled my face with his hand. "I love you."

Tears wet my eyes. Since when had sex turned into this life-altering, incredibly beautiful experience? It had never been like this for me. It had never been soul deep and breath-stealing—a complete and utter connection on every single level—before. But that was always how Wyatt was. He defied every norm I had. He broke every rule and exceeded every expectation. He was and had been and would always be my exception.

And I loved him for it.

I loved him too.

His thumb brushed over my cheek and I realized it was wet. He caught a tear that I had shed. Oh my God! I was crying during sex! He'd actually broken me.

But instead of embarrassment, I was overcome with joy. Wyatt loved me.

"I love you too," I whispered to him, barely able to speak through the lump in my throat. "I think I've loved you for a while now."

"Good," he said with a blinding smile that made my heart flip flop inside my chest. And then he moved. And didn't stop moving.

We clung together in a sweaty, tangled mess until we were both panting and desperate and taut with desire. He pushed me over the edge, sending me into a dizzying, blinding whirlwind of electric sensation. And then he followed me, groaning my name and another I love you in such a way that I knew I would never be the same, that this was the moment that changed me forever and ever amen.

His head landed on my heart as we both came down from life-altering orgasms that were about five years in the making.

"Knew it would be that good." His words rumbled against my skin.

I laughed, but it was breathy and weak, like my entire body. "The question is, would you still love me if I was bad at sex."

324

His head lifted, and he grinned at me. "Who said you were good at it?"

I slapped his arm and glared at him.

Settling in against my side, he slid his bicep under my head and pulled me against him. "Kaya, I would of course, still love you if you were bad at sex. I'd just make you practice a lot. You know, so you could get better. I don't want you to be deficient in any area. I'm nice like that." His fingers brushed over my stomach in a hypnotically soothing kind of way. "Now that I'm thinking about it though, there were actually several things you could improve. We should probably spend a significant amount of time working in that area. Practice makes perfect and all that."

I opened my mouth to say something about how he could just be celibate for the rest of his life, but a dinging in the kitchen interrupted my thoughts.

"What is that?"

"The quiche!" He hopped up so quickly, my head bounced back on the pillows. He jumped out of bed completely naked and I had the immense pleasure of watching him sprint from the room—with the perfect view of his muscled, bare ass. "Don't move!" he shouted at me.

My sweat had started to cool, so I slid beneath his comforter and pulled it to my chin. Five minutes later, I hadn't moved. Instead, I found myself smiling at my lap while my fingers traced circles in the blanket.

I'd agreed to a date with Wyatt, but what I'd actually gotten was sex, love, and a relationship. A seriously committed relationship.

And I couldn't have been happier.

When he came back, carrying two plates that smelled like heaven and looked like pieces of priceless art, I'd decided that this was what "making it" must feel like, finally reaching all my goals and aspirations. This was what living the dream felt like.

For so long I had been obsessed with my career and getting to the next level and creating a legacy for myself that I hadn't even noticed what my life

325

had been lacking. Yes, my career was important. And yes, I would continue to work as hard as it took to get the things I wanted. But this was what life was about—relationships. And doing them well.

I almost had my career goals within my grasp, but without Wyatt I would have been lonely and hung-up on the past. I would have existed but my insides would've been empty.

Wyatt fulfilled so many depleted places of me that it was honestly hard to comprehend how whole I felt. Maybe for the first time in my entire life, I felt like my career wasn't the shining star of my life and that maybe, possibly, there was more to me than just cooking.

Wyatt seemed to think that anyway.

And I also knew that one person could not fulfill all my emotional, physical, and spiritual needs. I knew I had a lot of work to do to make myself whole. But I also knew that Wyatt was a good place to start. And he would be a good cheerleader as I waded through the rest of the bog and tackled my issues one by one.

This wasn't only a new relationship. This was a new beginning for me. And with Wyatt by my side, I finally believed I could start over. I knew we could tackle this life together and take whatever we wanted from it.

He slid into bed beside me, burrowing beneath the comforter too. I mourned the loss of his body on display, but the quiche was so hot it was steaming. I figured that was a dangerous game to play with all our bits on display.

I accepted the massive plate of food from him. "Good thing I'm starving," I told him.

He waggled his eyebrows at me. "I figured we worked up a pretty good appetite."

"Good point."

I settled the plate on my lap, the bottom of it burning through the blankets to warm my legs. The heat felt good, and the quiche was everything it should be. Light and fluffy, packed with veggies and bacon. The crust turned out exactly right. Apparently, Wyatt hadn't been lying. He knew how to cook an amazing quiche.

Smiling around my first bite, I realized I shouldn't have been surprised. The man could literally do anything he put his mind to. However, quiche was such a strange dish to claim. I had expected him to have signature short ribs or beef bourguignon. Instead, it was quiche. And adorable.

And it tasted amazing. "Yum."

He nudged me with his elbow. "Told you."

"Mmm," I agreed around another bite of too-hot deliciousness. "Maybe tomorrow you can make me a casserole. You know, round out your style for me."

His rumbly laugh filled the room and he leaned over and bit my bare shoulder. "Maybe you should cook for me tomorrow," he suggested.

"You already judge my cooking every night," I reminded him. "At least I didn't yell at you across the house."

"I never yell at you."

"Umm, sometimes you do."

"Maybe I raise my voice, but it's never out of anger."

I lifted an eyebrow and gave him a look. "What is it out of then?"

"Sexual frustration?"

Shaking my head at him, I laughed again. "Does that mean you'll be cool as a cucumber from now on?"

He stuck out his lower lip and thought about it. "Maybe," he conceded. "As long as you keep me satisfied."

I thought about calling him on his bologna, but I was having too much fun razzing him. "Great," I sighed. "Lilou's going to implode, all because Wyatt is finally getting laid consistently."

"Hey, if I had to choose one or the other, pretty sure I'm going with getting laid."

"It doesn't matter to me," I laughed, "I won't be there for much longer anyway." As soon as the words were out of my mouth I wanted to shove them back in. *Abort, abort!* blared through my head, but it was too late.

I'd already said the stupid thing.

And Wyatt picked up on it immediately.

He set his plate down and slowly turned to face me. The humor had drained out of his expression and his eyes were that swirling storm I knew to be careful around. "What does that mean?" he demanded.

I took another bite of quiche and hummed my approval at the delightful ratio of bacon to mushrooms. "This is so good, chef. I can't believe how good it is."

"Don't try to sweet talk me now, Swift. Spit it out."

"The quiche?"

"The truth, damn it."

Nerves swirled in my belly and my skin felt hot and itchy and too tight. Was this the moment I ruined everything again? Was this my bad luck on repeat?

Wyatt and I had finally found this amazing, wonderful, incredible thing and I was going to leave him to work at Sarita. Hopefully. Okay, to be fair, I wasn't leaving the city. But with our crazy schedules, I might as well have been leaving him to move to Mars.

"Kaya," he growled impatiently.

I blew out a quivering breath and decided it best to just rip off the Band-Aid. This was a fantastic morning. I would probably remember every detail of it for the rest of my life. I honestly had no idea how Wyatt would react to my secret. Although, we had discussed the possibility of me leaving at some point for my own restaurant, it had only been hypothetical until now.

"Sarita," I blurted, anxiety getting the best of me. "I'm trying out for Sarita's executive chef position."

"Sarita?"

I shrugged.

"Is that where you've been Sunday evenings?"

I squinted and tried to keep my voice from quivering from fear of his reaction. "Vera's been, er, kind of training me to take over. Hopefully."

"Sarita?" he repeated as if it were the most unbelievable thing he'd ever heard.

I shrugged again. "I don't know… yeah…" Confidence bloomed somewhere near my knees and started walking its way up to my heart, one baby step at a time. "Sarita. I like her a lot. She has more of a vibe I can relate to. And I love the design of her menu and bar. I… the position opened up and I knew I wanted it. Ezra's interviewing me next Monday." I sucked on my lip ring for a second and then added, "Oh, so I need that day off too."

His expression remained unreadable, mysterious and closed off. "Are you sure you want to work for Ezra?" he asked. "He's pretty much the worst."

Good question. But I already knew my answer. "I get that. But he also has some of the best restaurants in the city. Maybe even the country. I want to run one. I want to do the awards and the magazine spreads and make a name for myself. Ezra might be hard to work with, but I know I can reach my goals in one of his restaurants. Plus… I can't explain the connection I feel with Sarita. It's like we bonded on a spiritual level. I was made for her. And she was made for me."

"What if you don't get the job?" he asked.

"Then I quit cooking. Completely." I laughed at my joke, but he didn't seem to find it as funny. In fact, he didn't laugh at all.

"Be serious, Ky. What if he doesn't give it to you?"

What if? What if what if what if what if?

The words had been bouncing around in my head for weeks. Hell, maybe I'd been facing them for years. What if I had stayed in Hamilton? What if Nolan had moved to Durham? What if I wasn't so defiant and at the same time, paralyzed with the fear of failure?

But for the first time in years, the question didn't hit me quite so hard. "I keep working for you," I told him honestly. "Or Vera and Killian. Vera has done everything but flat-out offer me the sous chef position. At least that's a lateral move."

His eyes narrowed. "Fuck Vera and Killian."

"Wyatt!"

His smile took the edge off his harsh words. "Seriously though, they're trying to poach from me already? Filthy rat bastards."

I pressed my lips together to hide my smile. "I think they're trying to find people they can trust."

He grumbled more curse words, but eventually he said, "That job would never have any advancement. Vera and Killian will always be ECs. You'll only ever be a sous chef there."

Nodding, I said, "I realize that. That's exactly why I'm not seriously considering the position. I was flattered she asked, but the position isn't for me."

"She would ask. She'd be dumb not to," he grunted. "You're too fucking good for your own good."

His words were meant as an insult, but they hit me right in the chest with hope and truth and a whisper that maybe Sarita wasn't impossible.

"Sarita?" He grunted for the third time.

330

"I'm not going to apologize," I told him preemptively. "I need my own kitchen, Wyatt. I feel stifled working for you and it's not even you. What kind of chef would I be if I didn't want my own kitchen? Besides, I have a problem with authority." I tilted my head and smirked at him to lighten his cloudy expression.

He made a sound in the back of his throat. "That's an understatement."

I frowned at his attitude. "I'm sorry if this changes things for you, but I—"

"Yeah, I have to find a new sous chef. I guess there's Benny, but I don't know if he wants that much responsibility. And he won't be half as good as you. I can't hire fucking Charlie—"

"Dillon."

He turned to me, pausing mid-rant at my suggestion. "She's not a permanent solution."

"But she'd be good enough for right now."

He rubbed his knuckles over his scruff thoughtfully and I realized we'd gotten way off topic.

"I meant, I'm sorry if this changes things between us. Between our relationship."

His gaze was laser sharp and totally focused. "What do you mean?"

"Because I could possibly, hopefully, maybe be leaving Lilou for my own gig. I'm saying if I leave, and you know, that changes things for you…"

"Why would that change anything for me?"

"I mean with our relationship."

"I understand what you're saying," he quipped. "I just don't understand why you're saying it. Kaya, you could open a kitchen on the moon and I would still want you. Did you not hear when I said that I love you? That we're a forever thing now? This"—he wiggled a finger back and forth between us—"isn't contingent on proximity. It's based on how much I care

331

for you and how important it is to me to spend my life with you. If you leave, and you probably will and should if you want the job, then we'll make it work. If you don't get Sarita and find a job across the country. We'll make that work too. Woman, I love you. And you love me. That's all that matters."

I breathed in deeply and it felt like my first big breath of my whole adult life. Collapsing against him, he wrapped his arms around me and I inhaled him. His body was so warm, and this feeling was so right.

"I love you," I told him, even though he'd said it for me seconds ago.

His confidence was amazing when you compared it to how insecure I could be. Maybe we were matched head to head in the kitchen, but he had me beat in the relationship department by miles. But that was okay. As long as he was strong enough to stick around, I could heal through this. I could get there. I could find my footing once again.

If for no other reason than to keep him from beating me forever. I mean, I loved him, but that didn't mean our competition was over.

He kissed the top of my head and said, "You're going to have to up the sexual favors though or the kitchen is going to hate you when you leave. I mean, fine, I can admit that you belong at Sarita and you'll kick ass there and be a national success in no time. But my staff is going to murder you when they have to deal with me after you're gone."

I laughed at his exaggeration. "I can handle the sexual favors part, but I'm worried about your fragile ego when Sarita starts outperforming Lilou."

His body stiffened, not liking that idea at all. "I'm not worried, Swift. After all, I just grabbed my first James Beard and I'm pretty sure you don't even have the EC job yet."

I pinched his nipple and twisted. That was fair at this point, right?

"You didn't tell me you got the James Beard!"

"Rising Star Chef of the Year."

"Holy shit, Wyatt! Congratulations!"

"Uhm hmm. You see? You've got a way to go before you catch up."

I pulled back, so he could see me roll my eyes. "You're making it hard to be happy for you."

He smiled, and I melted into a pile of sticky, happy goo right there on the bed.

"Do you want to go over your menu?" he asked. "When did you say you're interviewing?"

"Monday." I thought about his offer. How cool would that be for Wyatt to go over my menu with me? This was one of those reasons that we would make not just a good couple, but a great power couple. But, I couldn't accept his help. This was something I needed to do totally on my own. I needed to set myself apart from Wyatt and Lilou and sous chef. I needed to show Ezra that I was innovative in my own right and talented without holding the hand of a better chef. I needed to show him I had the guts and grit to take Sarita and turn her into her best version. "And I, uh, I think I got the menu on my own."

"Oh, yeah? Are you sure?"

I settled back against him and laid my hand over his heart to catch my balance. "Yes, I'm sure. I think he'll appreciate the menu more if I'm solely in charge."

"Yeah, okay. I can see that."

"Thank you though."

He kissed the top of my head. "Any time."

Tilting my head back, I caught a close-up version of him. It was beautiful and right and I was so grateful for this man I got to finally call mine. "I love you, Wyatt."

His lips lingered on mine, kissing me to oblivion. "I love you too, Kaya. I'm looking forward to all the different ways you're going to drive me wild."

Assuming that was a challenge, I kissed him this time and didn't stop until we were sated and exhausted once again. We curled up in each other's embrace on the bed, surrounded by plates and quiche crumbs and fell asleep. We spent the morning like that and were so enraptured with each other we ended up being late to work for the first time ever.

I was already embarrassed and flustered, but then Wyatt walked into the kitchen and announced to every single one of his staff and my coworkers that we were officially together.

His exact words were, "Kaya and I finally figured our shit out. We're together now. Deal with it."

That was approximately the time I burst into humiliated flames and braced myself against lighting the entire kitchen on fire.

But then, everyone cheered for us and forgave us for being two hours late. And I was able to relax in my own skin and this new, wonderful, crazy relationship with my boss.

Dinner service was not my best. And it wasn't Wyatt's either. But for the first time since I could remember, neither of us cared about the potential critics or the reputation of the restaurant or even our professional legacy.

Instead, we spent the night stealing glances and secret smiles and dreaming about later—when more sexual favors would be exchanged.

I had Sarita to worry about, and he had his changes at Lilou to implement, but suddenly none of that felt impossible. This great big thing in my life had finally happened and I could relax about my dream job.

At least temporarily—until I had to finalize my tryout menu and cook it for Ezra.

Chapter Twenty-One

A bead of sweat rolled down my spine and I contemplated puking. I set

the plate down, brushed my hands over my chef coat with trembling hands

and then tucked them quickly behind my back.

This afternoon had been the single most terrifying experience of my life.

I'd arrived in the Sarita kitchen at nine this morning and started serving Ezra

at three. He'd given me sixteen chances in the form of unique dishes to blow

his mind.

I hoped to do it in twelve.

It was risky.

After setting the last and final dessert in front of him, I started second guessing everything I'd done and didn't do. Every tiny, insignificant decision. From where I'd gotten my prosciutto for the fire-roasted Padrón peppers that I'd tossed in sea salt and turmeric, finished with mint, to the firmness of the goat cheese I used for the honey dipped goat cheese balls I lightly fried and served with a mint cream sauce.

But I'd especially second guessed my choice of using only twelve dishes. Three appetizers, four second plates and five thirds. Oh, and then the dessert course, which I didn't really count since it barely passed as servable.

Ezra eyed my bite-size *tres leches* cakes and churro fries with caramel crema dipping sauce. I didn't know what he'd been expecting, but I had done the desserts in the tapas style of the rest of the meal. Little bites that were meant to be shared around the table.

They weren't the most inventive of desserts ever created, but pastries were not my specialty. I also knew Ezra hired a pastry company to handle the sweet courses throughout the harem, including Sarita. This course was a test to see how well-rounded I was. That was fine. My caramel dipping sauce was spectacular. And my churro fries had turned out perfectly. I had made the cake bites yesterday, so I sincerely hoped they hadn't dried out yet. But they looked pretty.

I'd had a third dish planned, some puff pastry fritters with a custard drizzle. I was going to cut them in little S's and wow him with my ability to theme like a boss. But I'd scrapped the idea when I realized they were too similar to the churros. There was no point in ending the meal with a fried-food-fest that could rival the county fair.

Ezra turned to the other two judges with him and I felt like I'd accidentally signed up for a cooking reality show on Bravo.

Killian sat to his right, serious and intimidating. He wouldn't go easy on me no matter how much he liked me. And he knew all my weaknesses from my years of working under him.

As if he wasn't bad enough, Arón Delgato sat to his left. Delgato owned three Spanish restaurants in the Charlotte area and a pretty famous flagship out of Raleigh. I'd sat in a lecture he did when I was in culinary school and he'd intimidated me back then. Now my knees trembled, and I had started mentally willing my body to stop sweating.

This was the end, I reminded myself. For better or worse, I'd managed to get through the entire service without a major calamity.

After the first courses of goat cheese balls, Spanish Rioja-glazed chorizo, and chickpeas, and then heirloom tomatoes and spring onion toast with brazed manchego cheese shavings, I had relaxed into doing what I do best.

Other than having to serve the three judges myself and explain each dish, I'd spent most of the day in the kitchen with my head down. It had felt amazing to finally cook in Sarita. I took full advantage of the huge space, even if I didn't have it all to myself.

Vera had the kitchen staff prepping for the night on one side of the big space while I took up the other half. They pretty much stayed out of my way except to offer encouragement or loud whistles when I'd done something that especially impressed them.

That was probably the best part of the day—working near the staff I was coming to appreciate and respect. Vera had done some whipping into shape with their preparation and skills, and they'd seriously cleaned up the kitchen in her short tenure. But they were also good people. Talented people. I knew that if I had the opportunity to lead them, we could do some incredible things.

"Did you find that you had enough time to prepare for this meal?" Killian asked after he'd sampled both desserts.

I thought back to the last week of frantic prepping. Wyatt had given me some wiggle room at Lilou so I could spend more time at home perfecting the dishes I wanted to make. But I hadn't left him totally high and dry. The current state of my apartment verged on catastrophic. And laundry would need to be done ASAP. I was presently wearing my last pair of clean underwear.

Not that Wyatt would have complained if I suddenly started going without.

"Of course," I told him.

His lips twitched. He knew I was lying, but he thankfully didn't call me on it. "Where did you get the idea for the caramel crema? I enjoyed the way you tweaked a more classic dessert."

I shrugged and attempted a wobbly smile, admitting the truth this time. "My head. It's a dish I personally enjoy. I wanted to bring in the elements of all of my favorite things and showcase my personality in them."

"You've done that," Delgato murmured. It was impossible to tell if he was complimenting or insulting me. "And the crispy squid? Actually, just walk us through the second course."

My brain blanked on what I'd even served for the second course. It didn't feel possible to have done all of this in one day. And yet, somehow, I'd created the best meal of my entire life.

There were things I would have done differently now that I was on this side of the mayhem. But I'd given it everything I had and was super proud of what I'd accomplished.

"I wanted something light and edgy, but also balanced. There was a lot of pressure to impress you with just this one meal." I laughed lightly, and they smiled at my honesty. "I also wanted to bring in some other cultural flavor profiles. I know this is a traditionally Spanish restaurant, but one of my favorite things about cooking is bringing different tastes together and making them work to feature the best of everything. Crispy squid is one of my favorite dishes. I served it with the harissa aioli to cut the richness of it and then squeezed some lemon over the top for that acidity that I feel all fried seafood needs. Another favorite flavor profile of mine is artichokes and bacon." I grinned again. "Okay, I'm a big fan of bacon in general. But the crumbled smoked bacon and gorgonzola over grilled artichoke hearts is a particularly heavenly combination. Patatas bravas seemed like an obvious choice. But I julienned fingerling potatoes, so they would present nicely with the roasted serranos. The smoked paprika aioli and fried egg over the top was an idea inspired by Wyatt's asparagus on the Lilou menu. Seafood is such an obvious choice for tapas, but I wanted to stretch some of the concepts already on the menu. That's where I came up with the cold PEI mussels. So, I cooked them first in red wine and chopped tomatoes, onions and pineapple. I bulked up the broth while they simmered and then quick-cooled all of it. I finished the dish with fresh coriander."

"Those were my least favorite," Arón commented.

I nodded, accepting the criticism without defending my dish. I knew I was taking a risk with the pineapple and the temperature. But I hadn't wanted to play it safe or predictable.

"I liked the pineapple," Killian added thoughtfully. "I mean, I don't think I want to eat mussels cold every time I have them. But the dish itself was interesting enough to catch my attention and boasted the chops to back it up."

"Thank you, chef," I said quietly, demurely, with all the decorum in the world. On the inside, I'd thrown my hands in the air and was basically twerking in celebration.

Ezra didn't comment one way or the other. "And the third course?"

I went over my stuffed sardines with chorizo and poblano peppers; the prawns tossed in a garlic-chili-lemon glaze; the cheese and cauliflower fritters with a mint yogurt dip; and the marinated saffron lamb skewers and salsa verde. I'd also served the Padrón peppers with that course.

They said even less about my third plates. Other than Ezra's casual, "There was a lot of mint throughout."

"My attempt at cohesion," I answered lamely.

Ezra pushed the dessert to the middle of the table and folded his arms over his chest. His eyes moved over the dishes I'd slaved over that sat mostly untouched. They'd been picked at and ripped apart, severely inspected for mistakes and flaws.

I didn't know what they found. And I couldn't have told you if anything had turned out like it was supposed to.

The temptation to second guess every single thing I'd done and thought and approved today was so strong, I felt strangled by it. Instead, I forced my brain to focus on the technical aspects I knew I could control. The pepper was perfectly tender. The lamb was finished exactly right. My mint yogurt dip required exactly this amount of chopped mint leaves.

My execution was perfect. TBD on what any of it tasted like.

"What makes you think you can handle a kitchen like Sarita?" Ezra asked in a voice that was calm and direct. I'll admit I was terrified.

This was it. My chance. I thought of Wyatt's text this morning. **Don't fuck it up, Swift. You deserve this.**

Such a charmer.

Still, I smiled like an idiot at his straightforward advice. That he believed I deserved a kitchen of this caliber said everything I needed to hear. And the advice was sound. Don't get in your own way. Don't overthink it. Don't let them intimidate you into cooking anything less than your very best.

And I didn't.

I'd given it all today. Now I just needed to prove to Ezra that I would give it all every day.

340

Smiling to soften what I was about to say, I swallowed the remaining fear and embraced this thing I wanted so badly. "I like to believe I could handle any kitchen given the chance. I've spent the last five years at Lilou, some of that time as sous chef. I've worked under two of the best chefs in the industry." I wasn't even trying to butter Killian up. It was the truth. "I've learned from them, I've grown under their guidance and expertise, and I feel ready to take the next step to executive chef. I want that to be at Sarita because I get her. I get her vibe. I feel the connection in our souls. I know I would be a great asset to her kitchen. But more than that, I know I would be good for her. I want her to grow. I looked at her stats over the last two years and they're not impressive. There's no reason she shouldn't be getting awards and accolades. There's no reason she shouldn't have one of the best menus in the country. I believe I have the ability to give her those things. My background is in Latin cooking. I fell into Lilou on a fluke. And while I've loved working there, I have more potential than that kitchen." I caught Killian's direct gaze and remembered the advice he'd given me. "That said, I think Sarita is already doing a lot of things well. I don't want to step in here and change everything. I just want the opportunity to expand and mature what you're already doing here."

Ezra nodded, accepting my answer. I couldn't be sure, but I thought his shoulders might have relaxed some and the look in his eyes had softened. He went on to ask me about work habits and hours, how I felt about putting in the time and energy it took to be executive chef. And then he asked me how I thought I would fare working alongside him.

Clearing my throat, I gave him the nicest answer I was capable of giving him. "To be honest, I've watched Killian and Wyatt work with you and I've seen them both frustrated with their inability to independently create. If you micromanage everything I do, I think I'll end up just like them. But I hope that you would trust your hiring process and me. Sarita has all my best

341

intentions. I only want great things for her. I'd love to be as autonomous as possible. Let me find the menus that work the best. Let me have complete creative control. And let me show you I know what I'm doing."

He rubbed his eyes with his thumb and forefinger. "Good god, you sound just like Wyatt."

I smiled at my feet. Killian saved me from responding by saying, "She has a point. Stop nit-picking your chefs into insanity."

Ezra turned a glare on him that was clearly meant to shut him up. "Your opinion isn't necessary on that particular subject."

"Just sayin'," Killian muttered. "We all leave for a reason."

Ezra ignored him. "Thank you for your time, Kaya. I'm going to review my notes, discuss the meal with my associates and when the interview process is completed, I'll let you know what I decide."

My mouth went dry and I resisted the urge to chew on my lip ring. "Thank you. And thanks for this opportunity. I appreciate it."

I turned and walked to the kitchen. Keeping my pace even until I was out of sight, I held my chin up and managed to keep it from wobbling. As soon as the door swung shut behind me, I collapsed against the counter and let out a shaky breath.

"Hey superstar!" Molly called across the kitchen from where she stood with Vera.

I looked up and resisted the urge to beg her to make Ezra give me the job. Instead, I smiled, even if it was trembling, and said, "Congratulations, Molls! Engaged!"

We met each other in the middle of the kitchen and hugged. It was short a short hug though, because I needed to grab her hand and check out her gigantic ring.

"A pearl?"

"My choice," she explained. "I'm not a fan of diamonds."

"It's gorgeous. I'm so happy for you."

"I'm so happy for *you*!" she countered. "There are so many rumors flying around about you right now, I don't which one to grill you on first."

"Wyatt!" Vera shouted. "She's banging Wyatt!"

"Oh my God." If my cheeks hadn't already been the color of raspberries, they would have quickly blazed with embarrassment. "That's not true."

Molly pulled back, confused. "You're saving yourselves for marriage?"

"No, I mean… Yes? I mean, fine. We're banging. But that's not all we're doing. We're also dating. In like an actual relationship. With real commitment."

Molly turned back to Vera, her long dark hair whipping me in the face. "Did you hear that, Vere? They're in an actual relationship with real commitment and everything."

"You guys are the worst." I laughed. "And the meanest! I'm a wreck right now. It's unfair to pick on someone so emotionally fragile."

"There's that too!" Molly squealed. "You're taking over Sarita? That's so exciting!"

"Er, no. Again, your facts are wrong. I feel like you would have made a terrible PI, Molly."

"You've never seen me Facebook stalk someone," she countered seriously. "I can find anybody on the internet. I mean, anybody."

"It's true," Vera corroborated. "And also freakishly scary."

"What I mean is that, I'm interviewing, but who knows who Ezra will pick. That man is an enigma."

Molly laughed. "Hardly. Which is why I'm confident you'll get the job."

"We'll see." I sighed.

Vera waved her hand dismissively in the air. "You got this, champ. I didn't raise no fool." At Molly's confused look, she added. "I've been mentoring her for the past few weeks. She's amazing now."

343

"She's always been amazing." Molly laughed.

"Also, mostly you just made me bus tables. There wasn't a whole lot of mentoring going on."

Vera waved a butcher knife at me. "I mentored the shit out of you. I want full credit when you get the job."

"I've missed so much," Molly lamented.

"Well, that's what happens when you go on vacation for six years," Vera snapped back.

"Tell me all about it though! Vera and I will never get a vacation like that. I want to know every single detail. I mean, did you read any good books? Or take any naps? Explain in detail to me what it was like to take a nap. I can't remember."

She rolled her eyes, but thankfully launched into the story of what it was like to relax while I cleaned everything up from my day of cooking. She sat with me for over an hour until her fiancé realized she was hanging out in the kitchen and came to haul her out.

"Molly," Ezra growled her name upon entering the kitchen.

She hopped off the counter where she'd been happily chirping every detail of their Virgin Island getaway. "I just got here!" She winked at me and hurried from the kitchen. "I'll put in a good word for you, Kaya!"

Ezra stared at the swinging door in horrified awe of the woman he loved. "I don't know what to do with her."

I pressed my lips together and decided not to comment.

To me, he said, "I just wanted to thank you again, Kaya. You really impressed me today."

Setting my roll of knives down, I accepted the hand he'd extended toward me. "Thank you for the opportunity, Ezra. It would be a dream come true to run Sarita's kitchen."

He smiled, real affection for his restaurant shining through. "Do you have your references? I mainly need the one from Wyatt."

Clearing my throat, I pulled out the sealed envelope from my purse. Wyatt had given it to me yesterday. We'd discussed what to do about our relationship and if Ezra really needed to know that we were dating. Honesty was always the best policy, but our relationship was so new. It hardly seemed fair to compromise Sarita because of my love life.

And yet, given the choice, I knew I would pick Wyatt. Sarita was important to me, yes. But Wyatt was everything to me.

Staring at Ezra's polished shoes, I confessed, "You should know that Wyatt and I made our relationship official this week. We're dating."

His silence said more than words ever could. Especially when he finally spoke, it was a stilted "Oh."

Lifting my head to at least pretend I had courage, I quickly explained, "I realize this might affect your decision, but I wanted to let you know anyway. Wyatt and I have worked together for the last five years and I feel as though his opinion of me will remain objective, but we've also had feelings for each other for a while."

He made a sound in the back of his throat. "I know."

It was my turn to say, "Oh."

He smiled at me and I was taken aback so strongly I nearly lost my balance. "I might not have known about your feelings for him. But it's no secret he's been harboring a crush on you for ages. That said, if he's written his recommendation with hearts over the I's, I'm going to ask you to find someone else."

I laughed, and it felt real and genuine and so light. "Thanks, Ezra."

"Be good to him," he ordered. "He's as persnickety as they come, but he cares about you, Kaya."

"I care about him too," I said honestly, my body warming with just the thought of him.

"Good to hear." He patted me on the shoulder. "We'll talk soon."

I went straight to Lilou after I left Sarita. I had to see him. Today had been crazy and all I wanted was Wyatt and his arms around me.

I was dressed for work because I'd worn my usual coat and black pants to interview today. Driving like a maniac, I slammed my car into an employee parking spot and snuck in through the side door of Lilou. Nobody noticed me. They were too busy with what they were doing.

Dinner service had just started, and the crash and clatter of the kitchen filled my ears immediately. I paused just inside the door to watch the beautiful chaos that defined my life. Rarely did I take a moment to savor the hustle and bustle. I was always a part of it, swept up in the movement and focus.

Everything felt familiar and foreign at the same time. I watched Dillon throw things in a pan and whisk furiously at the sauce just beginning to simmer. Benny stood over a huge rib roast, slicing off ribeyes to order. Endo hurried back and forth as he kept his dishwashers and bussers in line. Charlie murdered duck after duck after duck.

Wyatt really needed to fire him.

My gaze fell on my boyfriend and even in my head the word felt strange. But it also felt like not enough. After all these years, it was bizarre to think of Wyatt, my one-time nemesis, my one-time friend, as my boyfriend. The word and description felt juvenile, immature… lacking.

He was so much more than a boyfriend. He was my rock. He kept me grounded when all I wanted to do was fly off the handle. He was the man that had healed me and saved me from myself. He challenged me, always pushing me to get better, and be better. He made me want better things. He was my heart and my hope and my future.

346

And what we had together wasn't just a relationship, it was the beginning of something so beautiful my heart felt like it could burst.

I had never been in a relationship that felt so perfectly right. Not that we were perfect. We couldn't have been further from it. We still bickered and argued. We were still constantly trying to one up the other. But that only made our story more incredible.

My past had damaged me in a way I hated to admit. Nolan's dismissal of what I thought had been love had gouged my self-worth with an icepick. He'd made me feel less than, unwanted. He'd broken me.

Wyatt did the opposite. He filled in those holes in my chest and promised he would keep filling them in for as long as I needed him. He didn't let distance scare him or allow change to get in our way. He embraced our differences and cherished the person that I was. He made me feel loved and worthy and wanted. He healed me.

Our love healed me.

I watched him lean over a plate as he worked the finer details and garnishes, and then he wiped the edge of the plate with a towel. His profile was cast in bright light from above, sharpening his jawline and nose, highlighting his masculine cheekbone and the shaved side of his head. His tall toque stood at attention, and his crisp jacket hugged the lines of his muscular body. I watched his steady hands slash sauce over the protein and then delicately sprinkle microgreens, turning an ordinary looking dish into a work of art.

I was so lucky to know him. Not just because I loved him, but because he was so good at what he did, so dedicated to perfecting his craft and being the best possible chef out there. I had never met a man I respected and loved more.

And I knew going forward, no matter how mad he made me, I still would never meet another man that could compare to him.

347

Feeling my gaze on him, he passed the plate to a server and turned to face me. His mouth split into that breath-stealing grin and he cocked his head in wonder. "How'd you do?" he asked without saying hello.

I lifted one shoulder in a shrug. "It's hard to tell."

"Did you kick ass?" he asked.

Nibbling on my lip ring, I shrugged both shoulders this time. "Hopefully."

He started nodding and laughing. "Yeah, you kicked ass."

His confidence in me burned a blush on my cheeks and I realized the whole kitchen had paused to watch us.

Wyatt jerked his chin and said, "Come here."

It was that small command that ruined me. He'd stopped caring about his kitchen and the food piling up in front of him. He didn't notice his staff watching us or the clamor of diners on the other side of the in and out doors. All he saw was me.

All he wanted was me.

And so I did what any sane, rational girl would do. I ran to him, leaped into his arms, and let him catch me.

His arms wrapped around my legs and held me there as our mouths crashed together. We kissed like we always kissed, desperately and voraciously and like we'd been waiting for this moment our entire lives. I held his face in my hands while I tasted him, butterflies swarming my belly and heat pooling between my legs.

God, how did he do this to me every single time? Would it always be like this?

Yes, I instinctively knew. Yes, with Wyatt, I would always want him this badly and love him this madly and drive him this crazy. And he would do the same to me.

348

The kitchen erupted with whoops and hollers and lewd suggestions. We pulled apart and smiled at each other.

"I love you, chef," I whispered to him.

His eyes darkened, and he squeezed my ass. "I love you, Ky. Want to get out of here?"

"And go where?"

He set me down but pulled me against him immediately. "Anywhere."

"What about the kitchen?"

"Fuck the kitchen," he laughed. "We need to go celebrate."

"Celebrate what?"

His smile twitched with mischief. "You finally quitting."

"It's not final yet!"

"A guy can hope."

I laughed because he was ridiculous and funny and *mine*. "If we both leave, who will run service tonight?"

He turned his head and yelled, "Dillon, you're in charge!"

"What?" was her shrieked reply.

Wyatt turned to Benny. "Can you help her out, man?"

Benny grinned. "My pleasure."

"What?" Dillon repeated even louder.

I smiled at my friend. "I owe you one."

She rolled her eyes and straightened her bandana. "You owe me at least ten."

Wyatt pulled his hat off and tossed it at her. "Try not to set the place on fire."

"No promises." She swore under her breath.

Wyatt grabbed my hand and smiled at his staff. I was positive they all assumed he was having a stroke. He had never smiled this much at them ever.

349

I mean ever.

"I'll be back tomorrow," he promised. "You've got twenty-four hours with Glinda the Good Witch but if you fuck anything up for her, you're fired. See you tomorrow."

Then he pulled me from the restaurant and we escaped into the night. We stripped out of our bandanas and chef coats and had a proper date in the sweaty clothes we had underneath. We laughed over street tacos and walked around downtown. Then we grabbed a few drinks at Craft, the bar that Killian had been poaching for. Apparently, Wyatt knew the owners too.

At the end of the night, I followed him to his house in my car where we stripped out of the rest of our clothes and spent the entire night not arguing once.

Chapter Twenty-Two

Three weeks later, Wyatt and I were on another morning date. And it was another surprise date. Although he'd promised me he wouldn't murder me. I'd made him swear by his favorite set of knives before I let him put the blindfold on me.

Because seriously, a blindfold?

It took all my trust to let him do it. I didn't want to say I wasn't a trusting person by nature, but let's be real, I was not a trusting person by nature. Or by force. And the blindfold I was currently wearing was testing every ounce of my patience.

The car turned off and I put my hands to my temples. "Now?"

Wyatt's deep chuckle chased a tingle down my spine. "Not yet."

"This is cruel and unusual punishment."

His hand rubbed down my thigh and then back up, settling in the crease of my thigh. "I promise it will be worth it," he murmured into my ear. I twitched at the tickle his breath caused.

"Okay," I whispered. Maybe I didn't trust the blindfold, but I trusted him.

The last month had been the best of my life. Wyatt and I liked to fight with each other, but it turned out, we liked to get along even more. We'd spent as much time as we could getting to know each other. Sure, we'd known each other for five years, but there was so much yet to discover.

And I knew it would always be like this with him. I would always want to know more. I would always want to see more of him and spend more time with him. I would always want him to know more of me.

In the few spare moments of free time we had, we were inseparable. But even during working hours, it was hard to pull us apart. Part of it was the honeymoon bliss, but we also knew I wouldn't be staying long at Lilou.

I hadn't heard anything from Ezra about Sarita. And Dillon remained tightlipped no matter how much I pestered her to interrogate him. My other friends were quiet too. I'd even forced Wyatt to set up a double brunch date with Killian and Vera, so I could grill the two of them.

Nobody had heard anything.

Not knowing if that was good or bad, I'd started looking around at my options and lightheartedly applied to places I could see myself working at. Wyatt and I knew we couldn't continue to work together. Not just for the sake of our relationship, but the sake of our staff.

We weren't Vera and Killian. We had chemistry that sometimes bubbled over. And sometimes exploded. Both in good ways and bad ways. We didn't want to make our staff suffer in the overflow.

Besides, my ambitions would never let me get comfortable as second in command. I wanted EC. And now my life felt very much like I had everything I wanted except that one thing.

Granted, it was a giant, life-accomplishment kind of thing. But still. Not having it only made me want it more.

I'd had three call backs from jobs I'd applied for. But when push came to shove, and I was invited to an interview, I'd ended up turning them down. Those weren't the jobs I wanted. And if I wasn't going to settle in at one of the best jobs at one of the hottest restaurants in the nation right now, I wasn't going to settle for a mediocre executive chef position either.

Not only that, but I *wanted* Sarita. I'd gotten a taste of her. She was in my blood now. I couldn't even entertain another restaurant until I heard about my fate for certain. But as the days stretched on and I ran into Ezra more and more and he didn't even offer so much as a hint or a smile or a word of encouragement, I started to give up on my dream job at Sarita altogether.

Wyatt's fingers on my chin, nudged my mouth toward his where he pressed a quick, hot, delicious kiss to my mouth. It ended too soon and made me curious about what he had planned for today. "Don't move," he ordered, before climbing out of the car.

My door opened, and I felt his hands on me again. "Ready for this?"

"For a surprise trip to Greece?" I guessed.

He laughed and made a buzzer sound. "Wrong."

Letting him guide me from the car, I guessed again. "You're forcing me to become a drug mule to carry heroine over the border?"

He paused mid-step. "Which border?" I could sense him shake his head at the ridiculous question. "Never mind, no. Obviously not. If I was going to make you smuggle anything it would be nuclear weapons."

I smiled and then felt like an idiot because I couldn't see anything. "Are you going to propose?"

He barked a laugh. "Only you would try to ruin the proposal surprise by guessing what I was doing before I did it."

"So that's a yes."

He pinched my side making me squirm. "Sorry to disappoint, but I'm not proposing today."

"You are proposing though, right?"

He sighed, exasperated with me. But this was his own fault for blindfolding me in the first place. "I'm proposing you stop asking so many questions."

I felt him lean past me and open a door. His hands gripped my waist and he walked behind me, guiding me the entire way. Even with the blindfold, I knew the room was darker than outside. Everything dimmed. I strained to hear something that would give me a clue as to what we were doing, but it was quiet.

He carefully maneuvered me through a darkened space and then drew me to a stop. "I hope it's something kinky," I told him.

His surprise laughter on the back of my neck made me wonder if we weren't alone. "That's for later," he whispered. And then he removed the blindfold.

I blinked at the scene in front of me, trying to make sense of all the people standing there. My parents were here. And my sisters. Killian and Vera. Ezra and Molly. Dillon. Benny and Endo and the rest of the Lilou staff. Even Jo was here. What in the world?

My first thought was that I had forgotten it was my birthday. "It's not until November," I told them. They were smiling like idiots, all of them, but my statement confused them. "My birthday, I mean."

Wyatt wrapped his arms around my middle and squeezed. His chin rested on my shoulder and filled in the blanks. "It's not a surprise party. If you stop guessing I can tell you why we're here."

I pressed my lips together. I wanted to call him a liar for telling me he wasn't proposing to me when obviously he was, but he was right. It would help everything if I just shut up.

Ezra stepped out of the crowd and somebody turned the lights all the way up. Sarita. Oh, my god, we were inside Sarita.

"Welcome home, chef," Ezra greeted, reaching out to shake my hand.

"No way!" I squeaked while my friends and family cheered loudly. Wyatt squeezed me tighter and I had the suspicion it was because he thought I was going to topple over in surprise. "No way!"

Ezra took my hand, which currently felt like a limp noodle, and shook it firmly. "I hope you don't mind the crowd," he murmured. "Wyatt thought it would be a fun surprise."

"I'm going to kill him," I told Ezra. Wyatt's dark chuckle in my ear told me he didn't believe me.

"No, I can't lose another chef," Ezra groaned. "I finally have two I can count on." He winked at me, letting me know I was one that he meant.

Me.

I was one of his chefs.

Oh my God!

A smile broke free on my face so big and wide and bright I felt like it was going split my head in two. "Okay, fine. He can stick around."

Wyatt hugged me tighter. "Congratulations, chef," he murmured in my ear.

I shivered at the heat in his voice and the way he said chef. I finally got the appeal. And good lord, I was going to need to hear it just like that again and again.

My family approached. "We're so proud of you, Kay-bug!" Wyatt let go of me, so my dad could pull me into a hug. "Always knew you'd make something of yourself," he preened. "Wait till I tell all the guys at the club, my girl's such a big deal in Durham."

I smiled against his barrel of a chest and savored the praise. "Thanks, Daddy."

My sisters were next. Cameron first because she was like an excited puppy that couldn't be contained. "Yay!" she cheered. "You're so cool, Ky. Like the coolest. I want to be just like you when I grow up!"

Claire was next. She hugged me tightly, tighter than she'd ever hugged me before. "Congrats," she said sweetly. "I'm so happy for you."

"Thanks," I told them both. Cameron beamed, but Claire looked different for some reason. There was something off with her. "Hey, are you okay?" I asked.

She shrugged and smiled, but it was forced, vacant. "I'm fine."

But she wasn't. My heart pinched with concern for her and all I cared about was making her feel better. "Hey, Mom and Dad mentioned that you wanted to come spend some time with me this summer. Is that for real?"

Her chin wobbled, but she caught it quickly. "I need a break, you know? Would that be okay? I'll try to impose as little on your life as possible."

"I'm busy," I told her honestly. "You could move in with me permanently and I would hardly notice. I'd love for you to come stay with me. For as long as you'd like." The best part was, I meant it.

"Okay," she whispered. "Thank you."

I had no idea what that was about, but I didn't have time to figure it out right now because my friends descended on me and pulled me into a hug all at once. Dillon, Molly, and Vera surrounded me with their congratulations, jumping up and down and screaming in my ear all at once.

"I told you!" Molly beamed.

"You're welcome," Vera teased.

356

"You did it!" Dillon laughed. "Oh my God, you actually did it. Kaya, you're my hero."

Laughing and crying and sniffling all at once I just looked at them. They had each played a part in this success. I couldn't have done this without them.

Molly had been my friend for a while now. And she had always encouraged me, always put up with me, even when I was snarly. I had no doubt she'd also whispered high praise into Ezra's ear. Because that's how she was. So giving and generous.

Vera had taken me under her wing and pushed me toward my goal. She'd inspired me to get to know the restaurant, all the ins and outs and ups and downs, and then she'd showered me with invaluable advice.

Dillon was my ride or die. She was always there to challenge me and help me get better. And she'd put the very idea in my head.

I was nothing without these incredibly, super talented women by my side. None of this would have been possible without them cheering me on and pouring into my life.

They were the kind of friends that would mark my life forever. One day, I would look back and see that some of my best moments were because of them and with them. I could have done this on my own. It probably would have taken longer. And it would have hardened me in a way that could have made me bitter.

But I preferred this way. I preferred having friends I could count on and lean on. I preferred not being able to take all the credit myself because I'd rather share it with these wonderful women.

The Lilou staff was next. I hugged so many people, I knew the Free People maxi dress I wore was wrinkled to crap and I smelled like a kitchen again, even though I'd showered and dressed for a date with Wyatt.

"Hey, if you get tired of him," I pointed to Wyatt across the room, "You can always come work for me. I promise to be nicer. And not to yell as much."

Benny laughed. "Don't make promises you can't keep, chef. Besides, he doesn't yell nearly as often now that he's getting action on the regular."

I stared at Wyatt across the room. "Yeah, those hookers I'm paying for nightly are really doing wonders."

"Ridiculous!" Benny groaned. "Happy for you two," he murmured and then disappeared.

I turned around and found my mom waiting for me. "Er, hey, Mom."

"Kaya," she said stiltedly. She held a glass of wine in her hand and a napkin with a shortbread on it. Wyatt had made his staff cater this little party. One last hoorah from Lilou. "This is quite the party in your honor."

My cheeks hurt from smiling so much, but I couldn't stop. This was too much. I didn't know it was possible to be this happy, this excited for life. My little Grinch heart grew fifty whole sizes and I knew one more piece of good news would tip me over the edge and I would just explode into itty bitty pieces—like a human confetti cannon.

Which I realized was a super gross analogy if you got into the logistics of it, but also legitimately how I felt.

Feeling extra forgiving in light of my new job, I said, "I'm sorry about how we left things the last time you were in town."

She raised a single eyebrow, surprised by my apology. "How did we leave things?"

She was going to make me say it. "With you mad at me over Nolan, because I don't want to marry him. Or move back home to be with him."

She waved her shortbread around. "Oh, Kaya, I wasn't mad at you because you don't love Nolan."

358

I resisted an eye roll. Yeah, right. Her pushing Nolan on me has only been a constant conversation since I left Hamilton. "Mom, I know you love him. I know he's like… the son you never had. But we were never meant to be together."

"Kaya, stop." She sighed. "All I have ever wanted was for you to be happy. Maybe I got it wrong, but I thought Nolan made you happy. The last time I really saw you excited about anything was when you two were together. You know, I don't get to see you cook. And I'm not a part of your life here. So maybe you're those things when I can't see you, but from my perspective you were so much happier at home. I just wanted you to have that light back in your eyes again. It had nothing to do with Nolan." She made a sound in the back of her throat. "Honestly, I could take him or leave him."

Emotion rushed through me, testing the boundaries of my body. "Oh, Mom." I sniffled, pulling her into a tight hug. Her arms swung wide to protect me from the wine and dessert. "I am happy. I've never been happier."

I pulled back and I was shocked to find real tears dampening her eyes. "I see that now." We simultaneously turned our attention to the party, both of us embarrassed to be caught teary-eyed. "And this new boy you're with? What's his name?"

"Wyatt Shaw," I told her.

"Wyatt. He's nice?"

I ran my lip ring through my teeth. "He's amazing."

"I'd like to get to know him better," she insisted.

He turned to face me from across the room, and I wondered if he'd felt my gaze on him, if he was always as cognizant of me as I was of him. "I'd like that."

Wyatt crossed the room in long strides as if sensing my desire to be with him again. Or maybe he just had the same intention.

When I introduced him to my mom for the second time, she was much more pleasant. She even laughed when he made a joke about how difficult I was to work with. My dad joined us and then my sisters. We spent the rest of the afternoon laughing over drinks and yummy food that was familiar for probably the last time.

But by three p.m., it was time for everyone to get to work. We'd put it off for as long as possible, but dinner service waited for no one.

I said goodbye to my parents, my sisters, my friends, and the staff at Lilou. I would cook tonight with Vera so she could show me the ropes and help me get familiar with the menu. Ezra wanted me cooking on my own by the weekend. That meant I had a lot of work to do over the next few days.

I walked Wyatt to his car while my new staff trickled into the kitchen and began quickly prepping for tonight's service.

"How long have you known?" I demanded when we were all alone.

He glanced at me out of the corner of his eye, a smile already dancing across his mouth. "Three weeks or so. Give or take."

"Three weeks!" I gasped. "You knew right away?"

He shrugged. "I mean, if we're honest, I knew you'd get the job as soon as I found out you wanted it. Come on, Kaya, was there even a question?"

"Yes! Yes, there were many questions! Starting with if you knew three weeks ago, why did it take so long for me to find out?"

"Well, we had to plan a party," he explained evenly, like it wasn't the most insane reason ever. "And that took time." He sensed my annoyance and quickly added. "And Ezra really did interview other candidates, but obviously you were the front-runner. Ezra felt the same way." Before I could launch into another round of arguments, he pulled me into a hug and said, "I'm so goddamn proud of you, Kaya. You're going to kick ass at this job."

I wrapped my arms around his neck and held on tight. "I'm scared," I told him honestly. "I don't want to mess this up."

He laughed and squeezed me tighter. "Then don't. Don't mess up. Just do what you always do, and everything will be fine."

He was right. Ezra wasn't looking for reasons to fire me. He wanted every reason in the world to keep me. I needed to do what I always did—cook amazing food—and everything would be fine. I smiled again, and my cheeks ached with exhaustion. "I love you, Wyatt. Thank you for all of this and for believing in me."

"I love you too." He pressed the sweetest kiss to the corner of my mouth. "More than I ever knew was possible."

We stood like that for a very long time, but eventually he pulled back. He had a restaurant to run. And so did I.

"This feels weird," I told him. We stood next to his driver's side door, holding hands. I didn't want to let go. It felt oddly permanent. Not in a bad way, but like the beginning of a new chapter. I wasn't sure I was ready for it yet.

"It will feel good soon enough," he countered. "As soon as you step into your kitchen, you'll get over the weirdness."

My heart kicked, knowing he was right. My kitchen. Mine.

Just like this man was mine.

"I think I might miss you though. Maybe a little bit."

He smiled at me, his mouth full of joy and wicked secrets and everything I loved so dearly. "I think I might miss you too. But more than you'll miss me."

"Obviously."

He chuckled and wrapped his arms around my waist. "Come over tonight," he suggested. "I want to hear all about your first day."

I had been nibbling on his ear, but I perked up at the prospect of a night with him. "Liar," I teased him. "You don't want to talk."

"I'll talk for a little bit," he laughed. "Then we'll get to the good stuff."

Pulling back, I met his warm, wonderful gaze. "I thought this was the good stuff."

His brown eyes were all promised heat and bright, beautiful future. "Oh, it is, chef. This is the very best stuff."

Then he kissed me into oblivion and I couldn't have agreed with him more.

Thank you for reading The Problem with Him! This series has been an incredible outlet for me to not only create sweet, steamy, super fun love stories, but to highlight issues that women everywhere are facing every day.

Wyatt and Kaya are one of my most favorite couples to have ever written. But I especially love Kaya. As a difficult, headstrong, ambitious woman, I loved creating and developing and getting to know a difficult, headstrong, ambitious woman in the pages of one of my novels. And I hope you did too!

And to the other difficult, headstrong, ambitious women out there—Never feel bad about wanting something big and impossible. Never feel bad about fighting for it with all of you, for letting it take over and consume you until you've done all that you possibly can to get it. Never feel bad about being a driven, informed, feisty woman that owns her seat at the table. You're amazing and worthy and I wish you the absolute best in this beautiful life.

The fourth and final book in the Opposites Attract Series, The Something about Her, is coming in February 26th, 2019. Each book is a standalone romance following a different couple! Keep reading to find out more about Dillon Baptiste and Vann Delane.

I quit life. Or at least my new job.

My fancy head chef position at one of the most acclaimed restaurants in the city is not turning out like I'd hoped. I'm a mess. Totally out of my element and underqualified, I've been thrown into a fiery kitchen and I'm not sure I can handle the heat.

But I owe my brother. And since it's his restaurant and he's my favorite person in the world, I can't walk away.

Even though I'd love to do just that. If we're being really honest though, it's more than just my kitchen. It's the bad date I went on last week. And my building superintendent that won't fix my heater. It's the creepy guy from my gym. But mostly, it's my friend's brother who keeps showing up in all the worst places.

I've never claimed to have it together, but I certainly don't need a man to rescue me every time I get my heel stuck in a sewer grate. Except that's what keeps happening.

Vann Delane is pushy and stuck up and thinks he knows everything there is to know about everything. And for whatever reason, he keeps saving me.

Not that he's happy about it. He's made it clear what he thinks about my money and dream job and the designer shoes he saved last weekend. He's not impressed with me or my penchant for disaster.

I've decided to stay away from him. I've got too many other fires to put out to worry about the something between us that doesn't have a name.

So he can give his knight in shining armor kindness to someone else. He can save those intense glances and butterfly-inducing smiles for the nice girl he's looking for. And he can deny it all he wants, but I know he likes me.

He says I drive him crazy. But I know there's something about me that he can't deny.

Rachel's next project, a second chance romance is coming October 23rd, 2018! This heartwarming love story is about a small town and a big second chance.

Trailer park born and raised. It's my legacy. That's how my mama lived. And how her mama lived. It's the life I was born into and it's the life I swore I would leave the second I was old enough to make it out.

Only legacies have a funny way of sneaking up on you. An innocent decision the night of high school graduation led to a series of complications in my plans to escape.

Seven years later, I've resigned myself to this small town and the roots I'm tied to. Nothing could make me leave. And nothing could make me spill the secrets that keep me here.

Until he walks back into town with a chip on his shoulder and a stupid hunch nobody else in town has been smart enough to follow.

Levi Cole is my opposite. Born on the right side of the tracks with family money to spare, he's the kind of black sheep that can afford to be rebellious—because his family will always pay for his mistakes. He's also the only living heir to Cole Family Farms, after his brother Logan was killed in an accident seven years ago.

He sees something in my life that he thinks he has a right to. But he's wrong. And obnoxious. And he needs to take his stubborn good looks and that intense way he stares at me and go back to wherever it was he came from.

I know better than to trust men like him. I was born and raised in a trailer park, I know nothing good happens to girls like me—girls with trailer park lives and trailer park hearts. Especially from gorgeous, kind, pigheaded men like him.

Acknowledgments

To my God and for this blessing of needing You. Every book, every day, every hour.

To Zach, thank you for all the ways you take care of me and our family and the house while I hide away and pull my hair out. You're the reason our kids eat supper, the reason the house isn't falling down and the reason I can write such incredible, swoon-worthy heroes. Thank you for being a better grown up than me. I love you.

To Stella, Scarlett, Stryker, Solo and Saxon. Thank you for delaying your summer fun so I could finish this book and for letting me leave every evening to find some quiet. You're chaos and mayhem and crazy all at once and I love you more than anything else in this world. Thank you for letting me kiss you in public, for thinking our handshakes are the coolest thing ever and for always forgiving me when I forget birthday parties and doctors' appointments. You're my favorite. Each of you.

To my mom, for being the strong, independent woman who raised a strong, independent woman. You taught me how to work hard and to sacrifice for family and the things that I want most. You taught me how to be resilient. You taught me how to be relentless. But most of all you taught me how to love recklessly. And thank you for the days you took the kids and made it possible to finish this book!

To Katie, Tiffany and Sarah Jo, my prickle. Thank you for our hours of laughter and our commitment to friendship and for all the big plans we have for this small life. You girls are friendship I didn't know was possible and I am so grateful for the grace and encouragement you give me daily. #squadlife forever and ever amen.

To Georgia, Shelly, Amy and Samantha, thank you for always being there for me, for always listening when I freak out and for always supporting me through everything. I could never survive this job without you. Your wisdom, your sane advice and your laughter saves me on a daily basis. I'm working on an island for us.

To Lenore, the best beta reader on the planet and my all-time favorite Canadian! Thank you for dropping everything for me, for finding all the last little mistakes I would never see and for being such a kind, gracious, amazing human. You are my people. And I am so blessed to know you. Also, yay to being almost-on-time!!!

To Amy Donnelly from Alchemy and Words, thank you so much for pushing me beyond where I'm comfortable, for demanding more from my words and characters and stories. Thank you for being an editor invested in your work, willing to sacrifice for your clients and for all around, being a truly upstanding woman. I fully acknowledge what a nightmare I am to work with, thank you for taking the job anyway.

To Caedus Design Co, hey, another great cover! Good job. Thank you for never giving up on me when you ask me to describe the book and I don't. Thank you for the endless teaser pictures and covers and all those times you make the business better and more efficient than I ever could. And thanks for putting up with all the people that ask if you're the cover model for The Opposite of You. Have I told you lately that I love you?

To the Rebel Panel, thank you for sticking around and sticking by me despite how entangled in life I am. Thank you for continuing to love my characters and read my stories and for never giving up on me. You ladies are a group of women I am proud and honored to be a part of. Thanks for being some of the best women I have ever had the pleasure to know!

To the bloggers and reviewers, thank you for your time and energy and for investing in my words when I know you have a million other things to be doing. Thank you for taking time out of your life to write a review and post a teaser and support not just me, but all of the authors you work with. Your encouragement and kindness means the world to me. I am so blessed to be a part of this industry where you exist in such incredible ways.

To the reader, thank you for taking a chance on me and on Wyatt and Kaya. Thank you for picking up one of my books or all of my books or some of my books and reading words that have come straight from my soul. Your time and support, your reviews and messages, are the fuel that keeps me going. You're the best readers on the entire planet and I am beyond honored that you would pick one of my books, but especially this one.

Rachel Higginson was born and raised in Nebraska, but spent her college years traveling the world. She fell in love with Eastern Europe, Paris, Indian Food and the beautiful beaches of Sri Lanka, but came back home to marry her high school sweetheart. Now she spends her days raising their growing family. She is obsessed with reruns of *The Office* and Cherry Coke.

Look for Constant and Consequence LIVE NOW!

Rachel's next release, Trailer Park Heart, a breathtaking second chance romance is coming October 23rd, 2017. And The Something about Her, the fourth and final standalone in the Opposites Attract series coming February 26th, 2018!

Other Books Out Now by Rachel Higginson:

<u>Love and Decay, Season One</u>

Volume One

Volume Two

<u>Love and Decay, Season Two</u>

Volume Three
Volume Four

Volume Five

Love and Decay, Season Three

Volume Six

Volume Seven

Volume Eight

Love and Decay: Revolution, Season One

Volume One

Volume Two

The Star-Crossed Series

Reckless Magic (The Star-Crossed Series, Book 1)

Hopeless Magic (The Star-Crossed Series, Book 2)

Fearless Magic (The Star-Crossed Series, Book 3)

Endless Magic (The Star-Crossed Series, Book 4)

The Reluctant King (The Star-Crossed Series, Book 5)

The Relentless Warrior (The Star-Crossed Series, Book 6)

Breathless Magic (The Star-Crossed Series, Book 6.5)

Fateful Magic (The Star-Crossed Series, Book 6.75)

The Redeemable Prince (The Star-Crossed Series, Book 7)

The Starbright Series

Heir of Skies (The Starbright Series, Book 1)

Heir of Darkness (The Starbright Series, Book 2)

Heir of Secrets (The Starbright Series, Book 3)

The Siren Series

The Rush (The Siren Series, Book 1)

The Fall (The Siren Series, Book 2)

The Heart (The Siren Series, Book 3)

Bet on Love Series

Bet on Us (An NA Contemporary Romance)

Bet on Me (An NA Contemporary Romance)

Every Wrong Reason

The Five Stages of Falling in Love

The Opposite of You (Opposites Attract Series)

The Difference Between Us (Opposites Attract Series)

Constant (The Confidence Game Duet)

Consequence (The Confidence Game Duet)

Connect with Rachel on her blog at:

http://www.rachelhigginson.com/

Or on Twitter:

@mywritesdntbite

Or on her Facebook page:

Rachel Higginson

Keep reading for an excerpt from Rachel's thrilling romantic suspense, Constant, book one in the Confidence Game Duet.

Constant

Scheme.

Scam.

Con.

Long or short, we're talking about the same thing—the confidence game.

A petty criminal doesn't understand the nuances that go into creating the flawless con. Conning isn't a last-minute misdemeanor or the consequence of a faulty moral compass. No. A true confidence game takes skill, finesse, hours of planning and plotting and finally, when your team has been assembled and the stars align and the wind blows just right, it takes perfect execution.

The morally upright, law-abiding citizens of the world look down their noses. They assume the worst, believing that con artists are nothing more than depraved and corrupt. Social outcasts that can't keep real jobs. But by assuming the worst, they're ignoring the most important trait this type of person possesses—they are artists.

377

A true confidence game isn't haphazard or carried out thanks to a penchant for laziness. A real con is carefully pieced together over months. Tireless preparation and cautious consideration form the bedrock of every game. But even the most prudent con can't plan everything. The fates throw their hand in too. Kindly or maliciously, the artist depends on them for grace.

And in the end, the game must be played perfectly. Everything must go according to plan. Everything must fall into place and happen exactly right. The stakes are high. The risks are great.

Yet the consequences are not enough to turn us away.

We've heard the siren's song and responded to her deathly lure. We're not criminals. We're artists.

Con artists.

At least I was once upon a time. Before different realities surfaced, forcing me to reprioritize. Maybe that's the difference between criminals and good people—what they have to lose and how desperately they're willing to gamble with it.

I had been willing to gamble before. I had chanced everything often and won every single time. Until one day, the reward wasn't worth the risk. Until I knew I had to leave the darkness behind, even if it meant giving up the game.

Not that the game had been all that great. It was a tangled web that left me empty and shallow, wrapped up in the chains of my own making. The game was greedy, all-consuming, demanding blood for payment and my soul for insurance.

There had been moments during that time I thought I wouldn't survive. I stood at the precipice of death and peered over the edge. One misstep or ill-timed gust of wind and I would have tipped over, fallen down the black abyss and never resurfaced.

Sometimes when I looked back at those moments, those infinitely dark and twisted times, I couldn't breathe. I would feel my heart shatter all over. I would experience the tearing, crushing, ripping apart of my limbs and muscles, my tendons and veins, my heart and my mind. I would forget how to breathe.

I would forget how to be.

Until I remembered him.

He was the one constant in my life that had pushed me through the darkness. He was the one constant in my life that loved me beyond everything else, beyond what I was or had been or could ever be. He wanted me to be better. He wanted to be better for me.

The problem was he was as tangled in the madness as I was.

I didn't live that life anymore. I had broken free and found something safe to build a new foundation for myself. But I couldn't remember the past without imagining his smile or his eyes, his touch. I couldn't think about where I had been without thinking of where we were supposed to go.

Where he was supposed to take me.

Sometimes life doesn't work out the way you plan. Sometimes circumstances change and sometimes they're for the better.

But he was my constant then and he is the constant ghost that haunts me now.

I might not be with him, but he will always be with me.

Chapter One
Fifteen Years Ago

Awesome. Another back alley.

There were only a handful of activities that regularly occurred in the darkened backstreets of downtown DC and none of them were appropriate for a ten-year-old girl.

I knew that well, since I had witnessed my fair share of seedy behavior from this city. But that had never stopped my pops from dragging me along with him to all of his work dealings.

"Keep up, Caro," he snapped when his crew came into sight.

The morning sun didn't reach this alley, and the cool air pulled the hair to standing on my bare arms. "I should be in school, Dad. I have a science test today."

He glanced quickly over his shoulder at me, his expression only marginally apologetic. "I called them this morning. Told them you had strep."

Anger burned beneath my skin, turning my face red with frustrated emotion. I ducked my head and let my short bob fall over my cheeks.

"Relax. It's a free day off school. You should be thanking me. When I was a kid I would have killed for my old man to call in for me. The test'll be there tomorrow."

"That's not the point. I don't care that I'm not there. I don't want to be *here*."

He grunted. "Yeah? Then you shouldn't be so good at what you do."

I stopped walking and ground to a halt. He was blaming this on me? *Me?* I didn't even know what to say. The words and arguments and furious thoughts I wanted to throw at him tangled on my dry tongue, a retort-worthy traffic jam.

Sensing that I wasn't following him, he turned around and walked the few steps back to me. He shot a glance to the cluster of men hovering between a rusted metal door and an oozing dumpster.

"Come on, Caro, I'm just kidding," he insisted, even though we both knew he was not. "This is a favor to Roman, all right? There's this truck. The cargo is… worth our time, yeah?"

I lifted my chin defiantly. "I thought you didn't do this stuff anymore. I thought you got promoted."

His bulbous nose turned red. "I did get promoted. This is a one-time thing. They need me. And I need you."

My dad, Leon Valero, had recently been bumped up from high level lackey to bookie. He worked for brothers that ran an organized crime syndicate in the underbelly of Washington, DC. They weren't the biggest outfit or the most infamous, but over the years they'd developed a reputation that held weight.

My dad had worked for them way longer than I had been alive. Bookie was supposed to be a better job than whatever he was doing before. Bookmaker meant more respect in the organization, a bigger cut of the paycheck. He took bets on anything you could take bets on and paid out winners and beat the crap out of you if you couldn't settle your debt.

This promotion was supposed to mean more stability for me. He wouldn't be gone as much. He'd make more money. He wouldn't need me for jobs anymore.

Promises, promises.

"Look," Dad coaxed. "Frankie's here."

I glared over at the only other girl my age I was allowed to play with. Her long hair was somehow darker than mine, and I had always considered mine black. Hers was more like ink. Or oil. Today she hid it beneath a hat. "That's 'cause Frankie will do whatever it takes to prove she's not a princess."

My dad ignored my comment. He knew I was right. But the problem was she *was* a princess. At least as far as the two of us were concerned.

"We need you, Caro." His voice dropped when he continued. "Frankie and Gus ain't got half the set of balls you do. This can't happen without you."

I rolled my eyes and turned to glare at the ivy clustered brick wall that lined the alley but something else captured my attention instead. Not really something, but someone. Someone new.

I could recognize all the usual players. They were guys my dad and his bosses trusted. Most of them were grown-ups that I was supposed to call uncle. As if making them part of our already dysfunctional family somehow made them better humans. They were low-level goons at best—murderers, criminals and drug dealers at worst. But I went along with the lie. Uncle Brick. Uncle Vinny. Uncle Fat Jack. My life was a cautionary tale.

Then there were the kids. Frankie was the only other girl I really knew. There were girls at school, but none of them paid attention to me. I was the poor, tragic outcast that cut her hair short because she didn't have a mom around to teach her how to braid it or hell, put it in something as simple as a ponytail. Frankie and I were close for that reason. It wasn't easy being raised by this pack of animals. But she didn't go to my school. She went to some swanky private school that made her wear skirts and knee-high socks every day. As the orphan niece of the three brothers that ran the syndicate, she was basically royalty as far as I was concerned, and way higher up on the food chain.

Then there were Atticus and Augustus—known as Gus—brothers and sons of the *derzhatel obschaka,* the bookkeeper, Ozzie Usenko. He held one of the highest positions in the *bratva.* Even though the brothers weren't much older than me, they were already in training to be regular, paid members of the crew.

Especially Atticus, even though he'd just turned sixteen. He was born for the life. I saw the hunger in his eyes every time we were allowed to be part of a job. He wanted this. He wanted to be one of the soldiers.

Gus wasn't as serious about it. He wasn't really serious about anything. Atticus was scary and intense and so devoted to the brothers. Gus just didn't want the shit beat out of him by his dad should he choose not to participate.

It was a worthy pursuit. His dad was mean as hell.

The syndicate didn't enlist kids to help with big jobs often. It was usually just me or the brothers. There was less at stake if they lost one of us. It sounded harsh, but I knew it to be true. And I was the most expendable of them all. I was a minor and the daughter of a bookie, a position easily replaceable and not all that important. Which was why I made it a point to never get pinched. They might not care what happened to me, but I did.

The brothers that ran the syndicate would always protect Frankie—the only surviving child of their beloved dead sister. The only reason she was allowed to go along for the ride was because nobody wanted to tell her no. Although they were going to have to start soon. Frankie hated her uncles. She blamed them for the death of her parents. Her mom was killed by soldiers from the Italian family competing for the same foothold the *pakhan,* her brothers, also known as the bosses, were. And her dad, who happened to be Italian, died at their hands in retaliation. Frankie only did this shit to punish her uncles.

The kid against the wall was probably Gus's age. Although it was hard to tell. Despite his height, he was half-starved and too skinny. His gangly arms and legs looked like I could snap them in half if I put enough pressure on them. But then his face looked old. Older than Gus and Atticus, maybe even older than my dad. His eyes were tired and his mouth pulled into a tight frown that was both sad and scary at the same time.

"Who's that?" I lifted my chin in the direction of the kid.

Dad shook his head. "We need someone skinny for the back end."

"He's *bratva?*"

"Nah, he's a stray. Jack found him digging through a dumpster and offered him a meal for his help."

I looked at my Uncle Jack who happened to be the size of a dumpster and wouldn't know the first thing about living on the streets and starving. Not that I did either. For all of Dad's shortcomings, he had at least always made sure we had a place to stay and food to eat.

But this kid screamed street urchin. He had that cagey look about him that said way more about his current lifestyle than he wanted anyone to see. I would have bet anything that a hot meal had sounded like winning the lottery. I could imagine Uncle Jack's promises of low risk for a big reward.

Of course the kid would say yes.

The problem was, I knew my Uncle Jack and there was no way he was going to waste another second on this kid once the job was done. Unless it was to tie up loose ends, which meant the kid would disappear.

Forever.

My stomach turned uneasily. "The Smithsonian," I looked my father in the eye. "If I help you, you take me to the Smithsonian."

"Again?" I stared him down. He rolled his eyes. "Is that it?"

"And I want to bring Frankie."

His frown turned into a grimace. "Yeah, well we'll see what Roman has to say about that."

Her oldest uncle would say yes. After I gave Frankie the opportunity to spend the day with me and my dad, she wouldn't care where we were going. And Roman wouldn't be able to tell her no. He never could.

"So you're in?"

It pained me to agree to today's activities, but I did. I didn't really have a choice anyway. "What's the job?"

"The Screaming Eagle," he explained. "The mark is that electronics store next to the 7-Eleven. They got a big truck of TVs coming in."

My lips parted and I breathed a slow, steady exhale of relief. As far as jobs went, the Screaming Eagle was low risk, little more than normal kid stuff. The most danger I would see was having my ass chewed by the electronics store manager.

But I couldn't let my dad know that. If he even got a whiff of my relief, he wouldn't hesitate to force me into more if this crap.

Instead I asked, "It takes all of us to pull off The Screaming Eagle?"

He made a sound in the back of his throat. "Lest I insult your ego, it will only be you, Gus and Frankie on the inside. Atticus is here to drive the truck."

"And the new kid?"

Dad glanced at him one more time. "Don't worry about the new kid."

I looked at Frankie so I could check out the new kid one more time without being noticed. If Dad didn't want me to worry about him, the kid must have a super bad part today. Or for after the robbery.

Leon was many things, but he always shot shit straight with me.

The kid in question stared down at his sneakers that were full of holes. His dark hair was long and shaggy over his ears, and his skin had that dull quality that happened when you didn't eat healthy food. He'd shoved his hands into his jeans pockets, but his thumbs stuck out revealing dirty fingernails and grimy fingers.

"What's the hold up, Valero?" Vinnie called from the back of the alley.

My dad didn't even spare him a glance, just shouted over his shoulder. "Just a minute." He turned to face me. "I'll let you know when we're ready to go. You good with everything else?"

I wasn't good with any of it, but I nodded anyway.

Dad left me to go talk to the guys. To be honest, what I did was a small part of the job. I created a distraction by causing a scene—classic misdirection. While everyone's eyes were on me, the rest of the guys slipped inside and took what they wanted.

It sounded simple. But it wasn't. There was finesse to it, skill. Frankie and Gus could make a lot of noise, but rarely could they capture an entire store's attention for the necessary amount of time. The real reason Dad kept me out of school today was because I was the best damn liar he'd ever met.

Frankie and Gus started walking over to me. Frankie looked pissed as usual and Gus looked like he could care less. Like usual. But my eyes were on the new kid.

My dad's words bounced around my head like a pinball in one of those trucker games at the arcade. He'd said not to worry about the new kid.

Yeah, right.

His eyes darted around the alley as I approached him, like he was trying to look at anything but me. He bounced up and down on his heels, his elbows locked at his side. He was getting ready to run.

Seeing his nerves made me slow my approach. I'd met plenty of street kids over the years. The syndicate always seemed to have low risk, odd jobs for them that paid in hot meals or a ride somewhere. The kids got something out of it and the syndicate got practically free labor from minors that didn't know anything about the organization. It was a win for everybody but the FBI who would rather arrest someone integral to the brotherhood, someone that they could prosecute. As long as they were low level jobs, I never worried about what happened to the kids. But this was different.

Pulling one into an actual con meant an extra witness, someone that hadn't pledged their loyalty to the crew.

I smelled him before I reached him and my heart kicked in my chest. He was like a stray puppy. With a broken leg. And someone had just cut off his tail, stolen his bone and then dragged him through the sewer.

Seriously, what was that smell?

"Hey," I called out softly, trying not to spook him. "I'm Caroline."

His Adam's apple bobbed up and down as he swallowed. "Uh, hey."

He looked away again, dismissing me. I recognized the look. I was dismissed a lot around my dad's associates. Nobody thought much of the little girl that was always tagging along with her part-time loser of a dad. Nobody noticed me when they talked business in hushed tones or passed money back and forth in dimly lit bars that smelled like piss and old men. I was just the sometimes useful child of a bookie.

But it irked me that this homeless kid treated me the same way.

At least I had showered this morning.

"I've never seen you around before," I pushed, my voice harder, my body stiffer.

He tipped his head back and looked at the narrow strip of sky visible between the two tall buildings surrounding us. "Huh."

He kept his mouth open and I got a good look at his teeth. He had all of them that I could see, which was surprising. And even more confusing was that they were mostly white. He smelled bad, but with teeth like that, he couldn't have been homeless for too long.

"Do you have a name?"

"No."

I resisted the urge to growl. "If we're going to work together, I should know your name."

His head dropped and he finally met my eyes. Bright, deep, impossibly blue. I wasn't prepared for eyes like that. Against his dirty face, they shined like lasers. "We're not working together. I'm doing something different."

My curiosity jumped inside me, like bubbles fizzing in a Coke. "What are you doing?"

His gaze shifted to Jack and Vinnie. "Something different."

I had decided to kick him in the shin when Frankie and Gus stepped up next to us. Irritation buzzed beneath my skin. I liked Frankie. I did. But she was so pretty. And now the new kid would only pay attention to her and I would never figure out what his role was.

Or what his name was.

"Who's your new friend, Caro?" Gus asked, all wide smiles and happy energy.

Frankie adjusted her worn baseball cap. "New recruit?"

The kid quickly shook his head. "Nah. This is a one-time thing."

The three of us exchanged a look. We'd heard that before. Not with kids our age, but men that got sucked into the life. Everyone said that. The job, whatever the job was, was always a one-time thing. Nobody set out to live a life of crime. It was something you fell into ass-backward and then spent the rest of your life trying to figure out how to crawl your way out.

Or you just succumbed.

Either way, it always started out as a one-time-only promise.

"You hungry?" I guessed.

His too-bright gaze cut to mine. "Fucking starving."

I backed up another step at his harsh language. It wasn't the words that surprised me, it was how he said it. The tone that punched through the air and hit my cheek with a bruising blow.

This kid was desperate. And that made him something more than pathetic or worrisome. It made him feral. Predatory.

He wasn't here because he wanted to be, but because he had to do *something* to survive. And for some stupid reason, that made me want to help him.

I had a tiny, beat up little black kitten in the corner of my bedroom for the very same reason.

"Enough with the cats, Caro," my dad had groaned last week when I brought the battered thing home. "You can't save all the stray cats in DC. You know that, right?"

Maybe Dad was right about the cats, but I could save this kid.

"What's your name?" I asked him bluntly.

He glared at me until I wanted to look away, until I wanted to let him win this staring contest and pretend like I hadn't said anything. "Sayer," he finally admitted. "Sayer Wesley."

"Sayer Wesley," I repeated as if I couldn't help myself. The words whooshed out of me on a breath I hadn't realized I had been holding. It was probably a fake name, but it sounded so real. So right. Like the first real piece of truth I'd ever heard.

His expression turned into a sneer, "That's right, Caroline. Got a problem with my name?"

390

I felt Gus and Frankie look at me, their eyes curious and accusing. Nobody called me Caroline. Not even my dad. I was always Caro. But I had introduced myself to this kid as Caroline.

Why had I done that?

Feeling weird and off my game and completely unnerved by this street kid, I rolled my eyes like it wasn't a big deal. "Frankie, give Sayer your hat."

She tugged it down over her eyes. "No."

Shooting her a frustrated scowl, I jerked my chin at Sayer Wesley. "He's not doing what we're doing, and there are cameras all over those streets. Let him protect his face at least."

She sucked in her bottom lip and contemplated my suggestion. Turning to him, she asked, "What are they paying you?"

He lifted one shoulder, his jaw ticking near his ear. "Food. Maybe a place to stay tonight."

The three of us shared another look.

"Caro, Frankie, let's go!" my dad shouted from across the alley.

"Give him your hat, Frankie," I hissed. "At least give him a chance to get away from the cops."

Sayer's body had tensed at my words, keen awareness rocking through him and transforming his face from desperate to terrified.

Someone else shouted at us to hurry up. Frankie ripped off her hat, her black curls cascading down her back like a waterfall. I watched Sayer's expression, waiting for him to be momentarily mesmerized, but his expression stayed the same. He had a good poker face. I could give him that.

She tossed the hat at him. He caught it and slammed it on, pulling it low on his forehead.

"Let's go," Gus suggested. "It's not worth pissing them off."

391

Frankie and Gus turned toward my dad and the rest of the crew, stalking off down the alley already playing the part of obnoxious kids without supervision.

Sayer started to walk after them, but I grabbed his forearm, unwilling to let him enter into this unprepared. "Make them realize you're valuable," I told him quickly.

His eyes narrowed, but he didn't say anything.

Not knowing if he got it or not, I went on. "If you want food or a place to stay you have to earn it. And if you don't, they'll let you get caught." I glanced over my shoulder toward my dad and his associates. "Or worse."

When I turned back to Sayer, those freaky blue eyes were glued to me again. "Why are you telling me this?"

I shrugged. I didn't really have an answer. "You'd do the same for me."

His head tilted. "No, I wouldn't."

His honesty made me smirk. "Now you will." I leaned in, dropping my voice to a whisper. "You owe me a favor."

His eyes widened and his lips pressed into a straight line. I was too pleased with myself not to smile, so I quickly turned around and hurried to catch up with my friends.

"Let's go, kid!" Jack shouted after Sayer. He stepped forward, out of the alley and into the confidence game that would irrevocably change his life. The confidence game that would change us both forever.

I didn't know what happened to Sayer until later that night. Frankie, Gus and I did our thing. We walked into the electronic store and cased the joint for an hour. We never intended to steal anything, but we acted suspicious as hell until all of the store employees had their eyes on us. Just when the manager made a beeline over to kick us out, I pulled out pockets full of crumpled one dollar bills and with tears in my eyes, asked what I could buy my dad for his birthday.

He took me over to a display of watches and feeling sufficiently guilty, he gave me all his attention. Frankie and Gus crowded around when he bent over to pick one up for me and I pickpocketed his wallet just for fun.

I had a bad habit of taking something for myself whenever I was on a job. Frankie called them my trophies. But it wasn't like I wanted to remember the job or show off or anything. It was more like insurance or collateral. I needed to start saving for the day my dad stopped taking care of me or got himself killed.

I paid for a cheap watch with a black cuff and made sure to sniffle in gratitude at the counter. Frankie, Gus and I left the store. The alarm rang just as we stepped on the sidewalk.

A delivery truck driver came sprinting around the corner, shouting after his truck that was speeding off down the street, already lost in traffic.

After driving another block, the truck would pull into a parking garage that happened to have no working security cameras, where it would quickly be unloaded into another truck and abandoned for the feds to find.

Sirens blared through the afternoon bustle of downtown DC and two cop cars screeched to a halt in front of us. Frankie, Gus and I stared at the entire scene with wide-eyed fascination—like ten-year-old kids were supposed to do. We moved out of the way when asked, but hung around while the cops took statements and talked to witnesses and tried to figure out what had happened.

Turns out the security cameras had been turned off during the heist. And the delivery driver had been somehow locked in the dumpster behind the building. Nobody saw the thief or realized anything was wrong until the driver had been able to get free of his trash prison. Nobody could even identify the driver since it hadn't seemed that anything was amiss until after the truck was gone.

393

The manager of the store was dumbfounded. The driver understandably furious. And the cops totally befuddled.

They even asked us if we had seen anything. To which we replied, "No, officer, we were just buying a birthday present for my dad."

"Why don't you get on home then," they suggested. "You don't need to be hanging around a crime scene."

We nodded solemnly and headed off down the street. Our job was over so we had the rest of the day to kill. We decided to grab pizza at our favorite place.

Later that night, my dad would tell me what a great job I did and hand me fifty bucks for being such a good girl. I would ask him how much his cut was and he would smile slyly at me and say, "Don't you worry about it, baby girl. Just know that we don't need to worry about anything for a while."

That was always his answer. He was obsessed with this idea of not worrying about anything.

The irony was that because of his job, I worried about everything all the time.

But we didn't get caught today. So at least there was that.

And neither did Sayer Wesley.

I wouldn't know what happened to him for a couple of months, but I would think of him every day until then.

Made in the USA
Monee, IL
05 May 2021